Lincolnshire
COUNTY COUNCIL

disc

This book shou ore
the last

BIRCH

DOCTOR ON
THE RED CARPET

BY
ANNE FRASER

T

MILLS
BOON

Anne Fraser's new duet
Doctors to the Stars
has the inside scoop on stories the paparazzi can
only dream of uncovering…

DOCTORS TO THE STARS!

Amongst the glitterati of the rich and famous,
cousins Fabio and Kendrick are infamous
for their heart-stopping good looks and
dangerously tempting charm…

By day Fabio is a top-notch Harley Street doctor—
but by night he's an adrenaline junkie who's
utterly irresistible to women!

Kendrick, the unstoppable stuntman
for the world's biggest Hollywood blockbusters,
leaves broken hearts on every film location!

*But Fabio and Kendrick's roguish ways
are about to be tamed…!*

THE PLAYBOY OF HARLEY STREET

BY
ANNE FRASER

MILLS & BOON

First published in Great Britain 2011
by Mills & Boon, an imprint of Harlequin (UK) Limited,
Eton House, 18-24 Paradise Road, Richmond, Surrey TW9 1SR

© Anne Fraser 2011

ISBN: 978 0 263 88596 5

Harlequin (UK) policy is to use papers that are natural, renewable and recyclable products and made from wood grown in sustainable forests. The logging and manufacturing process conform to the legal environmental regulations of the country of origin.

Printed and bound in Spain
by Blackprint CPI, Barcelona

Dear Reader

Welcome to the next two books in my miniseries *Doctors to the Stars*!

I love writing about strong, alpha men who like to test themselves to the limit and in this book I have two of them. Thrill seeking cousins Fabio and Kendrick share a love of extreme sports—and women.

Enter Katie and Elizabeth, two women who are grieving and definitely not looking for romance. But just as it looks as if they have found love with two men who have issues of their own, life still has one more curve ball to throw their way.

Despite the difficulties associated with writing about bereavement and life-limiting illness, especially when children are involved, I had so much fun writing these books and I really hope you have as much enjoyment reading them.

I have tried to make sure the medical information is as up to date and accurate as possible. However, since I wrote *The Playboy of Harley Street*, there has been progress in the treatment of cystic fibrosis. Very good news for sufferers and their families.

Anne Fraser

CHAPTER ONE

KATIE SIMPSON looked around the luxury interior of the private jet and wanted to pinch herself. Dr Cavendish, the senior partner at the practice, had told her at her interview that she'd be expected to fly all over the world, but he hadn't said anything about private jets.

Katie jiggled her legs impatiently. Where was Dr Lineham? They had boarded the small plane ten minutes ago and there was no sign of her colleague. Opposite her, their patient was playing a game on her games console, looking completely unfazed by her surroundings.

Lucy Hargreaves was eight years old and suffering from cystic fibrosis. Katie and Dr Lineham were accompanying her to Monaco so that she could watch her father, a British racing champion, in a prestigious racing tournament.

Katie swivelled round in her seat at the sound of footsteps clattering up the aluminium steps.

Dr Lineham at last—and not before time. For the second time that day, Katie was taken aback. Instead of the older man she'd envisaged, Dr Lineham was lean, with thick, tousled dark hair that curled over his collar, olive skin, high cheekbones and a wide, full mouth. His tall, broad-shouldered frame filled the doorway as he paused to finish adjusting his tie and do up the top button of his shirt. He looked more like a film star than a doctor.

'Damn London traffic,' he muttered, before coming forward. He stopped next to Lucy and ruffled her hair. 'Hi, Luce. You okay?'

Lucy glanced up, her eyes crinkled in a smile. 'Hey, Dr Fabio. Where've you been? Late night out again?'

Fabio held a finger to his lips and pretended to frown. 'Luce, don't give away my secrets. For all you know, I've been in the hospital all night.'

He winked at the little girl and she giggled.

Oh, please, Katie thought. Couldn't he at least pretend to be more professional?

Deep green eyes swept over Katie. She was aware of him taking in her dark suit and sensible shoes and shifted uncomfortably under his appraising look. She hadn't known what to wear so had settled on the same outfit she had worn to her interview. Not that Dr Lineham had been there. Apparently he'd been away with a patient in Mauritius or some other exotic island.

'And is this our new physio, Lucy?' His voice was as smooth as warm chocolate with just a trace of an accent Katie didn't recognise.

'She says I can call her Katie,' Lucy replied. 'She's been here for ages already. She knows how to play games on my console. I think she's cool.'

'I'm pleased to meet you, Dr Lineham,' Katie responded, trying to keep the disapproval from her voice. Despite being told at her interview that the practice was friendly and informal, it had been emphasised that all the staff took their duty towards their patients seriously. Katie expected nothing less, but now she wondered if one of her colleagues didn't share that ethos. Imagine coming directly to work after being out all night! What was he thinking? He should have left home earlier if he didn't want to be late. Like she had. An hour and a half before she'd had to, and if it had meant she'd had to hang around the airport for quite a while, at least she'd been on time.

And didn't Dr Lineham need to check Lucy over or something? Katie was far from reassured by his casual approach. Between them, they had total responsibility for their patient.

Dr Lineham held out his hand and as Katie shook it, she was aware of the hardness of his skin, which didn't quite fit with his groomed exterior. 'And I am pleased to meet you too, Katie Simpson, but, please, call me Fabio.'

The way he said her name in an accent she still couldn't quite place sent an unexpected frisson up her spine.

'You have to strap yourself in,' Lucy reminded Katie, as Fabio settled himself into the seat opposite. 'Just for take-off.'

Lucy was pale and underweight for her age but with a wisdom in her indigo-coloured eyes that belied her years. Dr Cavendish, the senior partner, had briefed Katie the day before about the little girl's condition.

'Her CF is under control most of the time, but unfortunately she has had one or two bad chest infections and there is some scarring.'

'Should she be travelling?' Katie had asked.

'It makes her happy. And after all the trip is only for two days and as long as she gets regular physio and Fabio is there with her, there's no reason to think she won't be absolutely fine. Our clinic is set up so that we can allow our patients to carry on with their normal lives as much as possible.

'For those patients that can manage it, naturally we see

them at the practice, otherwise we attend them in their own homes or wherever they may be. Sometimes a patient may need us to travel with them and we do that too. We aim to be as flexible as possible.

'Mrs Hargreaves—Amelia—wouldn't be letting Lucy go if she didn't have medical support for her and absolute faith in us,' Dr Cavendish continued. 'Dr Lineham has been looking after Lucy for the last two years—a year before he joined us—and her parents have complete and justified confidence in him.' He smiled. 'Lucy has never seen her father race—at least, not apart from on television—so she's adamant she wants to go. As you'll learn, she's quite a determined child.'

As the plane gathered speed for take-off, Katie gripped the armrests of her seat. Fabio, on the other hand, was casually flicking through a magazine as if he didn't have a care in the world. His legs were stretched out in front of him and Katie couldn't help but notice how the material of his suit trousers clung to his thighs, emphasising the defined muscles. He had loosened his tie and discarded his jacket and looked very much at home. Something about him sent a shiver of disquiet through her.

'Don't be scared,' Lucy said, placing one of her small hands on top of Katie's.

Not good. The child comforting the adult. Katie forced herself to unpick the fingers of her right hand from the armrests and relax.

'I'll be fine. Keep it between you and me, Lucy, but I've never flown in a plane this size before. It doesn't even feel like a plane. I guess it just takes getting used to.'

Lucy had given her a quick tour before they'd prepared for take-off. There were twelve seats in groups of four with a table between them, a bar with fruit juice and snacks, and shelves with books and magazines. It reminded her more of a lobby of a hotel than a plane. The co-pilot, a slim, attractive woman who looked far too young to be flying planes, doubled up as the stewardess and had introduced herself simply as Fern.

As soon as they were airborne and the seat-belt lights switched off, Lucy put down her games console and showed Katie how one of the seats at the rear of the cabin could be made into a bed. 'That way I can lie down while you do my physio.'

'Have you been to Monaco before?' Lucy asked, as Katie worked on her.

Katie smiled. 'I've spent three weeks in Europe and I've just returned from working in Ireland, but that's about the limit of my travels, I'm afraid.'

'I haven't been to Monaco either. But I have stayed on the yacht we're staying on before when we've been on holiday. I like staying on yachts. Do you?'

'I did a trip on a riverboat with my parents when I was a little girl. It was wonderful. I loved it. It was so much fun. I remember my brother and I had to keep getting on and off to open the locks.'

At the memory, a stab of pain shot through her and her eyes filled. She was glad Lucy was lying on her stomach and wouldn't see the tears threatening to spill. Would she ever be able to think of Richard without wanting to howl? She doubted it. She breathed deeply, trying to keep her voice level.

'Okay, that's you.' Katie helped Lucy sit up.

'That was quick,' Lucy said. 'You're much better than the person who normally does my physio.'

Kate smiled. 'Maybe because I've had lots of practice.

My young cousin has cystic fibrosis too. I used to do her physio when they lived near me.'

'Want another shot at my game?' Lucy asked when they were seated again. 'I don't mind sharing.'

She really was an extremely likeable little girl. 'No, thanks, sweetheart, but it's kind of you to offer. I think I'll read for a little while.'

Katie tried to concentrate on the magazine she'd bought in Departures, but somehow her eyes kept on straying over towards her colleague as he chatted to Lucy. Dr Fabio Lineham was the most extraordinarily gorgeous man she'd ever set eyes on. And she bet he knew it too. No doubt he had a phone full of women's phone numbers. She started guiltily when he caught her flicking a glance at him and she made a show of being deeply engrossed in reading an article. Until she noticed the title—'How to Entice Your Man into Your Heart and Between the Sheets'. She slapped the pages shut when Fabio left Lucy playing her game and sat down beside her.

'So, Katie, I think we should get to know each other, seeing as we'll be working together.'

He smelled divine. A mixture of spice and lemons. Her heart gave a little run of beats and for some reason she felt the air had been sucked from the atmosphere, leaving her feeling breathless.

'What would you like to know?' Katie asked, relieved that her voice didn't give her odd reaction away.

'Everything.' He glanced at his watch. 'We've a couple of hours to go yet.'

'There's not much to tell, really.' At least, there wasn't much she *wanted* to tell him. She liked to keep her professional and personal lives separate.

'I've been working as a physio for four years. I specialised in sports injuries before moving to paediatrics.' There. Keep it to work. That was safe ground.

'I know that. It was all on your pretty impressive CV. By the way, well done on that paper you contributed to the *British Medical Journal*.'

The paper wasn't listed on her CV and she was surprised he knew about it.

'I enjoyed reading about bioethics and physiotherapy. It's not something I knew much about.'

So, he hadn't just glanced at it but read it. She looked at him more closely. Perhaps she shouldn't make up her mind so quickly? Didn't she hate it when other people did that? Just because he was good looking—strike that, amazing looking—it didn't mean he wasn't a good doctor. She relaxed a little.

'I'd like to know about you,' he added. 'Not just your professional résumé.'

She stiffened. Perhaps she should trust her instincts after all? She was right about one thing. He was the kind of man who couldn't bear to pass up a chance to flirt with anyone of the opposite sex. He was gorgeous and knew it. She distrusted men like that. Not that she had any experience of his kind of man.

'Not much to tell, really,' she said.

'Ah, I'm sure there is. What do you like to do in your spare time?'

Katie looked at him out of the corner of her eye. 'I exercise when I can. Swimming mostly. And I go out occasionally.'

'No boyfriend?'

It was none of his business. This was taking polite interest a step too far.

'No,' she replied shortly. 'Tell me about you.' It was a

safe ploy. Men like him liked nothing better than to talk about themselves.

To her surprise, he shook his head. 'Oh, no, you don't. I asked first.' He smiled and her pulse did another little run of beats. 'Tell me about the swimming. Do you go often? What else do you do to keep fit?'

The approval as his dark green eyes swept across her body brought a flush to her cheeks. Really, if she hadn't just met him, and he wasn't her boss, she'd be tempted to… What? Tell him to stop looking at her? It wasn't necessarily his fault her body was behaving in this disconcerting, alien manner.

'I swim almost every day. It's a habit I got into as a child and have somehow managed to keep up. I find it relaxing. Nothing to do except think about finishing the lengths. No noise. Just mindless rhythm.' At least, that was how it used to be. These days any silence was filled with memories of Richard and terrible, overwhelming pain, loss and guilt. No matter how hard she pushed herself, no matter how many times she pounded up and down the length of the pool, she could never exhaust herself enough to sleep without having stomach-churning, terrifying nightmares.

She forced herself to concentrate on the present. 'What about you?' This was more like it. Two colleagues exchanging polite small talk. 'I take it you're into the party scene?' She couldn't resist it.

Fabio leant over, his warm breath fanning her neck. It took every ounce of her willpower not to instinctively pull away from him as sparks danced down her spine. 'Don't tell Lucy—she likes to think I lead an exciting life of parties and balls, but…' he dropped his voice to a conspiratorial whisper '…actually, I had to attend a formal dinner last night but was called out in the middle of it to attend to a patient. I had to admit her to hospital and we were there most of the night. I didn't have time to go home and change.'

'Oh.' So she had got him all wrong. She felt a tell-tale flush colour her cheeks.

He resumed his normal tone. 'But to answer your initial question, I love all sports.'

'He goes BASE jumping,' Lucy interjected from across the way. She'd obviously been listening to their conversation while playing her game. 'It's how he met my dad. Dad used to do it too but Mum made him give it up. She said it was too dangerous and that it was bad enough him being a racing driver without that as well.'

What could be more dangerous than driving a racing car?

'What's BASE jumping?' Katie asked. 'I can't say I've ever heard of it.'

'It stands for Buildings Antenna Spans and Earth. I looked it up in a book,' Lucy replied.

Katie was none the wiser.

'Earth actually stands for cliffs,' Fabio said. 'You find a cliff with sheer sides and jump off it.'

'You jump off cliffs?' Katie couldn't keep the incredulity from her voice.

Fabio shrugged. 'It's not as dangerous as it sounds. I do wear a parachute.'

'I couldn't imagine in my wildest dreams throwing myself off a mountain with nothing but a flimsy bit of material strapped to my back.' Katie shivered. 'Bit of an extreme way to get a high, isn't it?'

'Some people get their thrills from a bottle. I guess I get mine at the top of a mountain.'

It was the way he said it that made Katie look more

closely at him. There was a far-away look in his eyes, a sudden seriousness that intrigued her. Suddenly she wanted to know what attracted him to such a dangerous sport.

Fabio seemed to give himself a mental shake.

'But we were talking about you. Where do you live? And what about your family? Are they nearby?'

Katie swallowed. 'I stay in North London, not far from where I was brought up. Dad was an accountant. Mum used to work as a nurse in the local hospital.'

'Used to?' Fabio looked at her sharply.

Oh, God, she always dreaded this question. It made people embarrassingly uncomfortable and they usually quickly moved the conversation to safer ground. Not that she could blame them—what was there to say? 'They died in a plane crash when I was thirteen.'

There was no disguising the shock and genuine sympathy in his dark green eyes. 'I am so sorry. That must have been hard, losing both of them.' Fabio touched her hand lightly.

'It was.' Her heart thumped against her chest. She guessed what was coming next.

'What about brothers? Sisters?'

Katie flinched and shook her head. He'd already elicited much more information than she was comfortable with—and what could she say to this virtual stranger about her brother? Especially when she was still so raw she could barely acknowledge the truth herself?

'No. It's just me.' Even as she said it, she hated that she couldn't yet bring herself to mention her brother. But she couldn't. Not without wanting to cry.

She needed to turn the conversation back to safe ground. Anywhere but on her family life. Forcing a smile, Katie turned to him. 'And you? Where are you from? Not England, I'm guessing.'

'So where do you think, then?' he asked with a crooked smile.

She leaned her head back and made a show of thinking. 'Portugal.'

Fabio wiggled his hand in a side-to-side gesture. 'Hmm, not quite. Brazil.'

Brazeel. The way he said it made it sound so exotic.

'That's a long way from your family.'

'My mother lives in Brazil most of the time, it's where most of her work is. My father died when I was in my teens.'

'I'm sorry,' Kate said simply.

'His mother is a film star,' Lucy piped up again. The child had remarkable hearing.

'Hey, don't you give all my secrets away, Luce,' Fabio protested.

Katie sneaked a sideways look at Fabio. It made sense he'd have an actress as a mother. That was probably where he got his stunning good looks. She raised an eyebrow, inviting him to elaborate.

'You might have heard of her. The actress Camilla Salvatore?' The way he said his mother's name, rolling the consonants around his tongue, his Brazilian accent becoming stronger, made Katie's toes curl, even as she wondered what had caused the bleak look in his eyes.

Camilla Salvatore—who hadn't heard of her? If Katie remembered rightly, she had been a model before becoming an actress, the wife of the equally famous Tom Lineham, who had been huge in the 1980s and whose hits were still popular even now.

Tom Lineham! God. That made Fabio his son.

Fabio must have read the dawning realisation in her face. 'Yes. 'Fraid so. They're my folks.'

Katie's head was spinning. The couple had been international celebrities. She remembered reading somewhere that Tom Lineham had died and that there had been some mystery surrounding the circumstances, but wasn't that always the case with celebrities? It was hardly something she could quiz his son about. It wasn't surprising she hadn't made the connection, between Dr Fabio Lineham and Tom Lineham. It had never crossed her mind that two famous people would have a son who had become a doctor. Why had he anyway? It seemed an unusual choice for the child of extremely wealthy parents.

'Yet you became a doctor,' she said.

He looked amused. 'As opposed to what? Being in the movies? A singer? Lolling about, living off my parents' money?' He smiled wryly. No doubt he was used to this reaction. 'I'm a lousy actor and my voice is worse.'

'So all this…' she waved a hand around the interior of the plane '…is pretty much old hat to you.'

''Fraid so,' he said again. 'I didn't even know there were commercial aircraft until I was thirteen or so.'

Poor little rich boy.

A flicker of a smile crossed his face. 'That didn't come out too well, did it? But I'm not going to apologise for the way I was brought up. There was money, yes. But as for…' He stopped suddenly but not before Katie thought a flash of pain in his eyes. Almost immediately it was gone and the mask was back in place. 'One thing I've learned, Katie Simpson. Never apologise for who you are. Or what you were. Never look back. It's the here and now that matters.'

What did he mean by that? For a second she wondered

if he knew about Richard. But that was impossible. She hadn't told anyone. She was beginning to get the unsettling sensation he could see inside her head.

'And, before you ask, no brothers, no sisters—only a cousin who lives in California.' Maybe he *could* read her mind.

'So what made you choose physiotherapy?' Fabio said, before she could question him further.

'My young cousin has CF. Like all sufferers, she has to get physio regularly. She's one of the lucky ones, though.'

Her cousin had escaped the relentless round of chest infections that most CF patients were susceptible to throughout their lives.

'What about you? Why did you become a doctor?' Katie tried to turn the conversation back to him. She was reluctant to share any more details of her life with this man. He already knew more about her than she wanted him to know.

'Pretty much the same reason as you—personal experience. I was ill as a child—nothing too serious. I found it really interesting what everyone was doing around me and decided I'd like to be on the right end of a needle.' His words trailed off and Katie thought something shifted in his eyes before his mouth widened in a smile. 'Seems we have more in common than just being colleagues.'

Katie was pretty sure they didn't have much in common. Apart from the fact they had both lost their fathers, his upbringing couldn't have been more different from hers. He was rich, sophisticated and probably used to socialising with the kind of people she'd only read about. Furthermore, the way he looked, the confidence that seemed to ooze from every pore, made her feel gauche and unsophisticated. He had no right to make her feel like that.

'I doubt that.' As soon as the words were out of her mouth she realised how abrupt she sounded. 'I'm sorry, that didn't come out the way I intended.'

'That's okay,' He gave her a puzzled look. He was probably wondering why she was so prickly. She wasn't sure herself. Ever since he'd stepped on board, she'd felt flustered.

She picked up her magazine again, making it obvious she preferred to read than chat.

Fabio gave her a long look before settling himself back in his seat and closing his eyes. He opened one briefly to look at Katie. 'Give me a nudge when we're about to land, would you? It was a hell of a late night last night.'

Before Katie could reply, the rhythm of his breathing changed and within seconds he was sound asleep.

CHAPTER TWO

As soon as the plane touched down, the co-pilot returned to open the door and release the stairs. As they left the plane, Katie saw the statuesque blonde slip a piece of paper to Fabio. Her contact details, no doubt.

Lucy let out a squeal of delight and almost ran down the steep steps towards a slim, elegant woman and a stocky man, who had to be her parents from the delighted expressions on their faces.

Lucy's father swung her into his arms and held her tight, whilst her mother smothered her with kisses.

Katie hesitated at the bottom of the stairs, reluctant to intrude. Tears clogged her throat as she watched their emotional family reunion, suddenly stricken by a sense of loneliness and longing.

But she couldn't let her personal feelings overwhelm her—she was here to do a job—and perform it professionally. Forcing herself to breathe slowly and evenly, Katie regained her composure. Besides, what would it be like to have a child not knowing how long she'd be with you? Unbearable. As bad as having a son or brother or any loved one in a war zone. Life had taught her one thing. Happiness wasn't guaranteed and even this couple, for all their fame and fortune, weren't immune to the roll of the dice. Katie prayed Lucy's parents would have their daughter for a long, long time to come.

'Fabio.' Amelia walked towards them, hand held outstretched. She seemed pleased, even relieved to see him. He bent to let her kiss him on both cheeks. 'How lovely to see you again,' Amelia said. 'We can't thank you enough for coming.'

Amelia looked elegantly cool in a vanilla-white trouser suit with just the merest pink lace of her camisole peeking out. She was made up but no amount of make-up could hide the fear and sadness in her eyes. She turned to Katie and held out her hand. 'Miss Simpson, I can't tell you how delighted I am that you could come too. Lucy has been dy…' she bit her lip '…longing to see her daddy race, but we couldn't bring her. Until now. I'm told that you are an expert in the field of physio for CF.'

'I'm happy to be here too, Mrs Hargreaves. I gave Lucy her physio on the plane. Didn't I, Luce?'

'Please, do call me Amelia.' She knelt beside her daughter. 'Did you sleep on the plane, sweet pea?'

'Yes. A little.'

'Hey, Fabio!' Mark called out. 'Great to see you again.'

Katie watched as the two men greeted each other warmly, hugging and slapping each other on the back. Fabio clearly had a stronger relationship with the family than most doctors did with patients and their families.

After introductions all round, Mark gathered Lucy up into his arms again. 'Sorry I have to leave you straight away, sweetie, but there's a team meeting I have to attend.' Giving his wife a lingering kiss, Mark sketched a wave and jumped into a low-slung sports car, then roared away.

'I'll take you to the yacht,' Amelia said. 'The firm my husband races for has given us sole use of it for however long we need, whenever we need it. There's plenty of room. I hope you'll be comfortable.'

They all piled into the back of a stretch limo. The limo was another first for Katie and she sank back in the leather seat.

As Lucy chatted away to her mother, Katie stared out of the darkened rear windows of the car. She had heard about Monaco. With its international reputation for being the playground of the rich and famous, who hadn't?

It was like being on a film set. Sleek sports cars purred around. She didn't know the names of most of them, but they could have come straight out of a James Bond movie. Most of them were open to the sunshine and were driven by men and women who looked as if they'd just stepped out of the pages of a glossy magazine or starred in that same movie.

Fabio found himself tuning out from Lucy's excited chatter, watching Katie instead. Every now and again, her eyes would light up and then just as quickly she would bite her lip and look anxious. It was extraordinary—and curiously refreshing—to see every reaction reflected in her face. Most women he knew thought it gauche to show emotion, especially to reveal that they were anything but bored by their surroundings. Katie Simpson intrigued him.

Not that she was his cup of tea. She was prim and serious in her buttoned-up suit, and there was that disconcerting shadow in her eyes. He liked his women sophisticated and, well, to put it frankly, not too deep.

And there were definitely deep layers to Katie Simpson. He had yet to meet someone who didn't enjoy talking about themselves but it was obvious that she was the exception to the rule. There were times on the plane when he could have sworn she was hiding something. Back there on the tarmac, he'd seen sadness wash over her face as she'd witnessed the Hargreaves' reunion. Was she recovering from a broken heart? A jilted lover, perhaps? It was a possibility. So that sealed it. Even if she had been his type, he would never have an affair with a vulnerable woman who was on the rebound. That was a complication he could do without. And he didn't do complicated.

Despite the evidence of wealth everywhere, nothing could have prepared Katie for the actual size of the yacht.

Moored alongside several others, it wasn't the biggest in the bay, but it was still larger than anything Katie had ever seen. More like a small cruise ship than a pleasure boat.

'I'll show you to your cabins,' Amelia said as she led them up the gangway. 'Then, if you think Lucy's up to it, I promised I'd take her to the track. Mark is due to start a practice session in an hour.' Her anxious eyes found Fabio's. 'If you think it would be okay for Lucy to be there? You will come too, won't you?'

Fabio touched her on the shoulder. 'Lucy's doing really well at the moment and of course we'll come to the track. That's what we're here for.'

'You're such a worry-wart, Mummy,' Lucy said. 'I keep telling you I'm okay. There's no way I'm not going to watch Daddy.' The little girl's mouth was set in a firm line. This was the determined side to Lucy Dr Cavendish had told her about. Determination was good.

'I guess all mothers and fathers worry about their children,' Amelia said lightly. 'Even when they're all grown up. It's part of loving someone very much.'

It was true, Katie thought, her heart twisting. Unfortunately all the worrying in the world didn't stop bad things from happening.

Amelia hooked her arm through Fabio's, leaving Katie to follow in their wake. To her surprise she felt a small hand slip into hers. She looked down to find Lucy looking up at her.

'Don't be sad,' she said. 'I'll look after you.'

Katie squeezed Lucy's hand. No doubt the little girl was used to seeing the hurt in adults' eyes. Katie gave herself a mental shake and forced a smile. For as long as she was there, she would make certain Lucy had one less adult to worry about.

'Sure,' Katie replied. She dropped her voice and bent to whisper in the little girl's ear. 'This is a bit bigger than the boat I was on as a little girl, you know.'

Lucy giggled. 'It's not that big, silly.' She pulled on Katie's arm. 'Come and see.'

It *was* that big. There was a hot tub surrounded by padded seating and a raised deck for sunbathing. To the stern was a covered area where, Lucy explained, they had breakfast. A number of white-uniformed staff drifted around with trays of cool drinks and Katie helped herself to a glass of chilled freshly squeezed orange juice. It was the perfect cure for her tight, aching throat.

After showing her the top deck, Lucy led her down some steps.

The inside was even more spectacular. An enormous lounge with what looked like a working fireplace was furnished with soft white leather couches and antique pieces, including a polished rosewood table that held a silver decanter and crystal goblets. The dining room was equally impressive. A chandelier hung over a French-polished dining table with matching chairs. It was big enough to seat sixteen. Katie hardly had time to take it all in as Lucy kept pulling her along until they came to a door. Lucy opened it with a flourish.

'This is your cabin. Dr Fabio's is right next door. And mine is across the passage, next to Mummy and Daddy's.'

Cabin wasn't the word Katie would have used to describe the room. There was a double bed, a sitting area with a television and a marble bathroom with a full bath and shower. Katie, with Lucy still watching her reaction, stepped out onto a small balcony. The marina was crammed full of yachts, most of which had people on the decks either sunbathing or sipping drinks while they chatted. Katie couldn't be sure, but she thought she recognised at least one famous actor.

'Wow!' she said to Lucy. She couldn't think of anything else to say.

Suddenly the little girl seemed exhausted and she sank back on Katie's bed. Katie was instantly alarmed. The long journey plus the excitement had taken it out of the child.

'Tell you what,' she said. 'While I unpack, why don't you have a nap on my bed before it's time to go to the race track? Then, if you don't feel better, I'll ask Dr Lineham to come and have a listen to your chest.'

'I'm okay,' Lucy said. 'But I will have a sleep. Don't say anything to Mum, will you? She's happy right now.'

Katie's heart went out to Lucy. Along the way she had become used to pretending for her mother's sake.

Lucy was asleep in seconds and Katie was covering her with a blanket when there was a knock on the door. She answered it and put her finger to her lips when she saw Fabio standing there. He'd changed out of his suit and into a pair of light trousers and an open-necked, short-sleeved shirt. Katie felt over dressed in her jacket and trousers.

He glanced over her shoulder and, seeing Lucy, tiptoed into the room. 'I was just looking for her,' he whispered. 'How's she doing?'

'Exhausted, I think. I suggested she have her nap here, where I can keep an eye on her. I think it's all been too much for her. The journey, the excitement of seeing her parents, as well as the prospect of watching her father race.'

Fabio scrutinised Lucy's face while feeling her pulse. He straightened and smiled at Katie. 'She's okay. Rest is good. I'll let Amelia know where she is.'

'I'll stay with her until she wakes up,' Katie said. 'Tell Amelia not to worry.'

Fabio nodded his head in the direction of the balcony and Katie followed him outside. He closed the door behind them.

'It's important we let Lucy do whatever she feels able to,' he said. 'It's what she wants. Understandably her parents would prefer to wrap her in cotton wool, but Lucy has let me know in no uncertain terms that she wants to be treated as if she were any child.

'She doesn't want us to treat her as if she's a patient,' he continued. 'She prefers to think of us as being friends of her parents, people who are here because they want to be, rather than because she's ill. I like to think of all my patients in terms of the family and not in isolation.'

That explained Fabio's informal and apparently casual attitude. Katie found herself revising her opinion of him once again.

'She's a brave girl,' Katie said. She looked around the marina, taking in the wealth all around. 'My guess is that her parents would give every penny they have to have her well.'

'And you'd be right. But they can't.' His expression relaxed. 'They're really glad to have you here, you know. They wouldn't have risked bringing Lucy out here unless they knew she could have professional physio on hand whenever she needs it. A lot of parents do the therapy themselves, but Amelia hates doing it. She's scared she hurts Lucy.'

'I can appreciate that, but I think we should encourage her to give it a go. I won't always be around to do Lucy's physio—at least, not as often as she needs it. Besides, once they learn how to do it and get confident, many parents become really good at it.'

He studied her as if he were truly seeing her for the first time and she shifted uncomfortably under the intensity of his gaze. 'You're a surprise, Katie Simpson, do you know that? I get the feeling that if anyone can persuade Amelia, it'll be you.' He looked as if he was about to add something but then he turned to leave. 'We'll be up on deck if you're looking for us,' he said.

By the time Katie had finished unpacking her few belongings and taken a shower, Lucy was awake again. Realising that her suit was totally inappropriate, Katie changed into a skirt and cotton blouse. They went back on deck to find Mark had returned and Fabio was chatting to both him and Amelia.

As soon as Amelia saw them, she rushed over to her daughter and hugged her tightly.

'Did you have a good sleep, sweetie?'

Lucy nodded. 'Katie let me use her bed.'

'Daddy is going back to the track to practise. Do you want to come and watch? Or would you rather stay here and wait to see him in the race?'

'Mummy, I said before, I'm coming and you're not to fuss,' Lucy said. 'I'm okay.' She softened her tone and smiled at her father. 'I can't wait to see Daddy practise.'

Mark scooped his daughter into his arms. 'And so you will. C'mon, then. Let's get going.'

The race track was only a short drive from the yacht, so close they could have walked, although it didn't seem to occur to anyone to do so. No doubt they were scared of tiring their daughter unnecessarily. As soon as Katie was out of the air-conditioned car, she smelled oil and rubber.

'Hey, Fabio. If you fancy a spin around the track, I'm sure I could arrange it.' Mark said.

Mark had to be kidding.

But Fabio didn't seem think so. A broad smile spread across his face. 'Fancy it? That's putting it mildly. I'd give my right arm for a go in one of those monsters you race.'

Mark laughed. 'I knew you'd be up for it. Okay, then, let's go and get you suited up.'

The two men left them to go and change.

'Can Mark do that?' Katie asked. 'I mean, let Fabio have a shot at driving the car? Surely there are rules?'

Amelia smiled. 'You'll soon learn that one thing neither Fabio nor my husband care about are rules. They're both adrenaline junkies.'

'So I heard on the plane,' Katie said. 'Lucy said that they met BASE jumping?'

'God, yes. I made Mark give it up as soon as I watched a video of him and Fabio doing it. It's a crazy sport. They throw themselves off these huge cliffs and wait until they're almost halfway down before they open their parachutes. So many people die, it's practically outlawed in some places.'

God, it sounded even more dangerous than Fabio had made out.

Lucy was skipping ahead of them, but to be on the safe side Katie lowered her voice.

'Aren't you scared something will happen to Mark when he's racing?'

Amelia's expression darkened. 'I'm terrified every time he goes out on that track, believe me, but he wouldn't be the man I love if he didn't do what he does. I couldn't stop him anyway. All I can do is pray that he'll stay safe.' She smiled briefly. 'But it's not as dangerous as people think. At least all the cars are going in the same direction and there are ambulances and people with fire extinguishers on standby the whole time. On the whole, I'm happier with Mark racing than BASE jumping.' She shuddered. 'Now, *that* terrified me.'

It wasn't exactly reassuring. Having a husband who was a racing driver must be close to having a brother in the army in Afghanistan. Why was it that some men needed to face danger to feel alive? Didn't they realise the agony they put their loved ones through? But people didn't choose who they fell in love with. Amelia had still fallen for Mark despite his chosen career, and Suzy had never tried to stop Richard from doing the job he loved either.

Katie vowed that when she fell in love it would be with someone she knew she had a good chance of growing old with.

At the race track, they were made welcome. They were offered a seat in the viewing area and a cool drink, but Lucy was keen to visit the pits, so that was where they headed.

The area was crowded with mechanics fiddling with

engines and chatting. Fabio and Mark were already there, suited up in similar overalls. Fabio looked in his element.

'I'd rather race,' he was saying to Mark. 'I know you'll beat me hands down but, hey, I'll never get another chance to race you again.'

'You wouldn't see me for dust, mate.' Mark's expression turned serious. 'These babies are worth a small fortune, Fabio, and with your track record you have to promise me you'll stay under a hundred and twenty. Keep behind me, but not too close. I don't want you taking me out by accident. And we're only doing two laps. Okay? Use the first to get used to how the car handles.'

A hundred and twenty! Were the pair of them out of their minds?

Fabio's eyes glittered. 'I'm not crazy, you know. I'll take it easy, I swear.'

The men were helped into the narrow cockpits of their separate cars. With his helmet on, only Fabio's eyes were visible. There was no mistaking the excitement in them. Katie seriously doubted he'd be able to keep himself or his car under control.

She was almost tempted to excuse herself—she really had no interest in watching her colleague fulfil a boyhood fantasy but for some reason she couldn't bring herself to leave.

The noise of the cars revving up would have been deafening had the staff not handed out ear defenders to everyone. With one final roar of the engines and the screech of burning rubber, the two men were off and within seconds had disappeared from view, already travelling at speed.

Less than two minutes later the cars came back into view, hurtling down the track towards them. Even with the sound muffled, Katie could still hear the tremendous whine of the engines, and she could feel the ground vibrating beneath her feet. The smell of burning fuel filled the air, adding to the sense of drama and excitement. Despite herself, Katie leant forward, hands clutched with tension as she tried to make out who was in front. As they roared past, Lucy was jumping up and down with excitement.

'Go, Daddy, go!'

Before Katie knew it, they were back and Fabio was climbing out of his car.

'Thanks, mate,' he said to Mark. ''That was some adrenaline rush. I wish I'd tried it sooner. Maybe I should take up rally driving instead.'

Fabio obviously had nerves of steel. He looked as unruffled as if he'd just been for a Sunday drive. Totally at ease in his black and red jumpsuit, the helmet casually tucked under an arm, he oozed sex appeal. He caught her looking at him and dropped his lid in a wink. Her heart gave another awkward thump and she looked away quickly.

At least she had a colleague for a little while longer. But what was he thinking? They were here to work, not have fun.

Another roar of an engine and Mark was off again. Fabio turned to Amelia, Lucy and Katie.

'Your dad is some driver, isn't he, Luce?'

'He's the best,' Lucy agreed. 'I just know he's going to win the race.'

'Of course he will,' Fabio said. 'If you'll all excuse me, I'll go and get changed.'

'Why don't we get some lunch upstairs, Lucy?' Amelia suggested. 'We'll be able to see Dad better from up there.' She turned to Katie. 'You'll join us? Mark'll be at least another couple of hours out on the track. They have to be sure the car is handling just right before the race.'

'When is it?' Katie asked.

'Tomorrow. Then he's off to Istanbul for the next one in a couple of weeks. Depending on how Lucy is, we might go to that one too. If you and Fabio are free to come too, that is?' Amelia watched her daughter who had skipped on ahead. 'You don't know how good it feels for us to be able to spend time as a family.' She paused and bit her lip. 'We don't know for sure how long Lucy might be with us, so we want to spend as much time together as possible.'

Katie touched her on the shoulder. 'Hopefully she'll be with you long enough to give you grey hairs. Children with CF are doing so much better now.' And she was being truthful. These days, around half of children with CF could expect to live to their late thirties and improvements in treatment meant that babies born today with the condition could expect to live much longer. In the 1960s a child was lucky to survive much beyond his or her fifth birthday. Of course, Amelia would know all that. Not that it was likely to be of much comfort. No parent would want to dwell on the fact that it was possible they would outlive their child.

After lunch, they all returned to the yacht. Lucy was due another round of physio.

Before Katie started, Fabio checked his small patient over.

'Chest sounds good, Luce,' he said, returning his stethoscope to his leather medical bag.

'Does that mean I can skip my physio?' Lucy asked hopefully.

'Nice try, kiddo. But you know it doesn't.'

'S'pose so. I need to use the bathroom first.'

While they waited for Lucy, Fabio turned to Katie.

'There's a drinks party this evening. I don't know if Amelia remembered to tell you.'

The thought of spending an evening with strangers panicked Katie. Especially as it would no doubt be crowded with the outrageously rich and famous glitterati of Monaco.

'I won't be expected to go, surely? If you don't mind, I'd much rather have something to eat in my room and an early night.' It wasn't just the thought of spending an evening with stars—she just didn't feel up to a party. Not that she wanted to share the real reason for her reluctance with Fabio.

'You don't have to stay long.' Fabio replied, leaning against her dressing table. 'You never know, you might even enjoy yourself.'

'I doubt it. It's just not my…scene.' Damn! That made her sound even more gauche and unsophisticated than she already felt.

'If you're worried about meeting some of the guests, believe me, they're all just ordinary people under their confident facades.'

'It's easy for you to say. You're used to this world. I'm not.' Oh, God, was he never going to give up? 'Anyway I didn't think to bring anything appropriate to wear.'

His look was appreciative. 'I think you could wear anything and still look good.'

Katie flushed. As soon as she found herself warming to him, he resorted to the playboy charm. It must come as natural to him as breathing.

'I'm sure Amelia will lend you a dress if need be.' He looked at his watch and turned to go. 'I'll let Amelia and Mark know that Lucy will be along after she's rested.' Then, whistling, he left Katie standing in her room, unable to think of anything to say.

CHAPTER THREE

FABIO stood on the deck with a glass of freshly squeezed orange juice in his hand and looked around the crowd of partygoers. There was the usual mix of sports stars, singers and actors. He knew a lot of them from other occasions. Although he'd told Katie she would find the other guests interesting, in many ways he found it boring. It was the same old crowd, the same old parties, the same chat about who was dating who, who had clinched the bigger deal, whose career was on the up, and more salaciously whose was heading down.

He had thought about phoning the co-pilot and inviting her, but had decided against it. He was at work and didn't like to mix business with pleasure. He'd wait until he got back to the UK before he called her.

Then he saw Katie step onto the deck. Her blonde hair, unleashed from the plait, was gleaming gold in the moonlight. Her eyes were wide with excitement, or anxiety—he couldn't tell which, although he suspected the latter. As she stood on her own, separate from the crowd, twisting a lock of hair between her fingers, Fabio felt an unexpected rush of protectiveness.

A simple sundress exposed her delicate collarbones and revealed shapely, lightly tanned legs. Although she wore none of the ostentatiously expensive diamond jewellery the other women did and he knew enough about women's clothes to know that her dress was no designer one-off, she outshone every other female on the yacht. Next to her the others looked overdressed and unnatural. He was stunned. Was this the same woman he had travelled with? As if sensing his eyes on her, she found his gaze and in that split second it was as if everyone else disappeared.

He pushed his way through the crowd until he was by her side.

'So you decided to make an appearance after all?' he asked.

She smiled up at him, relief at having a familiar face to talk to evident in her grey eyes.

'Lucy made me. She said if I stayed in my room she wouldn't come to the party either, so I promised I would come for a short while.'

Grabbing a glass of champagne from a passing waiter, Fabio passed it to Katie. She took it with a grateful smile. 'I still feel as if I don't belong.'

'Trust me, you're already attracting attention. From the women as much as the men. They're all wondering who you are. The men because they're planning how to move in on you and the women because they want to know who the competition is.'

'Don't be ridiculous.' She smiled at him and he felt the strangest feeling—one he didn't recognise—in the pit of his stomach.

'But I don't care if I do look like Cinderella. I'm here to do a job and if I have to join in, that's what I'll do.' Her smile grew wider and her eyes sparkled mischievously. 'I doubt I'll ever be as close to the rich and famous again, so I'm going to enjoy it. Now, won't you tell me who is who?

I don't want to embarrass myself or offend anyone by not recognising people I perhaps should. Later, I'm going to write it all down in my diary so I can tell my grandchildren about it.'

Fabio's pulse was still behaving oddly. All of a sudden he wanted nothing better than to be alone with Katie and find a corner where he could keep bringing that mischievous glint to her eyes. But he couldn't. They were both on duty. And…he groaned inwardly…she was a colleague. Hadn't he told himself earlier that an affair was out of the question? That it would only lead to trouble sooner or later? But that had been before, when he'd been sure she wasn't his type. Seeing her now was like a punch to his solar plexus.

He had to ignore the feeling in his gut, or at least he *should* ignore the feeling his gut. He wasn't at all sure he was going to be able to do so.

'Okay. See that couple over there?' He indicated a man and a woman who were surrounded by fawning admirers. 'You must recognise them. Every one in the world knows who they are.'

'Oh, my God, yes! They're on the front page of most newspapers. The golden husband and wife of the film world.' Katie replied. 'I just find it hard to believe that it's truly them and not a couple of look-alikes.'

'Come on, then, I'll introduce you.' He liked the way she wasn't scared to show her wonder.

Panic flared in her eyes and she shook her head. 'I'd rather not,' she protested. 'What on earth will I say to them?'

'I think you'll find that they are more than happy to have an audience,' Fabio said dryly, and taking her by the elbow guided her across to the couple.

* * *

As it turned out, Fabio was right. The couple were charming and did most of the talking. All Katie had to do was nod and smile in the right places. She'd been terrified when she'd first come up on deck. The yacht was packed with glamorous men and women: the women in designer gowns that shimmered as they moved, diamonds sparkling at throats and hands, or in shorter, figure-hugging dresses, exposing long golden limbs; the men in tuxedos, with crisp white shirts and bow-ties. Everywhere Katie looked she thought she recognised someone from the movies or television or the modelling world. Next to the expertly made-up women in their impossibly high designer heels, Katie felt completely underdressed in her last season's sundress, her face made up with only the merest slick of lipstick and mascara.

When she'd arrived, she had spotted Fabio immediately. Even next to the recognisable faces of well-known heart-throbs from the sporting and film world he'd stood out. Looking relaxed and assured in his dinner suit, his dark head bent to listen to something a flame-haired woman was whispering in his ear, he was the best-looking man on board. He must have felt her eyes on him because he looked up. Their eyes locked and her heart crashed against her ribs. Despite what she'd promised Lucy, she had been on the verge of hot footing it back to her cabin.

But before she could retreat, Fabio made a beeline towards her. Fleeing then would have made her look even more gauche than she already felt, and she was damned if she was going to let him see how unnerved she was, not only by the overwhelming number of beautiful people but the way the sight of him had stopped her breath. It had taken every ounce of her resolve to summon the smile she gave him.

Her heart was still pounding with excitement as the stars

talked about their latest movies. If it hadn't been for the music coming from a string quartet, she was sure everyone would have heard it beating.

'Your cousin Kendrick was the stunt co-ordinator on set, you know,' Oliver Douglas, one half of the fabulous couple, was saying.

'And how is Kendrick?' Fabio asked.

'Crazy as ever. He keeps pushing the boundaries as far as stunts are concerned, and the directors love him for it. So do we, don't we, darling? It makes us, or at least me, look better.' Oliver smiled at his wife with a self-deprecating grin. 'We're just surprised he doesn't get hurt more often.'

'I guess as he didn't manage to get himself killed when he was in the army, he'll probably manage to keep himself in one piece on the set,' Fabio said dryly.

Oliver frowned. 'Didn't he fly helicopters in Iraq or Afghanistan? Is it true he almost got killed rescuing some men who were pinned down by enemy fire? I heard something went wrong. That he went against orders and his commanding officers weren't too pleased.'

'My cousin has never been one to let orders get in the way of doing what he feels is right,' Fabio said. Although his voice was quiet, almost gentle, there was a steely expression in his eyes.

Katie's blood ran cold. She didn't want to hear about the army. She didn't want to hear about war. She certainly didn't want to hear about rescue operations that went wrong. Couldn't they find something more pleasant to talk about? Their movies, for example. Their houses in exotic places. Anything except war. Images of her brother flooded her head. The two of them laughing at an old movie. He cajoling her to join him on a huge roller-coaster at a theme park, and laughing till he cried at how she'd screamed. Unlike her, he hadn't been frightened of anything.

Now he was dead. He hadn't been playing a part in a movie. He was gone and he was never coming back. As tears burned behind her lids, she clenched her teeth so hard it made her jaw ache. She needed to get away. There was no way she could contribute to this conversation. Her head was spinning, making her feel dizzy, and she swayed slightly. Would her feet even obey her commands?

Fabio was looking at her through narrowed eyes. He took her by the elbow and steadied her. 'Would you excuse us? There's someone I have to introduce Katie to.'

Without giving the couple a chance to respond, Fabio steered Katie away towards a quiet area of the yacht. She gripped the rail tightly, trying to stop her hands trembling, taking deep breaths as she waited for the dizziness to pass.

'What is it, Katie?' Fabio asked. 'You look as if you've seen a ghost.'

Katie couldn't speak through her numb lips. She clenched her jaw, praying that tears wouldn't come. Not here, not in front of all these people, not in front of this man.

'You're shivering. Here.' Fabio took off his jacket and draped it around her shoulders. It smelled of him. Lemon and spice.

'Thanks,' she mumbled. She wished he would go away. Then she could slink back to her cabin and give in to the tears.

'Do you want to talk about it?' His voice was gentle.

Please, she thought, don't be nice to me. Anything else—flirt, whatever—just don't be kind. If he was kind, it would undo her.

She gave a vigorous shake of her head.

'Okay, then, I'll do the talking for a while.' He indicated a man well over six feet five with silver hair, who was leaning nonchalantly against a polished railing. 'See him? Do you know he used to be a baseball star before going into the movies?'

Fabio stood next to her, not quite touching, but almost. He carried on, his voice calm and soothing, until eventually she felt some of the tension leave her body.

'And the red-haired woman in the black dress?' He tipped his head in the direction of a film star who had been nominated for several awards. 'I heard tonight that's she's planning to divorce husband number five. I can't imagine marrying once, let alone five times!' He kept pointing people out, dropping in little bits of gossip and wry remarks until Katie had to smile.

'That's better,' he said, noticing.

'Thanks for staying with me.' She cleared her throat. 'And thanks for not asking me any questions. I'm going to go back downstairs and check on Lucy.' She shrugged out of his jacket and held it out to him. 'Please, go back to the party. I've monopolised you enough.'

He tipped her chin and looked into her eyes. 'I'd rather stay with you. I can party anytime.'

The touch of his fingertip on her skin sent a spark down her spine. How could she go from thinking her heart was breaking to feeling like this all in a matter of a few minutes? How could this man have such an effect on her?

'No, please. I'm really tired, Fabio, but thanks.'

His eyes glinted in the moonlight. He leaned towards her and for one heart-stopping moment Katie thought he was going to kiss her. Instead, he brushed his lips against her forehead. It was just the lightest of pressure but enough to send a flash of heat through her.

'Sleep tight. I'll see you in the morning,' he said lightly, before walking away.

Katie was rooted to the spot as she watched him disappear into the crowd. Although she barely knew him, he was making her feel as if he was pulling her into his orbit, from where there would be no escape.

CHAPTER FOUR

THE next day everyone was up early and Katie found them all gathered for breakfast on deck.

A white-uniformed crew member pulled out her chair for her and asked her what she would like to eat. Katie looked at the side table, which was groaning with platters of fruit, pastries and cheese and cold meats.

'Coffee and a couple of those delicious-looking pastries, please,' she said.

Fabio was reading the paper, clearly having long since finished his breakfast, and looked up in surprise.

'I know I shouldn't,' she said defensively. 'But they just look so good.'

'Hey, I like a woman who enjoys eating. Most of the women I know, with the exception of you, Amelia, barely consume enough calories to keep themselves alive.'

The grin he gave her made her heart thump. She had been feeling anxious about seeing him after almost making a fool of herself the evening before, but he was clearly happy to pretend nothing out of the ordinary had happened and she was grateful to him.

Last night had been the first time she had slept without waking with tears on her pillow. Instead she had slept soundly, dreaming of dark green eyes and a full mouth.

God, she realised, feeling a warmth rush through her body, she had been dreaming of being held in his arms, of him kissing her with a ferocity that made her heart sing. She looked away, terrified he could read her mind.

Even though she had clearly lost it. The dream had been so erotic—and so real—it made her blush to remember it. Perhaps it was transference or whatever it was called. Fabio had been so kind, staying with her until she'd got herself together—never mind what he must have thought of her odd behaviour the evening before. She cringed inwardly. So much for presenting a professional front at all times. The last thing she wanted was for him to think that she wasn't up to the job.

Avoiding his eyes, she looked out to sea. The sun bounced off the water, making it sparkle. To her surprise the yacht was no longer moored. Some time through the night it had moved from the marina out into the bay.

'Daddy races today, but not until this afternoon,' Lucy said. 'Mummy and I are going to stay on board this morning.' Lucy looked contented with her world.

'We thought Fabio could show you around the town. Would you like that?' Amelia suggested, smiling at her daughter.

Katie glanced at Fabio, uncertain. After last night and her dream, she felt shy and awkward in his presence.

'Shouldn't we stay here?' she asked.

'I'm sure Amelia and Lucy would be glad of some time together,' Fabio said. 'But I'm sure they won't mind if you want to stay and sunbathe. You can swim from the side of the yacht if you like.'

'Or you can do both,' Amelia said. 'Have a dip, then go and see a bit of Monaco before the race. It's entirely up to you.'

Katie stared across at the clear blue water. The thought of cooling off was extremely appealing. There was only one problem.

'I didn't think to bring my bikini,' she said. 'It didn't occur to me.'

Amelia smiled. 'Luckily I have a drawer full.' She eyed Katie. 'You and I are about the same size. You're a bit shorter and smaller, but I don't think there's much in it.'

Fabio was studying Katie speculatively. 'Didn't you tell me you swim every day? I wouldn't mind a swim myself and I'm sure Lucy will join us.'

'C'mon, Katie.' Lucy added her entreaties. 'Mummy doesn't like to swim and it'll be more fun if you and Fabio come in too.'

'Okay, then.' Katie gave in. Exercise was good for Lucy.

After breakfast, Amelia helped Katie select a bikini. Although they were all more beautiful than anything Katie had ever worn, they all seemed slightly on the skimpy side, but seeing that she had no real choice she chose one that appeared to offer the most coverage.

By the time she'd changed and come back on deck, Lucy and Fabio were already in the water.

'C'mon, Katie,' Lucy implored. 'We're waiting for you.'

Fabio was treading water. With his dark hair slicked down with the water, he looked different—more vulnerable, more human. And, if it were possible, even more sexy.

'Yes, *vamos*. Or do I have to come up there and get you?' he threatened with a glint in his eye.

Katie had no doubt he would do as he said. She balanced on the edge of the yacht and taking a deep breath dived straight in. She gasped as she hit the cool water, but moments later it felt deliciously cool and refreshing.

She bobbed up within inches of Fabio. He was still looking at her with a gleam in his eyes. 'That was some dive,' he said appreciatively. His expression grew serious. 'Are you okay?' he said. His genuine look of concern rattled her. She didn't want him to think she needed looking after. Last night had been a glitch. In future she'd be more careful to keep her feelings under control.

'I'm fine. I was tired, that's all. It was a long day,' she replied, keeping her voice matter-of-fact.

He looked at her searchingly for a moment. She was sure he didn't believe her. Then, as if he knew he wouldn't get more from her, the teasing look was back in his eyes.

'Want to race?' he said.

Lucy had eased herself onto an airbed and was paddling towards them.

'If you race, I'll be the judge,' she offered.

Katie was about to refuse when she read the challenge in Fabio's eyes. Her heart started pounding.

'Okay.' She pointed to a buoy in the distance. 'What about to that marker and back?'

'Done. I'll give you a head start if you like,' Fabio said with a smile.

'Not needed.' Katie retorted.

'Okay, ready, steady, go!' Lucy shouted, cupping her hands around her mouth.

Without waiting to see what Fabio was up to, Katie set off at a fast crawl. Each time she lifted her face to the side to suck in some air, she looked for him, but he was nowhere in sight. Good. She must be in front. But when she touched the buoy, she saw that he had been ahead of her and was turning back already. Damn. She increased her speed, putting every ounce of energy into making her legs and arms move faster. Soon she was alongside him, and then with a last effort past him. That would show him.

But just as Lucy, and the finishing line, was within easy reach, a hand grabbed her foot and she was tugged under.

Twisting out of his grip, Katie bobbed to the surface. Fabio had started swimming away from her and would easily cross the finishing line before her. The cheat! Well, two could play at that game and perhaps it would convince him that her emotional wobble the evening before was well and truly in the past. With a wink at Lucy, she let out a loud yelp and pretended to grab at her calf.

Fabio stopped swimming and turned towards her. He frowned when he saw the fake agony on her face. 'Katie! What's wrong?'

'Cramp,' Katie groaned, sliding a look at Lucy, who hid her giggles behind her hand.

Fabio swam back towards her and his arm snaked around her waist. 'Hold onto me,' he said. The heat of his bare skin against hers was sending little bolts of electricity shooting through her, almost making her forget about the race. For a moment the world stood still as she looked into his heavily lashed eyes. Confused by the sensations running through her, Katie pulled away. 'Got you!' she yelled triumphantly. Kicking her legs as fast as she could, she swam towards Lucy. She ignored Fabio's shout behind her, aware that if she stopped even for a second he would catch up.

'I win!' Her ruse had worked. She grinned as Lucy high-fived her.

When Fabio arrived seconds behind her his expression was dark and dangerous. Katie's pulse beat even faster.

Lucy slipped back in the water and swam away.

'You cheated,' he said.

'You cheated first!'

'Ah, but winning is all that matters,' he drawled. 'At least as far as I'm concerned. I should warn you, I don't believe in rules.'

He was still looking at her as if he was contemplating what to do to her. Her heart was behaving as if someone was drumming out a rock song on it.

'Maybe you don't know me as well as you think,' she said. Now she was flirting back.

Once more Katie was acutely conscious of Fabio's nearly naked body only inches from hers, and to her dismay, something that felt very close to lust curled in her pelvis.

'I…I should go after Lucy,' she managed, mortifyingly aware that her voice was husky.

The way Fabio was looking at her suggested he knew exactly what effect he was having on her. Damn the man and his gorgeousness.

'She's fine, Katie,' he murmured, holding her gaze, his eyes sparking with mischief. 'Payback time.'

His arms shot out and holding her tightly against him he sank with her beneath the surface of the water. She fought to wriggle free, every thrust of her body bringing her closer against him and adding to the clamour of sensations sweeping through her. When they bobbed back to the surface, something shifted in Fabio's eyes and his grin faded. Knowing she had to get away from him, Katie pushed him away and swam towards the yacht as if the hounds from hell were snapping at her heels. By the time she arrived next to Lucy she was breathless and she knew it wasn't from swimming.

While she and Lucy splashed in the water, Katie watched her patient carefully for any signs of breathing difficulty. There were none.

Having taken possession of the airbed, Fabio lay on his stomach, using his hands to propel his way towards them.

When he reached them, he turned over and lay on his back, shielding his eyes from the sun with his hand.

Katie and Lucy looked at each other and with one accord they ducked under the water and came up next to him, pushing over his makeshift sunbed and tipping him into the water.

Fabio came up gasping and shaking the water from his eyes. He gave Katie and Lucy a wicked grin, before grabbing the child and tossing her into the air.

Then his hands spanned Katie's waist.

His touch sent her already thumping heart rate into overdrive and she found herself looking into his eyes, almost unable to breathe again. His mouth was inches away from hers. Was he going to kiss her this time? She couldn't move, couldn't breathe. But then with a look of what she could have sworn was regret he dropped his hands.

'We'd better get back to the yacht.'

Dismayed at the thud of disappointment she felt, Katie could only nod.

Back on board, Lucy went to have a rest while Katie changed into denim shorts and a white cotton shirt. For the first time in as long as she could remember, she felt almost light-hearted. The morning had been fun—if unsettling. Back there, in the water, when Fabio had held her, she'd had the strangest sensation of coming home, which was crazy. Men like Fabio were heartbreakers and she needed to remember that. Her heart was in bad enough condition as it was—the last thing she needed was more pain.

Back on deck, Fabio had also changed, his short-sleeved white shirt emphasising his bronzed chest.

'Are you ready for lunch ashore?' he asked. Katie was perplexed. The yacht was still out in the bay and she wondered how they were supposed to get there. Surely Fabio didn't expect them to swim?

'There's a little boat we can use,' Fabio said, as if reading her mind. 'The crew are happy for me to take us, if you trust me, that is?'

No, she didn't. Not after that morning. But even Fabio couldn't get up to any mischief in the short distance to shore. Or so she thought.

The small boat wasn't small at all. It was a rubber dinghy but one with a powerful outboard motor. Fabio suggested she sit behind him at the wheel and she did so, trying to keep as much distance between her body and his as was possible on the narrow seat, but when he revved up the engine so hard it almost reared in the air Katie squealed and wrapped her arms around his waist, acutely conscious of the hard muscles of his abdomen under her fingertips.

Instead of turning towards the shore, Fabio headed further out to sea and opened the throttle. Soon they were bouncing along like a bucking bronco on the waves.

Resigned, Katie gave herself up to the sensation of speed and the wind in her hair. As they scooted over the waves, she let herself enjoy feeling free and happy. It had been so long since she'd felt that way.

Eventually Fabio turned the boat round and headed towards land.

He turned to grin at her. 'Sorry. Just couldn't resist giving her a little run. You didn't get wet, did you?'

Katie's legs were like jelly as she stepped ashore, but whether it was because of the adrenaline rushing through her body or because of the memory of Fabio's body against hers, she didn't want to think about. Did this man have to live every minute in the fast lane? Was he ever happy to be at peace?

At least there was little he could do to agitate her as they walked in companionable silence around Monaco. The shops were amazing. Filled with clothes and jewellery that didn't deign to have price tags, Katie guessed that if anyone needed to ask the price they couldn't afford it.

'It's all kind of make-believe,' she said finally. 'Almost like a film set. Everything about this trip feels unreal.'

Fabio studied her through half-closed eyes, a small smile playing on his lips. 'Don't you like it?' he asked.

Katie thought for a moment. 'It is beautiful but, no. I don't think I'd feel comfortable living here. I think being surrounded by so much wealth all the time feels a little obscene when there's so much poverty in the world. What about you?'

Fabio looked thoughtful. 'I always thought I liked it, but I understand what you mean about not wanting to live here. As for the wealth and it being obscene, I feel like that sometimes about Brazil. People there are either enormously rich or pretty impoverished. Not easy to live with.' His words surprised her. He seemed so comfortable with the rich and glamorous lifestyle.

Fabio stopped next to some tables and chairs of an outside café and raised an eyebrow. 'Ready to eat?'

'I'm okay. But something cool to drink would be good.'

Unsurprisingly, there were no prices on the menu. After they had ordered their drinks, Katie leaned back in her seat and turned her face to the sun.

'Tell me more about Brazil,' she said. 'Is there really such a divide?'

Fabio nodded. 'I wasn't aware of it until I qualified as

a doctor. I spent a year working in the inner city and it opened my eyes. Maybe one day, I'll go back and work there again.'

Katie regarded him through half-closed eyes. 'What? And leave all this?' She indicted the square with its magnificent fountain and the immaculate buildings with a wave of her hand. 'All this luxury?' Could he be pretending to be something he wasn't in order to impress her? If that was the case, she didn't know whether to be flattered or annoyed. She was in a state of constant confusion around him. One minute his natural mode of operating seemed to be to flirt with every woman he met—she had no illusions she was special in any way—although when she was with him he made her feel as if she was the only woman on the planet. On the other hand, he seemed to genuinely care about Lucy and her family. She sighed inwardly. Men like him were beyond her scope of understanding.

The sun was warm on her face but a gentle breeze coming off the sea kept it from being too hot. She closed her eyes again, breathing in the scent from the baskets of flowers and taking in the sounds, content to feel at peace, even if only for a little while.

Fabio sipped his coffee and studied the woman opposite him. When he'd seen her poised at the side of the boat in her borrowed bikini, the sight of her had blown him away. Her petite figure was just as curvaceous as her sundress the night before had suggested. She had tied back her blonde hair in a ponytail, exaggerating her high cheekbones, and when she had dived into the sea, he had caught a glimpse of her sexily rounded bottom emphasised by the high cut of the bikini.

It wasn't just that she was sexy and cute in way that made

him want to kiss her senseless. He loved watching her in her unguarded moments when her eyes would light up with wonder at everything she saw, although he believed her when she said it wasn't for her. Every moment he spent with her, she intrigued him more and more. Most of the women he dated were only too happy to talk about themselves, but not Katie. What caused that sad look in her eyes when she thought she wasn't being watched? The one that made him want to make her laugh instead? And why had she become so upset last night? What secrets did she have? He wanted to know.

He gave himself a slight shake. He had to remember that she was out of bounds. He was pretty certain women like Katie weren't into casual relationships. When they fell in love it was for ever, and one thing he could never promise was a happy ever after.

Later that day, after they'd watched Mark's race, which to everyone's delight he had won, and they were back on the yacht, Fabio checked Lucy over. Announcing himself satisfied, he left Katie to give Lucy her physio. Katie organised some pillows on the deck to do postural drainage.

'Isn't it great that Dad came first?' Lucy said. 'I wish I could have gone to the party with them.'

They'd all been invited, but Katie had opted to stay behind with Lucy. Fabio reappeared, wearing a dinner suit and bow-tie, just in time to catch Lucy's words.

'I think you've had enough excitement for the day. We all have,' Katie told Lucy.

'I'm too excited to go to bed. Can't I stay up? We could all play a board game. You, me and Fabio.'

'I think Fabio is going to the party, Luce.' Katie glanced at Fabio, suppressing a smile as she saw the fleeting look of horror on his face. No doubt staying in and playing a board game was as far away from a night out as was possible for him.

But to her surprise, Fabio loosened his bow-tie and shrugged out of his jacket.

'Sounds cool. I'm sure your folks won't mind me not going, Lucy. I'll let them know and I'll meet you ladies in the lounge.'

Realising her jaw had dropped, Katie quickly recovered. This was more like the behaviour she expected from Lucy's doctor, although, to be fair, participating in a board game went beyond the call of duty. She decided to ignore the little surge of pleasure she felt that he'd chosen to spend the evening with her and Lucy instead of at some glamorous event.

The three of them gathered round the coffee table, sitting on piles of cushions scattered over the thick pile rug. Soft lamps glowed in the corners and the lights of Monaco twinkled outside in the distance. For the first time in a long, long while, Katie felt almost happy.

'No cheating this time, Fabio.' Lucy giggled. 'Katie and I are on to you.'

Fabio mimed shocked horror. 'I'm a genius at Scrabble! I don't need to cheat.'

Lucy's first word scored eleven, Katie's nineteen and, much to their delight, Fabio's five. The next few rounds saw him lag even further behind, until he pulled a big word score out of nowhere.

'Hey! What does that word mean?' Lucy asked, suspicious.

'It's Portuguese,' Fabio replied, doing his best to look innocent. 'It's a term for a beautiful woman.'

Katie and Lucy nodded at each other. 'Get out the

dictionary!' they shouted in unison. Lucy looked up 'quezob'. 'Nice try, Dr Fabio, but no such word exists.'

The rest of the game descended into a chaos of laughter as they all vied to win by cheating and using the most outrageous made-up words.

Finally, Fabio held up his hands in submission. 'I surrender—I can't compete with you two ganging up on me.'

'I think it's time for bed, Luce,' Katie said a short while later, noticing how tired the girl looked suddenly. A yawning Lucy allowed Katie to lead her away to bed, where Katie left her sleepily watching a movie.

When Katie returned to the lounge, she hesitated at the door. Fabio was sitting on the floor, leaning against one of the sofas with his arms behind his head. How could anyone seem so relaxed yet like a coiled spring at the same time? He was a mass of contradictions. Part of her wanted his company, but being alone with him suddenly seemed too intimate; too intense.

He jumped to his feet when he noticed her. For a moment they stood looking at each other and Katie's heart kicked against her ribs. He stepped towards her.

'I think I'll follow Lucy's example and have an early night,' she said, backing away quickly. His expression was unreadable.

'Did you have a good day?' His voice was low as if her answer really mattered to him.

'It's been wonderful.' She sounded breathless, even to her own ears. 'Goodnight, Fabio.'

But once in her bed, sleep evaded her. She was feeling very restless. Slipping on her dressing gown, she stepped outside her cabin and onto the balcony.

'Hello.' His voice came out of the darkness. 'Couldn't sleep?'

Fabio was sitting on his balcony, leaning back in his chair with his long legs propped up on the railings. Her heart started its annoying thumping all over again. If it wouldn't have looked crazy for her to head straight back inside, she would have.

She shook her head. 'No. I thought some air would help.'

'How is Lucy?'

'Fast asleep. Tired out from her day.'

'She's a good kid.' Fabio stood up and leaned his back against the railing so he was facing her.

'My heart goes out to her and her parents. I don't know how they manage to keep everything so normal. If this can be called normal.' Katie indicated the sweep of the marina with the thousand lights sparkling from the hundreds of yachts.

'It's normal for them. Don't let all of this fool you, Katie. Amelia and Mark love their daughter very much. They won't have any more children because they can't take the risk of having another child with CF. They both have to be carriers for Lucy to have inherited the illness in the first place and they have a one in four chance of having another child with CF. It's not a risk they're prepared to take I suspect they'd swap places with you in a heartbeat.'

She sucked in a breath. Would they? At least, for the time being, *their* family was safe and together.

'Maybe, maybe not,' she replied. As soon as the words were out she could have bitten her tongue. God, that sounded callous.

Fabio vaulted over the railing, joining her on her side of the balcony. He was so close she could smell his expensive aftershave, almost feel the heat of his body. Her heart went into overdrive. Why couldn't he have stayed where he was?

He tilted her chin gently so he could hold her gaze. 'Something is making you sad. Do you want to tell me what it is?'

Katie shook her head and stepped away. She wasn't ready to share what had happened to Richard with anyone, least of all him. Keeping everything locked up inside was the only way she knew how to cope with her grief. She was terrified that once the floodgates opened, she'd fall apart.

'I don't think it's something you'd want to hear about,' she said quietly.

'Don't judge me too quickly, Katie.' Although his tone was light, his expression was deadly serious.

He seemed so sincere, she found herself wanting to confide in him. But talking about it wouldn't change anything. It wouldn't bring Richard back. And Fabio was a colleague. One she barely knew. She'd already revealed more to him than she wanted to. 'Thanks, but I'm fine, Fabio.'

He took a step towards her and her heart almost stopped beating. For a moment it was as if she was being held in his arms and he wasn't even touching her. She needed to keep her distance from this man in more ways than one.

'I'll see you in the morning,' she said, and before he had a chance to respond, she was back inside her cabin.

Back on his side of the balcony, Fabio stared up at the sky. Katie wasn't the only one who was struggling to find sleep that night. Perhaps it was because he couldn't stop thinking about her. Which was ridiculous.

Wasn't it?

Why was he letting her get under his skin? Okay, so something was upsetting her, but that wasn't his problem.

There was no reason on this earth that he should feel this sense of protectiveness. No reason at all that he should keep imagining the feel of her lips, the touch of her fingers, the sensation of her hair on his chest, the swell of her hips under his hand. No reason why he should be remembering her bare skin with little droplets of water rolling down between her breasts.

He had almost kissed her back there and if she hadn't turned away, he would have. Even if he knew he was playing with fire. *Deus!* There were plenty of women he could be dating. Women equally as beautiful and far less complicated. So why didn't any of them make his pulse beat the way Katie did?

Fabio stood up and with his hands thrust into his pockets paced the small balcony. He'd had a surprisingly good time earlier that evening. Who would ever have thought that Fabio Lineham would enjoy playing Scrabble with Katie and Lucy more than any other date he could remember in the last year? He chuckled as he remembered the heated look on Katie's face when she'd caught him cheating. The impish smile as she'd tried to get her own back by nudging his letters away from the triple-score square.

At one point, when Katie had been frowning over her letters, it had struck him that this what being part of a family must be like for most people, and for the first time in his adult life he'd experienced a stab of envy.

He had to stop thinking like that. He had to get Katie out of his head and there was only one sure-fire way left to cure himself of his desire for her. As the thought flashed through his head, he felt an unexpected prickle of shame but quickly dismissed it. She would have to take her chances.

CHAPTER FIVE

THE flight back home to London was uneventful, except that this time Amelia was with them. A car picked them up and, after dropping off Amelia and Lucy, along with Fabio who said he wanted to give Lucy a quick once-over at their mansion, carried on towards the part of London where Katie was staying with her sister-in-law.

Katie stood at the front door of the little maisonette in the gathering darkness and took a deep, steadying breath. Richard and Suzy had only moved in eighteen months ago and she still remembered how excited they'd both been with their first home. As soon as they'd decorated, they'd announced they were trying for a baby and they had both been so happy when Suzy's pregnancy had been confirmed. How could they have known that less than a year later it would all fall apart?

Swallowing the lump in her throat and plastering a smile on her face, Katie let herself in.

She wasn't surprised to find that her sister-in-law was still up, little Rick cradled in her arms.

'Oh, hi,' Suzy said lethargically. She was clutching a crumpled letter in her hand. 'How was your trip?'

Katie felt a rush of sympathy and immediately dismissed her own fatigue. 'I'll put this little one down, shall I, and make us a snack, then tell you all about it,' she said, holding out her arms for her nephew.

Gently, Katie removed the sleeping baby from Suzy's arms. She breathed in the particular baby smell and her heart contracted as two small eyes, exact replicas of his dead father's, opened and fixed on hers. Recognising his aunt, Ricky fell back to sleep.

She put him down in his cot and returned to the sitting room. Suzy was still sitting in the same position as when Katie had left her.

'His commanding officer wrote to me.' She waved the pages of the letter listlessly. 'He's going to recommend him for some medal. As if that would make things better.'

A crushing sense of guilt threatened to overwhelm Katie. If Richard hadn't needed the money to support her as well as himself, he would have never joined the army. But that wasn't all. When Richard had been offered the chance to serve abroad, before he'd fallen in love with Suzy, he'd come to Katie and asked her what he should do.

'I don't want to leave you on your own, kiddo,' he'd said. 'But this is something I need to do.'

'Hey, I'm all grown up now. I'll be fine,' she'd said, although she'd wanted to beg him not to go. He had looked after her practically all his adult life, supporting her, encouraging her to follow her dreams, and it had only been fair that she should let him follow his.

Crouching by her sister-in-law's side, Katie took the pages and read. As Suzy had said, Richard's commanding officer was recommending Richard for a medal. It was pretty much as they'd been told. Her brother had been stationed at a forward operating post when some of the soldiers under his care had come under fire. Without regard for his own safety, Richard had left the protection of the FOB and rushed out to pull one of the injured soldiers to safety. Then he had gone back for another. It had been at that point he had been shot and killed.

'I'm so angry with him,' Suzy said softly. 'I know it sounds crazy, but he was a doctor, not a soldier. He didn't have to do what he did.'

Katie rested her head against Suzy's shoulder.

'He had us to come home to,' Suzy continued. 'All he had to do was keep himself safe for another two weeks then he would have been back where he belonged. Here. With his family.'

'I know,' Katie said.

Suzy sighed deeply. 'But he wouldn't have been Richard, would he, if he hadn't done what he did? He wouldn't have been the man I loved. Whatever you think, Katie, Richard wouldn't have been happy doing anything else.'

Her words were an echo of Amelia's. A reminder that loving brought pain and that you couldn't help who you fell in love with. An image of Fabio floated into Katie's head. In many ways he reminded her of Richard. He had that same insatiable desire for excitement and danger as her brother had had. However much he made her nerve endings tingle, however much she was drawn to him, she had to remember he wasn't the man for her. For all sorts of reasons.

Tears were running down Suzy's cheeks and Katie knew that, despite her best efforts to be strong for her sister-in-law, her own cheeks were wet.

'Oh, Katie, how am I going to live without him?' Suzy wailed.

And then the two women were in each other's arms, seeking comfort that they knew they could never find.

* * *

When they had dried their tears and made some tea, they made themselves comfortable on the sofa.

'So tell me about your trip. Was it fun?' Suzy said.

Suzy was always trying to get Katie to get out and start enjoying life again, so Katie told Suzy about the yacht, Monaco and the people she had met. She tried to make her stories as amusing as possible and was rewarded when Suzy laughed.

'And this Dr Lineham—Fabio? Tell me more about him. I'm guessing he's gorgeous. Your eyes light up every time you mention him.'

Suzy had always been too perceptive for her own good. Katie felt her cheeks redden.

'He's good looking, but not my type.' She went on to tell Suzy about Fabio and the race with Mark. 'He also BASE jumps, which as far as I can gather is one of the most dangerous sports a person can do. So put any matchmaking thoughts out of your head. When I fall for someone, it's going to be a man whose idea of a crazy risk is doing the lottery once a week.'

Suzy laughed. 'I wonder.' Then her expression grew serious. 'You know Richard wrote to me not long before he died and said that if anything ever happened to him, I was to move on with my life, and that's what I'm trying to do. Oh, I'll never forget him and I doubt I'll ever love again, but I have Ricky to live for. But apart from Ricky and I, the person Richard cared about most, Katie, was you. He'd want to know you were happy. He'd want you to live your life to the full. Maybe this Fabio is a chance for you to move on with your life.'

Katie hugged her knees to her chest. 'He's a risk-taker, Suzy, and that's only one of many reasons there could never be anything between us. Even if he wanted there to be, which I very much doubt. He has that same reckless streak that Richard had.' Katie's breath caught. 'If only Richard hadn't joined the army because of me, he would still be alive.'

Suzy had never once blamed her for Richard being in the army. Never once given any indication that she held her responsible for Richard's death. Katie had tried to tell her how she felt, but Suzy had refused to listen.

'You have to stop blaming yourself, Katie,' Suzy said. 'Richard was born needing to challenge himself, and that's why I know the army was the right place for him. Even if it hadn't been a way to put himself through medical school while supporting you, I think Richard would have found a way to be in the army one way or another. He was an adrenaline junkie before he joined the forces. You have to stop tearing yourself into tiny pieces.'

Although Suzy meant what she said, and even if, deep down, Katie knew her guilt was illogical, she'd never stop feeling that some of the responsibility for Richard's death lay at her feet.

Katie reached for Suzy's hand. 'I couldn't put myself through the endless worry all over again. I couldn't be you, or Amelia for that matter, never knowing whether today is the day you get the call you dread. I've lost three people I love much too soon and I'm not going to risk having my heart ripped out again.' She sighed. 'I don't know how you go on, left alone to bring up your baby.'

'I have Ricky and you and my parents, Katie. I have every reason to live. Loving Richard was the best thing that ever happened to me, even though losing him broke me into little pieces. Fabio may or may not be the right man for you, Katie, but at least promise me that you'll open your heart to the possibility of falling in love one day, whatever joy and sorrow that might bring.'

Katie managed a wobbly smile. 'I promise. Just as long as you know it won't be with Dr Fabio Lineham.'

Katie looked over her list of patients for the day. It was an easy schedule, a couple of footballers and an Olympic swimming hopeful who were coming to the practice for their physio. In the afternoon she had a home visit scheduled to an elderly patient who was recovering from a stroke and couldn't make it to the practice.

Even her experience of Monaco hadn't prepared her for the number of celebrities, sport stars and aristocracy that came through the doors.

When she'd come for her interview a couple of weeks earlier she'd known immediately that this was no ordinary practice. To begin with, instead of a formal interview with one or two of the most senior doctors sitting opposite her behind a desk, all of the staff had been there, seated comfortably in armchairs. Dr Cavendish, the senior partner, a suave, elegantly dressed man in his early thirties who looked happy with his lot in life; his wife Rose, who was currently heavily pregnant and who was one of the nurses as well as the practice manager; the receptionist, a lively-looking girl called Jenny in her late teens or early twenties with a startling haircut and a tattoo; and, finally, Vicki, the other nurse. The only one missing had been Fabio.

They had all gone out of their way to make her feel part of their small team and, Fabio notwithstanding, Katie was enjoying working there.

The footballers, whose names she didn't recognise but who caused a flutter with Jenny, arrived first. Katie ignored their teasing as she gave them their physio. It soon transpired that one was married and more than happy to exchange small talk about his wife and children as Katie worked on him. The other asked her to dinner, and seemed genuinely put out when Katie said no. No doubt he wasn't used to being refused. Tough. He was a patient and, besides, Katie instinctively knew that he was trouble. Nevertheless, she framed her refusal in a way that wouldn't cause offence. However, she had to admit it was good for her ego to be asked out.

Her next patient wasn't as straightforward as Katie had hoped. Gillian Blake had been pre-selected for the British Olympic swimming team and had a punishing schedule.

'I get up at five every day,' she told Katie, as Katie put her limbs through a series of passive movements, 'swim for six hours, come home, have something to eat, relax for an hour or two, then it's off to the gym for another couple of hours. It's great that you're here now. Before this, I had to go all the way across London for my physio. As you can imagine, that ate up a chunk of the day.'

'I like swimming too,' Katie told her, 'but my efforts amount to thirty laps at the most in the pool before or after work. It's the way I switch off from the world. I can't imagine doing it for hours and hours, every day of my life.'

'It's what I have to do if I want to stand a chance of getting a medal,' Gillian said. 'Thank goodness for the sports council grant. Now I can get some proper back-up to my training.'

Katie's hands paused at Gillian's knees. There was slight swelling and it felt hot to the touch.

'Gillian, have you injured your knee recently?' she asked.

The Olympic medal hopeful shook her head. 'No. At least, I didn't think I had. But it's been a bit sore over the last couple of months. It aches for a couple of days then the pain goes away. I wondered if there was something wrong with my technique. I asked my coach and he said no. It was him who suggested I come for a bit of physio and massage. It's probably overuse.'

'Mmm,' Katie said. 'Too much training could be the problem, but to be on the safe side I'd like one of the doctors to check you over. Would you be okay with that?'

Gillian frowned. 'I really don't think there's anything to worry about.' But Katie could see the doubt in her eyes.

'Let's just say I'd be happier if one of them had a look. You lie here and relax for a few minutes and I'll go and see who's free.'

Katie tapped on Fabio's door after checking with Jenny that he was alone. He had his feet up on the desk and was leaning back with his hands behind his head.

He leaped to his feet when she came in. Whatever else she thought about him, he had good manners, although she wished he wouldn't do that jumping-up thing every time she entered the room. It really was quite unnerving.

'Katie, what brings you into the lion's den?'

She wished he wouldn't take that flippant tone either. Since they'd returned from Monaco she had gone out of her way to avoid him, preferring to go to Jonathan Cavendish when she needed a medical opinion. She hoped that time would cure her of the peculiar way Fabio made her feel whenever he was around, particularly when they were alone. Unfortunately, today Jonathan had gone out to see a patient. Not that she could always avoid Fabio. She just had to keep their encounters on a professional footing.

'I'm with a patient at the moment. She's a swimmer who's hoping to win a medal in the games.'

His eyes had lost that sleepy look. He was immediately

alert. When he wasn't assuming his cat-like repose position, he was like a curled up spring. Was there no happy medium with this man? 'Something's bothering you?'

'Yes. When I was doing her physio I noticed some swelling of her right knee. It's hot to the touch as well.'

'What are you thinking?'

'I'm thinking that there might be something going on with her. Like rheumatoid arthritis. I know it's a bit of a leap, but I wondered if you'd mind having a look. I don't want to take any chances.'

'Sure. No problem. My next patient isn't due for another ten minutes and she's always late anyway. C'mon—let's go and see your girl.'

She had to admire the way patients responded to Fabio. When he was with a patient he lost that teasing predator look and became the consummate professional. Not that he lost any of his charm—it was just that he was good at putting patients at ease.

When she noticed his eyes narrow almost imperceptibly as he examined Gillian's knee, after asking her searching questions about her general health, she knew she had been right to call him.

He hid his concern from his patient. 'I would like to take some blood for testing if that's okay, Gillian.'

Gillian sat up on the couch, looking alarmed. 'Why? What do you think is wrong? As I said to Katie, I'm sure it's no more than overuse. I'll cut back on practice a little and you'll see—the stiffness will go away.'

'You could well be right,' Fabio said evenly. 'But isn't it better to get these things checked out properly? Especially for athletes. Why don't I send some samples of blood to the lab and we can arrange for you to come back and see me in a day or two. That way we can all be reassured.' He smiled and Gillian relaxed. 'After all, we want to keep you in peak condition.'

'I suppose,' Gillian said reluctantly.

Katie could tell that the thought of anything interfering with her training was difficult for this young, driven woman. Then something struck her. 'Gillian, when you train, do you go running?'

'Yes. And go to the gym and do weights.'

'And when you go running, is it on a track? Or cross-country?'

'Across the fields near where I live. Why are you asking?'

Fabio and Katie exchanged a look. He nodded, inviting Katie to go on with her line of questioning.

'And these fields, is the grass long sometimes?'

'No,' Gillian replied. 'It would interfere with my running too much.' Her reply wasn't what Katie had hoped.

'But,' Gillian added, 'I do take a short cut home through the long grass as part of my cool-down.'

'Have you noticed a rash?' Fabio asked, and Katie knew he was thinking along the same lines she was.

'Come to think of it, I have. At least, my mother noticed it on my back. I didn't think anything of it. Do you think it's important?'

'It might be,' Katie said. It was just possible Gillian had been bitten by a tick and her symptoms had been caused by tick fever. In which case, it was good to catch it early and with the right treatment Gillian's sore joint would heal. To be certain, however, they would ask for Gillian's blood samples to be tested for the disease.

'I could give your knee some ultrasound treatment after Dr Lineham's taken some blood. That might well help. And

I'll schedule you in for more when you come back to see the doctor for the results. How does that sound?'

Gillian nodded and quickly Fabio reached into the cupboards and pulled out a syringe and some vials for the blood.

'We should have the results tomorrow, if I rush them through,' he said, and after explaining what he was going to do slipped a needle into a vein in Gillian's arm.

'Okay, I'll get these over to the lab. Make sure you make an appointment to come back and see me the day after tomorrow. You can bring someone with you if you like.' He squeezed her shoulder. 'I know it's difficult and easy for me to say, but try not to worry.' With a last smile he left the room, taking the samples with him.

'He's kind of cute, isn't he?' Gillian said wistfully.

Katie smiled back. 'I can't say I noticed,' she lied. 'Come on, then, let's get some ultrasound on that knee.'

After Gillian had made another appointment and left, Katie went in search of Fabio. She knew the patient he had been waiting for had been and gone. She found him in the small kitchen drinking a glass of water.

'Thanks for seeing Gillian,' she said.

He held out a glass and raised an eyebrow. When she nodded he poured her a glass of water from the fridge.

'Never, ever think twice about seeking a medical opinion from one of us,' he said. 'Jonathan wasn't kidding when he said that we want our patients to get the best possible care and attention.'

Katie returned his look. 'Which is why I agreed to come and work for this practice,' she responded, her voice cool.

Fabio smiled sheepishly. 'Forgive me. I didn't mean that to come out the way it did. We wouldn't have employed you if we hadn't been convinced you were the best fit for us. There are too many people who are willing to take money from patients for unnecessary treatment.'

'Do you think there's a chance she might have rheumatoid arthritis?' Katie asked, trying to ignore the way something in her stomach was performing little pirouettes every time he looked at her.

'I think it's possible, but it was a good call to check for Lyme disease. We can't be sure what it is until we've done all the tests and have the results back.'

'Poor Gillian. If she does have rheumatoid arthritis, this could mean the end of her dreams, couldn't it?'

'Let's not get ahead of ourselves, Katie.'

'But if…' she persisted.

His eyes were almost the colour of grass, Katie thought. Now, where had that come from? She had to remember that not only was Fabio her boss, and off limits for that reason on its own, but he was the kind of man who broke hearts. She had more than enough to deal with at the moment without developing a crush on her new colleague.

'If she does have arthritis then, yes, it won't be good for her career,' Fabio admitted. 'On the other hand, Lyme disease and a host of other possible conditions are easily treatable. And she will have you to thank for spotting it so early. But until we know what we're dealing with, I refuse to make any predictions. Rest assured, I'll do anything in my power so that she doesn't have to give up the sport she loves.' He pushed himself upright. 'Do you always worry so much about your patients?' he asked.

'I can't help it,' Katie admitted. 'These days I worry all the time, about everyone.'

He looked puzzled.

'Any particular reason it's *these days*?'

She was surprised he had picked up on her slip. Yet she felt this strange connection between them. The silence stretched between them as he studied her intently. 'Are you sure there's nothing you want to tell me?'

Katie shook her head. She didn't want to let him into her head any more than he was already.

'You can't go through life worrying about what might happen. If you do, you'll end up missing what *is* happening,' Fabio continued softly.

He was right. Of course he was right. It was the same thing Suzy had said but that didn't mean she could change how she felt.

'I'll bear that in mind,' she said tightly. It was easy for him to say. Who did he care about?

Fabio gave her a sharp look but said nothing. He finished writing the labels for the bloods he had taken earlier and popped them in the tray to be collected for the lab. When he turned back to her the teasing look was back in his eyes.

'How do you fancy coming for a drink with me tonight? I have passes to the VIP area of Vipers.'

Katie's pulse thrummed. He was asking her out!

'I suspect you could do with some cheering up.' His eyes softened.

He was asking her out because he felt *sorry* for her? She wasn't going out with anyone just because they thought she needed cheering up. She had her pride after all. So much for thinking there was something between them. But neither, as she seemed to have to keep reminding herself, was she interested in him.

'I'm sorry, I can't.'

'Can't or won't, Katie?' He tilted her chin, forcing her to meet his eyes, and a flash of heat spiralled through her body.

She pulled away from him, needing to put distance between them. 'Won't. If you'll excuse me, I have a home visit to do.'

'Ah, yes,' Fabio replied. 'Lord Hilton. Actually, we're both going to see him. He had a stroke three weeks ago and you're scheduled to take over his daily physio. I need to check how he's doing. After that, we have a singer who was involved in a car accident a few weeks ago. She broke her arm, it's in a cast and I want to check and see how she's doing. She also needs some physio.'

'What sort of residual damage does Lord Hilton have?' Katie was glad to get the conversation back on neutral ground.

Fabio flicked a glance at his watch. 'He's expecting us in an hour. It will take us that long to get to his place. Why don't I bring you up to speed on the way?'

CHAPTER SIX

FABIO's car was a surprise. Instead of the sports car she'd assumed he'd be driving, it was a perfectly respectable, solid family saloon. Fabio must have noticed her raised eyebrow. 'Not mine. It belongs to a friend. The one I usually drive is in the garage, undergoing repairs for a…er… scrape.'

Katie couldn't bring to herself to ask him what had happened. She wondered if Mark had known about the so-called scrape before he'd let Fabio anywhere near his racing car. The rueful look in Fabio's eyes made her smile. Whatever his faults, there was no denying there was something terribly attractive about him. No doubt most women found him irresistible.

As promised, Fabio launched into details of the patients they were going to see, while he weaved his way through the heavy London traffic.

'Lord Hilton is first on our list. Luckily he's staying with his sister-in-law here in London while he recuperates, so we won't have to drive to his estate. His sister-in-law, Lady Hilton, is a big fan of the practice.'

'How bad was Lord Hilton's stroke?' Katie asked.

'It could have been worse. Apart from some residual weakness on his left side that makes it difficult for him to walk without help, he got off lightly. Unfortunately he has a fondness for cakes and pastries and no matter how often I tell him that he needs to reduce his cholesterol, he won't listen.' Fabio glanced at Katie through his thick, dark lashes. 'Perhaps he'll listen to you.'

'Me? I doubt that. If he's going to listen to anyone, surely it'll be you, his doctor.' And not just because he was his doctor. Katie was increasingly certain that Fabio could charm the birds out of the trees, young or old.

Fabio grinned. 'I might have been able to persuade him if it wasn't for the fact he's known me since I was in short trousers. My father's mother was his cousin. I think he still finds it difficult to accept that I'm old enough to be a doctor.'

Somehow Katie could simply not see Fabio as a child. She was sure he must have sprung from his mother's womb beautifully dressed and immaculately mannered. The image made her giggle.

'What's funny?' Fabio asked as he swung the car down a broad street lined with Georgian townhouses.

'Nothing.' His glance told her that wouldn't do. 'Sorry. The image of you in a sleepsuit. I couldn't help myself. It's a little different to the way you are now.'

Fabio pretended to look offended, then smiled back. 'Any image of me that makes you laugh has to be good. I like to see you smile.'

Katie's pulse skipped a beat and for a moment the air between them was thick with something she couldn't quite put a finger on. Flustered, she turned her head away and stared out of the window.

Now, what had made him go and say that? Fabio chided himself. His teasing comments clearly made her uncomfortable, but he couldn't help it, no matter how often he told himself she was off limits. He wanted to see her smile. Since the evening in Monaco when he'd decided that sleeping with her was the only way to get her out of his system, he'd revised his plan. He couldn't bring himself to seduce her. Since meeting Katie, he wanted to believe that he was better than that. He wanted *her* to believe he was a better man than he was. For the umpteenth time, he found himself wondering what was causing the sadness that was always lurking, even when she smiled. Had someone hurt her? It made him want to grab whoever it was and shake him by the throat. Any fool could see that she was different from other women. She was shy and reserved and…honest. When Katie gave her heart, it would be without pretence or guile. Women like her deserved better.

Why was he tying himself in knots over her anyway? She was beautiful, not in the way other women were, her mouth was slightly too wide, her nose had a little bump that stopped it from being perfectly straight, and she had the tiniest gap between her two front teeth. For some reason, he found the whole package incredibly attractive. But it wasn't just that he found her sexy as hell, she had this unsettling effect on his psyche. She made him introspective, made him think about stuff that he had spent most of his life trying not thinking about. And—maybe this had more to do with his attraction than he wanted to admit— she seemed completely unfazed by his attention. That in itself made her different—and a challenge. He'd had his fair share of kiss-and-tells, some of the women whom he dated obviously finding the lure of who he was, or rather who his parents were, irresistible. One or two had even thought he would use his connections to kick-start their acting and singing careers. Those were the women who, once he'd steered them towards someone who might be able to help, he dropped like hotcakes. While he didn't mind non-serious relationships, indeed made it clear from the get-go that he wasn't into marriage and babies, neither did he like the feeling he was being used.

He slid a glance at his companion, who was staring out of the window. He was certain that she couldn't care less who his parents were or who he was connected to. Come to think of it, she didn't seem that impressed with him either. He hadn't intended to ask her out earlier, but somehow he had found himself doing exactly that. And she'd said no! Her refusal had taken him by surprise. *Porra!* One way or another, he had to cure himself of his growing fixation with Katie Simpson before it got completely out of hand.

CHAPTER SEVEN

THE visit to Lord Hilton took longer than Katie had expected. The effects of his stroke had made him irritable and out of sorts. Thankfully Fabio had been able to cajole him into accepting the need for regular physio and once Katie had put him through a set of passive movements, Lord Hilton seemed to relax and was even grudgingly grateful.

Back in the car, Katie sighed. 'That was a bit uncomfortable.'

Fabio smiled again. 'Don't worry about Lord H. His bark is worse than his bite. He liked you.'

'Liked me? I doubt that.'

'Trust me, he would have evicted you promptly if he hadn't been happy. He told me when you were washing your hands that you weren't too bad for someone of your age and that he supposed he'd be happy with you doing his physio. Believe me, that's praise coming from Hugh.'

It was all right for Fabio, Katie thought grumpily as they sped towards their next patient. He was clearly used to having people eating out of his hand.

Their next patient was a singer who had a car accident a number of weeks before. The singer, so famous even Katie had heard of her, was staying in one of London's leading hotels while she recovered.

'She has a house in London, as well as in New York and Los Angeles,' Fabio said, 'but she often stays in a hotel while she's touring in England.'

'Do you know her well?' Katie asked, trying not to show how starstruck she was.

'Not very,' Fabio said. 'She came to me with a medical problem the last time she was in London. Up until this accident she's been touring non-stop. In many ways it's not a bad thing her accident happened when it did. I warned her she had to slow down. People think it's all glamour, but the schedules some of these stars lead can be killers.'

'Was it like that for your father?' Katie asked.

A muscle twitched in Fabio's cheek and he frowned.

'I wouldn't know. Between my father's career and my mother's, I didn't see that much of them.' Although his voice was light, Katie thought she saw a shadow cross his face, but before she could be sure, it was gone. 'On the other hand, whenever I was with them life was always exciting.'

And Katie knew how much Fabio craved excitement. However, she wasn't convinced by his glib response.

'But as a child? What was it like for you?' she persisted. 'What about school and friends? Did you travel with your parents?'

Fabio steered the car though the heavy traffic before replying.

'I travelled with them on and off until it was time for me to go to school. Then I went to boarding school, along with several others who had parents in show business. Jonathan was there too. It's how we met. I spent some school holidays with my folks. Mostly in Brazil. Sometimes in London.' As a life story it was short and to the point. Clearly Fabio didn't like talking about his past.

'Do you go to Brazil to see your mother?' Katie persisted. His reluctance to share the details of his life made her even more curious.

Once again Fabio paused. 'I haven't seen her for years. We don't really have much to say to each other.' He drummed his fingers on the steering-wheel. 'Maybe it's time I did something about that.' He sounded surprised, as if the thought hadn't crossed his mind before.

Katie wanted to probe deeper, but before she could they pulled up in front of the hotel and a doorman rushed to open the car door for them.

'I'll get someone to park your car for you, sir,' the doorman offered. Fabio tossed him the keys and led Katie into the hotel.

'Tamsin has a suite on the top floor,' Fabio told Katie.

Her head swivelled as she caught sight of various famous faces in the lobby, some of whom waved at Fabio as they passed by. She even thought she saw a minor royal sipping coffee. It was all head-spinning stuff. Like being in a dream. She only wished she were. Then Richard would still be alive and everything would be as it should be.

As the lift glided up to the top floor Katie was acutely aware of Fabio. He confused her. When she'd first met him, she'd thought she'd dislike him. He'd appeared to be the epitome of a playboy, but she was beginning to realise that there was far more to this man than his gorgeous looks. He was kind and thoughtful and sympathetic. No wonder his patients, even grouchy Lord Hilton, seemed to adore him. But how much was a facade? What was underneath?

'You should be aware, if you don't already know, that Tamsin is going through a messy divorce at the moment. She's pretty cut up about it,' Fabio said.

It seemed that celebrity status and wealth was no barrier to pain.

Tamsin opened the door to them and invited them in.

Katie had never been in a hotel room like it before. In fact, it wasn't a room but a suite with breathtaking views of the Thames and London Bridge.

'Fabio, thanks so much for coming here,' Tamsin said with a genuine smile of gratitude. 'I couldn't face running the gauntlet of the paparazzi at the moment. They wait for me everywhere.'

Katie felt a stab of sympathy. It must be horrible enough to be going through a divorce without having all the details spelled out in the papers for everyone to read.

'This is Katie, our physio, Tamsin,' Fabio introduced her. 'She's going to have a look at your shoulder and leave you some exercises to do.'

Tamsin smiled again. 'I can't afford to have my shoulder seize up,' she said. 'It's the one I hold the microphone with. I'm due to sing at a concert in a couple of weeks.'

'There's no reason why you shouldn't have full use of your arm once the cast comes off,' Katie reassured her. 'The exercises will help you regain full mobility that much quicker, that's all.'

'How have you been, Tamsin?' Fabio asked. 'Are you getting some rest?'

Tamsin shrugged. 'I could do with some sleeping pills if you have any in that magic bag of yours. I had to cancel some venues but my sponsors have slotted in some extra dates to make up for the ones I've missed. I really need to be at my best if I'm gong to cope.'

Fabio's expression darkened and he shook his head. 'I'm sorry. I don't think sleeping pills are a good idea. Perhaps if you could get some exercise, that would help you sleep.'

Tamsin pouted. 'Are you sure you can't give me some? I can't even leave the hotel to see you, let alone to exercise. My personal trainer comes here, but there isn't much I can do. Not with my arm in a cast. Go on, Fabio, be a sweetie.'

But Fabio shook his head again. His mouth was set in a grim line. 'I can't stop you going to another doctor who will give you sleeping tablets, but I'm afraid I won't. It's too easy to become dependent on them.'

Tamsin sighed. 'I don't want another doctor, Fabio. I trust you.'

Fabio checked Tamsin's shoulder as well as taking some blood. 'I want to make sure there isn't another reason for your tiredness apart from a too-hectic schedule,' he explained. When he'd finished, Katie put Tamsin through some passive movements.

'When does the plaster come off?' Katie asked.

'A week tomorrow, thank God. You have no idea how difficult it is to bath and dress while keeping a cast dry. And,' she added, 'it is not a good look with an evening dress. Which reminds me...' She eyed Fabio hopefully. 'I have tickets for Vipers tonight. Everybody is going to be there. I hear that waste of space who used to be my husband is going with his latest fancy. I don't suppose you'd be willing to accompany a woman in an evening dress and arm cast, would you?'

'Sorry, Tamsin, but you know the rules. You're my patient.'

Tamsin pouted but clearly realised Fabio wouldn't change his mind. 'I could always change my doctor,' she said teasingly.

Fabio smiled coolly. 'Still wouldn't be allowed, Tamsin. Sorry.'

Katie hid a smile. At least there were some rules Fabio wasn't prepared to break.

'So what do you think of Tamsin?' Fabio asked as they waited for his car to be brought round to the front of the hotel. 'Is she like you imagined?'

'Not at all,' Katie admitted. 'The newspapers make her out to be some kind of monster, but I liked her.'

'The newspapers are wrong about a lot.' Fabio's lips thinned. 'I've been on the receiving end of their fabrications more than once.'

He tipped the doorman and opened the car door for her.

'You'll find that the patients we deal with, although often rich and famous, are, under the surface, like most people. Perhaps a little more insecure than most.' He smiled at her. 'More insecure than you, at any rate. You have a natural way with them. It's good that you don't let their celebrity status get in the way of how you treat them. It would be easy to be bullied into doing what they want rather than what's right for them.'

'Like Tamsin and the sleeping pills?'

'Exactly. There are plenty of unscrupulous doctors out there who are prepared to give those rich enough or famous enough anything they ask for. Even if it ends up killing them.' The bleak look she thought she'd seen earlier was back. It made Katie wonder how much of the rumours and speculation surrounding his father's death were true. The papers had reported his death as being the result of an accidental overdose. In that case, no wonder Fabio had taken a firm line with Tamsin.

'But they trust you.'

'It helps that I'm part of their world. They know I'd rather lose them as a patient than compromise my ethics. And if they don't…' he shrugged '…they can go elsewhere.'

She believed him. Underneath his light-hearted demeanour ran a thread of steel. It would have been better had he not been someone she could admire. Far, far easier to resist the magnetism that radiated from his every pore.

'That's us finished for the day. How about I run you home?' Fabio suggested.

'Oh, there's no need. Just drop me at the tube station.'

Again that dazzling smile. 'It's no problem. You've had a busy day and at this time the tube is packed.'

'Don't tell me you know from first-hand experience. I won't believe you.'

He pulled a face. 'No, you're right. The last time I used the tube was years ago and nothing would tempt me to use it again. It takes far too long, apart from anything else.'

'In which case, a lift home would be very nice.'

'Are you sure you won't change your mind about tonight?'

'So you can cheer me up?' She couldn't keep the asperity from her voice.

He looked at her in surprise. 'Because I like being with you,' he said softly.

The world seemed to shrink until it contained only them. Katie's heart tumbled in her chest. She didn't know how to behave, what to do with this man. Every instinct was screaming to keep their relationship professional while another part of her wanted nothing more than to be with him.

She forced herself to listen to her brain. Much more sensible.

'I can't, really.' She smiled. 'But thanks for asking.'

He looked at her, the expression in his green eyes

unreadable. After what seemed like minutes, but could have only been seconds, he bent over and touched her cheek with his lips.

'Goodbye, Katie. I'll see you on Monday. Have a good weekend.' Then, with a casual wave of his hand, he was gone.

Katie touched her cheek with her fingertips. Every minute she was becoming more confused by him. Did he really want to spend time with her, or was he just being friendly to a colleague he knew was going through a bad time? And why did it matter?

The next morning Fabio was up and out before it was light. He'd spent the night tossing and turning, trying not to think of Katie. It hadn't worked. He kept thinking about the way he felt when he was with her. Peaceful was the word that sprang to mind and since when did he do peaceful? On the other hand, the way she kept probing into his life, while studying him with those steady grey eyes, unsettled him. Already he had shared more with her about his life than he had with any other woman. And no matter how often he told himself that she was off limits, he kept looking for opportunities to be alone with her. It was as if his head and his heart belonged to two different people.

At dawn he'd given up on trying to get back to sleep and after dressing quickly had jumped into his car. Driving at speed, he had reached the cliffs just as it was getting light.

He checked the buckles of his parachute once more. Everything was secure. It had to be. In this sport, nothing could be left to chance. It was risky enough as it was.

He walked across to the side of the cliff and studied the contours of the mountain one final time.

There was plenty of clearance as long as he jumped away from the cliff and turned the right way. He would open his parachute about halfway down. Adrenaline rushed through his body, almost making him giddy. He loved the feeling. He never felt more alive than when he was jumping or surfing one of the big waves.

Although he wasn't his father, perhaps they were more alike than he wanted to admit. Dad had needed constant excitement in his life in ever-increasing amounts and he himself did too. But he chose to get his thrills from testing himself against the elements—unlike his father who had found his escape in drink and drugs until eventually they had killed him. Far better to die doing something like this than by drinking yourself into an early grave. At least *he* had no child, neither would he ever have one, to worry about leaving behind. No woman either. Or none that were ever likely to be a permanent feature. They were a necessary and enjoyable part of his life, but as soon as they got too serious he broke it off—he didn't want or need emotional entanglement. He didn't want to be responsible for another human being and especially not their happiness. Why then did he have to keep reminding himself of that these days?

All he could remember from the time his parents were still together was raised voices, slamming doors and then his father staring into the fire with a drink in his hand. They'd been exciting but indifferent parents. He missed the excitement, but as for the indifference, he'd learned from early on only to rely on himself. That way no one got hurt.

Recently he had started wondering if he was drawn to extreme sports because something was missing in his life.

Fabio knew he and the other small select band of BASE jumpers were alike underneath. They were all always looking for the next challenge, taking ever-increasing risks, needing bigger and bigger thrills. Sometimes these risks paid off and new records were broken; sometimes they didn't and people died. It was an acceptable part of their sport. Although the authorities never saw it that way. They were always trying to limit access for the jumpers. Not that Fabio really wanted to jump off buildings. He preferred being out in the open, away from the city.

He took one last deep breath and flung himself into the air. God! There was no feeling in the world that could ever replace what he felt at this moment.

CHAPTER EIGHT

'HEY, anyone seen the latest photo of our Fabulous Fabio?' Jenny plonked the tabloid newspaper down in the staff kitchen where they were all gathered, with the exception of Fabio who hadn't yet arrived, to discuss the day's patients.

Jonathan picked it up and grinned. 'What's he been up to this time?' He let out a low whistle. 'That's some stunner he's with. He didn't tell me he has a new woman.'

'Not that you could keep track, darling, even if he did. We both know Fabio changes his girlfriends the way other people change their socks,' Rose said with a mischievous smile. 'I'm just glad the paparazzi aren't so interested in you these days.'

Jonathan wrapped his arms around his wife's shoulders. 'Not very playboy to have a heavily pregnant wife, is it? *Oof.* What did you do that for?' he grunted as his wife elbowed him in the stomach. 'You know which one I'd rather have on my arm any day of the week.'

Katie sneaked a look at the newspaper. Her heart thudded uncomfortably against her ribs when she saw that the picture was of Fabio and the co-pilot they'd met on their trip to Monaco. He had an arm around her narrow waist as she leaned against him. Almost matched in height, the blonde still managed to look as if she was gazing up at Fabio adoringly. And as for him, he was grinning down at her as if he couldn't tear his eyes away.

She felt disappointed and hurt and angry. It wasn't as if Fabio and herself were anything more than colleagues. Why then did she want to tear the paper into tiny little shreds? Now she knew for certain why he had asked her out. Out of sympathy—that was all. He'd probably been relieved when she'd said no so he could take Miss Drop-Dead Gorgeous. She should have trusted her instincts. Fabio Lineham was not a man to rely on and the photograph was a timely reminder of that.

'She's gorgeous,' Jenny was saying. 'Does anyone know who she is? I don't recognise her.'

'She's a pilot,' Katie said, and blushed as curious eyes turned to look at her. 'She was the co-pilot on the trip we made to Monaco.'

Jonathan laughed. 'Trust Fabio never to miss an opportunity to get himself a date with a beautiful… *Oof*,' he gasped as Rose elbowed him again. 'I mean a horrible, not-my-type-at-all woman.'

Vicki was also studying the photograph. 'I think she's got a mean look to her, if you ask me,' she said. 'Why can't Fabio find a woman who he can fall in love with? He can't go on playing the field for ever.'

'Who can't?' Fabio asked as he came into the room. He took the newspaper from Vicki and tossed it on the coffee table. 'You guys, of all people, should know not to believe everything you see in the papers.'

'So, you're telling us the picture is made up?' Vicki teased. 'Too bad we all know you too well.'

'Anyway, back to work,' Rose said. 'I thought I should tell you that as we've agreed, we're advertising for some more staff. A paediatrician to take over some of the children and an obstetrician and gynaecologist. More and more of our ante-natal patients are wanting the practice to see them all the way through labour and beyond.'

'And a new nurse?' Vicki said hopefully. 'It's not long until you go on maternity leave, Rose, and we have more than enough patients as it is.'

'That too.' Rose smiled and pressed a hand to her belly. 'I think he just kicked me!'

As the rest of the staff, with the exception of Fabio, crowded around the expectant mother, Katie slipped outside into the reception area.

'You okay?' She whirled round to find Fabio standing behind her, studying her quizzically.

'Sure. Why shouldn't I be?' Just because I thought you cared just a little for me—she thought the words, knowing that she would never say them.

Fabio looked as if he was about to say something, but just then the bell on the door rang, announcing their next patient, and Jenny rushed into the room.

'Cripes,' she said. 'I almost forgot. Sheikh Mustaf is bringing his two children to see you, Fabio. It's a first visit, so we'd better not keep him.'

Later, after Katie had seen the three patients scheduled for treatment, including Gillian, who did turn out to have Lyme disease and whose stiff limbs were improving. Just as Gillian left, Fabio popped his head around the door.

'I have two tickets for a film premiere next week and I'm looking for company. My cousin Kendrick is in it and I promised him I'd go.'

'What about Drop-Dead Gorgeous?' Katie muttered under her breath.

'Who? What did you say?' Fabio looked perplexed as

he walked towards her. Katie stared. There was something wrong with the way he was moving. Yes, he was decidedly favouring his left leg.

'What's wrong with your leg?' Katie asked, her chagrin with him momentarily forgotten.

'Nothing much. Now, what were you saying? Something about dropping dead? I hope that wasn't directed at me?'

'Sit down on my couch and either roll up your trouser leg or take your trousers off,' Katie said firmly.

'You want me to undress?' Fabio's eyes gleamed. 'Are you sure this is the time or the place?'

Katie gave him a none-too-gentle shove. 'Sit,' she said. 'Can't you do as you're told for once?'

Something in her expression must have warned him she was in no mood for joking around. He sat on the couch and rolled up his left trouser leg. 'See? Nothing wrong.'

'The other one, please, Fabio.'

Reluctantly he did as she asked. Katie bent and studied his ankle. It was swollen and badly bruised.

'When and how did you do this?'

'On Saturday,' Fabio conceded. 'But it's nothing. You should see—' He broke off.

'See…?' When he remained stubbornly silent she asked him again. 'What happened?'

'I was jumping at the weekend and let's just say there was a rock where the ground should have been flat.'

'You should be more careful,' Katie said tightly.

Fabio shrugged. 'What's the fun in being careful? Ouch! That hurt.'

Katie was unaware that she was squeezing Fabio's injured ankle, but she gave it another squeeze for good measure. It was only a sprain but, knowing Fabio and his recklessness, it could just as easily have been broken.

She stood up abruptly. 'Ice is what you need for that ankle. But you know that.'

'Hey, what did I say?' Fabio looked genuinely baffled. 'You're mad at me. Why?'

'You shouldn't be doing stuff that might stop you from working. You have a responsibility to keep yourself fit. How else are you going to look after your patients?'

'I don't take unnecessary risks, believe me.' He studied her through half-closed eyes and a slow smile spread across his face. 'Don't tell me you're worried about me.'

'Of course I'm not.' Katie turned away so he couldn't read her expression. She was angry with him, but whether it was because of the photo in the paper or the fact he didn't seem to care what he did with himself, she didn't know.

Fabio hopped off the examination couch, grimacing as he put weight on his ankle. Katie felt his hand on her shoulder and he whirled her round so she was forced to look into his eyes.

'*Te, te, te, minha linda*, don't care about me too much.'

And then he dropped his hand and, leaving her speechless, left the room.

The days settled into a rhythm. In the mornings they would meet over coffee and discuss the patients who were expected in for treatment as well as those requiring home visits.

Katie was kept so busy it hardly gave her time to think. When she wasn't seeing patients at the clinic, she was either out seeing patients in their homes on her own or with Fabio or another doctor at the clinic. Little Lucy was doing well and Katie often went to their house to carry out her physio.

One day Fabio sought her out.

'I have a couple of tickets for that movie premiere and I

wondered if you'd changed your mind about coming with me. My cousin is in it. He'll probably be there as he's between movies at the moment.'

'Your cousin is a movie star?'

Fabio grinned. 'Kendrick's not exactly a film star. Although he could have been.'

'I'm confused.'

'He's the stuntman. If you think I like risking my neck, I can assure you I have nothing on Kendrick. I don't think he's happy unless he risks it at least once a day.'

Then the memory of the film star on the yacht talking about Kendrick came back to her. Kendrick was the cousin who'd been in the army before becoming a stuntman. She shuddered. 'What is it about some men that they can't be happy unless they're behaving like Rambo? I feel sorry for his wife.'

'Kendrick hasn't got a wife. Not the marrying kind, I guess. Doesn't seem to run in our family for some reason.'

It was another subtle reminder—as if she needed one—that whatever this was that was between them, it wasn't to be taken seriously.

'I'm sure you'll find someone else to take easily enough,' she said stiffly.

'I'd like to take *you*.' A smile played on his lips. 'I promise you I'll be a perfect gentleman. You'll be perfectly safe with me. Just two colleagues having an evening out together.'

Katie tried to ignore the disappointment she felt at his words. Hadn't she decided that she and Fabio had very little in common?

'Please,' he said again. 'I really would enjoy your company tonight. I can relax when I'm with you. Unless, of course…' his smile widened '…you don't feel that you can trust yourself with me.'

He really was the most arrogant man.

'Don't be ridiculous,' Katie retorted, stung. 'I wouldn't fall for you if you were the last man on earth—whatever misapprehension you're labouring under.'

That told him. But it made her sound about three years old. His eyes had widened with surprise and was it something else? Satisfaction? Damn. Even to her own ears her protestation sounded remarkably like a case of the lady protesting too much.

'I'm sorry,' she added hastily. 'I don't know where that came from. It was rude and unnecessary. Of course I'd love to go.' Now, that was better. That was the normal response to a colleague who was being friendly. It wasn't as if they'd be alone. Surrounded by people, he wouldn't be able to tempt her with his dark green eyes and dangerously sexy mouth. And if her heart bumped against her ribs, it was nothing to do with wanting to spend time with Fabio. Nothing at all.

Katie was nervous as she dressed for her date. Not that it was a date, she reminded herself. He needed a companion for the evening, that was all.

Suzy had put Ricky down for the night and was perched on the edge of Katie's bed with a mug of cocoa.

'Now, you have to note everything,' Suzy said. 'I want to know it all. Who was there, what they were wearing. *Especially* what they are wearing.'

Before Suzy had gone on maternity leave she had been a buyer for one of the more upmarket fashion chains. She had always been bringing home clothes and up until her pregnancy and Richard's death had been one of those women

who looked stunning whatever they wore. Suzy had loved
Katie's descriptions of the people at the party on the yacht
and waited eagerly every evening to hear about the women
who came to the clinic.

'I don't know, Suzy. I think I should phone him and tell
him I can't go. I don't want to leave you on your own and,
besides, the thought of being in the company of all those
beautiful people terrifies me.'

'Don't be ridiculous,' Suzy said firmly. 'You can out-
shine them anytime. As for me…' she reached over and
touched Katie on the hand '…I'm doing okay. It's you I'm
worried about.'

When Katie went to protest, Suzy cut her off.

'I know you feel the pain of Richard's death as much
as I do. I'm trying to look to the future, even though the
fact it doesn't include Richard hurts like crazy. I know in
some ways it's worse for you. At least I have Ricky and
my parents, but Richard was the only family you had left.
I made a promise to him, remember? Part of that promise
is pushing you to get on with your life too. So think of
tonight as you doing it for me, okay?'

A lump in her throat, Katie reached over and the two
women hugged briefly.

'Okay. For you. And because Richard would never forgive me if I didn't,' Katie said. 'Now, what *am* I going to
wear?'

Suzy had insisted that they go shopping for something new
for Katie to wear to the premiere. It had taken longer than
any other shopping expedition Katie could remember, but
Suzy wouldn't give up until they'd found the perfect dress.
It was an off-the-shoulder, two-tone, silky, floor-length
evening dress in blood red. Not something Katie would

have ever chosen for herself, but she had to admit it made her feel sexy and sophisticated.

Fabio collected her, and when she came down the stairs, he whistled under his breath.

'*Deus*, you look stunning,' he said simply.

'You don't look too bad yourself.' Katie smiled back. He was wearing a dinner jacket and a crisp white shirt open at the neck.Five o'clock stubble shadowed his chin, if anything making him look more dangerously sexy than before.

Katie noticed that Fabio was driving a sports car. He must have retrieved it from the panel beater. At least in London he couldn't drive as if he were on a racing track. He opened the door with a flourish and, feeling a bit like Cinderella, Katie slid into the soft leather seat.

'I wondered if you'd change your mind,' he said as they pulled away.

'I did think about it, but here I am.'

Fabio slid her a glance. 'I'm very glad you are.' The smile he gave her made her heart hum and she was thankful that the darkness hid the heat that rose to her face.

Although Katie had seen clips of film premieres on television, the experience of actually being there was something else entirely. She doubted whether she had ever seen so many photographers in one place before.

It was impossible to ignore the cameras, seeing as the minute they stepped out of the car flashbulbs popped and dazzled like a million exploding stars as the photographers pointed their cameras at them.

'Fabio! Look this way! Who's the lady? What is your mother up to? Does she have another film lined up?'

Fixing a smile on his face, Fabio gripped Katie by the elbow and steered her along the red carpet.

'Just look straight ahead and try to smile,' he whispered

in her ear. 'They'll soon turn their attention to someone else. There are plenty bigger fish here tonight than me.'

It was easy for him. He didn't have to worry about getting four-inch heels stuck in the hem of an evening dress that had cost Katie almost a month's salary, only to have the picture appear in a newspaper. She smothered a giggle. Who would have thought only a couple of weeks ago that she'd be worried about having her picture in a newspaper?

'Pretend they're all naked—it works for me,' Fabio whispered in her ear, making her laugh, and she relaxed. It was surreal, being here, being photographed alongside the rich and famous. It would be another memory to stash away for her grandchildren.

Nevertheless, by the time they were safely inside, away from the photographers' lenses, she found herself sympathising with those in the public eye. Although she knew that many sought publicity, it couldn't be easy to be constantly under scrutiny. Was that what it had been like for Fabio when growing up? No wonder he seemed so self-assured.

Just then a tall, muscular man in his early thirties approached them and flung his arm around Fabio's shoulder.

'Fabio, good you could make it.' Piercing blue eyes turned on Katie and the man gave her an appreciative look. 'And who's this?'

'Hands off, Kendrick. She's with me,' Fabio growled. 'Katie, I'd like you to meet my cousin, Kendrick. Kendrick, this is Katie.'

'Pleased to meet you, ma'am.' The accent was mildly American and the voice held an undercurrent of amusement. Kendrick grinned at Katie. 'Any time you get tired of going out with this Pom, I'd be glad to show you around.'

Another flirt. Did every man in Fabio's family behave the same way?

'You must be the stuntman,' Katie said. 'I'm really looking forward to seeing your film.'

'You won't even see me,' Kendrick warned. 'It's my job to make it look as if the hero is doing it all himself. I wouldn't have come to London to see it except I happen to have heard there's some good waves in Ireland this weekend.' He turned to Fabio. 'Are you up for it?'

Fabio grinned. 'Count me in.'

'You surf too?' Katie asked.

Kendrick flicked his eyes at Fabio. 'I guess some people would call it surfing. Others call it Big Wave. Regular surfing is for ladies.'

What was that supposed to mean?

'I've got a 'copter lined up and a couple of jet skis,' Kendrick continued. 'So we're sorted.' He looked at his watch. 'If you'll excuse me, the film is about to start and my date is waiting.' He nodded across to a film star with a metallic dress who, although surrounded by adoring men, kept looking Kendrick's way.

'It was good to meet you, Katie. I hope to see you again.' There was no mistaking the speculative look in Kendrick's eye as he glanced at Fabio. 'Something tells me I'm going to.' And with that he threaded his way back into the crowd.

'What does he mean, some people call it crazy? What kind of surfing needs a jet ski and a helicopter?' Katie asked Fabio.

'Pay no attention to Kendrick,' Fabio said evasively. 'Let's go and take our seats.'

As soon as the film started, Katie knew she had made a dreadful mistake. Why hadn't she thought to look it up? The title, *One Saturday in December*, hadn't given any indication that it was a movie about war. She gripped the edge of her seat as images spooled in front of her. Men under fire. Men being shot. Men flying in the air as bombs exploded all around them. She felt sick. Was that how it had been for Richard? The noise, the flying dirt, the relentless fear? Had he been terrified in those last few minutes of his life? Had he been in pain? Calling out for Suzy? Knowing he would never see Ricky or any of his family again? Katie's heart felt as if it was shattering into tiny pieces.

Unable to bear one more minute, she knew she had to get out of there.

'Excuse me,' she whispered to Fabio. 'I have to get past. I need to go.'

Immediately he was on his feet. Ignoring the impatient sighs of the audience, she shuffled up the row. Her hands were clammy and she felt physically sick. She stumbled outside, taking deep breaths of fresh air, trying to get herself back under control.

'What is it?' Fabio was by her side, his steadying hand on her elbow.

She couldn't speak. She could barely breathe. She had to get away, find some corner where she could be alone.

Fabio hailed a passing taxi and ushered her inside. 'I'm taking you home.' Long fingers felt her pulse. 'Your pulse is racing,' he said.

'Not home,' she whispered. She couldn't let Suzy see her like this. She couldn't face her until she got herself under control. Suzy needed her to be strong. Not this falling-apart wreck she was right now.

She was aware of cool fingers on her overheated skin as he touched her forehead.

'A bit clammy. A touch of flu maybe.' He frowned. 'At

least, that's what I would think if you hadn't been okay before the film started.'

'It's not flu,' Katie said miserably.

'Driver, take us to Tower Bridge,' Fabio told the driver.

She was grateful for his silence as the taxi drove towards the river. Katie wanted to be outside. She needed fresh air and the darkness.

By the time the taxi dropped them she knew where she wanted to go. Somewhere she went almost every week since she'd come back to London. On the Thames Riverbus, going up the river and returning without getting off, surrounded by strangers, was the one place she could be alone with her thoughts and memories.

'You can go back to the movie,' she said to Fabio. 'I'm going to take the riverbus. I'll be fine, I promise you. I just need to be alone. Or at least not with anyone I know.'

'If you think I'm going to let you go anywhere by yourself, you're crazy.' His mouth tipped up at one corner. 'Anyway, I've never been on the riverbus.'

Katie didn't have the strength to argue with him; besides, she knew she'd be only wasting her time.

They found a seat right at the back where they could be on their own. The tourists were happy to get the best seats near the front. As they passed the Parliament buildings, Fabio leaned back and placed his arms behind his head.

'This is cool. Why have I never thought of doing this before?'

'Because it's not your style?'

'Hey, how do you know what my style is?'

He was right. She still knew very little about him, even if she felt as if they were connected by a gossamer-fine thread.

He said nothing as the boat continued upriver. She knew she owed him an explanation for her behaviour, otherwise he was going to think his colleague was seriously kooky. But what could she say?

Right now she was grateful for his silence.

Eventually he spoke.

'I can tell you're hurting. *Porra!* A blind man could see it. I think you should tell me.'

The darkness of the night, the sympathy in his voice, this connection she felt with him, whatever it was, at last she knew she was ready to tell him.

'On the plane to Monaco I told you I didn't have any brothers or sisters. It wasn't the truth. I had a brother. A much-loved brother. He died a few months ago.' Her voice caught on the words. It was still so difficult to say. So difficult to believe. 'He was a doctor in Afghanistan.'

His hand covered hers and she was grateful for its warmth. 'It still hurts. When our parents died, it was only me and him. Kind of the two of us against the world. We had no one else to depend on, so we relied on each other. He was older than me, eighteen to my thirteen. Somehow, I don't know how, he persuaded the authorities that I shouldn't go into care. That he would look after me. He was about to start med school. He gave up any social life he might have had so he could be there when I came home from school. He was the one who told me about boys,' She attempted a smile. 'Not that it did me much good.' She swallowed the lump in her throat. 'He was the one who was there when I went through puberty, the one who comforted me when I wanted my mum, the one who dried my tears when my first boyfriend dumped me. He was there. He was always there.'

Fabio's arm came around her shoulder and as she leaned into him it felt the most natural thing in the world.

'Our parents left us the house so we had somewhere to stay, but money was tight. When I told Richard that I wanted to be a physio, he agreed to let the army put him through medical school in return for staying with them after he'd graduated.'

Fabio pulled her closer. She closed her eyes, remembering. 'He said he didn't mind. He loved being a doctor—he was an A and E specialist, and he knew he was playing his part, helping the troops. He always claimed it didn't matter whether you believed in war or not, the soldiers deserved the best medical care the country had to offer. And he was one of the best.'

She could feel Fabio's heart beating through the thin material of his shirt.

'That's what Kendrick believes too,' Fabio said. 'He hated the fact of war but always said someone had to do it. He was a career soldier, though. He knew the risks. Unlike your brother.'

It was too dark for Katie to read his expression as she continued.

'It wasn't just the funding that attracted him to the life. He loved it that he could spend his weekends outdoors learning new sports. I still remember how excited he was about his first jump from a plane.'

They were both silent for a while as Katie struggled to find the words. 'Before he went to Afghanistan for the first time, he met the woman who was to become his wife. My sister-in-law, Suzy. He was so happy. He promised he'd do a couple of tours and come home. Then, just before his second tour, Suzy told him she was pregnant. He was so excited. We both were. He was going to have his own family, one that he made very clear I'd always be part of. I was going to be an aunty, my brother had found the perfect woman, I had qualified as a physio. Life was good. We never really thought about the possibility he'd be called up to work in a war zone, never mind have to go where the fighting was the fiercest. But of course they need doctors as close to the soldiers as possible. Not that Richard told us that he was expected to go there. He let us believe that he was safely in at base camp. I don't know if you know it, but it's well protected and the medical staff there are believed to be pretty safe.'

Her throat was so tight she could barely speak.

Fabio squeezed her hand and waited silently for her to continue.

'What we didn't know was that Richard had to do a stint at one of the forward operating bases. That's in enemy-held territory. You know, with the troops as they go on patrol. It's a job for doctors who are soldiers too.'

'So I've heard,' Fabio said.

'Knowing Richard, they wouldn't even have had to ask him. He would have felt it was his duty to go. If soldiers in his regiment were putting their lives at risk, he would have wanted to be there to help them if they needed it.'

Her voice was shaky and she turned away from Fabio, trying to hide the tremble in her hands.

'To cut a long story short, he was with them when they came under attack. Richard could have stayed safe until it was all over, but, no—' she couldn't keep the bitterness from creeping in '—he had to go out under fire to pull an injured soldier to safety. Not once, but twice. It was on the second occasion that he got shot. The only good thing is that it was instantaneous, or so they say…'

'They wouldn't lie to you about that.' Fabio pulled her

more firmly into the crook of his arm. 'If they say it was instant, you should believe them.'

Katie tasted the salt of her tears. She hadn't even realised she was crying.

'The two soldiers he went to save are going to be okay. One had to have a leg amputated and the other was in hospital for a few months, but they say he's going to be fine, so at least Richard didn't die for nothing. We find some comfort in that.'

'So you're all alone. Parents dead and now your only brother.' He let out a low whistle. 'My poor girl. It's not fair. How old are you? Twenty-four?'

'Twenty-six.' She managed a smile. 'I'm older than I look. Life isn't fair,' she added quietly. 'I don't know why we think it should be. Richard wasn't the only person to be killed that day. There were four others who died along with him. Four other families going through the pain of losing someone. Fathers, mothers, sisters, brothers, children.' Her voice hitched and she drew a shaky breath. 'At least he died doing something he loved and there was some purpose to his death. I try to take some comfort from that.'

Fabio took his arm from her shoulder and turned her so she was facing him. He took a clean handkerchief from his pocket and gently dabbed the tears away.

'He must make you very proud,' he said finally when he'd finished.

'He does. But that doesn't make up for the way I feel. Right now, I would give anything to have him back. Anything. And I'm sure the families of the other men who died that day feel the same. As for Suzy—all her dreams are shattered. Instead of bringing up Ricky with Richard, she's going to have to do it on her own. How can any of that be right?' She sniffed loudly and took his handkerchief from his hand and blew loudly. 'What I find difficult to understand is how Amelia can watch Mark race and not be terrified. What if he's killed? She'll be just like Suzy. Left with a child to bring up on her own. It's even worse for her, knowing that she could lose Lucy too. I could never, ever do what she does. Especially not now. One thing is for sure, I will never, ever marry a man who puts himself in danger. I won't go through what Suzy did and what Amelia does. I'm not strong enough.'

'I think you're stronger than you think, Katie. You'll feel differently in time. The pain will go, I promise. Not completely, I'm told it never does that, but it will get better.'

Suddenly conscious that she was holding his sodden hanky in her hands, Katie was horrified. It was completely inappropriate, never mind unprofessional, to break down in the arms of her colleague, no matter how kind and sympathetic he'd been. She pulled away from his embrace and stepped away.

'I'm sorry. I don't know what you must think. Someone you hardly know, and a colleague to boot, crying all over you.' She dabbed ineffectually at the front of his damp white shirt with his hanky and steadied her breathing. 'I can assure you, if you can believe me, that it's not something I usually do.'

'Don't worry about it. I'm kind of used to women crying,' he said.

She stepped away. Of all the insufferable comments. Trying to make out he was used to women breaking their hearts over him. Just as she was beginning to think she'd misjudged him all along.

'I bet you are,' she said stiffly.

His eyes were amused. 'I'm talking about patients,' he said. 'What did you think I meant?'

She was always misreading him. After he'd been kind. 'I think I'm ready to go home now,' she said.

Fabio dropped Katie at her sister-in-law's house and sent the taxi away. He would walk the five miles to his flat. It had taken all his willpower back on the riverbus not to take Katie in his arms and kiss the tears away. Instinctively he'd known it wasn't the time. When he kissed her for the first time, he didn't want it to be because she was vulnerable.

Deus. How many times did he have to remind himself that kissing Katie would lead to a relationship, which would lead to trouble? He forced the image of her mouth out of his head.

No wonder Katie was guarded. The loss of her brother explained a lot.

At least Richard had died for something he'd believed in. What did *he* believe in? Nothing. Only living life to the full. The next thrill. The here and now—his sport. Certainly not the future. He didn't want happy families. Not that he believed happy families truly existed—even if Katie seemed to think her brother's marriage was different. His parents had torn each other apart even before his father had become dependent on drugs. At least at boarding school he hadn't had to witness his parents fighting. He remembered hiding in a cupboard once, terrified that his parents' arguing was about him and that if he disappeared, perhaps they would be happy. At boarding school he'd been lonely at first. He'd thought his parents had sent him away because they didn't love him. It had hurt, but if it meant the arguments would stop, it was worth the empty feeling inside he had for most of his childhood. But his parents had divorced anyway and no one had come to fetch him back from school. It had taught him one thing. To rely on himself. Not to count on anyone else for happiness.

Fabio let himself into his flat, flinging his car keys onto the coffee table where they landed with a clatter. It was so quiet in here. Why had he never noticed?

Ignoring the red light on his phone that indicated that there were messages waiting for him, he went into the kitchen and poured himself a fruit juice. He never drank alcohol. With his father, he had seen first hand what a reliance on chemical stimulants could do to a person. Not that he was at all concerned if others chose to drink—that was up to them. It was just that he much preferred to get his highs naturally.

Taking his cold drink, he crossed over to the window and looked out at the lights of Westminster blinking below.

Why was he feeling so unsettled? Somehow he had become involved in another person's life, and that was something he'd sworn he'd never do. But he'd never felt so drawn to a woman before. She was beautiful, there was no doubt about that, but he had dated more beautiful woman than her and he'd never felt the need to make them part of his life. At least, not a permanent one.

When he was with Katie something deep inside him quietened and felt at peace.

Not that he was feeling peaceful right now. She made him think about stuff he didn't want to think about. Like his childhood. Making him feel that he was missing out some-how. That having someone in your life who cared might be a good thing. That he wanted to be a better man.

The thought scared him more than any cliff or big wave. He valued his independence too much. No, he was attracted to her because she was a lovely, kind woman who needed a friend. It was her vulnerability that was making him feel this way. That was all. He thought the realisation would make him feel better, but it didn't. Probably because he had the uneasy feeling he was lying to himself.

Later, after Fabio had dropped her off at home, Katie crept up to her room, thankful Suzy was in bed. She would only have to take one look at her face to know she'd been crying.

Katie thought about the evening. Fabio had been kind and understanding, and it had, she admitted, been a relief to finally talk to someone about Richard.

There was so much more to Fabio than she'd given him credit for. He was sensitive and thoughtful and easy to talk to. That connection that she'd felt almost as soon as they'd met was growing stronger every time they were together.

That wasn't all. When she was with him, she felt happy again. As if life had meaning once more. As if there was a future to believe in.

His presence banished the shadows from her life and her world came alight whenever he was around.

She groaned and buried her face in her hands. Despite everything she'd told herself, she was falling in love with him. She could no longer keep pretending to herself.

But that didn't change the type of man Fabio was or the reasons why she shouldn't let herself care more deeply about him than she already did. Not only was he a risk-taker, he'd made it very clear that he wasn't into serious relationships.

Remembering what Kendrick had said about big wave surfing, she logged onto her computer and ran a search. A link to a video clip came up and she clicked the play button. What she saw made her feel as if someone had dropped ice cubes down the back of her neck. A surfer was being towed by a jet ski out to the biggest wave Katie had ever seen. The surfer let go of the tow rope and proceeded to surf down a sea of water that looked the size of a mountain, or a six-storey building. Katie held her breath for the interminable seconds it took the surfer to ride the wave. Were they crazy? Anybody could see that all it would take was one wrong move and the surfer would be buried under a wave from which there was no hope of escape. According to the report, a crazy few extreme surfers went all over the world in search of exceptional waves that could only be reached by helicopter and jet ski. Ireland was one of those places.

As she watched the clip again, Katie's blood ran cold. Then she typed in 'BASE jumping', and if anything that made her feel worse. Only a week ago somebody had been killed during a jump. If ever she needed a reason to stay away from Fabio, this was it. No way could she ever trust her heart with someone who risked their life for fun. Why, then, did she feel as if someone had removed her heart and trampled all over it?

CHAPTER NINE

A COUPLE of days later, Fabio came to find Katie. She had gone out of her way to avoid him since the night of the premiere, terrified he'd read how she felt about him in her eyes.

He'd phoned to make sure she was all right, but they hadn't spoken since. At least, not about anything except work.

'I've just had Amelia on the phone. She's worried about Lucy. Says she's not her usual self. I'm going out to see her—are you free to come too?'

'Of course I'll come. I have one more patient then I'm all yours. I won't be more than thirty minutes. Will that be okay?'

Fabio nodded, looking worried. Despite his nonchalant manner, Katie had seen from the way he was with Lucy that the little girl was more to him than just a patient. She hoped Lucy hadn't caught a chest infection. Every time she did, it carried a risk of additional scarring to the lungs. The more infections, the worse the ultimate prognosis. Not that there was anything anyone could do to stop a sufferer of CF getting chest infections. It was impossible unless the patient spent their life in a bubble and the effect on the quality of life had its own drawbacks.

Alone in the car with Fabio, Katie switched on the radio,

pretending to find a news item fascinating. She needn't have worried. Fabio seemed preoccupied with his own thoughts.

Every time Katie went to Lucy's home she was stunned all over again. A little outside London, it had its own private gated entrance, enormous manicured gardens, a swimming pool and tennis courts.

Amelia met them at the door. If anything, she was paler than ever and for the first time Katie saw her looking less than immaculate. Her hair was scraped back in a ponytail and instead of her usual stylish trouser suits she was wearing a pair of jogging trousers and a T-shirt.

Fabio jumped out of his car as soon as it stopped and went over to Amelia.

'Hi, Amelia. Where's our patient?' he asked.

'Thank God you're both here. I didn't know what to do. I wondered if I should take her straight to hospital, but when you said you could come, I knew it was better to wait.'

'Why don't I go and see her before we make any decisions?' Fabio asked. 'Is she in bed?'

Amelia nodded. 'That's how I know she isn't well. Normally I can't keep her inside, especially on a day like this.' She indicated the garden with a sweep of her hand. The June sunshine bathed everything in light, but Katie felt a shiver of dread.

Katie followed Amelia and Fabio up the sweeping staircase. She hoped that Amelia was being over-anxious, and who could blame her? But equally Amelia had enough experience of her daughter's illness to know when she should seek medical help.

Lucy was sitting up in bed, looking listlessly out of the window.

'Hey, Luce,' Fabio said, crossing the room. 'Mum tells me you're not feeling too good.'

'Hey, Dr Fabio,' Lucy replied softly. 'I'm just a bit tireder than usual. I told Mum I'll be all right by tomorrow.'

'I assume you've being having your physio regularly? When Katie hasn't been doing it?' Since they'd returned from Monaco, Katie had been teaching Amelia and Lucy how to do Lucy's physio. Under Katie's supervision Amelia had soon gained the confidence to do it herself and they had agreed that they would do it themselves two days out of three, with Katie coming every third day.

Amelia nodded. 'If anything, Lucy has been having it more regularly since I can do it.'

'We all know that it is an unfortunate part of CF—that despite the medication and the physio chest infections can still occur,' Fabio said as he slipped a stethoscope from his bag. 'Why don't I listen to Lucy's chest and then we can see what's what?'

When Fabio finished his examination, he looked up and smiled. 'You do have a very mild chest infection, Luce, but I don't think it's too bad. I'm going to give you some antibiotics, up your dose of mucolytics and come back and see you tomorrow, but I think we caught it in time to get on top of it quite easily. In the meantime, I'm afraid, Lucy, you need to rest. Not necessarily in bed, though.'

'I could make you up a little bed on one of the couches outside by the swimming pool,' Amelia suggested. 'How about that?'

'I don't know, Mum. Maybe tomorrow.'

Fabio, Katie and Amelia looked at each other. This behaviour was unlike Lucy. Katie wondered if something else was bothering the little girl. Something she didn't want to share with her mother.

'Why don't I give you some physio while your mum and Dr Fabio have a chat?' Katie suggested. Perhaps if she got Lucy on her own she might share whatever it was that was troubling her.

'Okay, sweetie, do you want to tell me what's really up?' Katie asked as she percussed Lucy's chest.

Lucy was quiet for a moment. 'There's this girl at school. I thought she was my friend.' Katie waited for her to continue. 'She said she overheard her mum and dad talking about me.' Lucy's bottom lip wobbled and her eyes were damp. Katie stopped what she was doing and sat on the bed alongside Lucy and put her arm around her.

'Go on, Luce. You can tell me. What did she hear?'

'Her mum's a doctor. I don't know what kind. Anyway, they were saying that they were sorry for Mum. That not only might she lose me but even if I did live into my thirties she would probably never know what it was like to have grandchildren because I would almost certainly never be able to have babies.'

'Oh, sweetie,' Katie squeezed her tighter. 'We don't know that.'

'I don't even know how you have babies,' Lucy said, 'but I think one day I'll want to be a mummy.' She was quiet for another moment. 'I'm sorry for Mum and Dad too. I know that I make them sad. I don't want to make them even sadder if I can't have babies.'

For a moment Katie couldn't think of anything to say. What was there to say? Children with cystic fibrosis often did have trouble conceiving, but many went on to have perfectly healthy pregnancies. At this stage only time would tell. Lucy was far too young to have to worry about stuff like that at the moment, but on the other hand she was wiser than her years and didn't deserve to be palmed off. How could she give the child the comfort she needed right now? Only by telling her the truth.

'We don't know how your illness is going to progress, Luce. What I do know is that medical science is making huge advances in the treatment of CF every day. All we can do is try to keep you as healthy as we can and trust that you are going to lead a long life that includes all you ever dreamed of. I wish I could promise you right now that everything will be okay, but I can't. What I do know for sure is that your mum and dad love you very much and that they would rather have you the way you are than a different child. As for thinking that you make them sad, you don't. You bring so much joy and happiness to their lives you should be proud. Of course I know that if they could take away your illness with a magic wand, if they could do anything to make you better, they would. But if it is a choice between having you, Lucy, and not having you at all, there's no contest.'

Katie hugged Lucy tighter. 'You know, Luce, one day you'll meet someone and fall in love.' She smiled as Lucy pulled a face. 'And if he's worth loving he will want to share his life with you regardless of whether you can have children or not. That's the important thing to remember.'

Lucy smiled wanly. Then, in the way of children, she picked up her games console and eased her legs out of bed.

'I think I'll do as Mum suggested and rest outside by the pool.'

'You should tell your mum and dad what you told me,' Katie said, helping Lucy into her dressing gown. 'They will be able to reassure you.'

'Maybe.' She flung her arms around Katie and squeezed her so tightly Katie stumbled back a step or two.

'Whoa, Lucy. You're stronger than you think.' But Katie was delighted to see that Lucy's apathy seemed to have disappeared. For the time being at least. No doubt there would be many times over the coming years when the child would have to face up to the effects of her illness. However, she was a tough kid and somehow Katie knew she would deal with whatever life threw at her.

'C'mon, then.' Lucy smiled. 'Let's go and see if Mum has a snack for us.'

After they had driven away, leaving Lucy tucked up on the sofa outside with Amelia reading to her, Fabio turned to Katie.

'What happened back there? One minute Lucy was looking miserable, the next she was more like herself.'

'We had a chat while I was doing her physio,' Katie said. 'It seems that some kid at school said something about her not being able to have children.'

'*Porra!*' Fabio said. 'Poor kid. How did you deal with it?'

'The only way I knew how. I told her that it was far too early for anyone to know whether her illness would affect her fertility—not in those exact words, though. I said that when she grows up and meets someone who falls in love with her, if he's any kind of man at all, he won't care whether she can have children.'

Katie slid a glance in Fabio's direction. He was frowning as he concentrated on the road ahead.

'A small percentage of children do suffer fertility problems,' he said after a while. 'It is something Lucy might well have to face later on.'

'It's so unfair. The way life can turn out for some people,' Katie muttered.

'One thing I do know, Katie, is we have to make the best of what we have. Life can be fun and exciting and we should make the most of any time we might have.'

'Is that why you go big wave surfing and BASE jumping, or whatever they call it. Just for the excitement? Don't you care that you could be killed?' Katie burst out.

Fabio held her gaze for a second. 'Of course for the excitement. What other reason could there be? I am not planning on getting myself killed, though. I manage the risk.'

'Manage the risk! From what I saw on the internet, there is no way you can manage the risk. Too many things can go wrong. Men like you just don't think.' She couldn't help it. She was so frightened for him. Not that she could admit it.

Fabio brought his car to a stop and swivelled in his seat.

'You looked it up on the internet?' His lips twitched briefly.

Damn. She hadn't meant to say that, but he was always doing strange things to her head.

'You're really upset, aren't you?' he continued with wonder in his voice. Then a look of remorse crossed his face. 'Of course you're thinking about your brother. But, Katie, this is different. I really don't take crazy chances.'

Anger was still boiling up inside her. Not least because she was furious with herself for showing him that she cared. 'What you do has nothing to do with me. If you want to break your damned neck, that's entirely up to you.'

Despite her best efforts, hot tears were burning behind her eyes. She looked out of her side window and blinked rapidly. *Please. Don't let me make a bigger fool of myself than I've done already.*

'Katie,' he said softly. 'I warned you not to care about me. I'm not the kind of man you need.'

When she said nothing—he wasn't to know she couldn't speak—he started the car and headed back into the traffic.

After Fabio dropped Katie off at home he sat in his car for a while, drumming his fingers on the steering-wheel, feeling restless.

He wondered what Katie would think if he told her that he had suffered from the effects of having mumps as a child. Not that he intended to tell her. It wasn't as if he had any plans to get married and have children. But she would one day and that was the problem. Whatever she'd told Lucy about not caring whether someone could have kids when you were in love with them was naïve. Surely that was the only reason most people got married? Otherwise why bother?

He glanced at his watch. Six o'clock. It would be daylight for another hour or so. Not for the first time he wished he lived closer to the sea. Taking a board out and pitching himself against the waves, or flinging himself off a cliff, always helped clear his head, but that would have to wait to the weekend. Perhaps he would go for a ten-mile run. Maybe after that he would be able to sleep without thinking of sad grey eyes and a wounded expression.

Fabio, with Kendrick behind him on his surfboard, drove the jet ski at speed towards the wave. It was one of a set of five and Kendrick was determined to ride the wave of his life. After he had finished it would be Fabio's turn. The wind rushed through him, filling him with exhilaration. This was just what he needed to get Katie out of his head.

The ten-mile run the night before hadn't helped him to get to sleep or prevent his dreams from being filled with Katie.

Kendrick had hired a helicopter to take them to the west coast of Ireland, where he'd heard that the waves were, in his words, 'awesome'. He'd been right. There was no way they could catch the waves by paddling out to them—hence the need for the jet ski.

Fabio towed Kendrick on to the lip of the second wave and raced the jet ski out of the way. As he turned back to watch, he felt a sickening jolt of dread. Kendrick was in trouble. The drop of the wave was so huge there would be no time for his cousin to surf under the curling lip of the wave before it crashed down on him.

It seemed that this time they had taken one risk too many.

His heart pounding, Fabio watched as Kendrick did the only thing he could—he dived straight into the wave, hoping to come out the other side. But it wasn't to be. The wave hit Kendrick with such force it sent him and his board shooting into the air.

Fabio gunned the jet ski and headed back towards his cousin. Kendrick had been hit by his board and was bobbing around semi-conscious. Summoning all his strength, Fabio grabbed the neck of Kendrick's wetsuit and dragged him onto the front of the jet ski. He had to get him to dry land before he could assess how badly his cousin was hurt. He glanced around for help but knew it was useless. There was no one else crazy enough to tackle the waves that morning.

It seemed to take for ever to drag Kendrick back to shore. Once he was as close to the beach as he could manage, he still had to get him onto to the beach and Kendrick was a big man.

To his relief, Kendrick was coming round.

Fabio cut the engine of his jet ski, hoping that the tide wouldn't pull them back out.

'Kendrick!' he yelled in his cousin's ear. 'Are you with me?'

Kendrick groaned and opened his eyes. 'Hey, man, what happened?'

'Can you wade to shore?'

Kendrick pushed himself off the jet ski and although he swayed a little he managed to stay upright long enough for Fabio to jump into the water and get his arm around him for support. Together they staggered to shore and collapsed on the beach.

Fabio took a look at Kendrick's head. It was bleeding but should only require a stitch or two. Fabio knew it was only a matter of luck that they were both still in one piece.

Kendrick eased himself to his feet and smiled down at Fabio.

'Some wave. D'you fancy giving it a go?'

For the first time Fabio wondered what he was doing. He would always love the excitement of pitching himself against nature but, hell, he didn't want to die.

'You, my friend, are going nowhere—except to the hospital, where we can get that head wound stitched,' Fabio said.

Kendrick looked as if he was about to argue, but then he grinned. 'Okay, but once I'm fixed up, can we go back in?'

As Fabio waited in Casualty a little while later for Kendrick to be fixed up, he knew that he would be going back to London that evening.

For some reason, big wave surfing had lost its appeal. Perhaps it was because Katie wasn't there. Perhaps it was because these days he was getting more of a buzz by being with her than any extreme sport could give him. The realisation turned his blood to ice. Damn the woman, he couldn't stop thinking about her, wanting to be with her. What was going on? Lust had never done this to him before. *Deus!* He was falling for Katie Simpson and he didn't like the feeling one little bit. All he knew for sure was that he had to see her.

CHAPTER TEN

KATIE was taken aback when on Saturday evening she opened the door to find Fabio standing there.

'Will you have dinner with me tonight?' he said.

Katie's heart did a little roll of beats. When he smiled like that, it undid her.

'I'm sorry, I can't. I promised Suzy I'd babysit. She's going out with a friend for the first time since...' Her words tailed away.

He looked disappointed and uncharacteristically unsure of himself.

'But there's no reason why I can't cook for us here,' Katie said impulsively. 'If you like baby food, that is. I don't think there's very much else.'

'Tell you what. Why don't I cook?'

When he grinned at her, Katie knew astonishment was written all over her face. Fabio could cook?

'I know it's a surprise, but I can make a mean feijoada. It's a typical Brazilian dish.'

'What's in it?'

He grinned again and if anything Katie's heart beat faster.

'You'll find out,' he said. 'Give me an hour and I'll be back.'

After he'd left Katie leaned against the door. He was making it clear that he was interested in her and the realisation churned her up inside.

'Was that Fabio's voice I heard?' Suzy came into the room, towelling her hair. Although her sister-in-law's eyes were still shadowed with grief, she was beginning to go out with her friends again, and was even talking about returning to work. And as for her? She still couldn't think of Richard without experiencing a stab of pain that took her breath away, but since the night she'd confided in Fabio, she was beginning to see a future that wasn't clouded by grief.

'I've invited him here for dinner,' Katie said. When Suzy's eyebrows shot up, Katie added hastily. 'He's doing the cooking.'

'Just as well. Although you have many talents, my dear sister-in-law, cooking isn't one of them.'

'I can make pasta. And toasted sandwiches,' Katie protested, before answering the smile in Suzy's eyes. 'Okay, so he's had a narrow escape.'

'He likes you,' Suzy said.

Katie's heart kicked against her ribs.

'You don't know that.'

'I think I do. What's there not to like? You're beautiful and kind—okay, you can't cook but, hey, we can't all be perfect.'

Katie turned away. 'He's just being a caring colleague, that's all. Anyway, he's not for me.'

Suzy studied her thoughtfully as if she knew Katie was lying. 'He's gorgeous, rich, a great doctor, and he cooks. What's not to like?'

Katie sighed. There was no point pretending with Suzy. She'd always been able to read her like a book.

'He does make me laugh. More than that, he turns me to jelly. But he's reckless and a womaniser. He's made it crystal clear he's not interested in a serious relationship. I don't want to fall in love with someone like him. One way or another, he'll end up breaking my heart.' The words came out almost like a wail. 'I'm sorry, I don't know where that came from. I'm just so emotional these days. I've had enough grief in my life without inviting more.' Katie picked up some toys and baby odds and ends from the floor and dropped them into a basket.

'Something tells me it might be too late,' Suzy said, so softly Katie couldn't be sure she'd heard right. 'Why not just go with the flow? Have a fling. Have fun. God knows, you could do with some of that in your life right now.'

'But I work with him, Suze. It's not a good idea to have a fling—as you so quaintly put it—with a work colleague. And you know me. I'm not the fling type.'

Suzy smiled. 'Maybe it's about time you were.'

After Suzy had left, Katie finished tidying up before showering, taking the time to shave her legs and wash her hair. Whatever Suzy said, she was so not going to have a fling with Fabio. This was dinner with a colleague. What could possibly happen when there was a child in the house? Katie had to smile at the thought of using her nephew to keep Fabio at arm's length. What kind of wimp did that make her? But she'd do whatever it took. Ricky was sleeping through the night now and was unlikely to wake up, but just in case she was careful to keep the baby monitor switched on and close by.

Now, what should she wear? Something that didn't scream date but that she felt good in. Eventually she settled on the sundress she had worn that night on the yacht.

She had only finished putting the finishing touches to her make-up when Fabio arrived back, carrying bags of shopping. Judging from the faint scent of spice and lemon, somehow he too had found time to shower and change. He was wearing tight, faded jeans and an open-necked white silk shirt. Katie's throat went dry at the sight of him.

'Just put the bags over on the worktop,' she said, leading him through to the kitchen. 'Would you like something to drink?'

Fabio shook his head. 'I don't drink and anyway I'm driving, but feel free to have one yourself.'

Katie poured herself a glass of cold white Pinot Grigio from the fridge and took a bigger gulp than she'd intended, spluttering as it went down the wrong way.

'Are you all right?' Fabio asked, patting her on the back.

She nodded. Great start. Here she was with the most sophisticated man she had ever met and she couldn't even manage to take a sip of her drink without choking.

'Okay,' he said, pointing to a bar stool by the counter. 'You sit there, well out of danger's way, while I get cooking.'

'Don't you want a hand?' she asked.

His mouth tipped in a smile. 'I can cope. I hope you like Brazilian food.'

'Can't say I've ever tried it, but I'd like to.' She squinted at him. 'Tell me more about Brazil. What's it like? Do you go there much?'

'Not as much as I should, but I'm thinking of taking a trip there in a week or two to see my mother.'

Katie felt a thud of dismay. She hated the thought of not being able to see him most days.

'And as for as what it's like, you should visit one day.'

A glow spread through Katie. Did he mean that? Impossible though it seemed, was he envisaging a future for them? She dismissed the thought. Hadn't she told herself repeatedly Fabio was not for her? Why couldn't her heart keep in tune with her head?

'We have the greatest footballers in the world,' he continued as he assembled the ingredients he'd brought.

Katie hid her disappointment. Was she always going to be reading more into his words than he intended?

She rolled her eyes. 'Don't tell me you're one of those men who can't bear to miss a match.'

'You are kidding! Unless I can't help it, I never miss a game.'

'There must be more to Brazil than football.'

'A lot more. You'd love it. Think of the clearest seas, white sands, palm trees, and you've pretty much got it.' He paused his stirring and looked at her. 'Not that it's paradise. As I told you before, there's a huge difference between the rich and poor that is almost scandalous.'

'How did your parents feel about you becoming a doctor?'

'They were a little surprised, I think, but doctors are held in high esteem in Brazil so they didn't think it was too much of a drop in status,' he said with a twist to his lips. 'Besides I suspect they thought I'd give it up sooner or later.'

'Tell me more about your mother. I know she's stunningly beautiful, but what's she really like?'

Fabio placed the lid on the pot and leaned back against the counter, studying her through narrowed eyes.

'My mother? Yes, she is beautiful. Even in her late fifties. But I guess I don't really know her that well. She wasn't around that much when I was a child. When she and

Dad split up, they divided my time between them, but that didn't work in too well with their careers so they found me a boarding school.'

'That must have been difficult.'

Fabio's expression darkened. 'Not half as difficult as it was living with them both, witnessing them tear each other apart.' Although he smiled, it didn't quite reach his eyes. 'Enough of that. What do you mean, you don't understand the rules of football?'

Katie was just clearing away the dishes from the dining table when she heard Ricky cry. 'If you want to go to him, I'll finish here,' Fabio said.

Katie picked Ricky up and quickly changed his wet nappy. He was due a feed and Suzy had left a bottle in the fridge to be warmed up. Carrying the crying baby over her shoulder, she went into the kitchen, where Fabio was stacking dishes on the counter. Amused, she noticed he wasn't quite domesticated enough to put them directly into the dishwasher, but that was okay. His cooking had been a treat.

'You couldn't hold him while I warm his bottle, could you?' she asked.

'Sure,' Fabio said, taking Ricky from her. 'How are you, little man?' As she set about warming the bottle she looked over at Fabio and her heart lurched. His dark head was bent over Ricky, who had grabbed Fabio's ear and was tugging it as if he wanted it to come off. Her heart splintered. There was something about this man, who radiated masculinity on the one hand yet wasn't scared to show a gentler side, that she couldn't resist.

Having warmed the bottle, Katie took Ricky back from Fabio and made herself comfortable in one of the armchairs.

As the baby sucked greedily on his bottle, she looked up to find Fabio's eyes on her. He was watching her with a strange, inscrutable expression.

'What?' she asked.

He shook his head. 'Nothing.' He turned away and looked out of the window. 'I think it's time I was going,' he said.

Katie was disappointed, but who could blame him? Fabio wasn't someone who would be comfortable in a scenario of domestic bliss. He was more at home in a posh bar. When she saw him glance at his watch she wondered if he was planning to drop in at some club before going home. That was much more his scene.

'Thank you for dinner,' she said. 'I had a lovely time.'

'I'll let myself out, shall I?' he said, and before Katie could respond she heard the soft click of the door as it closed behind him.

Fabio paced his flat. This was becoming a habit, he thought grimly. The more time he spent with Katie, the less the idea of late nights and bars appealed to him.

The image of her sitting in the armchair with Ricky in her arms just wouldn't go away. It had looked so right, so natural.

Then again, everything about her was so natural. Whenever he was with her he felt as if he were in an oasis of peace and calm, and when he wasn't, he felt like this; restless and out of sorts.

In another life, he would have wooed her, but what did he have to offer? No doubt one day she'd want children of her own and it wasn't as if he could give her a family. And as for being dependent on someone else to make him happy—well, since he'd been a child and had had to get used to dealing with life on his own, he'd promised he would never rely on anyone and, more importantly, not let anyone depend on him. He was happy the way he was. Wasn't he?

He drained his orange juice in a gulp. For a second he thought about phoning Fern but only for a second. These days other women had lost their appeal. His mind kept returning to Katie and the sight of her with the baby. He had never given children much thought, knowing it was almost certainly impossible. But, for the first time, he wondered whether there was a chance. Things had moved on since he was eighteen. The way his mind was going jolted him. Thinking of babies and families. All because of one grey-eyed woman. Had he lost his mind?

CHAPTER ELEVEN

As the days continued to pass, Suzy and Katie settled into a routine. Suzy and little Ricky were her family now and Kate felt closer to Richard just by being with his wife and child.

Fabio remained friendly but distant and every time Katie caught a glimpse of his dark head her stomach would flip. He hadn't asked her out again and she wasn't sure if she was disappointed or relieved. However, it was better this way.

One day as she was tidying up her treatment room he sought her out.

'Mark and Amelia are hoping to take Lucy with them for Turkish Grand Prix in Istanbul and were wondering whether you and I would go with them.'

Katie kept her back towards him. More time with Fabio wasn't really what she needed. On the other hand, this was why she'd been employed by the practice.

'When?' she asked. 'I'll have to check my patient list.'

'This weekend. I know it's unfair to ask you to give up your free time, but Amelia and Mark would appreciate it.' Fabio said. 'You could take time off at the beginning of the week to make up for it. Jenny would be happy to shuffle your diary around.'

Katie hesitated and then gave herself a little shake. She couldn't let personal feelings get in the way of her doing her job.

'I don't mind about working over the weekend and I was a little worried about Lucy's chest the last time I saw her. Do you think it's wise to let her go?'

'You know how Lucy feels about being able to do things with her parents. I'll be there to keep a close eye on her and you'll be there to do her physio. In many ways she couldn't get better care, even if she was in hospital. Amelia and Mark would be really grateful if you could go. Amelia only decided to go yesterday. Apparently, if Mark wins this one, and there's a good chance he will, then he's in the lead. They really want to see him do that.'

Boy, did Fabio know which buttons to press. He knew she couldn't refuse Lucy the opportunity to see her father. 'In which case, I can't say no, can I?' She was mortified to hear a touch of bitterness in her voice.

He placed a hand on her elbow and turned her so she was facing him. 'What is it, Katie? Something's up. Is it Suzy?'

How could she tell him that she didn't want to spend more time with him than necessary? How could she tell him that seeing him every day was torture?

Of course she couldn't.

She forced a smile. 'Nothing's wrong, honestly.' She should cross her fingers behind her back. 'Istanbul it is.'

And so, once again, Katie found herself ensconced in Mark's private jet. As before, they would be staying on board the yacht that Mark's sponsors had put at his disposal. Despite her reservations, Katie was excited. And, she had to admit, happy knowing that she would be with Fabio for a few days.

'Have you ever been to Istanbul?' he asked as they took off.

'To be honest, I've never been very far. I travelled around Europe with friends from university, but that's it really. What about you?' She smiled at him. 'I guess you've been everywhere.'

'Most places, but not Turkey. It's always somewhere I wanted to go, though.' He studied her from under his long, dark lashes. 'Maybe you and I could see some of the sights together?'

Katie's heart thrummed. She wanted to be with him, even though it was bitter-sweet. She hauled out her guide book and flicked it open. 'As a matter of fact, I've earmarked a couple of places I would like to see. The Haghia Sophia, of course, the Basilica Cistern, the Blue Mosque and the Topkapi Palace—and that's just for starters. I've been reading up about the Ottoman Empire since I knew I'd be making this trip and I'd like to see as much as I can squeeze in. I guess it depends whether Lucy wants to go too, or if she'd prefer to hang out with her parents.'

They chatted about what Katie had learned in the guide-book for a while, then she yawned.

'I think I'll nap for a bit, if you don't mind. Ricky was a bit unsettled last night. He's teething, we think, poor lamb.'

She rested her head and closed her eyes, wondering if she would be able to sleep. Despite her tiredness, every nerve in her body was intensely aware of Fabio next to her. She wanted to ask him to go and sit on the other side of the plane, but that would be ridiculous. She could hardly explain that his close proximity unnerved her to the point of not being able to think. Her thoughts drifted. She and Fabio were somewhere alone, a picnic perhaps, he was looking at her as if he loved her…

As Katie's breathing slowed to a regular rhythm Fabio studied her. Her long blonde hair had fallen over her face and she had a small smile on her face as if she was having happy dreams. She made his heart ache.

He loved the way everything excited her. She couldn't feign boredom if she tried. He still found it difficult to sleep at night. Every time he closed his eyes, her image would appear. Either laughing at some idiotic joke he'd made in an attempt to keep the sparkle in her eyes, or her face awash with sadness as if she was remembering her brother.

He was tempted to brush back the stray lock of hair that had fallen across her eyes, and only just managed to restrain himself. However he felt about this woman, it wouldn't be fair to start anything. Katie wasn't the kind of woman to fall in love easily and somehow he knew with unshakable certainty that when she did, it would be for ever. She would want children one day and if the thought that it wouldn't be with him made his stomach clench, that was too bad. He was many things, but selfish wasn't one of them.

The yacht was moored in the Bosphorus. By the time they stepped on board it was dark and the river twinkled with a thousand lights.

The sights, sounds and smells of Istanbul hit her the moment they arrived. It was as if she had been transported to the Ottoman period when the sultans had lived in palaces.

'I can just imagine the sultans and their wives living

here,' Katie breathed, as Amelia pointed out the Blue Mosque.

'You should visit the harem in Topkapi Palace if you want to see what it was like for the women at that time. I'm not so sure it was all that great for them,' Amelia said, before kissing her. 'Thank you both again for coming. I know you didn't have to, but it means so much to Mark that Lucy and I can be here.'

Amelia looked more relaxed than the last time Katie had seen her. Lucy had been keeping well and she knew Amelia put that down to the care the little girl received.

'I intend to see as much as I can squeeze in. Maybe tomorrow? Do you think Lucy would like to come too?'

Lucy was in bed when they arrived, having travelled with her mother the day before.

Amelia laughed. 'I'm not sure going around museums is my daughter's cup of tea. But you can ask her yourself tomorrow. Maybe we'll all go while Mark is practising.'

In the end, as her mother suspected, Lucy had decided not to come. ''S boring,' she said. 'But you can go, Mum. I'll be all right by myself.'

'Of course I'm not going to go without you. Anyway, I've seen it before.'

'Then I'll stay too,' Katie offered. She'd already carried out some physio on Lucy and had been pleased to see that her home routine was working well. Lucy's chest was clear. At least for the time being.

'No. You and Fabio go off for the day. At least if you're both seeing something of Istanbul, I won't feel too bad about dragging you out here on your weekend off.'

'I'd hardly call it dragging,' Katie protested.

'Still, I insist you go. Enjoy your day and we'll see you back here for drinks before dinner.'

* * *

The tender that belonged to the yacht dropped Katie and Fabio off at the harbour. It was thronged with tourists thumbing through travel guides and locals selling every imaginable delicacy from small stalls. In every way it was different from the sophisticated glitz of Monte Carlo, but Katie decided she liked it better. It was more authentic.

'Okay, where do you want to go first?' Fabio asked.

'I don't know—anywhere. Everywhere.'

'Okay, put yourself in my hands,' Fabio said, taking her by the hand. Katie felt herself go crimson. Whether it was because of the image that popped into her head of her in Fabio's hands, or whether it was because the feeling of her fingers in his was so deliciously secure, she wasn't sure.

Fabio steered her across the road. The cars made no attempt to slow down for them and Katie was relieved when, after dodging the traffic, they made it to the other side in one piece.

They went first to the famous Blue Mosque that dominated the city. Katie read snippets from the guide book as they roamed the impressive building with its thousands of blue tiles that gave it its name. After that they visited the underground Basilica to gawp at the hundreds of pillars and Medusa's head before heading to the Topkapi Palace. Fabio stopped outside to buy her some cut-up watermelon to quench their thirst and they sat on a bench, taking in the sights and sounds.

'It says here that the sultan kept as many as three hundred concubines in his harem,' Katie said. 'A bit much for most men, don't you think?'

Fabio grinned at her, his eyes creasing at the corners.

'I guess it depends on the women,' he teased.

'I suspect you would have been in your element,' Katie

said grumpily. 'A different woman for almost every day of the year.'

'That's a bit unfair,' Fabio said. Before she knew it he had taken a lock of her hair and tucked it behind her ear. 'I think if the sultan or whoever met the right woman, she would be enough for him. I know it would be for me.'

Her heart was hammering so hard in her chest Katie thought it might explode. If she hadn't known better she would have sworn that his eyes were full of meaning…and longing. But that was silly. If Fabio felt anything for her, he would have said—or done—something.

'Shall we go in?' she suggested, relieved to hear her voice was steady. As she got to her feet she found her legs were less so.

Fabio stood and kissed her lightly on the lips. '*Vamos!* Let's go!'

As he turned away Katie put a finger on her lips where his had been only moments before.

Damn, damn, damn. Why did she have to be falling for this man? Her heart stopped. *Falling* in love? She could no longer fool herself. Her heart had been no match for her head. She'd fallen hook, line and sinker. For ever.

After they had admired everything the palace had to offer, they stopped at the harbour for a fish sandwich. As Fabio watched Katie happily perched on a makeshift stool, eagerly waiting for her fish, caught only moments before, to be grilled and placed between two slices of bread, his heart cracked. She was everything he'd ever wanted in a woman, but hadn't known he did until he'd met her. Why did she have to come into his life when he'd thought he was happy? And now he knew he hadn't been. The restlessness, the constant seeking for new adventure, new thrills, new women had been a desperate attempt to fill the emptiness inside him that, until he'd met Katie, he hadn't realised was there. He wanted her more than he'd ever wanted a woman before. Not just in his bed, but in his life. But he couldn't have her. It wasn't fair to Katie.

Back on the yacht, Lucy was waiting excitedly, keen to hear about their day and to tell them about hers.

'I went on the small boat all the way up the river. It was so much fun. Mum came too. And then one of the crew brought his son to meet me. He didn't speak much English, but he knew how to play computer games.'

Fabio ruffled her hair. 'Sounds like you had a good day, sweetie. How are you feeling?'

Katie glanced at Fabio.

'I'm feeling good,' Lucy said.

'Then you won't mind if I listen to your chest later just to make sure,' Fabio said. Katie had also noticed that Lucy's breathing was more laboured than usual. Perhaps the humidity was affecting her chest. She desperately hoped it wasn't the first signs of a chest infection.

'I'm okay,' Lucy said, setting her mouth in a firm line.

'Mark and I have been invited to dinner with the rest of the team tonight,' Amelia said. 'You and Fabio are invited too.'

Katie rubbed her feet. They were aching from all the walking they had done that day. 'If you don't mind, I think I'll give it a miss. I'm shattered.'

'What about you ,Fabio?'

'Me? Oh, if it's okay with you, I think I'll stay here too. Keep Katie and Lucy company.'

'But I want to go to dinner with you and Daddy,' Lucy protested. 'Please, Mum. Can I?'

Amelia smiled at her daughter. 'If Fabio thinks it's okay and you're not too tired, of course you can come. But...' she wagged a finger at her daughter's smiling face '...you'll have to leave early. I want you in bed by ten at the latest.'

Lucy pouted but it was only for a moment. ''Kay,' she said. 'I'll probably get bored unless there's a kid my age to play with.'

Amelia puckered her brow. 'Would it be okay if I gave the staff the evening off? I usually do when we're all off the yacht, but I could ask the chef to stay behind and make you dinner before he joins the others.'

Fabio and Katie shook their heads in unison.

'Not really hungry...' Katie said.

'I can make supper,' Fabio said at the same time. Their eyes locked and Katie felt the air fizz between them. She wanted to be alone with him and it seemed he felt the same way.

'No.' Katie smiled. 'Don't worry about us. Have a good time.'

Fabio stood and stretched. '*Vamos*, Lucy. Let's check you over before Katie gives you your physio. We want you to be in tip-top condition for your evening out.'

When Fabio and Lucy left to go below, Amelia sighed.

'He's so good with her. I don't know how we would have coped without him these last couple of years.'

'You would have managed fine.'

Amelia shook her head. 'Until Fabio became her doctor, I wouldn't let Lucy do anything. I was always so scared. Mark was always asking us both to come and watch him race, but I was too nervous that Lucy would get sick while we were abroad.' She smiled wanly. 'Silly, isn't it? Most countries where Mark races have perfectly good hospitals, but it's not the same somehow.'

'No, I guess it isn't. Not that I'd know. I haven't travelled much before. Apart from a trip to Europe with friends from university and going to Monaco and coming here, I've always holidayed at home.'

Amelia took a sip of her drink. 'Are you seeing someone? Is that why you don't travel?'

Katie shook her head. 'I've never met anyone I've wanted to be with.' Until now, a small voice whispered inside her head. 'At least, not longer than six months.'

'What about Fabio?' Amelia asked with a teasing smile. 'You two seem pretty close.'

'Fabio!' Katie tried to fix an expression on her face as if it was the first time such a thought had crossed her mind. Unfortunately she could feel a tell-tale blush creep up her cheeks. 'Fabio and I are just colleagues.'

Amelia's smile told Katie that she wasn't fooled, but without saying anything else Amelia drained the last of her drink and got to her feet. 'I should go and shower and change, if I'm not going to be late.' She frowned at her watch. 'I wonder where Mark is? He should be back by now.' She sighed. 'I guess he must be chatting to his team.'

Although Amelia's words were light, Katie could see the anxiety lurking behind her eyes. Once again she thought of how much she'd hate to be in Amelia's shoes. It must be hell on earth wondering whether your husband was going to come back to you in one piece, however much Amelia claimed to be used to it.

'Would you mind telling Luce that I'll come and help her get ready in a bit?' Amelia said.

'I'll go and tell her now. Fabio will have finished checking her over, I'm sure.'

* * *

Katie found Lucy and Fabio sitting on Lucy's bed, arguing over a game on Lucy's games console. Katie suppressed a smile. Sometimes she wondered who was the biggest kid. Despite what Fabio had told her about not wanting children, he was a natural with them. Someday he would change his mind. At the thought her heart contracted. Fabio with a wife and children wasn't something she wanted to think about.

'Sorry to break this up, guys. But if you're going to have time to get ready for dinner, Luce, we should get on with your physio.'

Reluctantly Lucy put her game to the side. 'I was beating Fabio.'

'Were not. At least, I would have caught up eventually.'

'How is Lucy's chest?' Katie asked.

'A tiny bit more rattly than we would like, but nothing major. I've increased her antibiotics slightly and the physio should help.' He chucked Lucy under the chin. 'I'll leave you two girls to it. Remember to come and show me yourself in all your finery.'

He glanced at Katie. 'I thought we could eat about eight? I'll go and see what the chef has in the fridge.'

Later after everyone had left—Mark had been late but thankfully intact—Katie was unsure what to do with the couple of hours before dinner.

There was no sign of Fabio, who had disappeared once Lucy had modelled her dress for him, and Katie eyed the hot tub longingly. The light was fading, although it was still warm. A few minutes in the tub would be good before she got ready for the evening.

This time she'd remembered to bring her costume and,

nipping down to her cabin, she changed quickly, and went back up on deck, taking the white robe that had been left behind the door for her with her.

As she slipped into the hot water she sighed with pleasure. It was just the right temperature. She switched on the bubbles and rested her head against the tub rim and closed her eyes. Bliss.

'Do you mind if I join you?' At the sound of Fabio's voice, her eyes snapped open. He was standing in front of her, wearing his swimming shorts and holding a towel.

For a moment their eyes locked and Katie couldn't look away. She should get out, run for her life but her limbs felt heavy, weighted down. Her eyes were drawn to his chest, the way his swimming shorts hugged his hips, the dark silky hair on his lower abdomen. Hot sparks of desire were shot through her body. Knowing that if she tried to speak her voice would betray her, she simply nodded.

She closed her eyes again as he got into the tub. Although the tub could comfortably have held ten and there was plenty of space for him on the other side, he lowered his body onto the seat next to her.

She opened one eye and glanced at him. He was looking at her as if trying to memorise her face. Darkness fell and the moonlight seemed to light his eyes from within. The air between them fizzed and, as her heart leaped to her throat, Katie knew that she had been waiting for this moment all her life. A heady sense of inevitability drove any thoughts of danger from her head.

'*Minha linda…*' His voice was hoarse. 'What are you doing to me? Why can't I get you out of my head?'

She didn't want to be out of his head. She wanted stay there for the rest of her life. She wanted to be with him for ever. It was no use. She loved him. Hopelessly and for ever. Right or wrong—it no longer mattered.

He raised his hand and very gently pushed a lock of wet hair from her eyes. 'You know I want you, don't you? More than I thought it was possible to want a woman.'

Her heart was pounding so hard she thought he must be able to hear it.

He ran his hands down her face, letting them rest on either side of her neck. Slowly, ever so slowly, he brought his lips down on hers.

His mouth was warm and his lips soft—at first. He nibbled at her bottom lip then his kiss deepened and he explored her mouth with his tongue as if he couldn't get enough of her.

She kissed him back hungrily, tasting coffee and mint. Her head was spinning, her body straining towards him. He lifted his head and looked into her eyes.

'You are very beautiful,' he said huskily. 'Like a sea sprite.' His accent had thickened, his Brazilian accent coming to the fore.

He slid an arm underneath her bottom and lifted her onto his lap. She could feel his desire for her through the thin material of his swimming shorts.

It didn't matter that there was no future for them. All that mattered was the here and now and her aching need for him.

He pushed the top of her bikini away with his mouth and nuzzled her breasts. She threw her head back as a wall of desire took her breath away. She had never felt like this before. As if she was going to explode. As if she had no control over her body or her mind. She pulled back, terrified of the way her body reacted to him.

'It's okay, my love. It will be all right. I promise. Just give in to it.'

Trusting him, she gave herself up to the sensations. She could do nothing else.

He circled her nipple with his tongue and she moaned.

Then she gasped as his hand slid under her bikini. Involuntarily she parted her legs to give him better access.

He looked at her and as their eyes held, she was lost. She was drowning.

'Are you sure?' he asked.

She could only nod. She'd never been more sure of anything in her life.

'I think we should go somewhere less public,' he said hoarsely.

Taking her by the hand, he helped her out of the tub and down to his cabin. She could hardly breathe. Sensations were zinging around her body.

He'd barely kicked the door closed behind him before his hands were on her again. Touching, seeking out her secret places as he watched her response through half-closed lids. If he didn't finish what he'd started, she would scream with frustration.

He lifted her into his arms and laid her gently on the bed. His eyes glowed as he looked down at her. Reaching into a drawer, he pulled out a condom and lay down next to her.

Holding her gaze, he slipped his fingers inside her. She cried out as wave upon wave of pleasure rocked her body.

Then with one swift movement he tugged off her bikini briefs and slipped out of his own.

He pulled her on top of him so that she was straddling

him. He lifted her by the hips and then he was inside her and they were rocking together. She pushed back against his chest, wanting him, needing him deeper.

Once more he brought her to the edge where she cried out with her need, and then as he moaned and his thrusting became deeper, her body exploded with intense pleasure from the tips of her toes, coursing through her body right up to her scalp.

Gasping, they held each other. Katie felt her body turn to mush as the most incredible languid feeling spread through her body. She rested her head on his shoulder, hearing almost feeling his heart beating.

He stroked her hair wordlessly as she cuddled into him.

Suddenly shy, she buried her face in his shoulder. They stayed like that for a few more minutes, Katie savouring the feeling of happiness as she listened to the rhythm of his heart.

He lifted her chin with his finger and looked deep into her eyes. His expression held a look of wonder. 'My God, Katie. What are you doing to me? I don't think I've ever wanted a woman as much as I want you.'

Want, not love. She pushed the words to the back of her mind. He hadn't made any promises. What was the point in worrying about the future when you couldn't control it anyway? She knew now that happiness had to be found wherever and whenever.

'I don't know about you,' Fabio said, 'but suddenly I'm starving.'

'Me too,' Katie whispered. 'I didn't realise sex could give you such an appetite.'

Fabio grinned down at her. 'We need to keep your strength up. I'm not finished with you yet.'

Her body tingled when he said the words. She wanted

him again. She would never stop wanting him. This man was the person she'd been waiting for all her life. The other half of her soul. And if the thought made her ache with the knowledge he didn't share her feelings, hadn't she always known that she would only ever have a small part of him?

He eased himself off the bed and, despite what they had just shared, Katie blushed. He was so confident in his nakedness and why wouldn't he be? Every muscle was clearly defined without being too built up. His stomach was hard and flat, his legs long and lean.

Grinning at her scrutiny, he passed her his robe before wrapping a towel around his hips.

Still blushing furiously, Katie took the robe from him and slipped her arms in. Fabio took hold of the lapels of the robe and pulled her towards him. 'You have no idea how cute you look when you blush.' She shivered as he dropped a kiss on the side of her neck. If he carried on touching her, she would drag him back to bed.

Before she could act on the impulse, he released her and, taking her by the hand, led her back upstairs.

'The galley is in here. What do you fancy? Lobster? Langoustine? Something Turkish?' He opened the fridge with a flourish.

'Scrambled eggs will do me fine,' Katie said.

'That all?' he teased. 'I could eat a horse.'

Katie perched at the stainless-steel counter and watched Fabio as he whipped up some eggs and cut fresh bread. He looked perfectly at home. Was there anything this man couldn't do? Her body was still throbbing from the feel of him and she knew she wanted him again. She was in love with him, but he hadn't suggested she was anything except a casual fling. He had said lots of lovely things to her, but not that he cared about her. After this evening would he seek her out again, or would he be on to pastures new? Wasn't that how men like Fabio worked? Moving from one conquest to another? But she couldn't believe he didn't feel something for her. She'd seen the look in his eyes when he'd thought she wasn't watching and she'd seen the naked pain. That didn't fit with a man who didn't care.

If he had made no promises, neither had she. She should give it time. Wait and see.

Fabio piled creamy eggs onto a plate and passed it to her before doing the same to another plate and sitting down opposite her.

'I thought you'd be having something more substantial,' she said.

'And I found I lost my appetite. Funnily enough, I have other things on my mind.' He leaned across and removed a morsel of egg that had landed on the side of her mouth and popped it into her mouth before running his finger across her lips.

Katie was having difficulty swallowing, she was having difficulty thinking. She placed her fork down and, lifting her plate, scraped the remains of the egg into the bin. Now she was having difficulty breathing. Her head was whirling and her body was behaving in a way it had never done before. Her desire for him was pulling at her, and she couldn't think straight. She wanted to feel his skin next to hers, feel his hands caressing her, have his mouth on hers.

She felt him come and stand behind her. His warm breath caressed the nape of her neck and he murmured something she couldn't understand in Portuguese. His hands untied the belt of her robe and she leaned against him as her robe fell open. Strangely she no longer felt shy. She felt nothing except longing and wonder that he was there with her. She felt no shame, no embarrassment. Just lust.

His hands were on her breasts and her breath caught in her throat.

She turned around in his arms and looked into his dark eyes.

'Take me to bed,' she whispered.

Lying in his arms felt so right. Everything about being with Fabio felt right. But she knew deep inside that for him, at least, this meant little. Why of all people did she have to go and fall for him? He'd made no secret of the fact that he intended to stay single.

She was getting ahead of herself. They both needed more time to get to know each other. Not that it would make any difference to the way she felt.

Outside the water was lapping gently, almost mimicking the rhythm of Fabio's heartbeat.

Katie squinted at her watch, which was illuminated by the harbour lights outside. Nine-thirty. Lucy could return any minute.

'Fabio, wake up,' Katie whispered.

He moaned in his sleep and his arm pulled her closer. Katie would have liked nothing better than to stay exactly where she was, possibly for the rest of her life, but she didn't want Lucy to look for her or Fabio and find them. Some things were better left private.

Propping herself on her elbow, she looked down at his face. In sleep he was more severe looking, but there was a vulnerability about him she'd seen once before. 'You need to get up, Fabio,' she whispered again.

His eyes flickered open, and as he came to and saw her he smiled and pulled her towards him.

'You're pretty special—you know that, don't you?'

His words should have given her a glow, but they didn't. She wanted to be more than pretty special. She wanted him to love her, the way she loved him. Nothing less would ever be enough.

'You're not bad yourself,' she replied lightly. She leaped out of bed and tossed him her robe. 'Now, scoot. I'm going to shower before Lucy arrives back.'

Katie sat by the side of Lucy's bed and brushed away a lock of hair that had fallen over the sleeping child's face. As she'd expected, Lucy had rushed into her room as soon as she'd returned, wanting to tell her all about the evening. It had taken Katie all her persuasive powers to coax the excited girl into bed after more than an hour had passed and Lucy had begun to look exhausted.

Katie was surprised at how fond she'd become of Lucy over the last few weeks. For a while after Richard's death she had thought she would never be able to feel anything ever again. That she would never let herself get close to anyone again, in case she lost them too. Yet here she was, and despite herself she'd allowed two people into her heart. How had she let that happen?

Fabio wasn't in it for the long term. He'd never pretended otherwise. But she was sure she meant more to him than just an affair. Sighing, she stood and looked out of the window. She didn't really know for sure, did she? She'd never met anyone like him before. He was used to having relationships that weren't serious. She wasn't. She thought back to what he'd told her about his family. It couldn't have been easy for him as a child. Shunted between two arguing parents who had put their own lives ahead of their child. No wonder he had such a downer on marriage and no wonder he didn't want children.

But marriage didn't have to be like that. Her parents had been deeply in love until the day they'd died. And take Suzy and Richard. If Richard had lived…she swallowed the familiar lump in her throat…there was no way those two would have ever separated. Fabio shouldn't let his own experiences cloud his view of marriage. As she turned away and tiptoed out of Lucy's room, a thought crept into her head. Could she change his mind?

CHAPTER TWELVE

THE next day, they set off to where Mark's race was due to start at two. Fabio had left with Mark before Amelia and Lucy had been up.

As Katie had known he would, Fabio had come to her when everyone was asleep. They had made love again, before she'd fallen asleep in his arms. When she woke up he'd gone. She hugged the memory of their night together, praying she hadn't given herself away to Mark by blushing furiously when she'd seen Fabio at breakfast.

Lucy could hardly sit still at the thought of seeing her father race.

'Mum says there's a special place for families to watch from. We can have ice cream—anything we want.' Katie and Amelia shared a smile. Despite being mature for her age, Lucy was still, at the end of the day, a little girl.

'And if he wins, he will be the champion!' Lucy bounced on her seat. 'And he'll be able to come home with us, won't he, Mum?'

'He'll be able to come home whether he becomes champion or not,' Amelia agreed with a smile. 'But let's hope he wins.'

The race track was already crowded with spectators by

the time they arrived. Someone met them at the entrance and escorted them upstairs to a small room with a balcony overlooking the race track. The sound of cars tuning up filtered through the window. A large flat-screen television rotated different views of the pits, where the crews and drivers were making last-minute preparations, as well of the track where the race would take place.

'At least it's not as loud up here,' Amelia said.

They were offered drinks and snacks and, to Lucy's delight, ice cream. They settled down to watch the TV screen. Not that it was very interesting. Just shots of helmeted and jumpsuited men working over sleek racing cars. But eventually the cars were lined up at the start of the race.

'That's my dad!' Lucy said excitedly, pointing to a blue car near the front.

'How do you know?' Katie asked. Apart from the colours, they all looked the same to her.

''Cos it has his number, silly.'

'The other blue one is his teammate,' Amelia said. 'I have to agree with you, Katie, they all look the same to me. I rely on the commentators to tell me where Mark is.'

'How many laps?' Katie asked.

'Fifty-eight. Do you want to watch the start from the balcony?'

Katie wondered what was keeping Fabio. He would miss the start of the race. Just then the images on the TV panned to the pit where Mark's crew were and Katie saw Fabio's dark head as he leaned in to hear what one of the pit team was saying. The sight of him sent her pulse thrumming as memories from the night before rushed back into her head. Not that she'd been able to stop thinking about him all day.

'Fabio's back. He must have decided to watch from down there,' she said, hoping she wasn't blushing again.

The cars started with a roar and after a warm up lap began to race in earnest, each one jostling for position. Katie caught her breath as a car passed the one in front seeming to miss it only by a whisker.

'It's hot. I think I'll go back inside,' Amelia said.

Katie stayed outside where she could enjoy the warmth.

Every few minutes a stream of cars would rush past. Having had enough of the sun, she was about to go back inside when the screech of a car in trouble caught her attention. Smoke was billowing from its engine as it careered across the track, forcing cars behind to swerve in order to miss it. Her breath caught as she noticed the colour. Blue. Was it Mark?

The driver fought hard to get the car under control, but as if it were all happening in slow motion, the car flipped several times before coming to rest the right way up against the barrier.

Feeling sick, Katie watched as men started to run towards the car. She felt even sicker as she recognised that Fabio was one of them. Was he crazy? Judging by the smoke coming from the engine, the car could explode anytime.

She was only dimly aware of Amelia and Lucy standing next to her. Amelia had turned a ghastly white and looked as if she might faint.

'It's all right, Mummy,' Lucy was shouting, pulling at her mother's arm. 'It's not Daddy.'

Amelia sank into one of the armchairs. 'Thank God.'

Katie shared her relief, but Fabio! He was putting his life at risk. Feeling increasingly nauseous, she couldn't tear her eyes away as he ran to the injured driver and leaned right into the wrecked car. Right behind him were men running, carrying fire extinguishers. What if Fabio couldn't get the injured driver out before the car was engulfed in flames? She knew he would never leave the man to die.

He was tugging and gesticulating. The other men were beside him now, helping him. With the sheer numbers they managed to extract the driver and were running away from the car, carrying the injured driver between them.

Run, God damn it, Fabio. Run!

Then with a blinding flash the wrecked car exploded into a sheet of flame.

Smoke billowed into the air, obscuring Katie's vision. She was only dimly aware that the race had been stopped. Her heart was crashing against her ribs so violently she thought she would be sick.

Please. Not again. Don't do this to me again.

Then out of the smoke the four men appeared, still carrying their patient, and Katie recognised Fabio's dark head. He was all right! He was alive. Katie sank back onto the chair behind her, placed her head in her hands and sobbed.

'What am I going to do?' Katie wailed.

Suzy put her arm around Katie's shoulder. They had returned home the day after the race. Mark had gone on to win, and the injured driver was doing well in hospital with surprisingly few injuries, but Katie couldn't bring herself to join in the celebrations. She'd excused herself and, apart from doing Lucy's physio, had remained in her cabin all evening. She didn't want to see Fabio, not until she knew what she was going to do. He'd knocked on her cabin door late the night of the race, but she'd feigned sleep. She'd felt relieved when the next morning she'd heard that Fabio had been called away to see another patient somewhere in Europe and had left already.

'Oh, sweetie, you do have it bad, don't you?' Suzy said sympathetically. 'But what do you mean, what are you going to do?'

'I love him, and I wish I didn't.'

'You can't help who you fall in love with,' Suzy said. 'Why don't you see where it takes you? From what you tell me, he isn't immune to you either.'

Katie sniffed. 'He doesn't love me. Even if he did, he's wrong for me, wrong, wrong, wrong.'

'You don't know that. Men like him do change their ways. When they meet the right person.'

Katie blew her nose. 'It's not just that. He reminds me so much of Richard. Fabio doesn't seem to care whether he lives or dies, and I can't bear the thought of something happening to him.'

Suzy stiffened.

'I didn't mean that. Oh, Suzy, I'm sorry. Of course Richard wanted to live. He had you and Ricky. He wasn't like Fabio at all. Fabio puts his life at risk for fun. And Richard, he put his life at risk because he had no choice.'

'Let me get this straight. You love Fabio, but you think he doesn't love you. You're scared he's going to break your heart. You're also scared he's going to kill himself in some mad adventure, leaving you all alone.'

'That's about it. Pathetic, huh?'

'I don't think there's anything pathetic about loving someone so much you can't bear to live without them.' Suzy's eyes grew moist. 'But if I had my time all over again—even if I'd known when I met Richard that our time together would be limited—I would have still wanted to be with him. There would never have been a choice.' Suzy blew her nose. 'Fabio didn't go after the racing driver out of some idea that it would be fun, Katie. He did it because he felt he had no choice. Would you rather he was the kind of man who stood back and let others take the risks?'

'No—I mean yes.' Katie shook her head, feeling miserable. 'I don't know. All I do know is that I couldn't bear it if someone close to me died again. I'm not strong enough.'

'I think you are,' Suzy said quietly, and Katie was reminded of Fabio saying the same thing to her that night on the yacht.

'Anyway…' she attempted a smile '…I guess I'll get over him. I have no choice. I've no reason to think I'm anything more than a passing whim as far as he's concerned.'

'Maybe he cares for you more than you think.' At the sound of cries coming from the nursery Suzy got to her feet. 'Baby calling. Katie, why don't you talk to him? Tell him how you feel. I can't imagine that Fabio will put his life in danger to save people from burning cars every day of the week.'

'I know he won't. But there's all this other stuff he does. One way or another. it looks like he's determined to kill himself.' Katie followed Suzy into the nursery. 'When he hurt his ankle it was because he was BASE jumping. The article I read said someone had died recently doing exactly the kind of thing he does. This recklessness of his—it's in him and it's never going to go away.'

Suzy picked Ricky up from his cot. 'The item you read could be exaggerating.' She placed her small son down on his changing mat and peeled off his wet nappy. Once he was changed and redressed in his sleepsuit, Suzy sat down and started breastfeeding.

'And even if it isn't, Katie, you have to accept that's who Fabio is and you have to decide whether it is better to live with him in your life, knowing that you will always worry about him, or whether it is better to live without him and all the joy and yes, pain, that love can bring. Unfortunately, loving someone comes at a price. I for one think that price is worth paying.' Suzy's voice hitched as she looked down at her suckling child.

As Katie watched mother and son her heart squeezed. One day she would like to have children. But please, God, she would have the children's father safe at home beside her. And right now all of it seemed like no more than a far-fetched dream.

'Anyone fancy going to Ascot?' Jenny asked, waving tickets in the air as if she'd just won the Lottery. 'Give us all a chance to dress up.'

Katie was getting used to the fact that their patients would drop off tickets for almost any event that she could imagine. Most of the time she declined.

Fabio had gone from his patient in Europe to Brazil for a couple of weeks and so she hadn't seen him. She didn't know whether she was dismayed or relieved by his absence. She only knew she missed seeing him every day.

'I don't think I'll bother,' Rose said, patting her ever-increasing girth. 'All I want to do these days after work is change into my pyjamas and have an early night. I went last year, though, and it was fun. You should go, Katie. Take your sister-in-law if she would like to go.'

Katie took the tickets from Jenny. 'I wouldn't want to stop anyone else from going,' she said.

'They wouldn't let me in probably,' Jenny grinned. 'I don't do dresses. Anyway, horses bore me.'

'What about you, Vicki?' Katie asked the nurse who was

writing up her notes at the desk. They weren't expecting any more patients and would be closing up soon.

'Can't. My husband is on duty that day. I've already checked. But he says if no one wants the tickets for the football game next Saturday, could he please have them?'

'They're his.' Jenny scrabbled around in a drawer before finding a bunch of tickets. 'And if anyone else wants to go, there's more where these came from.'

The footballers who Katie had been treating regularly dropped off tickets for their home matches. One of them kept asking her to go out with him, but she always refused. Maybe she should reconsider. The worst danger a footballer got themselves into was usually a sprained ankle or a torn Achilles' tendon. But she knew she never would go out with the footballer. The simple fact was he wasn't Fabio.

'I'll ask my sister-in-law if she fancies Ascot,' Katie said. 'Would it be okay if I let you know tomorrow?'

Jenny nodded. 'Take your time. Hey, does anyone know when Fabio is due back? Some of his patients have been phoning for appointments. Most are happy to see Jonathan if it's an emergency, but one or two are pretty adamant that only Fabio will do.'

Vicki looked up from her note-writing. 'Let me guess. The women.'

Jenny feigned innocence. 'Now, why would you say that?'

Katie forced a smile, even though it hurt her to think of Fabio with other women. He could have phoned her or texted her. Something. But he hadn't. Was he regretting sleeping with her? Even worse, now that he had, had he lost interest? Was she just another notch in his bedpost?

'He's due back tonight, so he'll be in tomorrow. I'm

surprised he didn't let you know, Jenny. It's not like him.'
Rose puckered her brow.

'Maybe he can't get a signal in Brazil.' Jenny sighed.

'Don't be a goose, Jenny,' Vicki said. 'Brazil isn't exactly
Third World.'

Katie closed her ears to the rest of the chat. Her stomach was churning at the thought of seeing Fabio again and
knowing that whatever had between them was over.

But wasn't that what she wanted? Hadn't she told herself that she would tell him that a relationship was impossible? She felt bruised and hurt that he hadn't given her the
chance. It seemed that her fears had come true. It was one
thing for her to decide she couldn't risk loving him, quite
another for him to treat her as if she meant nothing. Could
she bear to continue to work at the practice knowing she
would see him almost every day for the foreseeable future
and having to hear about his conquests, pretending she
didn't love him?

Her heart slammed against her ribs. How could she have
been so stupid as to fall in love with him? Now she knew
that he didn't need to die to break her heart.

She was putting Ricky down for the night when the doorbell
rang. Leaving Suzy to answer it, she carried on tucking her
nephew in. He was growing so quickly. Before they knew
it, he'd be toddling around.

'Katie, it's Fabio.' Suzy's voice came from behind her.

'Fabio!' Immediately her heart started racing. Had he
come to tell her it was all over? Before they came face to
face at work? Well, if he had, she wouldn't give herself
away.

A glance in the mirror confirmed her worst fears. She
looked as if she'd spent the night arguing with a hurricane.

Her hair was all over the place, she had a smear of baby food on her cheek and she was wearing her oldest pair of tracksuit bottoms. Bloody typical.

Noticing her hesitation, Suzy gave her a small push. 'He's waiting,' she hissed.

'I can't see him like this,' Katie hissed back. 'Can't you stall him?'

'What am I supposed to say? Could you wait half an hour while Katie dolls herself up for you?'

'I don't care what you tell him, just give me ten minutes—or fifteen,' she added when Suzy raised a sarcastic eyebrow.

'Can I help?' An amused voice came from the doorway.

Katie swung around with a little yelp. She had been so busy arguing with Suzy she hadn't heard him approach. Her nerves thrummed at the sight of him. He was just so damn sexy. And dear.

'It's okay. I was just putting Ricky down, but he's sleeping now.' She made a futile attempt to push her straggly hair behind her ear. 'Would you like a coffee? I was about to make one for myself.' Actually, she hadn't been. She simply couldn't think of anything to say.

'I wondered if you'd like to come out for dinner,' Fabio asked. 'I did try your mobile, but I couldn't get through.'

'Battery must be flat.'

Fabio seemed uncharacteristically nervous. No doubt this was where he gave her the boot. Of course he couldn't say anything in front of Suzy.

'About dinner?' If he'd noticed that dinner was the last thing she was ready for, he gave no sign of it.

'Tell you what, guys,' Suzy interrupted. 'Why don't I leave you two alone? There's a casserole in the oven you could have and I'm overdue a visit to my folks. Would it be all right if I left Ricky? I don't want to wake him.'

'Sure,' Katie said. She didn't know which was worse. Being alone here with Fabio or being in a restaurant.

'Home cooking sounds good to me,' Fabio said. 'If you're sure? I don't want to chase you out of your home.'

Suzy picked up her handbag and started putting on her coat. 'Honestly, I could do with a change of scenery. I've got my mobile, Katie, if you need me,' And with a last wave she was out of the door, leaving Katie facing Fabio.

'I should go and change,' Katie said. 'I don't suppose you could give me a few minutes?'

'You look perfect the way you are.' He stepped towards her. 'Even the crusty baby food suits you.' He licked his finger and rubbed at her cheek. Her skin sizzled where he'd touched her.

'Now I'm definitely having a shower.' If he was going to tell her that sleeping with her had been a mistake, at least she wanted to feel less at a disadvantage. 'Could you listen out for Ricky for me?' She picked up a pile of magazines and shoved them at Fabio. 'Something to read while you wait.'

Fabio's mouth twitched. '*Cosmopolitan*? *Mother and Baby*? Not my usual reading material.' Then his eye caught one of the feature headlines—'How to please your man'— and his smile widened. 'This one sounds interesting.' He shooed her away. 'Go. I'll be fine.'

When Katie emerged from the shower, Fabio was walking up and down with a crying Ricky on his shoulder. Katie hadn't heard the baby above the noise of the shower.

She went to take him from Fabio but he shook his head. 'He's settling,' he said quietly.

Katie went into the kitchen and set plates out, checking on the casserole. It had another twenty minutes to go.

Back in the sitting room, Fabio was still pacing, with Ricky draped over his shoulder. Katie scooted around to his back to check that Ricky was asleep, only to be met with the solemn, wide-awake but content eyes of her nephew.

'Every time I try to put him back in his cot, or stop pacing, he starts crying again,' Fabio said. 'I think it's safer just to leave him where he is for the time being.'

Katie smothered a smile. Ricky had left a trail of re-gurgitated milk down the back of Fabio's shirt. This time it was his turn to look less than immaculate. She peered at him. Something was different. He was growing a beard or something. Well, not exactly a beard. More like six o'clock shadow. Whatever it was, it suited him. He had never seemed more sexy to Katie than now, with baby vomit and a couple of days' stubble on his face.

'I could always walk alongside you and feed you mouth-fuls of casserole if you're hungry,' Katie offered.

Fabio grinned and her heart flipped, then his expression turned serious. 'I'm not very hungry,' he said. 'But I thought we should talk.'

A shiver of apprehension ran up Katie's spine. This was it. The part where he told her it had all been a mistake and for the sake of their working relationship, could they just be friends? She steeled herself to pretend she felt the same.

'The thing is, Katie. I think I'm falling in love with you.'

It was as if a string orchestra had set up home inside her chest. He was falling in love with her!

'But it's not going to work,' he added quickly

Her heart plummeted. She knew now without a shadow of doubt that although she had told herself many times he wasn't the man for her, it was too late. Her heart had betrayed her. Reckless and a womaniser he may be, but she loved him. She would rather risk her heart with this man than spend her life safe but without him.

'And I think you care about me too,' Fabio said, his eyes searching hers.

'Really?' she prevaricated. 'What makes you say that?' If she was going to get the brush-off then she was going to damn well hang onto some dignity.

His smile was sad. 'Oh, Katie, do you really think you can hide your feelings? It is the thing I love about you the most. The way you can't pretend to be anything except who you are. Being with you is like being in a harbour. A place of safety from the storm.'

'So why can't we be together?' Katie sank down on the nearest armchair as Fabio continued to pace.

'For all sorts of reasons. First, I'm not the marrying kind. I don't believe that two people can live together without tearing each other apart.'

Marriage! Did he say marriage? Her mouth went dry.

'Who said anything about getting married? Don't you think you're jumping the gun a bit?'

'I'm just trying to be honest. I need you to know that wherever this goes, it can't be permanent.'

'Why? Why do you say that?'

He smiled, but there was no humour in his eyes. 'I saw the way my parents almost destroyed each other. They were in love once, they must have been. I was very young when they separated, but I still remember the fights.'

'Lots of couples make it. Your parents had different stresses. It couldn't have been easy for them to follow careers that took them to opposite parts of the world.'

Fabio stopped pacing and looked at her. 'I know my

parents weren't like everyone else's.' He started pacing again. 'Like many in his line, my father lived life too fast. Do you know what I'm saying?'

Katie shook her head, bewildered. 'I think you're going to have to spell it out.'

'My father took drugs and drank himself to an early grave. I watched him destroy himself. I swore then that I would never find my thrills in the bottom of a bottle or in chemicals. That's why I surf and take risks. It's the way I get my highs.' He paused. 'At least, it used to be. These days I get more of a buzz being with you.'

Katie's heart did a little dance and then fell over. He loved her, but he couldn't be with her.

Ricky whimpered and Fabio started pacing again. 'I know that marriages can break down, and that my parents had more pressure than most. God knows, I see enough of it every day, but that's not the only reason we can't be together.'

Katie's head was beginning to ache. If only Fabio would stop walking up and down.

'Go on,' she said quietly, knowing that whatever he had to say, she needed to hear it.

'My folks were so caught up in their own lives that when I got mumps as a child they didn't even notice. They left me with the housekeeper while they went away for the weekend.'

He took a deep breath, 'To be fair, they didn't know how sick I was going to get. They thought it was a simple case of mumps. Naturally it hadn't occurred to either of them to get me vaccinated.'

'Was this when you were in hospital? When you decided to become a doctor?'

He smiled. 'You remembered.'

As if she'd forget anything he'd ever told her.

'That came later,' he said. 'At first I was too sick to know where I was. All I remember is wanting my mother, and she wasn't there.' His voice thickened. 'I'm not telling you this, Katie, because I want your sympathy. I just need you to understand.'

When Fabio turned round, Katie saw that finally Ricky had fallen asleep. Gently she lifted him from Fabio and, going to the nursery, placed the baby back in his cot. When she returned to the sitting room, Fabio was staring into space. She had never seen him like this and her heart ached for him. She crossed over to his chair and, sitting on the floor, placed her head on his lap. His hand came out to stroke her hair.

'What happened while you were in hospital?' Katie asked, knowing Fabio hadn't reached the end of his story.

'Most kids who get mumps only get mild symptoms. I was one of the unlucky ones. For a while the nurses thought they were going to lose me. This time my mother did come. And my father. I have a vague recollection of them both sitting by my bed. I was happy. I thought it meant that they were going to get back together. If getting sick meant I would live with both my parents, then I was glad.' He sighed heavily. 'But as I got better, they started arguing again. Each blaming the other for my illness. The nurses had even to evict them at one point. Not exactly what a child wants to happen.'

His hands stilled in her hair. 'I got better, obviously, and I think I grew up then. I decided I would never rely on anyone again. It's also when I decided to become a doctor. I saw it as a way out. It gave me hope that I could lead a life far removed from that of my parents. You asked me if

I ever wanted to be a singer or an actor—believe me, there was nothing I wanted to do less.

'When I got better I returned to boarding school. Most people hated it there, but I liked it. There was no shouting, no arguments, and if there wasn't love either, that was better than the pain I felt living with my parents. I learned how to depend only on myself.'

'So now you know how not to be with your children. You would be a very different parent from what they were, I think. You'd have to stop taking risks, or at least not as many, but perhaps it would be worth it.'

His hands gripped her shoulders briefly, before they dropped to his sides. 'Katie, how simply you see life. Living with me would destroy that. I would end up tearing you in two. I can't change and you want me to. Despite what I told you about my parents, I will never be the pipe-and-slippers type.'

Katie scrambled to her feet, feeling a warm tide of anger wash over her. Placing her hands on her hips, she turned to face him.

'I'm sorry, Fabio, but all this sounds like so much hog-wash to me. An excuse why you can't try and have a loving, committed relationship. If it can't be with me, that's one thing, but pay me the respect I deserve, and don't lie to me.'

He looked up at her with such an expression of regret and sadness it took her breath away.

'Tell me, Katie, do you want children in your life?'

The question took her by surprise. 'I always did. Growing up with only Richard, I always wanted to be part of a big family one day. It scares me sometimes now, especially when I think of Lucy and Richard, and know that I will go through my life terrified that something will happen to my child. But now you ask, I guess it is a fear I'm prepared to live with. I would just need their father to tell me when I was being over-protective.'

'I thought so,' Fabio said slowly. 'Anyone who sees you with children knows that you are meant to have them. Three or four, perhaps.'

'Hey, I'm only coming to terms with the fact I might have them one day, I'm not planning to get pregnant any time soon.' She tried to keep her tone light, but her voice came out with a wobble. The feeling of dread was getting stronger.

'And that's the problem. It's not just that I'd be a hopeless risk as husband material, I can't have children, Katie. The mumps I had as a child left me sterile.'

CHAPTER THIRTEEN

'How can you be sure?' Katie's head was spinning.

'When I was eighteen a girl I slept with told me she was pregnant. As you can imagine, I was stunned. I saw my life going up in smoke. When I told my mother, it was the first and last time I had gone to her for advice, or financial support for the girl at least, she told me that she didn't think it could be mine. Then she explained about the mumps.

'In some ways, although I wasn't ready to become a father, I was devastated. I had become used to the idea that there was going to be a child in this world who had my genes and I knew that I wasn't going to be like my parents and put my own needs first.

'I didn't believe my mother. I suspected she just wanted me to get out of having a responsibility for the child, in the same way she'd abandoned her responsibility, so I decided to get my fertility checked.' His mouth twisted in a parody of a smile. 'As you can imagine, it took a bit of nerve for an eighteen-year-old to put himself through what I had to do. Donating a specimen in a room, knowing that there were people almost right outside, wasn't exactly conducive to producing the specimen.'

He rubbed a hand across his cheek. 'Turns out that my

mother was right. My sperm count was so low as to be almost negligible.'

'I'm sorry, Fabio. That must have been hard.'

'It wasn't so hard at the time. In a way I was almost relieved. At least I knew the child couldn't be mine, and when I challenged the girl, she admitted there was no baby. It was all a bit of a con to try and extract money from my family.'

'And now?'

His smile was ghostly. 'I got used to not being able to have children. I didn't see the point in marrying. So it didn't matter. Until now.'

He stopped his pacing and came to crouch at her feet. 'I thought it was only fair to tell you.'

Katie reached out and brushed a lock of hair from his eyes.

'Thank you for telling me,' she said, 'but there are other ways to have children, you know. Besides, I don't care. I love you. You're enough for me. Can't you see that?'

He took her hand and placed it back in her lap. 'But for how long, Katie? We can't take the risk that one day you'll want more. *You* can't take that risk. I won't let you.'

The blood in Katie's veins turned to ice. She couldn't accept what he was telling her. Wasn't her love enough for him? It should be. He was enough for her.

Fabio sighed heavily. 'One thing I have done is to make my peace with my mother—and my childhood. And while I was in Brazil I got to thinking about the kids who don't have parents. So I've set in motion a project to build a home for these kids, one where they'll get love as well as the best education money can buy. My father left me a lot of money, but I never wanted to touch it. I think he would be pleased that the money he left and the money his estate still makes through royalties will be used to do some good. So, at least if I can't have children of my own, I'm making a difference to some child's life. I have you to thank for that, Katie. Somewhere along the way, you've made me believe I can be a better man.'

'You were always a good man, Fabio, you just didn't know it,' Katie said.

Fabio half smiled. 'If I were a good man, I would have never let you love me. The only thing left for me to do is set you free.'

After the door closed behind Fabio, Katie sat deep in thought.

What would it be like to know that children were never going to be part of her future? Because if she and Fabio did find a way to be together, that was what life would be like.

She stood and crossed over to the window. A car passed in the otherwise deserted street.

Did it matter? A life without children if she had Fabio? Of course it did, but, as she'd told him, she would rather a life with him than without. And there was the project he'd spoken about. Those children would always be part of their lives.

There was adoption too, of course. That would be a possibility. But the feeling of unease she'd had since they'd spoken wouldn't go away. Why was he telling her this? Was it just an easy way out of a relationship he didn't wish to pursue? She shook her head. She couldn't believe Fabio would be so cowardly.

He had no right to decide what she could or couldn't cope with. Although the thought of never having children of her own saddened her, she knew that she could never walk away. All she had to do now was make him see sense.

Fabio studied the nervous man sitting opposite him. Luke, the son of a famous TV presenter, had asked specifically for Fabio when he'd made his appointment.

After spending a few minutes on small talk, Fabio decided it was time to get to the bottom of whatever was bothering this otherwise fit and healthy-looking specimen in front of him.

'Would you like to tell me why you're here?' he asked.

A deep red washed up Luke's neck and face.

'Whatever it is, Luke, you can tell me. I promise you, there's nothing I haven't seen or heard since I qualified as a doctor.'

'My girlfriend and I were—um—having sex last night when she felt something that didn't seem right.'

'In your testicles?' Fabio guessed.

Luke nodded miserably. 'Is it cancer?' he said.

'We won't know until I've had a look and done some tests. Why don't you get up on the couch so I can have a look?'

Luke did as he was told. As soon as he'd felt the lump Fabio knew instantly it would require further investigation.

'It could be a cyst,' he told Luke, 'but we won't know until we do an ultrasound at the hospital. I have to be honest with you, though, it feels a little too solid to be a cyst.'

'I'm supposed to be getting married in three months,' Luke said as he pulled his trousers up. 'What if it is cancer? What then? Will we be able to go through with the wedding? What about children? God, this is such a shock. Could I die?'

'If you have testicular cancer,' Fabio said, 'and at this stage it's only an if, and we've caught it early, then there's a good chance that you will be okay. You may need chemotherapy and you will have to have an orchidectomy—that's a procedure to remove the affected testicle—but it will be straightforward. One thing you will have to consider is whether to have your sperm stored before treatment. Unfortunately the chemo does tend to make you infertile, but if you freeze sperm it gives you an excellent chance of having children later on once the treatment is over.'

He waited until Luke was sitting down again. 'I know there's a lot to take in and you'll want to talk it over with your fiancée, but I need to get you seen at the hospital as soon as possible. Luckily my colleague, Dr Cavendish, works there. I'll give him a ring and see if he can squeeze you in this afternoon.'

Luke was pale now. 'Won't it look horrible—disgusting, even—if they remove one of my testicles? What if it puts my fiancée off? What if she decides she doesn't want to marry someone who is half a man? Could I even blame her?'

Fabio went round to Luke's side of the desk and squeezed his shoulder. 'She'll hardly notice, I promise. They reconstruct the testicle after surgery so it looks almost as it did before. And if she loves you, and seeing that she's agreed to marry you, it seems she does, she'll just be glad to have you fit and well again.'

'She agreed to marry me before she knew I was sick. It's not fair to keep her to her promise now, especially if I get sicker.' He stood up. 'Thank you for seeing me, Doctor,' he said heavily.

Luke seemed so dazed and frightened that Fabio's heart went out to him.

'Look, take a seat in the waiting room,' he said, 'while I make some calls. If they can see you this afternoon, and if I can clear my diary, I'll come with you to the hospital. That way we can discuss your options as soon as we know what exactly it is we're dealing with.'

For the first time since Luke had entered Fabio's consulting room, he looked relieved. 'Would you, Doc? I can't tell you how much it would mean to me. That way I don't need to call Clarissa until I'm sure what I want to tell her.'

'Take a seat outside. I'll be out shortly.'

Five minutes later Fabio replaced the receiver and leaned back in his chair. He had managed to arrange an appointment for Luke that afternoon. They would do an ultrasound first to rule out a cyst and then they would take it from there. All that remained was for Fabio to clear his diary so he could be with Luke when he got the diagnosis—good or bad.

His mind went back to the day he'd found out he couldn't have children. His mother had been away filming, so he had phoned Kendrick. It was always Kendrick he turned to when he was in trouble. They'd been at boarding school together and had got into mischief together and were closer than most brothers. Kendrick had been due to leave for America that afternoon but had changed his flight immediately.

'Can't let you go through this on your own,' he'd said.

Kendrick was the only person who knew what it had been like for Fabio, growing up without his parents being around. His mother and Fabio's father had been brother and sister, but where Fabio's father had little interest in anyone except those directly involved in the music world, Kendrick's father was overbearing and controlling. It was hardly surprising Kendrick had managed to get drummed out of the army. As far as Fabio knew, his uncle rarely spoke to his son.

When Fabio had been told that his sperm count was so low as to make the chances of having children almost impossible, Kendrick had called for him and then they had gone out and for the first and only time in his life Fabio had got plastered, along with his cousin.

So Fabio knew what Luke was going through. How much worse for Luke that he was engaged to someone who expected that they would have children. But as he'd told his frightened patient, even if he turned out to have testicular cancer, and Fabio was pretty sure that would be the case, at least there were other options. Children could still be part of his future.

And maybe they could be part of his. He hadn't been able to stop thinking of Katie's face since he'd spoken to her. Maybe he was being a coward, refusing to face life, whatever it brought? In that way, Katie was far braver than he was.

CHAPTER FOURTEEN

As HE'D promised, Fabio accompanied Luke to the hospital. It was just as well he did, because he was sure that Luke would have crashed had he driven himself.

'Isn't this going beyond the call of duty?' Luke said. 'I mean, you can't go with your patients to hospital every time, can you?'

'It's all part of the service, although…' Fabio hesitated. 'I like to pop in every now and again anyway to keep in touch with the staff, so don't worry. If it makes you feel any better, it's not just for you.' But that wasn't the whole truth. As he'd been talking to Luke an idea had formed in his head. If Luke was going to see the fertility specialist about storing sperm, perhaps Fabio should have a word too. Sometimes, not often admittedly, sperm counts improved over time and there was always that small possibility that his had. He thought back to what Katie had said about getting on with life. She was right. At the very least he would have his infertility confirmed. Knowing kids were out of the question might make his decision to keep away from Katie easier. It was bloody hard. Every time he saw her, he wanted to pull her into his arms and when he wasn't with her, she was always in his mind. He could barely sleep these days for thinking of her. Hell, even big wave surfing had lost its charm.

At the hospital, he left Luke in the capable hands of the surgeon Jonathan had arranged for him to see. He had an hour or so before Luke would have his diagnosis.

Feeling a little like a thief, he found his way to the fertility clinic. He referred patients there fairly regularly and so knew the doctor who ran the clinic.

'Fabio! Good to see you. Have you come to check up on us?' Dr Aubrey was in her fifties with penetrating blue eyes and a ready smile.

'Not exactly. Look, is there somewhere we can go to talk?' he asked.

Dr Aubrey frowned. 'Sure. Come this way.'

When they were settled and had finished discussing the possibility of Luke storing sperm, which as Fabio suspected would be straightforward, Fabio cleared his throat.

'I wanted to ask you whether you'd do a sperm analysis on me,' he said.

'Not a problem. You know the procedure?'

When Fabio nodded, Dr Aubrey went on. 'I could do with a little medical history, Fabio. It will help the embryologists.'

'Mumps when I was a child. Had a sperm analysis when I was eighteen Very low motility. So low as to make the chances of conceiving almost negligible.'

Dr Aubrey placed the fingertips of her hands together and tapped them together gently.

'That was, what? Ten years ago?'

'About then.'

'We've come a long way since then. It's certainly worth getting it checked out. Even if there are one or two motile sperm, we could use them to achieve a pregnancy using ICSI.'

'I've been reading about it. I didn't think too much about it…until now.'

'You've met someone and now children seem less like a crazy idea. Am I right?'

Fabio managed a smile. 'That's about it.'

'Okay. You can do it now if you have time. Or would you prefer to do it at home and bring it in first thing? You know it has to be with us within an hour of production, but we can give you everything you need.'

Riding ten-metre waves had never felt quite this terrifying.

'Home, I think.'

'Okay let's get you the pack. It has all the information you need on it. Hand it in tomorrow morning and we should have the results by the afternoon.' Dr Aubrey held out her hand. 'Good luck.'

After leaving his pack for the morning in his car, Fabio returned to the outpatient clinic to track down Luke.

He was just in time to see him emerging from the surgeon's office looking distraught and shocked. 'It's definitely cancer. But luckily it's early stage and there's time for me to deposit some sperm before I have to start treatment. They're going to do some procedure—an orchid—something early next week.'

'An orchidectomy,' Fabio filled in. 'They remove the testicle.'

'Then they're going to start with chemotherapy. They say that there's a good chance I will be sterile after that so, as you said, they advise storing as much sperm as I can before treatment starts.'

Luke sank down on a chair. 'I still can't believe this is happening to me.'

Fabio sat down next to him. 'Life can be awful sometimes. But you can store your sperm for years—until you're ready to have children. You might not even have to have IVF either. They could use it to do IUI.' Seeing that Luke was looking bewildered he added, 'Intra-uterine insemination. It's where they kind of squirt the sperm straight into the uterus at the appropriate time in your partner's cycle.'

'I don't know what to say to her. I don't know what I should do. Maybe I should walk away and let her get on with her life. Why should she be saddled with someone sick? She's young. It isn't fair. I love her too much to put her through all that.'

'And she loves you enough to want to go through it with you. If you leave her now, if you exclude her from everything—your life, your illness—she'll be hurt. You have to at least talk to her. Tell her what's going on in your head. You might be surprised to hear what she has to say.' As he said the words, Fabio knew he wasn't just speaking about Luke, he was talking about himself. One way or another, he and Katie had a whole lot of talking to do.

Fabio delivered his specimen the next morning on his way to work. Then he set off in the opposite direction to see Lucy. Amelia had phoned him to say that the little girl was wheezier than usual and she was worried, so would he mind calling in? He'd suggested that she call Katie and ask her to come out too. The thought of Katie made him feel warm. Being with her felt good. Everything about her felt good. More than good. When he was with her it was as if he'd come home. If, and he knew this was a long shot, the sperm sample he had delivered showed that there was a chance he could father children, then there was no reason why he and Katie couldn't be together. Up until he had fallen in love with her, he'd thought that he would never trust enough to commit to marriage but he knew deep down that Katie would never let him down. Not even if her life depended on it. On the other hand, if, as was likely, the results of his specimen test came back negative, he would walk away from her. He loved her that much.

Amelia met him at the door, her eyes shadowed with anxiety. 'Lucy doesn't sound good,' she said. 'Katie's here and is giving her some physio to help clear the secretions from her lungs.'

Fabio hugged Amelia. 'I'll go up and see her straight away.' He knew better than to offer Amelia false reassurances. She knew almost as much about her daughter's illness as most experts.

Upstairs, Katie was just tucking Lucy into bed. Although, along with her nebuliser, she had her computer games in her lap, she was making no attempt to play with her game. Even from the doorway Fabio could hear her rasping breaths. He was immediately alarmed.

'Hey, Luce,' he said, careful to keep his voice level and his face expressionless. 'Mum says you're not feeling too good.'

He could see his concern reflected in Katie's eyes. He'd seen Lucy a couple of days ago and her chest had been fine then. But that was the nature of this illness.

'My chest feels tight. It's a little better since Katie gave me a long session of physio.' She looked at him with tears in her eyes. He couldn't recall seeing Lucy cry before and it alarmed him even more than her breathing. 'I won't have to go into hospital, will I? I don't want to. I want to stay here.'

'I'll have to examine you, Luce, before I can make a decision about what we're going to do, you know that, but if we can keep you at home, we will.' He took his stethoscope out of his medical bag. 'Could you lift your PJs while I have a listen to your chest?'

He wasn't surprised to hear crackles. There was no doubt Lucy had a chest infection. He checked her pulse and respirations. Not as high as he'd feared. 'Tell you what. I'm going to give you mucolytic through your nebuliser and some antibiotics. I'll come back to see you this evening and assess how you're doing. If there's an improvement, then fine, you can stay at home; if not, I may have to admit you to hospital.' He lifted her chin, cutting off her protests and forcing her to look into his eyes. 'You trust me, don't you?'

Lucy nodded, her mouth trembling.

'Okay, then. We'll get you sorted for the time being. We'll decide what to do later. If that's okay with Mum?'

Amelia nodded too.

'You can get me on my mobile if you're at all worried,' he said. 'And I'll come running. That's a promise.'

Mother and daughter seemed reassured. In many ways Fabio would have liked to have taken the easy way out and admitted Lucy to hospital, but the easy way out for the doctor wasn't always what was best for the child.

Leaving Amelia with Lucy, he took Katie aside.

'Are you comfortable with what I'm proposing?' he asked. 'You have as much say in this as the rest of us.'

Katie looked at him with her clear grey eyes. 'Hospitals aren't always the best places for children. She's scared to death of going there. I think I'll hang about here for the rest of the afternoon and give her some more physio.'

Despite the reassurances Fabio had given mother and daughter, he was relieved that Katie would be on hand. She would see any change and get in touch with him immediately.

'Don't you have somewhere else to be?' he asked.

'I did,' she said softly, 'but right now it's Lucy who needs me most.'

There was something in her expression that made him pause. But she pushed him gently towards the door. 'I know you're on call for the practice today, so get going. I'll call you if I need you.'

He looked at her one final time. He wished that was true.

With a heavy heart Katie watched Fabio's car pull away. She did have somewhere she should go. Somewhere important, but if she'd told him, he might have changed his mind about watching Lucy at home for a bit. Today was the day that Suzy had been invited to Buckingham Palace to collect the medal for Richard on his behalf. Suzy's mum and dad were going too, and Suzy also wanted Katie to be there.

Still, it couldn't be helped. As she'd told Fabio, it was the living that mattered. Loving Fabio had made her believe that and, besides, Suzy would have her parents. But today would have been a final goodbye to Richard, not that she would ever stop grieving for him.

She made her way back upstairs. If only things could have been different between her and Fabio, she could have found comfort in his arms today when she needed it most. Her heart ached as she recalled the words she'd said to him. *I'll call you if I need you.* And so she would. For a patient, but never, it seemed, for herself.

***

Fabio felt distinctly unsettled all day as he saw the patients who swore they couldn't go another day without seeing him. It was mainly sore throats, colds and the odd request for sleeping and slimming pills. The last two he always turned down so you'd think word might have got around by now. He had a letter from Luke's surgeon on his desk and his surgery was scheduled for the end of the week in order to give him time to produce three samples to be frozen. Luke had phoned him to say that he had talked to his fiancée and she was adamant that nothing, not even the possibility of never having children, would come between them and that he was relieved and feeling more optimistic about the future.

There was a tap on the door and Rose stuck her head around. 'Finished for the day?'

'Apart from one or two home visits.' He explained about Lucy and that he had left Katie keeping an eye on things until he was able to pop back.

'Katie?' Rose frowned. 'Katie is with Lucy? But she's off duty.'

'I know, but apparently Amelia phoned her after phoning me. They've come to rely on her a lot.'

Rose was still frowning. 'But she'll miss the medal ceremony.'

'Medal ceremony? What medal ceremony?' It was the first he'd heard about it.

'The one for her brother. He's been awarded a Conspicuous Gallantry Cross. The presentation is at the palace this afternoon.'

Fabio was stunned. Katie had given up her afternoon, and not just any afternoon, so that she could help Lucy and her family. Her unselfish behaviour made him feel small. How often had he put the needs of others before his own?

And wasn't that what he was doing, seeking her out when he knew he had nothing to offer her?

'She can't miss the ceremony,' he said, getting to his feet. He looked at his watch. Two o'clock. 'What time did you say it was due to start?'

'About four. I think there's tea in the garden or something beforehand.'

'Look, Rose. I know you have enough on your plate at the moment, being pregnant and due to deliver almost any day, but could you do me a favour?'

'Whatever you want.'

'Could you ring the lab and get me Lucy's results?'

'No problem. Anything else?'

Fabio hesitated. 'I'm going to collect Katie from Lucy's house—she'll need a dress or something for the palace. Could you help me pick one out? And then could you stay with Lucy and Amelia until I get back there? I'll drop you off, see how she's doing, take Katie to the medal ceremony and then drop back in on them on the way back.'

Rose was already on her way out of the door. 'I gather her invitation was for her plus one, so you could stay.' She paused. 'She might need a shoulder to lean on, and I'm guessing the shoulder she needs is right in front of me.'

Fabio's phone was ringing but he ignored it. 'Would you ask Jenny to field my calls? Perhaps Jonathan could pick up any patients who need seeing.' He stopped. 'I owe you both. Meet me outside. I'll bring the car round.'

Rose was waiting outside the clinic and jumped into the car as Fabio screeched to a halt.

'The results for Lucy show a slightly elevated white count and CRP but nothing to cause concern. I can organise another blood sample while I'm there if you like.'

'Did I ever tell you that I love you, Rose?'

Rose smiled. 'You did once—at my wedding, if you remember.'

Fabio pointed his car in the direction of Katie's flat and pressed his foot to the accelerator. Too bad if he got a speeding ticket.

'A Dr Aubrey called to speak to you. I asked if it was urgent and she said no, but you should ring her at home when you got a chance.' She passed Fabio a slip of paper with a number. 'Nothing I can do, is there?'

He shook his head. 'Not right now. Maybe later.'

'You're in love with Katie. Aren't you?'

Fabio didn't bother to pretend. He knew Rose would see right through him.

'Yes,' he said simply.

'So what are you going to do about it?'

'I don't know. All I know is that making her happy is the most important thing in the world to me and if I can't do that, she's better off without me.'

Rose touched his hand lightly. 'Why is it you men think you know what is best for us?'

'You can talk,' Fabio retorted. 'Didn't you think you knew what was best for Jonathan when you kept your illness secret?'

'Touché. Are you telling me you have something wrong with you?' Her voice was anxious. 'Because even if you don't want to tell Katie, and I think you should, you should tell me, or Jonathan. Especially if it's something that might affect the practice.'

Fabio smiled grimly. 'I promise it's nothing that will affect my ability to see and treat patients.' He took a deep breath. Maybe it was time he shared his conflicted feelings with someone else. And who better than this woman, the wife of his friend, who had been through so much herself?

'I'm infertile. At least, I'm ninety-nine per cent sure I am.' The tyres screeched as he turned a corner. 'Sorry!'

'I think Katie would prefer to have you arrive in one piece than not at all,' Rose remonstrated. 'Have you told her about your infertility? Wait a minute! Dr Aubrey—is that why she was phoning?'

Fabio slowed the car to a reasonable speed. Killing Rose or injuring an innocent driver was not going to help matters. Jonathan, for all his laid-back manner, would take him apart piece by piece if anything happened to his beloved wife.

'Yes. I decided to have a sperm test so I can be sure.'

'Have you told Katie about this?'

'Some of it. I don't want her marrying someone who can't give her children.'

'So you want to marry her.'

'More than anything in this world. She makes me…feel complete.' He felt a bit of an idiot saying the words but it was true. Without Katie he'd never be completely whole.

'You should tell her,' Rose said. 'At least she'll know you love her.'

Fabio brought the car to a halt in front of Suzy's house. 'What? Like you did with Jonathan? From what he told me, that's why you ran away from him. Because you thought you were going to die. And it's partly why you had the operation. So you could give him children.'

'You two have been talking! But it wasn't as simple as that. C'mon. Let's grab something for Katie to wear.'

Fabio slapped his hand against his forehead. 'I haven't been thinking straight. How are we supposed to get in?'

But Rose just smiled and got out of the car. She walked over to a plant pot and lifted it. 'Ahah! One key!' She held it up for Fabio to see. 'She told me one day that she left a spare there. Said she was always managing to lock herself out. I did warn her it was the first place a thief would look, but she wouldn't listen. Seems your luck is changing.'

When they let themselves into the sitting room Fabio saw an outfit was draped over the back of the sofa with a pair of matching shoes placed neatly next to it. Fabio recognised the dress at once. It was the one she had worn that night on board the yacht. The night when he had truly seen her for the first time. It was perfect.

'There's a handbag too. Looks like she had it all laid out ready.' Rose smiled. 'OK, lover boy, let's get going.'

Once again Fabio drove as fast as he could without risking crashing the car. It was almost four o'clock. They had thirty minutes to persuade Katie she had to go, get her into her outfit and get to the palace. Given the London traffic it would be close. Amelia answered the door looking far happier than she'd looked that morning.

'Fabio, I didn't expect you back until later.' Her eyes creased with anxiety. 'Is there anything wrong? Are the blood results bad?'

'Don't worry, Amelia, nothing's wrong. The blood results are fine. Honestly!' Amelia peered behind him, noticing Rose for the first time.

'Rose! What brings you here? Now I'm really worried.'

Quickly Rose explained why they'd come. Amelia was immediately contrite. 'Katie never breathed a word. Of course she must go!'

'The trouble is,' Fabio said, glancing at his watch again, 'I don't think we're going to make it.'

'You leave getting there to Rose and I. Mark and I owe

you both so much, do you think we're going to let Katie miss this?'

Fabio left Rose and Amelia conspiring and ran up the stairs to Lucy's bedroom. Katie and Lucy were reading a book together and Fabio was relieved that the little girl's breathing was back to being as close to normal as it ever was.

'Hi, Luce. Feeling better?' When Lucy nodded he took a surprised Katie by the hand. 'I just need to borrow Katie for a few hours. Is that okay? Rose is here and she'll stay with you until I get back.'

'Rose? Here?' Katie let Fabio pull her outside the room before turning to him. 'I think you should tell me what's going on. Has something happened? God, I can see by your face it has. What is it? Suzy? Ricky? For God's sake, Fabio, tell me.'

'Why didn't you tell me your brother was being awarded a posthumous medal this afternoon?'

Katie's face registered shock. 'How did you know?'

'Rose told me. *Vamos!* We have half an hour to get you there.' He started leading her down the stairs, but Katie literally dug her heels in. 'I'm not going. I'm staying right here. Who do you think you are to tell me what I should do? You have no right.'

'I have more right than you think, woman,' he growled. 'We haven't got time to argue.'

Still looking mystified, Katie let him lead her down the stairs. 'But I haven't got anything to wear. There's no way I can turn up at the palace like this.' She indicated her work top and matching trousers. 'They'll throw me out.'

'We have clothes—and shoes and handbag. Downstairs.' As they reached the foot of the stirs Rose silently handed Katie the clothes they had taken from Suzy's house.

'How did you get these?'

'Key. Flowerpot.' Rose gave her a gentle shove. 'Go on, Amelia will show you where to get changed.'

'But there's no time,' Katie wailed. 'I was supposed to be there no later than four.'

'Mark has our helicopter and a pilot standing by,' Amelia said. 'It will take five minutes, and Jonathan's used his contacts to clear a landing space close to the palace. Now, c'mon.'

'Or do I have to get you dressed myself?' Fabio said.

Something in his expression must have made Katie realise he meant what he was saying as without another word she turned and followed Amelia.

It was the first time Katie had flown over London, but she hardly had time to take in the sights before they were landing. She'd been given headphones to wear to drown out the noise of the engine but that had made it impossible for her and Fabio to speak. Her heart ached. Whether it was because of how Rose, Amelia and Fabio had pulled together to make this happen for her, or whether it was because she was going to say another emotional goodbye to Richard, she couldn't be sure. All she knew was that everything Fabio did made her love him more. And she didn't want to love him at all.

The helicopter touched down and Fabio helped her jump to the ground—not an easy task in three-inch heels. And then a car was pulling up and Fabio was opening the door for her.

'You'll make it. Now go.'

She looked into his familiar eyes and knew, whatever the price, she wanted this man by her side. Through good and bad. Children or no children. He had her heart and without him life had no meaning.

'Come with me.' She held out her hand. 'Be with me.' She hoped he knew what she was saying.

He hesitated for a moment as if he was going to refuse. Then he grinned and jumped in beside her. 'The invitation was for you plus one, so I guess they won't evict me.'

Inside the palace, there were more phone calls where Jonathan had to pull strings once again to get Fabio inside. However, no matter how well connected Jonathan was as Lord Cavendish, even he couldn't get an unnamed guest into the room where the Queen was bestowing the medals.

'I'll be here. Waiting,' he said. He placed his hands on either side of her face and bent his head to kiss her firmly on the lips. 'Always.'

The ceremony was as painful as Katie had expected. When Suzy stepped forward to accept the medal after the citation about Richard's heroism was read out, she had to fight tears. They weren't the only ones there that day. Too many other families were receiving posthumous medals on behalf of their dead brothers, husbands, sons, daughters, wives and sisters.

Suzy's parents were distraught, and Katie stood between them, holding their hands throughout the ceremony. When it was finally over she was relieved. She didn't know how much more she could have endured without breaking down.

Outside, as promised, Fabio was waiting. He stepped forward and introduced himself to Suzy's parents.

'My deepest sympathies on the loss of your son-in-law. You must be very proud. I hope you don't mind me intruding on this day.' He looked at Katie. 'I just wanted to check Katie was okay, but I'll leave you now.'

Suzy reached out a hand and grasped his. 'We're going to my parents' house for a bit and then back to mine. Perhaps you'll join us there later?'

'I would be delighted,' he said. 'Would it be all right if I came, Katie?'

Katie could read the hesitation in Fabio's face. 'You'd be welcome,' she said softly.

What was going on with him? His usual relaxed charm had been replaced with awkwardness. He was almost shuffling his feet.

Before she had a chance to say anything, he sketched a wave and turned back to the waiting helicopter.

Later, after Katie and Suzy's family had spent an emotional couple of hours talking about Richard, Suzy, Ricky and Katie returned home. Although there had been tears, there had been laughter too as Katie had recounted childhood escapades. Katie knew that every day she was getting closer to accepting a life without her beloved brother.

'He's some guy, your Fabio,' Suzy said.

'I don't know how many times I have to tell you, he's not my Fabio,' Katie protested.

'I'm not sure who you're trying to kid. Anyone can see that the pair of you are crazy about each other. The way he looks at you. It's exactly the way Richard used to look at me.' Suzy's voice trembled and the two women hugged. They might be coming to terms with Richard's death but they were a long way away from being able to think of him without pain.

'I think he does love me. But he's made it clear that he doesn't want a future with me.'

'And you believe him?'

'He was pretty specific. His parents weren't exactly a

glowing example of how to bring up a family, so he pretty much thinks that no relationship can survive. And that's not all.'

'Go on,' Suzy prompted.

'He can't have children. And he says no woman should be married to a man who can't give her a family.'

'Phew!' Suzy said. 'I'm not sure if that's noble or selfish.'

'What do you mean?'

'Are you sure it's not because he doesn't want to consider adoption? Or sperm donation? There are a lot of ways of getting pregnant.'

Katie thought for a moment. 'Actually, where does he get off, deciding for me? If he loves me, he'll consider other options so we can have a family, and even if he doesn't, I'd rather have him and not have children than not have him. I don't want to be with someone because of the children they can give me.'

'Have you told him that?'

'No. I never got the chance. He's been keeping his distance. I'm not even sure that he does love me. All this could be a way of letting me down lightly.'

'Then I don't believe you know him as well as you think. C'mon, where's the Katie who would fight for what she wants? I don't know much, but I do know if you have a chance at love you have to grab it with both hands—whatever the cost.'

Katie grabbed her bag. 'You know what, Suze? You're right. If he doesn't want me, he's going to have to tell me that and I'll live with it. What I won't live with is never knowing what might have been. Now, where are my car keys?'

* * *

Fabio emerged from the shower, a towel wrapped around his waist. He couldn't put it off any longer. One way or another he had to know the results of his sperm test. He wanted Katie. Wanted her more than he'd thought it possible to want a woman. He wanted her with him every day for the rest of his life. But he wouldn't ask her to marry him as long as he knew he was infertile. He couldn't do that to her.

He picked up his mobile and studied it thoughtfully. The next few minutes could change the course of his life. Checking Dr Aubrey's number from the piece of paper, he dialled.

Katie tapped on the door, feeling nervous. All her earlier courage had evaporated. Despite her brave words to Suzy, she knew she'd be devastated if Fabio turned her down.

When he answered the door, wearing only a towel and looking as sexy as hell, it took every ounce of her resolve not to fling herself into his arms. Even if he didn't want a long-term relationship, something was better than nothing. But as soon as she thought the words, she knew she didn't believe them. She wanted Fabio, heart and soul, not just a little bit of him.

He was wearing a stunned expression on his face. No doubt he was surprised to see her here.

'Can I come in?' she said, and without waiting for a reply squeezed past him. As she did so, she caught the tantalising scent of soap.

'I was coming to see you,' he said.

'I saved you the bother.' She wasn't going to let him talk. She was going to have her say, come hell or high water.

She whirled round to face him. 'I know you love me, Fabio. I don't care what you say, I feel it in here.' She pressed a palm against her heart, knowing she was being dramatic, but she couldn't help herself. She had to make him accept that she wanted him, good or bad, madcap, reckless existence, infertility, the lot. The only part of him she would not accept, of course, was the playboy. That would definitely have to go.

'You do?' He was still looking bemused.

'Oh, yes. I may not have much experience with men but I know when someone is lying to me. You say you can't marry me, and it's something to do with not having kids and thinking that we will be like your parents and that we won't survive. I'm here to tell you that you're wrong. We will. Even if we never have children, we will be together for the rest of our lives. The children in Brazil can become our children. And…' She wagged her finger at him as he opened his mouth to speak. Was that really laughter in his dark eyes? This was so not a laughing matter. 'And,' she continued, 'we could have our own children if we both decide that we want to. We can adopt, we can use a sperm donor. There are ways. But…' her voice hitched '…I don't care about that. Not if I can't have you.'

He was looking at her in a way that made her already rapid beating pulse beat harder.

'You would give up the chance to have children for me?' he said wonderingly.

She nodded her head vigorously. 'I would even, God help me, put up with you doing that big wave surfing or whatever you call it—although don't expect me to go and watch because I couldn't. We don't choose the people we love, and when we do fall in love, we shouldn't want to change them.'

Her words dried up. She had no more to say. He was still looking at her with an odd expression on his face. Had she got it all completely wrong and made a prize fool of herself? She was offering him everything she had and still he made no move towards her.

Her throat tightened and she picked up her handbag. All she wanted right now was to escape so she could lick her wounds in private.

'I just wanted you to know,' she said stiffly. 'But we can forget I said anything. I'll start looking for another job tomorrow.'

As she turned away, he grabbed her by the arm and turned her, tipping her chin and forcing her to look into his eyes.

'Say that again,' he commanded.

'Which bit? The looking for a job or the other bit?'

'The bit about loving me. Whatever.'

'I love you, Fabio. Whatever.'

He crushed her to his chest so tightly she could almost not breathe.

'And I love you. More than anything in the world. I want you with me every day of my life. I want to make you laugh, I want to make you happy and more than anything I want a little Katie to love and cherish too. And if that means IVF, so be it.'

'You will think about it?'

'More than think,' he mumbled into her hair. 'I had my sperm retested and, while the count is still so low as to be almost negligible, Dr Aubrey says that there is enough that with the help of her team and a willing, loving woman there is no reason why I can't make a baby. Maybe two or three.'

He lifted her into his arms. 'My darling Katie. Will you marry me and think about having my babies? If I promise to do everything in my power to make you happy?'

Her heart felt as if it was going to explode. She wrapped her arms around his neck and brought her mouth up to his.

'My love, haven't you been listening to a word I said?'

DOCTOR ON THE RED CARPET

BY
ANNE FRASER

All the characters in this book have no existence outside the imagination of the author, and have no relation whatsoever to anyone bearing the same name or names. They are not even distantly inspired by any individual known or unknown to the author, and all the incidents are pure invention.

First published in Great Britain 2011
by Mills & Boon, an imprint of Harlequin (UK) Limited,
Eton House, 18-24 Paradise Road, Richmond, Surrey TW9 1SR

© Anne Fraser 2011

ISBN: 978 0 263 88596 5

Harlequin (UK) policy is to use papers that are natural, renewable and recyclable products and made from wood grown in sustainable forests. The logging and manufacturing process conform to the legal environmental regulations of the country of origin.

Printed and bound in Spain
by Blackprint CPI, Barcelona

Anne Fraser was born in Scotland, but brought up in South Africa. After she left school she returned to the birthplace of her parents, the remote Western Islands of Scotland. She left there to train as a nurse, before going on to university to study English Literature. After the birth of her first child she and her doctor husband travelled the world, working in rural Africa, Australia and Northern Canada. Anne still works in the health sector. To relax, she enjoys spending time with her family, reading, walking and travelling.

Recent titles by the same author:

THE DOCTOR AND THE DEBUTANTE
DAREDEVIL, DOCTOR...DAD!†
PRINCE CHARMING OF HARLEY STREET
RESCUED: MOTHER AND BABY
MIRACLE: MARRIAGE REUNITED
SPANISH DOCTOR, PREGNANT MIDWIFE*

The Brides of Penhally Bay
†*St Piran's Hospital*

CHAPTER ONE

DR ELIZABETH MORGAN stepped out the car, transfixed at the hustle and bustle in front of her. The desert heat of California smothered her skin like a blanket, making her damp blouse stick to her back. Rivulets of perspiration trickled between her breasts.

What was she doing here? She glanced wistfully at the driver as he unloaded her suitcases, tempted for a moment to tell him not to bother. She'd made a mistake, changed her mind—would he please take her back to Los Angeles International Airport? And straight onto a flight back to England.

But she couldn't do that.

Wiping the dust from her face with a tired hand, Elizabeth took a deep steadying breath. Right—the director must be somewhere amongst the crowd of people. Dragging her cases behind her, she picked her way along the rutted dusty ground, her feet throbbing in her unsuitable high heels. This wasn't what she'd expected. Weren't all movies made in a studio? Not out in the back of beyond near Palm Desert in what must be a rundown mining town. Hardly the glamour and sophistication she'd envisaged.

Not that she could bring herself to care. It was all she could do these days to put one foot in front of the other. If it hadn't been for the fact she'd known she would go crazy if she stayed in London, she would never have taken this job. Doctor on a Hollywood film set was as far away from what she used to do as it was possible to get. At least here there were no constant memories of the life she once led. And that was its attraction.

She screwed her eyes up against the harsh midday sun. Filming was in full swing, it appeared. Cameramen were perched high on top of mobile cameras, people stood in clusters, talking animatedly, and around what appeared to be the central filming area, large aluminium caravans stretched almost as far as the eye could see.

Just then a horse cantered by, kicking up dust and with someone clinging precariously to its neck. Elizabeth watched, heart in mouth, as the rider seemed to lose what little balance he had and slid further off the horse, before landing with a thump on the ground.

Elizabeth paused only to pick up her medical bag. Judging by the way the rider had fallen, he was bound to be badly hurt.

But to her amazement, before she had even crossed the few yards to his side, the man was on his feet, wiping dust from his trousers with a nonchalant flick of his cowboy hat.

'How was that, Philip?' he called out in an American accent. 'Was that realistic enough for you?'

Elizabeth slowed to a walk. He was big this man, well over six foot and powerfully muscled. He was wearing faded jeans that clung disconcertingly to his thighs and cowboy boots with spurs. He had short brown hair and a wide mouth and had such an air of masculine assurance about him that instinctively Elizabeth knew this was a man who broke hearts. Was he one of the actors? Silly question—he was bound to be.

He stopped swatting the dust from his clothes as she approached, and gave her a long slow stare. Then he grinned, showing even white teeth. If he carried on riding horses like that, Elizabeth thought testily, he wouldn't have perfect teeth for much longer.

'Howdy, ma'am. I don't think we've met. I'm Kendrick,' he said, holding out his hand.

Elizabeth's fingers were enveloped in his. For some reason the way he was looking at her was making her heart race. Then again, she *had* got a fright. She'd really thought that the way this man had fallen from the horse meant she would be fixing him up and calling an ambulance. And all before she'd even unpacked.

'Dr Elizabeth Morgan,' she replied. 'I'm the doctor for the set. Are you all right? Maybe you should sit down.' She glanced around. The only place she could see was a couple of camping chairs outside a trailer a few yards away. What if he collapsed before she got him there? She'd never be able to support a man of his size. 'Actually, back on the ground will do while I look you over.'

His grin grew wider. 'Now, come to think of it, ma'am, I think I did hurt my shoulder. Maybe you should have a quick look-see?'

Before she could say anything he whipped off the dust-smeared cambric shirt he was wearing, revealing a bronzed chest with a number of scars. His torso was muscled, not overly so but enough for Elizabeth to be able to detect each individual ridge. He wore his jeans low on his hips, and his abdomen was taut, with a fine sprinkling of dark hair disappearing into the waistband. She blinked.

This was a man who was perfectly aware of the effect he had on women—other women that was. He'd find out soon enough that she was immune to any man.

'I really do think you should sit down, Mr…?' she said. The ridiculous way her pulse was behaving you'd think it was her who had just fallen off a horse.

'It's Kendrick. No one calls anyone here by their last name.

You might be all formal in England…' He raised an eyebrow at her. 'You are from England, right?' When she nodded he continued. 'But we all use first names here, Lizzie.'

'It's Elizabeth. And I'd prefer you to call me Dr Morgan,' Elizabeth responded stiffly. When he quirked an eyebrow at her she flushed. Damn the man. Everything about him made her feel at a disadvantage. 'Now, which shoulder did you hurt?'

He stepped closer until he seemed almost to block out the sun. She resisted the impulse to move away.

'Come to think of it, the shoulder is fine. I was kidding.' His eyes glinted down at her.

'I'd rather you didn't waste my time, Mr…er…Kendrick,' she said, dismayed at the way her heart continued to race. 'You've heard about the boy who cried wolf, haven't you?'

Her words only made his smile wider. He turned to call over to a middle-aged man with long sideburns and a ponytail who was making his way towards them, accompanied by a young woman in the tiniest denim shorts Elizabeth had ever seen.

'Hey, Philip. We have someone over here who likes fairy-tales. Maybe you should explain who I am. I have a feeling this little lady isn't going to believe a word I say.'

Just who was he calling a little lady? Who did he think he was? Was he so absorbed in the movie he was acting in that he was getting it confused with real life?

The man he called Philip sauntered towards them with the girl in denim shorts, who was taking short, fast steps in outrageously high heels as she struggled to keep up with him, all the time passing him pieces of paper to sign as they walked.

'Okay, Sunny, that'll do for now,' Philip said. 'I'll catch up with you after lunch.'

Sunny?

The girl shot Kendrick a look from under thickly mascara'd eyelashes. Kendrick winked back, earning himself a blush before Sunny tottered away on her high heels.

'You must be Dr Morgan,' Philip said. 'Glad you made it here so quickly. I'm the director.' He waved a hand towards Kendrick. 'I see you've already met our stuntman and stunt co-ordinator. 'Kendrick, Dr Morgan has stepped in for Dr Marshall. You might want to keep on the right side of *her*, seeing as you're likely to need her services at least once during this movie.'

Kendrick flung his shirt over his shoulder and smiled again. 'You know I don't tend to get hurt, Philip, that's why you employ me.' Kendrick tipped his head at Elizabeth. 'Good to meet you, but if you'll excuse me I should get washed up.' With a casual wave of his hand he turned on his heel and strolled away.

There was silence as Philip and Elizabeth watched Kendrick's retreating back.

'He's right, you know. He rarely gets hurt—at least not seriously. But there's always the possibility. That's one of the reasons we need a full-time doc on set,' Philip said. He looked at Elizabeth. 'I'm sorry I wasn't here to meet you when you arrived, but nothing interrupts filming when we have the right light I'm afraid. I'm glad you were able to fill in for Dr Marshall at short notice.'

Elizabeth wanted to know what had happened to Dr Marshall, but decided not to ask. She would find out soon enough.

'Why don't I show you around then you can get settled in?' Philip said. 'I'll explain what it is we need you to do on the way.'

'I'd appreciate that.'

'The film we're shooting is an action movie, but you might have gathered that. It involves car chases, horses, a few explosions. That sort of thing. Kendrick does most of the stunts, although we have some others, including a stuntwoman. You'll meet her later. I understand that you have experience in emergency medicine?'

'I've completed training in emergency medicine.' She wasn't going to remind him that it had been a couple of years since she'd worked as a doctor. It was all in her CV. Besides, some things you never forgot.

'Good. A lot of what you'll do here is deal with sore throats, upset stomachs, fairly minor stuff, although at times you'll think your patients are at death's door from the way they complain. Having said that, I'm counting on you to keep our cast and crew healthy. Any time they have off costs the production serious money.'

They walked across an open stretch of ground and into a dusty street lined with wooden buildings. Elizabeth wondered if they were real or just facades. If so, they were remarkably authentic in appearance.

A tumbleweed rolled past. The heat was intense.

'We have our two stars, Jack and Tara, as well as about twenty other actors. Add in the supporting staff, camera crew, sound recordists, grips, runners and film extras and that takes the number to around a hundred. We'll keep you busy.'

'I'm glad to hear it,' Elizabeth responded honestly. Busy was exactly what she needed, and the busier the better.

Philip paused in front of a large tent. 'Most of us eat here together, but you have a kitchen in your trailer so it's up to you what you choose to do.'

Elizabeth nodded. Although she would have preferred to keep out of everyone's way when she wasn't treating them, she knew it would be difficult in such a small community. She didn't mind eating communally every now and again as long as nobody asked her too many questions. While she was here she intended to do her job and keep herself to herself.

'Okay, that's more or less it,' Philip said. 'Except for the medical trailer, where you'll work out of. It's on the other side of the camp. It's equipped with everything you could need. Anything serious, God forbid, we send into LA by chopper. There's always at least one available.'

'I'd like to see the medical facility now, if that's okay. Just to check that everything is there that I'll need.'

'Sure. I think you'll find it's better equipped than some small hospitals. Like I said, we can't take any risks with our cast, and that includes Kendrick. After you've had a look around, I'll ask Sunny to take you to your trailer, so you can settle in. You'll meet everyone at lunch or on the set. Filming starts again at two p.m. We'll need you to hang around for that. We're going to be shooting some stunts with Kendrick and knowing him there's bound to be a scrape or two that will need attention.'

Philip left her to look around the medical trailer, telling her that he'd send Sunny to take her to her accommodation. He had been right when he'd told her money hadn't been spared when it had come to fitting out the facility and Elizabeth was impressed. It was so well equipped she could probably deal with most scenarios. There was a defibrillator, monitoring equipment, basic drugs—just about everything she was used to having when she'd worked in a hospital.

And when Sunny returned to take Elizabeth to her caravan—or trailer as the Americans called it—it seemed no expense had been spared there either. Sunny had hurried off again as soon as she'd shown Elizabeth where she was to live for the next few weeks.

It was a relief to step out of the blazing sun and into the air-conditioned mobile home. A compact kitchenette was fitted with every mod-con and device ever thought of. Swinging open the cupboard doors, Elizabeth noted they were fully stocked. Did she have Sunny to thank for that? Comfortable couches lined three walls of a living room dominated by an enormous plasma-screen TV. DVDs and books filled a floor-to-ceiling bookshelf.

Slipping off her shoes, Elizabeth opened the door leading off the sitting room and found a bedroom complete with double bed and wardrobe. This was certainly a far cry from the cramped caravans she remembered from childhood holidays. It was more like a five-star luxury suite—with an en suite bathroom to boot. And someone had thoughtfully brought her suitcases in for her as well.

Maybe this wasn't going to be so bad after all.

Elizabeth reached into her handbag and retrieved the photograph of her daughter, placing it carefully on the bedside table. She touched a finger to her lip, then to the image.

'Morning, darling,' she whispered. 'Bet you never thought you'd find Mummy in a place like this, did you? I only wish you could be here with me.'

Elizabeth's throat tightened as she trailed her fingers over her daughter's face. No amount of longing or praying or wishing could bring the precious child in the photo back to life and into her arms.

Dragging her eyes away, she glanced at her watch. There wasn't time to unpack before lunch and filming, but she definitely needed a quick, cooling shower and a change of clothes.

Afterwards, feeling refreshed and slightly more human, she redid the plait in her hair, changed into a pair of white cotton trousers and a T-shirt and stepped outside, screwing her eyes up against the midday sun.

Kendrick rotated his shoulder and winced. Damn it. The fall had hurt him more than he cared to admit. He watched the new doctor come out of her trailer and whistled under his breath. She was a stunner. Even with her long blonde hair captured in a plait and wearing a simple white T-shirt and low-slung cotton trousers, anyone could see that she had a body that could drive a man crazy. Add the aristocratic nose and the cool, almost icy blue eyes and Kendrick knew she would be a challenge. But what the hell? That was what made her interesting. Years of dating women from all walks of life had honed his instincts and already he suspected that Dr Elizabeth Morgan might be his toughest challenge yet.

Elizabeth put a few pieces of fruit and cheese on her plate and looked around the mess tent for a place to sit.

She'd hesitated about going for lunch. She hadn't had much of an appetite over the last couple of years and the last three months had put paid to the little appetite she did have, but she knew she had to eat. She couldn't risk getting ill. She had no doubt, and neither could she blame them, that the film company would replace her in a heartbeat if they felt she wasn't up to the job.

However, she almost changed her mind when she arrived at the dining tent. It was crowded and she couldn't see an empty seat. As she was about to retreat back to her trailer Kendrick appeared by her side, his plate piled high with grilled chicken and rice. Unlike her, it seemed as if he had a pretty good appetite.

Catching her look, he grinned. 'Protein. Good for repairing muscle, isn't it?'

Elizabeth shrugged. 'Doesn't look as if you have much problem in that regard.'

When his grin widened, she realised that she had spoken without thinking. 'I mean…you assured me there was no damage after your fall,' she added hastily, annoyed to find she was flushing

'Tell you what,' he drawled, 'why don't we find a place to eat outside in the shade? It will be more comfortable, apart from anything else. The fans they use to try and keep the air circulating in here aren't much good.'

She didn't want to have anything more to do with Kendrick than she had to, but as she opened her mouth to refuse she saw that he had already turned away to go back outside. There was nothing she could do without seeming rude except follow.

He was right, there was more air outside. Moreover, a little breeze had come in from somewhere, cooling her overheated skin. Kendrick pulled out a folding chair for her, before easing his long, powerfully built frame into one beside her.

'So, tell me, Lizzie, what brings you here?' he asked, forking a piece of meat. 'All the way from England? I would guess London if I had to narrow it down.'

She noticed he was no longer speaking like a cowboy from a movie. In fact, despite the American accent, she could have sworn he had spent some time in the UK.

'You're correct,' she said. 'London. But I spent some time in America before…' She bit her lip. She didn't want to go there. She didn't want to talk about her life back then. She definitely didn't want to think about Simon and she couldn't bear to think about Charlie. 'Before going back to the UK,' she finished lamely.

Kendrick studied her thoughtfully for a moment.

'What about you?' she asked, before he could ask her anything else. 'If I'm not mistaken, you've spent time in the UK too.'

'And you'd be right. I went to boarding school in England. My parents travelled a lot and my mother is English. But we were talking about you.' Kendrick neatly turned the conversation back.

'Nothing much to tell.' At least, nothing much she wanted to tell. 'I went to medical school—St Bart's?' She raised her eyebrows in question. When he nodded, indicating he knew it, she continued. 'I trained in emergency medicine and then worked with the London Air Ambulance service for a year. That's about it.'

'Married? Kids?' His eyes dropped to the bare finger of her left hand. Elizabeth sucked in a breath.

'I was married but it didn't work out,' she said evenly. This was exactly the kind of conversation she wanted to avoid.

'I'm sorry.'

'Don't be. It happens.' She placed her plate to the side. 'Isn't it time for filming to start again?'

'It'll probably be closer to two-thirty before it gets under way. Our leading lady isn't known for her timekeeping.'

When he smiled at her, his eyes creased, revealing faint laughter lines. She wondered if everything amused Kendrick.

'In that case, I guess I'll go along to the medical trailer. There might be someone who wants to see the doctor before filming starts.'

'Do you know where it is? I could show you if you like.'

'Philip took me there earlier. Anyway, don't you have to be on set, getting blown up or something like that?' she said, more sharply than she intended. The trouble was, and she didn't know why, this man was getting under her skin, despite the fact she had just met him.

Kendrick looked baffled. He stood up, slapping the dust from his trousers.

'Sorry, Lizzie. I hope I didn't say anything to offend you.'

Elizabeth felt herself go cold with embarrassment. He was right. Despite his blatant interest and the way he looked at her, he'd been friendly and welcoming. He wasn't to know that she was barely holding it together. That since Simon had left her, she'd erected a shield around herself. And then as Charlie had become sicker and sicker… A wall of pain slammed into her and she swallowed hard.

None of that excused her appalling manners. Kendrick wasn't to blame for any of it.

'I'm sorry, that was rude of me. I'm just a little…' she struggled to find the right word '…out of sorts, that's all.'

The ready grin flashed, but before he could say anything, a loud screeching noise made them both whirl round.

'What in the name of…?' Kendrick said.

Philip was using some sort of megaphone in an apparent attempt to summon the cast.

'He needs to get that thing tuned.'

As they shared a smile, Elizabeth's heart missed a beat. He had the devil in his bright blue eyes, she thought irrationally.

'Have to go, I'm afraid,' Kendrick said, sketching a salute. 'We're going to need you too. Philip has been putting off this scene until you got here.'

'What kind of scene?'

'I have to drive a car off a cliff.' The matter-of-fact way he said it made it sound as if this was what most people did as a part of their daily routine.

'Oh, really?' she said with a lift of her eyebrow. He had to be winding her up again, but this time she wasn't going to fall for it.

'Don't worry. I jump out of the car once it goes over the cliff. I'm not actually in it when it hits the ground. Or at least I hope I won't be.' He muttered the last few words.

'Let me get this right,' Elizabeth said. 'You are in a car that goes over a cliff, but you jump out in mid-air? And how do you get back on the ground? Fly?'

'It's not as difficult as it sounds. They've removed the rear window. Once the car goes over, I climb out and sort of sky-dive to the ground. I'll have a parachute.'

She still didn't know whether to believe him. It sounded too fantastic.

But as the trucks, loaded up with cameras, cast and crew, including Elizabeth, rolled out into the desert coming to a stop at the top of a cliff, she realised that Kendrick hadn't been teasing her.

Philip was hustling everyone to get into position. 'We don't have much time, folks,' he said. 'And I don't want to do this more than once, so let's get it right.' He turned to Elizabeth. 'You better check with Kendrick where he'd like you positioned, just in case he has a problem.'

Elizabeth nodded. This was why she was here and she needed to be prepared for anything. Heaving her medical kitbag over her shoulder, she searched around for Kendrick.

Given his height, it wasn't difficult to spot him amongst the crowd of people. Although the set was buzzing with noise and activity, she could hear his distinctive voice coolly instructing his team above the clamour. As if he sensed her gaze, Kendrick looked over towards her. As their eyes locked, her pulse missed a beat. This was a man totally in control and completely in charge. What would it be like to have someone like him on your side? Someone to count on?

Almost immediately, Elizabeth shook the thought away. Where had that come from? She didn't really know anything about Kendrick. There was no way she was ever going to go down that road again. He was just a man, a work colleague.

She threaded her way amongst the crowd until she was standing in front of him.

'Where's the best place for me to wait in case I'm needed?' she asked.

He gave her a lopsided grin. 'Lizzie, if this goes wrong, no doctor is going to patch me up.' His voice grew serious. 'Not that anything will go wrong. But with a stunt like this, other factors come into play, so we have to be prepared for anything. We're cordoning off a safe area at the foot of the cliffs. Watch out for falling debris when the car falls to the ground—that's the biggest risk to the crew.'

'Okay.' The words 'Good luck' hovered on her lips, but she bit them back. Somehow she didn't think Kendrick would need it. Instead she made her way over to the base of the cliff and behind a toughened plexiglass screen. He'd certainly thought of everything.

From the bottom, the cliff looked even higher. Kendrick was right. If he didn't manage to get out of the falling car in time, or if his parachute failed, she doubted she'd be able to do much to help him. There was a very real possibility he could be killed. Her blood ran cold. But he was a professional. This was what he was trained to do.

After a tense hour and a half they were ready. The car rolled over the lip of the cliff and into space. An explosion splintered the sky, sending sparks of dazzling yellow and orange outwards and sizzling towards the canyon floor. A collective gasp went up from the onlookers, but still the cameras kept on rolling. After what seemed like an eternity, but could only have been a second or two, a figure clambered out of the rear window and launched itself away from the falling car. Elizabeth couldn't have pulled her eyes away even if she'd wanted to. There were a few heart-stopping seconds as the figure fell, hurtling towards the ground, and there was no sign of Kendrick's parachute opening. Elizabeth tensed, positive that the sound of the car crashing to the ground was going to be followed by the thud of his body. Only when his parachute whooshed open did she realise she'd been holding her breath. Kendrick landed lightly on his feet, several metres away from the burning wreck and only a short distance from her.

He sketched a bow as everyone applauded.

Relieved that for this scene at least her services hadn't been needed, Elizabeth crossed over to Kendrick, who was divesting himself of his parachute.

'Are you okay?' she asked.

He turned glinting eyes on her. She could tell that he'd got a kick out of what he'd just done.

'Perfect,' he said.

'That was crazy,' she said. 'I don't know why you let Philip talk you into doing it. No film is worth dying for.'

His eyes narrowed and he frowned at her. 'Relax, Doc,' he said.

Although his tone was light, there was an undercurrent of steel in his words. 'I have no intention of getting myself—or anyone else on my team—killed. We spend a lot of time discussing and planning the stunts beforehand to eliminate as much risk as possible. Then we deal with what's left. It's what stuntmen and women do. If you don't like it, perhaps this isn't the job for you.'

He looked over the top of her head. 'Hey, Josh, Immy. What d'you think? Did Philip get the shot he needed?'

He walked away, leaving Elizabeth feeling dismissed.

Who was he to tell her what job did or didn't suit her? But she had to admit he was right. Her job wasn't to worry about Kendrick or to tell the film producers what they could or couldn't do. Her job was to keep them alive long enough to get them to hospital should anything happen.

Filming over for the day, Elizabeth knew that this was the time that the cast and crew would be most likely to look for her should they require a medical opinion. She took a ride on the first truck heading back to the camp and, sure enough, she was kept busy until dinnertime, seeing members of the crew who had sore throats or sunburn. Nothing too serious and nothing that required more than some painkillers or advice.

When she was certain there were no more patients, she locked up. If anyone needed her out of hours, they knew where to find her.

She let herself back into her trailer and picked up the photo from the bedside table.

Charlie was staring into the camera, a small smile on her face. It had been taken just before she'd lost control of her neck muscles, but even then they had been deteriorating, giving her a lopsided look. But to Elizabeth her daughter looked beautiful.

Elizabeth started to unpack. On top of her clothes was Charlie's favourite soft toy, the ear lightly chewed and missing an eye. A crushing pain squeezed Elizabeth's chest as memories rushed back. Her daughter's little face looking up at her with incomprehension that Mummy wasn't able to help, the feel of her child's tiny frame in her arms as Charlie lost more and more weight. The last time she had held Charlie, knowing that she was slipping away and there was nothing, nothing anyone could do and that no amount of love or denial could stop her from dying. And then later the small white casket being lowered into the ground, the disbelief that she would have to live out the rest of her life without her daughter.

Elizabeth brought the soft toy to her face and inhaled the still lingering scent of her daughter.

In the weeks following Charlie's funeral Elizabeth had been almost unable to function. She'd wandered around the small house, alone and aching to touch her child. Just once more.

The nights were the worst. She'd find herself curled up in her daughter's bed, soaking the pillow with her tears. But eventually she'd known she had to do something. When she'd seen this job advertised it had seemed perfect. No chance of coming into contact with children, a limited contract that would give her breathing space to decide what to do with the rest of her life, and an environment where people knew nothing of her past and were unlikely to be interested.

As soon as she'd been offered the job and accepted, she'd put her terraced cottage on the market. With a bit of luck it would be sold before she had finished here. With Charlie gone, Elizabeth couldn't bear to live in the home that had once held such happiness. She didn't know if she could even ever set foot inside it again.

Her throat ached as she remembered sitting on the floor of Charlie's bedroom, tears pouring down her face as she'd packed away Charlie's clothes and toys. She hadn't been able to pack away the soft toy. Together with the photo, it was all she had brought with her to remind her of her darling daughter. Not that she needed anything to remind her of Charlie. Every second of Charlie's too-short life was burned into her soul. She kissed the photo one more time before replacing it on her bedside table.

Although so far her day had been mostly straightforward and the work nothing compared to caring for a severely disabled child twenty-four hours a day, Elizabeth was tired. But for once it was a nice tiredness. She had been able to forget for a few hours. The thought sent another shot of pain through her. Not that she wanted to or could forget her baby. Despite Charlie's disabilities Elizabeth would have given everything she had to have her daughter back.

But that wasn't to be. She had somehow to make some sort of life for herself, even if at the moment she didn't know what that could be.

CHAPTER TWO

THE weather over the next couple of days continued to be hot.
The nights were thankfully cooler but still Elizabeth found it
difficult to sleep. When she did it was to dream of Charlie.

She was getting to know some the cast and crew. Everyone
was friendly and good company. Somehow she was always
aware of Kendrick even when she wasn't in attendance for
one of his stunts. Often she'd see him walking around the
set, joking with the cast and crew or occasionally outside his
trailer, his long legs stretched out in front of him. Whenever
she walked past him, he seemed to know she was there, even
with his hat tipped forward, covering his eyes.

Kendrick wasn't the only stuntperson on set. There was
Imogen, who doubled up for Tara, the female star of the film,
and Josh, an older man who helped Kendrick with some of
the stunts. Gossip on the set had it that Josh had been a rally
driver before getting into stunt work and he took the lead in
most of the stunts involving high-speed chases. Elizabeth
was sure that there was an element of competition between
him and Kendrick. As far as she could see, they were always
trying to outdo each other in terms of who could do the most
difficult stunt.

Most of the filming took place during the day, although
Philip had warned her that some of it took place in the evenings, depending on the light.

One morning, Sunny came to see her before filming began.

'I haven't been feeling so good over the last couple of days. I don't know if it's the heat, but I feel as if I have a temperature.'

'Any other symptoms?' Elizabeth asked, taking in the young woman's pallor.

Sunny shook her head. 'Nothing specific. Just as if I'm coming down with flu. And I can't afford to be ill. We're already running behind schedule. If we don't catch up, Philip is going to insist on filming over the weekend and I want to get home to see my kids.'

Grief, Sunny had children? She didn't look old enough.

'Why don't you slip your blouse off while I check you over?' Elizabeth suggested, picking up her stethoscope. 'How many children do you have?'

'Two.' Sunny smiled wistfully. 'Sam is eight and Trixie six. I had Sam when I was seventeen, before you ask.' That made her twenty-five.

'You must miss them.'

'I used to bring them with me on a job and that worked fine until they started school. I could have employed a tutor to teach them on set, but I don't think that's fair, do you? Children need their friends and a routine, don't you think? I want them to have a better start in life than I did.'

Elizabeth's heart tightened as the never-far-away image of Charlie floated in front of her. What she would give to have had her daughter know what having friends felt like. It didn't stop her sympathising with Sunny, though. It had to be tough for the young mother, working away from her children.

'Philip has been good to me. He took me on as a gofer, now I'm his personal assistant. I kind of always hoped I'd be discovered one day, but I guess that's not going to happen now.'

Sunny squinted up at Elizabeth as Elizabeth took her blood pressure. That seemed normal too.

'Do you have children?' Sunny asked.

Elizabeth turned away and sucked in a steadying breath.

'No, it's just me,' she replied, picking up a couple of Vacutainers. It *was* just her—now. 'I'd like to take some blood before we finish if that's okay?' Something seemed a little off, but Elizabeth couldn't put her finger on it.

Sunny nodded. 'It would be good if you could take it where no one can see the marks. Just in case…' She gave a little smile. 'I still haven't given up hope they might use me in the film.'

'I'll try not to leave any, I promise.'

Elizabeth inserted the needle into the crook of Sunny's arm and filled three vials to send to the lab. She didn't think there was anything seriously wrong, but it wouldn't hurt to be thorough.

'I'm really looking forward to seeing the kids next weekend,' Sunny was saying. 'Hey, by the way, we're going to be filming in the studio in Hollywood and Jack is having a party for the cast and crew. I know he was planning to invite you. Everyone else will be there. Even my kids.'

Elizabeth smiled. 'I doubt he wants to invite me, he hardly knows me.'

'Then it's a good way for you to get to know him and the rest of us. He has a huge house on Mulholland Drive—you know, where a lot of Hollywood stars live. His parties have quite a reputation. Half of Hollywood would give their eye teeth to be invited.'

'I'm not really a party animal,' Elizabeth demurred. 'I'm more the kind to go to bed with a good book.'

'In LA?' Sunny didn't attempt to keep the incredulity from her voice. 'You have to be kidding me. Didn't you just tell me that you're footloose and fancy-free?' She nibbled on her bottom lip and studied Elizabeth through violet eyes. She might look innocent, almost naïve, but there was no mistaking the sharp intelligence behind the ditzy exterior. 'Or have you just recently had your heart broken?'

She narrowed her eyes when Elizabeth took in a sharp intake of breath. 'I'm right, aren't I? In that case, you have to come. It'll cheer you up, and who knows—you might meet someone else.'

That was so not going to happen. Never, ever would she give her heart to someone only to have it broken. The agony simply wasn't worth it. She was finished with men, finished with love. All she wanted now was to find a measure of peace.

'We'll see,' Elizabeth murmured, placing the blood samples into a specimen bag for one of the drivers to take to hospital. 'Okay, I should have the results for you in a day or two. In the meantime, if anything changes, let me know straight away.'

As she was escorting Sunny out of her trailer, Kendrick sauntered up to them.

'Hey, Kendrick, how're you doing?' Sunny greeted him warmly. 'I've just been telling Elizabeth about Jack's party, but she says she's not coming.'

Kendrick eyed Elizabeth. 'Maybe I can change her mind.'

Elizabeth shook her head. 'It's kind of Jack to think of me, but I'm not really the partying kind. I'm quite happy with my own company.'

'I'll leave you two to argue it out, but right now I could do with a lie down. I'm feeling yucky,' Sunny said

Kendrick took Sunny by the arm and turned her round. He peered into her face. 'You don't look too good. What did the doc say?'

'The *doc* hasn't said very much yet. We think it's a case of flu but just in case, the doc has taken some blood,' Elizabeth said, irritated.

But Kendrick was no longer smiling. 'What about your pee? Is it normal?' he asked Sunny.

Elizabeth was growing more indignant by the moment. Just who did he think he was?

'Well, now that you ask…' Sunny looked embarrassed. 'It's kind of dark.'

An alarm bell went off in Elizabeth's head.

'And when was it that you were in Tanzania for those few days' filming? Ten days ago, if my memory serves me right,' Kendrick continued.

'Yes. About then.' Sunny turned to Elizabeth. 'Philip had a couple of scenes he wanted to shoot there. Something about the light. Only Jack and Tara and a few of the supporting crew were needed, apart from me. Anyway, Kendrick, why are you asking?'

'I think I should have a closer look at you, Sunny,' Elizabeth said. Damn it, she had been so sure it was flu she hadn't even asked the obvious questions.

'Did you take prophylactic anti-malarial medication before you went?' she asked as a confused-looking Sunny let herself be led back inside.

'Yes. Of course. Why?'

Kendrick and Elizabeth shared a look. 'Doesn't necessarily mean anything,' Kendrick said.

He was right. Although prophylaxis helped, it didn't, contrary to what most people thought, mean you couldn't get malaria. Add the flu-like symptoms and the tiredness to the dark urine and malaria was seeming more likely.

'I think you might have to go to a hospital in Los Angeles to be checked out more thoroughly,' Elizabeth said. She could have kicked herself. Why hadn't she asked more questions? 'I should take you there. Is there a car we could use?'

'I'll take her,' Kendrick volunteered. 'I'll use the helicopter.

It'll be faster and more comfortable. I could be there and back in a couple of hours.'

'You can fly a helicopter?' Was there nothing this man couldn't do?

'I'm a qualified pilot,' he said briefly.

Elizabeth raised her eyebrows. What was a trained pilot doing working as a stuntman?

'If you could get Philip to agree, that would be a help.' Elizabeth placed a reassuring hand on Sunny's arm. 'It's best we get you to hospital as soon as we can, but it's only a precaution.'

'I'll tell Philip I'm taking it. Don't worry, he won't try and stop me. I fly it for him for his stunts and we keep it handy in case we need to get anyone to hospital in a hurry.'

Elizabeth guessed that the people most likely to require to be flown to hospital in a hurry would be the stuntmen. Kendrick in particular. She wondered if he'd thought about who would fly him if he got badly hurt.

'The cost of a trip to LA is nothing in the scheme of filming a movie like this,' Kendrick continued. 'Besides, sometimes I fly Tara and Jack to LA for the weekend to save them hiring their own planes. It's all part of the service. We stuntmen do all sorts of stuff on set.'

'In that case, would you clear it with him and let him know what's happening? Sunny, do you want to grab what you need for a couple of nights in hospital? You might want to phone your family and let them know what's happening. While you're doing that I'll speak to the admitting attending at the hospital so they know we're coming.'

By the time she'd spoken to the hospital, Sunny had packed a bag and was waiting by the door of the helicopter. Kendrick was in the pilot's seat, doing some sort of checks, or so Elizabeth assumed.

The helicopter was small with only just enough space for Sunny and Elizabeth in the back.

'Philip's not too happy about me going,' Sunny said. 'He depends on me. Are you sure it's necessary? I don't feel that bad.' Then she groaned. 'Just really, really tired. Is it okay if I lie down?'

'Sure,' Elizabeth said. Sunny was definitely deteriorating. It was good that they'd be at the hospital in thirty minutes.

Elizabeth's stomach dropped as Kendrick took off and she found herself clutching Sunny's hand.

'It's okay,' Sunny mumbled. 'I've see him fly. Believe me, we're in safe hands.'

As soon as they were airborne and the helicopter levelled out, Elizabeth was too busy monitoring her patient to worry whether they'd make it to the hospital in one piece. At least until they got into Los Angeles city and she saw that they were flying just over, and sometimes between, the skyscrapers. At that point she wished she could keep her eyes closed.

Kendrick put the helicopter down so gently Elizabeth almost didn't realise they had landed on the roof of the LA city hospital. Almost before the rotors had stopped turning, the hospital staff were wheeling a gurney towards them.

Sunny opened an eye and tried to protest that she could walk, but she didn't have the energy. Elizabeth quickly updated the doctor, who nodded. 'Don't worry, we'll take it from here. I'm afraid you're going to have to move that chopper from the landing pad. We're expecting another casualty in a few minutes.'

Although she knew the hospital was first class, Elizabeth didn't want to abandon Sunny. But she didn't really have an option. She bent over her patient.

'I'll phone and find out how you're doing as soon as I can.' She squeezed Sunny's hand. 'You're going to be fine.'

Kendrick had hopped out of the pilot's seat in time to hear the doctor's words.

'Jump in beside me, Lizzie. We'd better get out of the way,' he said.

Reluctantly, Elizabeth did as he suggested. She wasn't at all sure about being in front with Kendrick where she had a bird's-eye view of the buildings they had to negotiate their way through, but now was clearly not the time to argue. As Kendrick started the engine he passed her a pair of head-phones and indicated she should put them on. Then with an-other stomach-lurching lift, they were back in the air.

'I should have stayed with her,' Elizabeth shouted above the noise of the engine.

Kendrick winced. 'You don't have to yell.' His amused voice came over the head phones. 'Just speak normally. Sunny will be fine, I promise. Besides, you might be needed back on set.'

Elizabeth couldn't say anything as they flew between the buildings. She was clenching her jaw too tight. Thankfully, and not a minute too soon, they were leaving the city behind.

'How come you guessed it was malaria?' she asked as soon as she could speak.

'Saw a bit of it in the army.'

'You were in the forces?'

'Yup.' He didn't elaborate.

Kendrick surprised her more and more. Thank God he had recognised what could have turned out to be very nasty for Sunny if she hadn't been sent to hospital.

'I should have picked it up,' she said. 'I can't believe I didn't.'

'Don't beat yourself up,' Kendrick said. 'It happens.

'But not to me. I hate making mistakes.'

Kendrick's smile was back in action. 'I might not have recognised what it was if I hadn't known she was in Tanzania a couple of weeks ago, so I wouldn't call it a mistake, exactly.'

'What would you call it, then?' Elizabeth snapped.

Immediately she felt ashamed. She was tired and out of sorts but that didn't excuse any of it.

'I'm sorry,' she said, shaking her head. 'I'm not usually this touchy. It's just…' She stopped herself just in time. If her history got out, if people knew the real reason she was here, they would be sympathetic and want to know all sorts of stuff she didn't want to talk about. More worryingly, they might wonder if she should be back at work and if she was up to the job. Especially if they knew she had almost missed diagnosing Sunny immediately. Of course, as soon as the blood results had come back she would have known that there was something more seriously wrong than flu. But by then it might have been too late. She shivered. Sunny had two small children depending on her.

Kendrick was looking at her as if she puzzled him. It was hardly surprising. Her behaviour must seem odd at the least.

She forced a smile. 'Thank you for your help. I really appreciate it.'

Kendrick studied her intently for another moment, before touching his hand to his head in an informal salute. Elizabeth wanted to tell him to keep an eye on where he was flying but she had the horrible suspicion that if she did, he would tease her by doing some trick with the helicopter. It was just his style.

As they flew out over the desert Elizabeth began to relax. At least out here there was nothing to crash into.

'It's beautiful,' she said. 'I've never been in a place quite as desolate as this before, but it has its own magic.'

'I'll show you more of it when we have time off,' he said.

It was on the tip of her tongue to tell him that she wouldn't dream of spending a minute longer with him than she had to, but she bit back the words. She'd been quite rude enough for one day. It wasn't his fault that he made her feel on edge.

'I'd like that,' she said.

'It reminds me of my folks' home,' he continued.

'Where is that?'

'A few hundred miles to the north. My father has a ranch near the San Bernardino Mountains.' He glanced at her. 'Have you ever been to a working ranch?'

'No. I would love to see one, though.'

When she saw the satisfied smile on Kendrick's lips she could have bitten her tongue. Clearly the man thought he was making progress. Didn't he recognise a friendly, polite response when he got one? But anything she said now would only make it worse.

The rest of the short journey passed quickly. Kendrick made a short detour to point out the San Andreas fault.

'Have you ever experienced an earthquake?' Elizabeth asked. The thought of one happening, even though they were so close to the fault, didn't concern her. How could it? The worst had already happened.

'I was involved in the rescue mission after the quake in Kashmir. The army used the helicopters' heat-seeking equipment and radar to locate trapped bodies.' He brought his dark eyebrows together and his silver eyes darkened to pewter. 'It was tough. I sure hope we don't see anything like that here, even though they think it's inevitable.'

There was nothing much she could say in reply. The more she knew about Kendrick the more he surprised her. From helicopter pilot to stuntman? None of it seemed to fit. But the closed look on his face told her now was not the time for questions. If ever.

When they touched down they were surrounded by people wanting to know about Sunny. As soon as she'd updated them,

Elizabeth excused herself, saying she wanted to phone the hospital, leaving Kendrick to field their questions. Whatever he decided to tell them about her near miss was up to him. Somehow she knew he would make sure there was no blame attached to her and she didn't know how she felt about that. She didn't want to be beholden to this man.

That night, when Elizabeth was lying in bed, her thoughts kept drifting back to Kendrick. Thumping her pillow and throwing off her blankets didn't make any difference. Resigned to a sleepless night, Elizabeth made herself cocoa and took a seat by the window, gazing out at the thousand stars lighting up the cloudless sky.

Earlier she had spoken to the doctor at the hospital and he'd confirmed a diagnosis of malaria.

'Well spotted,' he said warmly. 'A day or two would have made a difference. She would have become a lot sicker. As it is, we should be able to discharge her after the weekend.'

'It wasn't me who spotted it,' she'd said. She couldn't sit back and take credit where none was due. 'It was one of the stuntmen. He was in the army and saw a lot of it there, apparently. He's the one who flew us down.'

'Well, whoever caught it, the result's the same,' the voice on the other end of the phone said. 'But tell him good job from me.'

Why did her thoughts keep returning to Kendrick? There was no doubt he was interesting. One minute he was acting like someone straight out of an action movie, the next he was being kind and perceptive and, she had to admit, good company. But that wasn't the only reason. There was a strength about him, an assurance, as if he was always in control, as if he'd never let anything bad happen on his watch.

In every way he was different from the man she had married. She couldn't imagine Kendrick walking out on his wife and child when that child had a life-limiting illness. But then again, what did she really know about the stuntman? He was clearly someone who liked his freedom. But that was okay. It wasn't as if she was thinking of Kendrick in *that* way. Being intrigued by someone was a whole different ball game to wanting to be with them.

She walked across to the bedside table and picked up the photograph of Charlie. Tracing the contours of her daughter's face with the tip of her finger, she smiled. From the first moment she'd held her daughter in her arms, she'd been overwhelmed with love. In that instant she'd understood when people talked about a mother's tigerish protectiveness. And when Charlie had finally been diagnosed with Gaucher's disease, that instinct had only grown stronger. She would have given her life for her child.

Simon, on the other hand, had been disbelieving, almost outraged. As it had become apparent there was something seriously wrong with their child, he'd insisted on getting a second and then a third opinion. But no matter how many doctors they had seen, the diagnosis had always been the same, as Elizabeth had known it would be. Charlie had inherited a rare gene from both her parents and there was nothing anyone could do to stop the illness taking its course. Finally she had put her foot down.

'Enough, Simon. She has a terminal illness and nothing's going to change that. She won't be with us for long, but whatever time we have with her, can't we just make the most of it? No more treating her like a pincushion. No more dragging her halfway across the world.' Seeing the grief in her husband's eyes, she had softened. 'Let's just love her.'

Simon had shaken his head and looked at her, his eyes filled with abject misery. 'I don't know if I can cope with all this. I know what that says about me, but I don't think I can.'

And he couldn't. He had tried at first, but soon he'd been

spending more and more time away from them and at work. Elizabeth had intended to return to her job with the air ambulance service when the baby was six months old, but that had proved impossible. Not that she'd minded. She'd wanted to make the most of every second she had of Charlie's life.

It shouldn't have been a surprise when Simon had left, but it had been. To be honest, she hadn't even noticed him drawing away from her until it had been too late.

His leaving her rocked her soul, but for Charlie's sake she had picked herself up and carried on. What else could she do? The last time she had seen her ex-husband had been at Charlie's funeral.

She would never love again, she knew that. It was too painful. So why was she even thinking about Kendrick? The man was clearly not her type. But wasn't that part of the reason she was attracted to him? At least he didn't pretend to be something or somebody he wasn't.

CHAPTER THREE

KENDRICK glanced over to where Jack was leaning against one of the cars they were using in the shoot, gesticulating with his hands as he talked. Next to him was Elizabeth but from her body language, arms folded, whatever Jack was saying was cutting no ice. For the first time ever, Jack's famous smile and charm was having no effect. Kendrick eyed Elizabeth speculatively. Most women were fawning, gibbering wrecks when Jack turned on his charm. But Dr Lizzie seemed less than starstruck. Kendrick grinned. The movie star was still persevering, but it would take more than his dazzling, whiter-than-white smile to thaw this particular ice maiden.

What was her story anyway? Why was she so cool and distant? Had she just come out of a broken relationship? It was the most likely explanation for her frosty exterior. If so, he knew exactly how to fix that.

He strolled across to Jack and Elizabeth and was pleasantly surprised to see the look of relief in her eyes when she noticed him and shot him a smile. He loved seeing her all-too-rare smile. It softened her mouth and lit up her eyes.

'Kendrick,' she said. 'Jack was just inviting me to his party next weekend. He says everyone's going.'

Sneaky so-and-so. Trying to get in there first. Thinking that an invitation to his mansion in Beverly Hills would tip things in his favour. His gut was telling him that it would take more than glitz and glamour to impress the doctor, but he wasn't going to tell Jack that.

'You're coming too, I assume, Kendrick?' Although the lead actor smiled, Kendrick could see that he didn't want him to get in his way. Every time they did a film together there would be this little unspoken competition about who would end up with the woman they both wanted. So far the score had tipped in Kendrick's favour, but Jack was only just lagging behind.

'Wouldn't miss it for the world,' Kendrick said easily. 'Would you excuse us for a minute? There's something I need to speak to Dr Morgan about. In private.'

'He's after you, you know that,' he said as soon as Jack was out of hearing.

Elizabeth shook her hand free and glared at him. 'I'm perfectly able to look after myself, you know,' she said coldly. 'And as for Jack *being after me…*' her voice was thick with sarcasm '…I can assure you I'm not interested. In him, or any other man for that matter.'

Ouch. There was no mistaking how she meant that comment. It was time to change tack.

'Look, I was just being a little over-protective. Can't help myself.'

'Not when a little lady might need to be rescued,' Elizabeth bit back.

Wow! She was prickly. This wasn't exactly going to plan. He changed tack again.

'Actually, I wanted to ask you about my arm.' Women couldn't resist a man in pain and as the doctor she had no choice but to take him seriously. 'When I did my latest stunt, I think I wrenched it again.'

Elizabeth's frown was replaced by a look of concern. Kendrick decided not to let the fact it was professional concern bother him. At least she was no longer glaring at him.

'Why don't you come into the medical trailer and let me have a look?' she suggested.

Kendrick raised a triumphant eyebrow at Jack, who was watching them closely, and fell into step next to Elizabeth. 'I'm pretty sure it's just a sprained muscle. Nothing a bit of massage won't help.' He shot her a look. 'I don't suppose you're into massage, are you, by any chance?'

Oops, perhaps he'd overdone it. The glare was back.

'I'm a doctor, not a masseuse!'

She stopped in her tracks and placed her hands on her hips. Kendrick was distracted for a long moment. Her hips curved in just the right places and a man could probably just about circle that waist with the palms of his hands. As for those legs. His eyes travelled down the length of her body and he swallowed a groan as a vivid image of those long legs wrapped around him jumped into his mind.

'When you're quite finished…' a cool voice said, and he dragged his eyes back to her face, only to find himself focusing on a mouth that just cried out to be kissed.

He shook his head. Now was not the place and certainly not the time. Dr Elizabeth Morgan needed a good bit more thawing before he would even risk a quick taste of those lips.

Inside her trailer, Elizabeth instructed Kendrick to sit on her sofa.

Trying to remember that Kendrick's torso was simply a mass of muscle and fibre, she ran her hands over his powerful shoulders. Then she noticed something odd. A star-shaped hole with lines radiating out from the centre just below his left clavicle. Although she had never seen a bullet wound before, there was no mistaking what this was. She touched the scar with her finger.

'Is this what I think it is?' she said softly.

Kendrick nodded. 'Got it in Iraq. Damn bullet chipped a bit of bone. That's what makes my shoulder stiff sometimes.'

Not just been in the army, then, but on active service.

So he hadn't been all together untruthful when he'd crashed from the horse a few days earlier. A wound like that was bound to cause problems. Especially since he insisted on battering it every day of the week.

'How does a helicopter pilot get a bullet wound?'

His expression darkened and for the first time Elizabeth wondered whether Kendrick was as easygoing as he liked to pretend he was.

'That's a long story. Can we save it for another day?'

This time Elizabeth was sure she saw a shadow cross his face. Did Kendrick have something in his past he didn't want to talk about? Maybe they weren't so different after all?

'Sure,' she said. He was entitled to his privacy as much as she was entitled to hers. Nevertheless, she found herself wanting to know more. Why had he gone from being an officer in the army, someone no doubt with a bright future ahead of him, to a stuntman? And why was she interested? It wasn't as if she was planning to get involved with him. All she wanted to do was to be left alone with her pain. If he had secrets of his own, it was none of her business and never would be.

Turning her attention back to what she was supposed to be doing—giving the man in front of her the best medical attention she could—she carefully felt along his shoulder, probing gently and asking him to lift and lower his arm. There was a little stiffness there, but nothing too worrying. She would like to have a look at his X-rays and medical records, though. Until she saw them she wouldn't be happy that he was working as a stuntman. Repeated banging of a damaged limb couldn't do it any good. She had an idea that Kendrick would somehow have managed to forget to tell the film producers about his medical history.

'Does Philip know about your shoulder?' she asked.

'No. And you're not going to tell him,' Kendrick said firmly.

'He should know. It's not a good idea to carry on working as a stuntman until I see your X-rays. You could damage your shoulder permanently.'

Kendrick's hand shot out and gripped her wrist so hard it was almost painful.

'He's not to know,' he said through clenched teeth. 'You're my doctor and bound by patient confidentiality, isn't that right?'

Surprised by the vehemence in his tone, Elizabeth removed her hand from his grasp. 'Of course I can't say anything, but I'd feel happier if I could get a look at your medical notes.'

Kendrick eased himself off the couch and picking up his shirt, shrugged into it.

'I have no idea where my records are. Even if I did, there's nothing in them that would give you any reason to worry. Stuntmen work with injuries all the time. If we stopped every time we hurt ourselves, we'd never work. Broken bones and other injuries are part of the job.'

'But not bullet wounds surely?' Elizabeth said sharply.

'No. They don't usually use live ammunition on film sets.' He shook his head in mock dismay. 'That would lead to too many dead actors.'

Elizabeth flushed. For some reason he was always wrong footing her.

'So, what about Jack's party? Are you going to come? Because if you are, we could travel down together.' The teasing look was back in his eyes. 'You don't want to stay here on your own surely? That's no fun.'

Fun? She wondered if she even remembered what that was.

'I'm more than happy to stay here by myself. I happen to like my own company.' She made herself smile. 'Honestly.'

Kendrick eyed her thoughtfully. 'I wonder,' he said slowly. 'At least think about it.'

Then picking up his hat and whistling under his breath he left her feeling as if she'd just done a couple of rounds in a boxing ring.

Kendrick strode back to his trailer.

Trust Lizzie to have picked up on the bullet wound. Despite her anxiety over almost not picking up Sunny's malaria instantly, he doubted she missed much.

He'd liked the feel of her cool fingers on his skin. The way a lock of hair had fallen across her face as she'd bent over. She intrigued him more and more. What was behind that guarded exterior?

Not that he wanted to know, he told himself. His interest in Lizzie Morgan was purely physical. The same as his interest in any woman since Amy.

He winced. Amy. His first love and his last. He would never feel that way again. He wouldn't let himself. Loving someone meant responsibility. Or should do. Their happiness, their life in your hands.

But he had been unable to save Amy. If he'd got there five minutes earlier, might he have been able to? He would never know.

Why was it coming back now? He'd thought he'd closed that particular wound—one that was worse than any physical pain he'd ever experienced. It didn't matter how many big waves he surfed, how many mountains he flung himself off, how fast he rode his horse, no rush of adrenaline, no losing himself in another woman's arms could completely wipe out the feelings of loss and guilt.

If the army hadn't stopped him from flying while they'd investigated, would he have stayed? There was no clear answer to that. Or not one he wanted to think about. At least working as a stuntman gave him a similar adrenaline rush to flying helicopters. He needed his daily dose or he'd go crazy. He grimaced. His father had been disbelieving and furious when he'd told him about his decision to leave the army, but that was too bad. All his life he'd tried to win his father's approval—and failed. Now he was living the life he wanted, with no responsibility for anyone but himself.

He let himself into his trailer and peeled off his shirt, feeling restless and on edge. He needed to be doing something. A workout would help. And after that? An image of blue eyes and a soft mouth jumped into his head. After his workout, he knew just what he needed to keep his head from going places he didn't want to go.

Elizabeth stroked the horse's mane and he whinnied with pleasure. After lunch she had walked around the perimeter of the camp until she had come across the stables.

'You like horses?'

She started as a deep voice came from behind her. She whirled around to find Kendrick standing there. Earlier she had passed him lying on a bench, dressed only in his army pants, concentrating as he lifted weights above his head. Happily he had been too preoccupied to notice her stealing surreptitious glances at him as each muscle in his abdomen and shoulders bunched every time he lifted the weights above his head.

The horse nuzzled its soft mouth into her hand and she pulled her hand away as its whiskers tickled her palm.

'Hey, it's okay. Buster won't bite,' Kendrick said, misreading her action.

'I know. I have ridden before.' Okay, so it was years ago and was only once, but he didn't need to know that.

Kendrick raised an eyebrow at her and his mouth turned up at the corners. Elizabeth's heart thumped against her ribs. It would be much better if he wasn't so sexy.

'Have you got anything planned for this afternoon?' Kendrick continued.

Why was he so damned determined to seek her out at every opportunity? Hadn't she made it crystal clear she wasn't interested?

'Just work. I'm employed here for a reason, you know,' she said testily, trying to ignore the uncomfortable racing of her heart.

He grinned down at her. 'Not this afternoon you're not. Philip is shooting a close-up that involves Jack and Tara in a love scene. Unless something happens there, like she bites his tongue when he tries to put it down her throat, which I wouldn't put past her—they have a bit of history—I think you'll be all right.'

'Why do you want to know?' Elizabeth asked. 'Do you need to see me again? Is your shoulder causing you more discomfort?'

'The shoulder's fine. I thought you might like to come with me to the desert for a ride. We could take the horses we've been using for the stunts. You've already met Buster here.'

Would he ever give up? On the other hand, she hated having time on her own, despite what she'd told him earlier. Without something to occupy her mind there was too much time for thinking, and thinking meant remembering....

'I don't know. It's a long time since I've been on a horse,' she admitted 'I wouldn't be surprised if it had me off in seconds.'

'No, he won't. The horses we use are like lambs—really well trained. Besides, we use western saddles. It's like sitting in an armchair.'

It wasn't just the horses that was making her hesitate. Although she wanted to see what was out there beyond the confines of the set, she wasn't sure why Kendrick was asking her. If he thought she was up for some brief romance with him, he was very much mistaken. Couldn't he see he was wasting his time pursuing her?

'It's only a horse ride—I'm not proposing marriage,' he said, as if reading her mind. 'Of course, if you're too chicken...' He shrugged, leaving the challenge hanging in the air.

Elizabeth made up her mind. Why not? It was unlikely that she'd ever be back here, so she should make the most of every opportunity that came her way.

'Who do you think you're calling chicken? I've a clinic to do first, but I can be ready about three.'

She turned away, knowing and having to admit liking it that he was staring after her. Was she nuts? Didn't she know that Kendrick spelt danger? On the other hand, Kendrick was no more looking for a long-term relationship than she was. In that respect they were two of a kind, even if for completely different reasons. And she could handle someone like Kendrick.

The clinic produced no more than the usual sore throats, sniffles and sore muscles, a sprained ankle and a paper cut. Despite the work being a little boring at times, Elizabeth was content that the cast and crew were keeping well. Especially after Sunny becoming ill. Although Philip's assistant was very much better, she remained in hospital.

Elizabeth was ready and waiting when Kendrick turned up with a riding hat.

She eyed the hat warily.

'I thought you said it was perfectly safe,' she said. 'I'm not intending to go any faster than a walk. You do know that?'

'Just a precaution,' he said. 'Anyone can fall off a horse. We need to make sure the set doc stays in one piece.'

'Where's yours, then?'

He looked aghast. 'When I said anyone, I didn't mean me. I've been riding all my life and only fall off when I mean to.'

Feeling less certain about the proposed adventure, Elizabeth waited while he fastened the helmet on for her. As his fingertips brushed against her throat, she felt goose-bumps pop up all over her body.

Now that she was committed to riding him, Buster looked bigger somehow and Elizabeth eyed him nervously. Maybe this wasn't such a good idea. But before she could do or say anything, Kendrick had taken hold of her leg and swung her into the saddle. He was right about that at least. It was like sitting in an armchair.

Kendrick adjusted the stirrups for her, lifting each of her legs in turn while he did so. Elizabeth felt a jolt of electricity each time his hands brushed her calves. Why did her hormones seem to have suddenly come back to life? And why with this man?

Once her stirrups were adjusted to Kendrick's satisfaction, he showed her how to hold the reins in one hand and the pommel of the saddle with another.

'It will make you feel more secure. If you want to go right, just pull the reins to the right and ditto for the opposite direction. You don't have to use your legs—he'll respond to your voice.'

Kendrick swung himself into his own saddle and wheeled his horse round.

'Just follow me.'

As they left the compound behind Elizabeth began to relax, especially when Buster responded to her voice and the slightest pull on his reins. She looked around. The desert seemed to stretch on for as far as the eye could see, with the mountains in the distance. She hoped Kendrick had water in his saddlebags. Of course he would have water. He wasn't the kind of man who would go into the desert unprepared. Risktaker he may be, but idiot he clearly wasn't.

He brought his horse next to hers. 'There's a canyon about five miles from here. I thought we could stop there.'

'Sounds good.'

'How does it feel? Do you think you could manage to post—I mean trot? Or a short canter?'

'I could try.'

'Don't try and rise or anything fancy. Just relax and stay with the horse's movements. I'll go in front. Buster likes to stay behind. If you feel yourself slipping, hold onto the pommel, say whoa and he will. Okay?'

Elizabeth's mouth had gone dry so she simply nodded. Kendrick kicked his horse on to a slow trot and Buster followed immediately. Elizabeth clenched her teeth before remembering what Kendrick had said about relaxing. She forced her body to go with Buster's rhythm and soon she found that it was okay. She could do this. All she had to do was concentrate.

Kendrick was riding with one hand on the rear of his saddle, looking back at her and watching to see how she was doing. If she'd dared let go of the saddle or the reins, she would have given him a thumbs-up. As it was, she managed a smile.

'Want to try a little faster?' he asked.

Not really. This was quite fast enough. But she surprised herself by nodding. Somehow she trusted him completely.

Cantering was more comfortable than trotting had been, even if it felt more like an all-out gallop. She let herself feel Buster underneath her, the way the horse seemed to know what he was doing, as if he wanted to make sure she was all right. After a while Kendrick slowed his horse back to a trot then a walk and Buster followed suit. There was a dodgy moment when the change in tempo made her lose her balance but it was short-lived. As Kendrick brought his horse back alongside hers she grinned at him.

'That was amazing. I loved it. Can we do it again?'

'If you like.' And then he was off again, with Buster following close behind.

They stopped near an outcrop of rocks and Kendrick jumped down, tying the reins in a knot near his horse's head.

He held out his arms and as she slid off Buster and into them, he held her against him, her feet not touching the ground. She could feel the hard muscles of his chest through the thin material of her T-shirt. Something deep in her belly sizzled. Dismayed, she wriggled until he placed her back on her feet.

'You're a natural,' he said approvingly.

She felt an unexpected stab of pleasure at his words.

He untied the saddlebags from his horse and passed her some water. Elizabeth drank thirstily.

'How far to the canyon?' she asked.

'Another mile or two. If you're happy to canter for some of it, it won't take too long.' His eyes glinted. 'I have to warn you, you're going to be stiff tomorrow.'

They rested against the rocks, which provided welcome shade from the relentlessly hot sun. Unfortunately, for them both to be in the shade meant that they were pressed close together. His jeans-clad leg was warm against hers and doing all sorts of things to nerve endings she'd thought no longer existed.

'So why did you leave the army?' Elizabeth asked. 'I'm only guessing, but I would have thought they'd be pretty keen to hang onto helicopter pilots.'

Kendrick stared off into the distance.

'I guess you could say that the life didn't suit me. I don't like doing what I'm told.'

Now, why didn't that surprise her?

His expression was closed, his eyes shuttered. The message he was giving was loud and clear.

'Why stuntwork, then?' Elizabeth thought it wise to change the subject.

'It seemed the natural thing. My aunt by marriage is an actress. She put me in touch with a director who was looking for someone who could fly a chopper for an army movie he was making. She suggested me. Then they realised I could ride horses too and all kinds of other stuff and I guess it followed on from there. The work suits me. I like the travelling. I like doing stunts. I'm good at it.'

He said the words matter-of-factly. He wasn't boasting. Just saying it how it was.

'What about your folks?'

His expression darkened.

'My father was in the army too. A colonel. He's retired. He works his ranch full time now.'

'Is that how you learned to ride?'

'Yes. I grew up with horses. My folks have always had the ranch.'

There was more to all of this than he was telling her. She was sure of it.

'And you? What about your family?' He turned the conversation back to her.

Elizabeth winced inwardly. Once she'd had a family—a husband and child. Now all she had left was her father.

'My mother died when I was sixteen. My father's pretty frail now. He lives in Canada, although he's American. From the East Coast. That's how come I can work here.'

'Do you see him?'

The last time she had seen her father had been at Charlie's funeral.

'Apart from one brief visit he made to the UK a few months ago, I haven't really seen him for a couple of years.' She hadn't been able to. Taking Charlie out of the country and away from her medical team had always been out of the question. 'But I'm hoping to see him when I finish here.'

'And then? Will you stay in the US or go back to England?'

Elizabeth sucked in a breath. 'I haven't thought that far.'

He was looking at her as if he wanted to know more. She jumped to her feet to avoid further questions.

'Shall we go?'

He said nothing as he packed away the water again. Not wanting to feel his hands on her again, Elizabeth slipped her foot into the stirrup and tried to mount. But the stirrup was too high for her to gain the necessary momentum to swing her leg across Buster's back. When she hit the ground, landing on her backside, she knew she should have waited for help. But she was used to relying on herself. Whatever Kendrick thought, she was no little lady needing some big strong man to protect her.

Kendrick helped her to her feet with a broad grin on his face.

'That didn't go too well, did it?' he teased. 'You should have waited for me to give you a leg up.'

Elizabeth dusted herself off and glared at him. Then she saw the funny side of it and laughed. She'd forgotten how good it felt.

This time, with Kendrick's help, she mounted without further mishap.

They cantered for a while before slowing to a walk again.

'The canyon is over there.' Kendrick pointed with a finger.

Just then Buster reared. It was so unexpected Elizabeth shrieked and dropped the reins. When Buster took off at a gallop, all Elizabeth could do was dig her hands into his mane and hold on for dear life.

'Whoa,' she shouted in the horse's ear, but it had no effect. Buster was making straight for the canyon.

Terrified, Elizabeth was only dimly aware of Kendrick shouting something at her. Probably telling her to pull on the reins. But there was no way she could let go of Buster's mane long enough to try and pick them up. If she did, there was no doubt in her mind that she would crash to the ground.

Suddenly Kendrick was cantering beside her. He pulled his horse close to Buster, reached over and with one arm pulled her off the bolting horse. It wasn't an elegant manoeuvre—Elizabeth was slung over his saddle like a sack of potatoes—but at least she was no longer being taken towards what she thought would be certain death.

Kendrick pulled his horse to a stop and let Elizabeth drop to the ground.

'Stay here,' he said. 'I need to get your horse.'

Buster, without her hanging on his neck and screaming in his ear, slowed to a canter and Kendrick took off after him. The horse was still heading for the edge of the canyon. Elizabeth didn't know how steep the drop was but it looked as if the horse was heading for certain death. Had she been on his back still, he'd be taking her with him. Did Kendrick know what he was doing? What if the panicked horse pulled him off his mount?

Her heart in her mouth, she watched as Kendrick got alongside Buster again and, leaning forward, almost completely out of the saddle, grasped the reins and pulled both horses away from the cliff edge. Another moment or two and they would have gone over.

When Kendrick trotted back with Buster, who was still rolling his eyes, Elizabeth's legs gave way and she sank to her knees.

'I thought you said he was well behaved,' she cried. 'Like a lamb, you said!'

'Didn't you see the snake?' Kendrick asked. 'The only thing this horse hates worse than tumbleweed is snakes.'

'Now you tell me.'

Kendrick leaped off his horse and came to kneel next to her.

'Are you okay? Sorry I had to kind of dump you back there, but I couldn't risk Buster going over the cliff.'

'I'll live. I guess.'

'C'mon, then. We should get back. It'll be dark soon. Are you okay riding Buster or would you prefer to ride with me?'

If he thought for one second that she was going to get back on Buster he had another think coming. What if there was another snake or, God forbid, a ball of tumbleweed? On the other hand, she didn't want to be so close to Kendrick either.

'Maybe I should walk.'

'Walk? It'll take hours.'

Elizabeth rubbed her backside. Boy, she was going to be stiff tomorrow. 'I think I'd rather walk than get on that horse again. What if there is another snake? There's no way I'm going to go through that again.' She eyed Kendrick suspiciously. 'Are you sure you didn't make him go off? Just to see me make an idiot of myself?'

'Hey, would I do something like that?' Kendrick feigned a hurt look then his face grew serious. 'I wouldn't do that. If you'd fallen you could have really hurt yourself. We need you in one piece. Philip would never have forgiven me if I didn't bring you back safe.'

Elizabeth looked into the distance. The plains stretched as far as the eye could see. Kendrick was right. It would take hours to walk back to the set.

'Okay, Buster, seems you and I are going to have to make this work,' she said into the horse's ear. 'Just promise me that if you spot any more snakes you'll stay calm.'

Grabbing the pommel of the saddle, she heaved herself up, relieved to find that this time she managed to make it without landing on her backside.

After giving Buster a pat, as much to reassure herself as him, she picked up the reins.

'Okay,' she said, pleased that her voice betrayed no hint of her nervousness, 'what are we waiting for?'

They made their way back to the camp at a more sedate pace and with Kendrick taking up the rear this time. As he watched Elizabeth adopt the British way of trotting, he smiled to himself. Had she any idea how cute her bottom was in her tight-fitting jeans? And that wasn't all that he liked about her. He was impressed by the gutsy way she'd insisted on getting back on Buster and riding back to the camp. Most women he knew would have refused point blank.

He was beginning to realise that there was more to Dr Elizabeth Morgan than he'd originally thought, and he was looking forward to finding out more.

CHAPTER FOUR

As SHE'D anticipated, Elizabeth was so stiff the next morning she could hardly put one foot in front of the other. If only there had been a bath somewhere on set she could have soaked her aching muscles last night and perhaps she wouldn't be feeling like this.

She hobbled over to the mess tent, trying her best to pretend that she wasn't in agony.

But she obviously failed miserably. Kendrick spotted her over the heads of the others and grinned. She scowled at him.

She helped herself to scrambled eggs and toast and found an empty seat close to where the breakfast buffet was laid out for everyone to help themselves.

She winced as her bottom hit the chair. Would she ever be able to sit down again without grimacing? Right now it didn't seem possible.

'Feeling a little stiff?' A familiar deep voice came from her left.

Elizabeth looked up to find Kendrick smiling down at her, his eyes glinting with suppressed laughter.

'I could give you a rubdown later, if you like. It always works for the horses.'

'Very funny and, no, thanks, I'll pass on the rubdown.' Before she could help herself an image of Kendrick's hands kneading her aching muscles flashed into her head and heat rose to her cheeks.

'Don't you have some stunt to do?' She waved her fork in the general direction of outside. If only he'd leave her alone, she might be able to relax a little. Whenever he was around, she felt on edge, as if her body didn't belong to her.

'I do, as it happens. Doing a fight scene with Josh. And then I need to set up Imogen's scene. She has to pretend to fall down the stairs.'

'In that case,' Elizabeth said, 'I'll see you on set.'

The man clearly didn't recognise dismissal when he heard it as he sat down next to her and stretched his long legs in front of him.

'No rush. We have an hour or two to go. Plenty of time.'

Elizabeth stabbed at the food on her plate with her fork. She hated the way he made her feel hot and bothered. In that moment she realised that at least she felt something, apart from grief and a numbness. These last months she had gone through the days on a kind of autopilot.

She didn't know if she wanted the numbness to go away. She didn't want to feel. Feeling was too hard. Charlie's death was like a wound. A wound she needed to leave alone. She had wrapped her heart in ice and she wanted it to stay that way. Thinking about Charlie, her appetite disappeared and she pushed her plate away.

'I have to open the clinic in fifteen minutes,' she said. 'So don't feel you have to keep me company.'

He was looking at her through slitted eyes, as if trying to work her out. Good luck to him. She could hardly work herself out.

'Are you always this grouchy in the morning?' he said eventually. 'I'll have to remember that.'

He grinned again and before she had a chance to think of

a retort he jumped up and, catching sight of Imogen, excused himself with a brief word of apology.

Elizabeth found herself following his progress as he walked across the room. Despite his size he reminded her of a cat the way he moved. A panther stalking its prey, creeping up when least expected. He was as dangerous as a wild cat too. Men like Kendrick used women. He would pursue them until they gave in then he would leave them. She knew it with absolute certainty.

She stood too, and dumping her tray on the counter walked as briskly as her tortured muscles would let her towards her medical trailer. Work. That was what she needed. Something to keep her busy and stop her from thinking.

'Okay, everyone,' Philip called from his position high above one of the mobile cameras, 'take your positions, please. Let's roll.'

Elizabeth settled in one of the camp chairs close by. She had finished her clinic. As usual there had been little for her to do except dole out some antibiotics and painkillers. This job was fine for the time being but once she was finished here she'd have to think seriously about which direction she wanted her career to go in. If she was honest, she missed the rush of emergency medicine. She also knew that she had been in no state to go back to that speciality straight after Charlie's death. At least now she was beginning to think about the future.

She turned her attention to what was happening on set.

Kendrick was made up to look like Jack while Josh was dressed to look like one of the baddies, and some of the other crew members had been drafted in as extras. Imogen was wearing a red wig to make her look like Tara.

The fight was taking place inside the mock-up of one of the buildings and everyone moved inside. The set had been made to look like a restaurant. Elizabeth had been given the script by one of the assistants and she found the scene. Apparently the hero—or Kendrick, in this instance—was to be set on by ten or so villains. He would fight his way out of trouble with his fists and in the middle there was a bit where he would leap from the balcony onto the shoulders of one of the baddies—in this case Josh—before ending up victorious.

Or so it was scripted.

A pile of cardboard boxes was being piled up at the foot of the balcony by Kendrick's team. He would have to fall just right so he didn't hurt himself.

The fight was so realistic that Elizabeth found herself sucking in a breath every time Kendrick took a blow.

At one point Kendrick jumped over the balcony and onto Josh's back. The next moment he and Josh were rolling around on the floor as if they were genuinely involved in a fight to the death. When Josh's fist actually connected with Kendrick's jaw, Elizabeth winced. That had to have hurt.

'Cut. Okay, folks, that's a wrap,' Philip called. 'Good job, everyone.'

Kendrick helped Josh to his feet. Elizabeth noticed a cut on Kendrick's forehead that was bleeding badly. She was on her feet in an instant, stopping only to reach for her medical bag.

'You're hurt. Let me take a look,' she said.

Kendrick reached a hand towards his head and seemed surprised when it came away sticky with blood. 'Hey, Josh, did you do this?' he said. 'I thought I'd trained you better.'

'You've got to be kidding me,' Josh retorted. 'If I'd connected with you, you would have known all about it. You must have hit your head on something.'

'It doesn't matter how you got it,' Elizabeth said. 'I need to clean you up.'

She slipped on a pair of sterile gloves. 'Come and sit down under the light so I can see it better.'

With a wink at Josh, Kendrick let himself be led over to a chair. Elizabeth angled the light so she could see better. Thankfully the wound wasn't deep enough to require stitches. There was also a bruise coming up on Kendrick's cheekbone.

'I'll clean the cut and apply some Steri-strips. I've got some arnica in my bag that I can put on the bruise. That should help.'

Kendrick leaned back in his chair and as Elizabeth bent to clean his head wound she was uncomfortably aware of his breath on her neck. She hoped to hell he wouldn't notice it was giving her goose-bumps.

'Take your time, Doc,' Kendrick drawled.

Kendrick leaned back, enjoying the feel of her cool fingers on his head. Normally he'd have cleaned it up himself and just stuck a sticky plaster on but he was enjoying this way too much to want to stop Elizabeth from doing whatever she was doing. The touch of her fingers made his gut clench.

Her perfume drifted across, intoxicating him, and when she bent over he could see the swell of her breasts just above the open button of her shirt.

What he wouldn't do to feel that soft, pale skin under his fingertips. To thread his hands through her thick hair, to take away that guarded expression from her eyes.

And he would. It was only a matter of time.

She had finished applying the makeshift stitches to his forehead and was pressing lightly on his bruised cheek.

He swallowed a groan.

Before he could stop himself he took her hand and held it away from his face.

'If you carry on doing that, I won't be responsible for my actions,' he growled. 'I'm only human.'

'Don't be ridiculous,' she replied, but not before he saw

the answering spark in her eyes. Perhaps the ice maiden was starting to thaw. Maybe on the next stunt he could really hurt himself. He was damned if he didn't want to see the look of concern in her eyes again.

CHAPTER FIVE

In the end the decision whether to go to Los Angeles was taken out of Elizabeth's hands when Philip announced late on Thursday evening that he'd decided to film a scene in the city.

The cast and crew drove down in convoy, leaving when it was still dark the next morning. Kendrick had offered to take Elizabeth on his motorbike, but she had refused politely. The thought of spending a couple of hours with her arms wrapped around his waist was unnerving. He hadn't said anything but his mocking eyes had suggested he knew exactly why she'd opted to travel with the crew.

They drove into LA and along Sunset Boulevard, with its giant boards advertising the latest movies, just as it was getting light.

The next part of the filming would take place in a studio on the outskirts of the city.

The stunt for the interior scene didn't involve Kendrick. The female stuntwoman, Imogen, who was doubling for Tara, had to fall down a flight of steps. Elizabeth thought they would use all sorts of equipment to mimic the fall and was surprised when Imogen stood at the top of the stairs dressed as Tara's character without any pulleys, wires or padding. Imogen was wearing the red wig again and from where Elizabeth was standing looked pretty much like the star. Kendrick had explained that while they tried to get doubles for the stunt that were close in appearance to the stars, make-up and wigs usually had to be added.

'It's not as if the camera gets a close-up of the doubles,' he'd said. 'We learn to keep our faces away from the camera. The success of the stunt depends on the audience believing that it really is the actor.'

Kendrick and Imogen had spent the last half an hour with Philip, discussing what the stuntwoman would do and where the cameras should be positioned in order to get the best shot.

'Okay, we're hot.'

'Everyone get clear.'

On command, Imogen pretended to fall down the stairs. She tumbled down, making no attempt to shield herself as her body bounced from wall to wall.

Elizabeth was shocked. She could break her neck. And as Imogen lay at the bottom of the steps, not moving, she thought her worst fears had been realised and started to move towards her. Forget Philip and his insistence she stay out of the shot until he gave the all-clear. She was here to make sure her charges stayed alive and no director, no matter how much of a Hollywood big shot he might be, was going to make her do otherwise.

But even as she was running towards Imogen, Philip was calling 'Cut' and the stuntwoman was getting into a sitting position, rubbing her wrist.

Before Elizabeth could reach her, Kendrick had got there first and was talking to his colleague.

Imogen brushed herself off and stood up.

'Did you hurt your wrist?' Elizabeth asked. 'Can I have a look?'

'It's nothing,' Imogen said dismissively. 'You want me to do it again, boss?'

When Kendrick nodded, Elizabeth couldn't believe what she was hearing.

She took Imogen by the upper arm and studied her wrist. It was already beginning to swell. Probably a bad sprain, but she should get it X-rayed to be on the safe side.

'I'm afraid no more stunts for you today. At the very least you need to get that X-rayed.'

Imogen winked at Kendrick.

'Tell her, boss,' she said.

'It's not broken. She can do it again,' Kendrick said.

Elizabeth felt the slow burn of anger travel to her chest.

'May I remind you that I am the doctor? You may have experience—first-aid experience—in the army, but there's no way you are competent to make that diagnosis. I'm forbidding Imogen to do that scene, or any other scene, until I'm satisfied that her wrist isn't broken.'

Before she knew it, Kendrick was hustling her away from Imogen. She tried to struggle out of his grasp but his grip was too strong. He waited until they were out of earshot of the others.

She rounded on him furiously. How dared he treat her like some sort of…? She couldn't think of the right word. She was too angry.

'What the hell do you think you're doing? How dare you manhandle me? How dare you drag me away from my patient?'

'How sure are you that Immy's wrist is broken?' Kendrick remained implacable in the face of her fury.

'I don't think it is, but I can't know for certain. Any re-sponsible doctor would insist on an X-ray.'

'If Immy doesn't think it's broken then it's not. Believe me, she's had enough experience of being injured to know.' He dropped his voice. 'Stuntmen and women get paid by the gag they do. If you take her off the set now, just to satisfy your own need for reassurance, she'll lose money.'

Elizabeth glared at him.

'Hey, Kendrick, we need to get on,' Philip shouted across. 'Can't you two leave any discussion for later?'

'I'm not going to let her do it again,' Elizabeth said. 'It's my decision.'

Kendrick looked at her for one long moment. Clearly he wasn't used to being told what he could and couldn't do. Then his face relaxed. 'You are one stubborn woman. Tell you what, I'll ask Josh if he'll do the stunt. I'd do it myself except I'm too tall to pass for Tara. I suspect Josh won't be too happy about dressing up as a woman but, hey, I owe him for that punch he landed on me. Will that keep you happy?'

He was putting her in a difficult position. If Josh hurt himself, she would feel responsible. She opened her mouth to protest but he cut her off.

'Lizzie, I'm not asking you. I'm telling you.' Now it was his turn to frown at her.

Kendrick turned away and, after a quick word with Philip, Imogen left the set. Philip was drumming his fingers on the camera. 'Can we get on, please? Will someone tell the doctor that she's not here to get in the way of filming?'

A flash of annoyance passed across Kendrick's face and he turned to Philip. 'If the doc says someone's not fit to do a stunt then we listen. Josh is going to do it instead.'

There was a moment when Philip and Kendrick faced each other, before Philip sighed loudly. 'Could you at least make it quick?'

A small smile crossed Kendrick's face. 'I just need five minutes to persuade him and get him into the right clothes.'

As Kendrick turned away he winked at Elizabeth and she glared back. She didn't want him running interference for her. She was perfectly able to stand up for herself.

'It's going to take time to get Josh organised.' Philip's look at Elizabeth left her in no doubt he held her responsible for the delay but she held her head high. What use was she to anyone if she let them push her around? She would rather pack her bags and leave than go against her professional judgement. Not that she wanted to leave, she realised with an unpleasant sinking feeling in her stomach. She liked it here. The last thing she needed or wanted right now was to be looking for a new job.

'Let's do the scene with Jack and Tara in the meantime,' Philip continued, with a last baleful look at Elizabeth.

Tough. They could all glare at her as much as they liked. It wouldn't change her mind. She crossed over to where Imogen was sitting, flexing her arm. From the movement Elizabeth knew it couldn't be broken. Still, she wanted to get it strapped. In her peripheral vision she could see Kendrick and Josh talking. From the heated look on Josh's face he wasn't too happy at having to stand in for Imogen. However, after a final word from Kendrick, Josh turned on his heel and stomped off towards the dressing area.

Elizabeth turned her attention to the injured stuntwoman. 'Hey, Imogen, you okay with me strapping your wrist?'

Imogen looked at her with a look of admiration. 'You did a brave thing back there. We don't usually see the medical support standing up to Philip. The only one who usually gets away with it is Kendrick. Philip knows he needs him, and us, to make the film look good.'

Elizabeth called to one of the production assistants for some ice. 'Keep your arm high and we'll put this ice pack on. It should alleviate most of the swelling. After that I'll strap it and if it looks okay, you might be all right for tomorrow's filming.'

'Sure hope so. We're doing some car-chase scenes and I need my wrist to be working. But I should tell you that this little bump is nothing compared to what I've worked through before. You'll find out that most of us carry on unless we're laid up in hospital. It's the nature of the job.'

When Elizabeth was satisfied that Imogen's wrist had been sufficiently iced, she took a bandage out of her medical bag and deftly strapped her affected limb. In the meantime, an unhappy-looking Josh, wearing a dress and red wig, strode back onto the set. Elizabeth and Imogen shared a smile.

'Ready when you are, Philip,' Kendrick called over. 'How's it going, Immy? That's a pretty neat bandage you have there.'

'The doc insisted,' Imogen replied. 'I did try to tell her it was nothing but a little bump, but she wouldn't listen.' She looked from Kendrick to Elizabeth. 'I suspect our doc isn't used to being told what to do any more than you are. That should make it interesting around here for the next few weeks.'

Elizabeth started. What did Imogen mean? Had she picked up on the tension between Kendrick and herself whenever they were together?

'I feel ridiculous in this get-up,' Josh complained. 'Maybe we should have got the doc to stand in for Immy.' He winked at Elizabeth to let her know there were no bad feelings. 'But can we get this over and done with so I can get back to being a man?'

Everyone laughed and Kendrick punched Josh lightly on the shoulder. 'I guess you'd better go and fall down some stairs to keep Philip happy. I'll watch it on camera. Make a good job of it and you won't have to do it again.'

Josh's fall was a repeat of Imogen's. Fortunately he seemed to survive his tumble unscathed. Nevertheless, it took another couple of attempts before Kendrick declared himself satisfied with the take.

'Okay, that's a wrap,' Philip called, after Kendrick and his team had huddled around the camera, checking that they were satisfied with the shot. Elizabeth had noticed that it seemed to be as much to do with Kendrick as Philip when it came to deciding whether a stunt was good enough not to require repeating.

'I need everyone back on set on Sunday lunchtime at the latest. I guess I'll see most of you tonight.'

As cast and crew began to disperse, Kendrick walked across to Elizabeth.

'How about I show you around?' Kendrick asked. 'I'm assuming you don't want to spend the rest of the day back at your hotel.'

'I'd planned to go and see Sunny at the hospital this afternoon.'

'So did I, so I checked with Sunny earlier. She asked if we could come for the afternoon visiting. Something about her having more than her quota for this morning.'

'In that case, I do have the morning free.'

'I could use one of the company's helicopters and take you up the coast,' Kendrick suggested.

Elizabeth gave a mock shudder. 'I'd really prefer something a little less exciting.'

Kendrick gave her a lopsided grin and clasped a hand to his chest. 'Hey, are you saying you don't trust me? I'm a pretty good pilot, you know.' He paused. 'I know a great restaurant overlooking the Big Sur. We could go there for lunch and then go for a walk on the beach.'

That sounded too much like a date.

'Maybe another time? I wouldn't mind just going for a walk and having a look around. I've always wanted to see Venice Beach.'

'Sounds good to me. I'll meet you outside in five minutes,' Kendrick said. 'I just need to change into something more modern.'

* * *

Venice Beach was a place Elizabeth had heard about but never seen. The strange but pleasing thing about Los Angeles was that everything was exactly like how it was depicted in the movies. She was beginning to see how some people might feel that they were living on a film set. There were beautiful women in shorts and crop tops rollerskating and Elizabeth couldn't help but notice that Kendrick's eyes were swivelling as they walked. A little further on was Muscle Beach. This time it was Elizabeth's turn to gawp at the bare-chested men lifting weights and lapping up the attention of the bystanders.

Along one side was a range of shops advertising the services of spiritual healers and psychics. There were even places offering therapy for pets. It made her smile. Only in California…

Leaving the promenade, they strolled onto the beach. The sun was high in a cloudless sky. Elizabeth slipped off her shoes, enjoying the sensation of sand between her toes. Neither said anything about their earlier difference of opinion. Elizabeth was sure Kendrick wasn't a man to harbour a grudge.

As they walked, several of the bikini-clad wannabe starlets who were parading their toned and tanned bodies gave Kendrick interested looks. He seemed oblivious to their unabashed admiration. Elizabeth could have sworn that Kendrick wasn't the type to pass up the opportunity to flirt. On the other hand, he was probably used to female attention.

'Do you have a girlfriend?' Elizabeth asked. The words were out before she could stop them. Great, he was bound to make some smart remark about why she wanted to know.

But to her surprise, instead of the usual flashing smile, a shadow crossed Kendrick's face. 'No,' he said quietly. 'Not any more.'

'Not any more' was an odd way to put it. Why not say 'Not at the moment'?

Once more she had the feeling that there was more to Kendrick than his easygoing exterior.

'Ever been married?'

'No, and not likely to be,' he said.

Elizabeth could have sworn something shifted behind his eyes. She had clearly touched a nerve. Perhaps he wasn't quite as tough as he liked to pretend? She had the distinct impression that there had been someone and the relationship hadn't ended well. But she valued her own privacy too highly not to respect his. If he wanted to tell her, he would. Nevertheless, she was intensely curious. She suspected that despite his playboy exterior Kendrick wasn't a man who gave his heart lightly.

'Are you ready for something to eat?' Kendrick asked.

'Sure. Where do you suggest? There appears to be a million restaurants and cafés.'

'I know just the place. I have a cabin along at Malibu. It's only a little further along the coast. It's quieter. We could pick up a sandwich and something to drink from one of the delis and have it on the beach.'

Elizabeth's heart kicked against her ribs. What was he asking? She was about to refuse when he turned his deep blue eyes on her.

'I need to pick up something from there to give to Josh.'

She hesitated for the briefest moment then gave herself a mental shake. As Kendrick had said, it would only take a few minutes and she found herself intensely curious to see where he lived.

'Lead the way,' she said with a smile.

'So this is where you live?' Elizabeth said, surprised. Whatever else she had expected, it hadn't been this small cabin perched on the edge of the beach. On the other hand, it was exactly where Kendrick would live. He would never do the conventional.

'It belonged to my folks, way back when they got married. Before this part became fashionable. I bought it off them as soon as I was earning money.'

He took Elizabeth by the hand and pulled her up the wooden steps and onto the deck.

'It's so, so…cute. I love it.' The small cabin was painted white with a picket fence and a deck overlooking the beach, which was only a short walk away.

'Cute?' Kendrick pulled a face. 'I don't want to live in a house that anyone calls cute.'

'Doesn't quite go with your image? Then I guess you shouldn't have painted that adorable picket fence. You should have put up a steel fence—all barbed wire and spiky. Would that have been better? More in keeping with the owner?'

Kendrick grinned at her, a deep dimple appearing in each cheek. On any other man this might have made him look feminine. On Kendrick, however, it had the effect of making him look ten times sexier. As if he wasn't sexy enough.

The air between them fizzed. Elizabeth could have sworn every hair on her body was standing up. Maybe it hadn't been a good idea to come here after all.

She must have been staring because he winked at her. She didn't want his swollen head getting any bigger.

'It must be worth a fortune,' she said, simply to say something.

Kendrick pretended to look shocked. 'Didn't think you were the type of woman who cared too much about that kind of stuff. Don't tell me I've got you all wrong, Dr Morgan.'

'Oh, I'm as venial as any other woman.' She grinned back at him. 'I need to be kept in shoes at the very least.'

Damn! That could definitely be construed as flirting, and Kendrick didn't need any encouragement.

'Can I see inside?' she said quietly. She was dying to look for more clues about this man.

'Help yourself, but there's not much to see.'

To an extent he was right. Along one complete wall of the sitting room were a number of surfboards propped up against the wall. On the other side were what seemed like sails for a windsurfer and still more equipment. The absolute minimum amount of space was left for a couple of armchairs that had seen better days and a TV. Clearly Kendrick wasn't home a great deal.

'You surf?' she asked, pointing to the boards.

'Whenever I can. Don't always get the right waves here, though. Sometimes I meet up with my cousin, Fabio, and go in search of the big ones.'

'What else? Windsurfing, by the look of this stuff.' She indicated the other side of the room with a sweep of her hand.

'Kite-surfing. You use a kite as well as a surfboard. It lets you do tricks. I could teach you if you like.'

Elizabeth shook her head. 'Oh, no, you don't. You've already almost got me killed once.'

Kendrick drew his eyebrows together. 'Almost got you killed? When?'

'When you took me out on the horse.'

He threw his head back and laughed. 'Believe me, you were in no real danger.' His expression grew serious. 'I would never let anything happen to you.'

The way he was looking at her was making her bones feel as if they were melting. She gave herself a little shake. She needed to remember Kendrick could no more not flirt than she could, what? Not be a doctor?

But it was as if there was a magnetic field surrounding him that drew her to him and her brain was sending wild thoughts to her heart. In this man's arms she could forget.

He hooked his fingers into the waistband of her jeans and pulled her into him.

She raised her head, meeting his eyes. They were as cool as the sea after the rain, and just as fathomless. Fathomless but she could tell that he wanted her. He looked at her for one long moment as her head continued to spin and she was powerless to stop him. She didn't want to stop him. Although her head was screaming that she should, her body seemed to have developed a mind of its own.

He brought his mouth down on hers. His lips were warm, soft and hard at the same time. His hands grasped her hips and pulled her even closer.

His mouth on hers was like an electric shock. Her body sparked and a liquid warmth spread through her as she moulded her body to his.

His hands were plucking her shirt from the waistband of her jeans, the rough skin of his fingers on her back before his hands moved across her stomach, lightly, gently, feeling her skin, his mouth never leaving hers.

She heard a moan come from somewhere and realised with a shock that it had come from her.

He lifted his head and his eyes glittered down at her.

It was enough. She pulled away, conscious that her breath was coming in little gasps and all too conscious that her body was screaming out to be touched again.

'No, Kendrick. Please. I can't.' She was aware the words were coming out in little, breathless gasps.

'Why not?' he said easily, reaching for her again.

She moved away from him, putting as much distance between them as possible. If she let him touch her again, she'd never be able to tell him to stop. Although she wanted the oblivion being in his arms would bring, it would be temporary. Giving in to him would lead to complications she didn't need.

'I just can't.'

The look he gave her was inscrutable. 'I would never force anyone. One day you'll want me as much as I want you. I can wait for then.'

His arrogance was breathtaking. But, then, hadn't she kissed him back with a passion that she'd never experienced before?

'I wouldn't hold my breath if I were you,' she said. 'Some women can resist you, you know. Women who have a bit of pride. Women like me.'

She made a show of looking at her watch. 'Isn't it time we headed to the hospital?'

The good thing about being behind Kendrick on his Harley-Davidson was that it made conversation impossible. The bad thing was that the feel of his body under her hands was doing nothing to calm her overheated libido. She was relieved when they pulled up outside the hospital and there was some distance between her and Kendrick once again.

Inside her private room, Sunny was sitting up in bed. Despite her pallor, she was clearly on the mend.

'The doctors say if you hadn't spotted that I had malaria when you did, it could have been really serious. Thank you both.'

'I think you have to thank Kendrick,' Elizabeth demurred. 'Without him, it would have taken another day or two for me to arrive at a diagnosis.'

Sunny raised her face to let Kendrick kiss her cheek. 'He's a bit of a dark horse our Kendrick, isn't he?'

Just then two children scampered into the room and Sunny held open her arms as they flung themselves on top of her.

'Hey, sweeties. Did you miss Mummy last night?'

Elizabeth felt a stab of pain so sharp it took her breath away. She would have given her life to be able to hold her daughter like Sunny was holding hers. Trixie was six. What would Charlie have been like had she lived? What would she have been like at six? At eighteen? As a mother? What would the future have held for her child?

It was pointless to torment herself like that. Turning away so no one would see the tears that burned behind her eyelids, she arranged the flowers she had brought in a vase one of the nurses had provided. When she swung around a few minutes later, it was to find Kendrick watching her speculatively. She got the impression that he didn't miss much.

'We should leave you to spend time with your family,' he told Sunny. 'We just wanted to say hello.'

'Thanks for taking the time, guys. But don't worry 'bout me. At least this way I get to spend time with these two,' Sunny said, hugging her children close. 'Although the doctors think I'll be able to come back to work next week, so I'll see you both then. As long as you promise to tell me all about the party the next time I see you.'

They left Sunny cuddling her children. When they were out of hearing range, Kendrick took Elizabeth by the shoulder and gently turned her so that she was facing him.

'What's wrong?' he asked. 'Back there, something upset you. Do you want to tell me what it was?'

Elizabeth forced herself to hold his gaze. 'There's nothing to tell. I'm just glad to see that Sunny is doing okay.'

She could tell that Kendrick didn't believe her. He looked at her intently for a moment but said nothing more.

'I'm fine, really,' she said again. But she wasn't—not really. 'I think I'll take a cab back to the hotel. I'm feeling a little bushed.'

'Forget the cab, I'll take you.'

Elizabeth panicked. She needed time on her own. Away from Kendrick's searching looks. Time to regain her composure. 'I'd much rather take a cab. You don't have to keep watching out for me, you know.' But didn't a small secret part of her like it that he did? It had been a long time since she'd been able to share her problems. She gave herself a mental shake. Her head was all over the place. She had to get away from him.

Kendrick frowned. 'Are you sure you're feeling okay? You don't look that great to me.'

'I promise you I'm fine,' Elizabeth said with as much conviction as she could muster. In some ways the flirting, teasing Kendrick was easier to deal with than the one who looked at her as if he could see into her head. If he was kind to her, she didn't know if she could stop herself from throwing herself into his arms and sharing her pain.

He let her arm drop. 'It's probably not a bad idea to get some rest before tonight.' His teasing smile was back. 'Jack's parties have quite a reputation. They often go on way into the next day.'

Elizabeth forced a smile. 'I'll look forward to it. In the meantime, I'm sure you have things you'd like to be getting on with.'

As soon as the cab dropped her outside her hotel, she hurried up to her room. Inside she leaned against the door, and the tears she'd been holding back came in deep painful sobs. Just when she had thought she was coping, something would happen: the simple sight of a mother holding her two healthy children had brought her carefully held-together veneer crashing down. Back there at the hospital, she'd been shocked at the raw jealousy she'd felt when she'd seen Sunny with her two children. She slid to the floor and buried her face in her hands.

'Oh, Charlie. When is it going to stop hurting like this?'

By the time the tears had stopped, night had fallen. She hadn't cried like that since Charlie's funeral and in an odd way it felt good. A quick glance at her watch told her that she had half an hour to get ready for the party.

Jack had insisted on sending a driver and limousine to pick her up at the hotel. She hadn't thought to pack a party dress, so black jeans, a glitzy belt and a silk blouse would have to do. After her shower, Elizabeth sat down at the dressing table, putting on her make-up. When was the last time she'd done this? It was hard to remember.

Her thoughts returned to the kiss she'd shared with Kendrick. She couldn't remember ever being kissed like that. The touch of his lips on hers had turned her into a quivering wreck. And that had just been a kiss. What would it be like to be loved by him? She shook her head. It was crazy to let her thoughts go in that direction. Hadn't she told herself over and over that getting involved with Kendrick wasn't an option? Given the state her heart was in, it was far too dangerous. But back then when he'd kissed her, the world had stopped and the darkness in her soul had disappeared. It had only lasted while she'd been in his arms, but she had to admit it had felt good to forget, if only for a little while.

Clipping on gold earrings, she surveyed her image with a critical eye. The hot Californian sun had dusted her skin with a light tan and highlighted her hair. At least she looked healthier than the washed-out, exhausted shadow of a woman of a couple of weeks ago. She looked like a woman who could be happy. The thought brought her up short. Slowly she unclipped her earrings and dropped them back onto her dressing table. Apart from having to face Kendrick, did she really want to spend the night talking to complete strangers? Maybe another time, but tonight at least she was better on her own. When Jack's driver came for her, she would tell him she'd changed her mind.

* * *

Kendrick tossed the keys of his motorbike to a waiting valet. Set high up in Beverly Hills, the driveway of Jack's multi-million-dollar mansion was lined with sports cars. Kendrick scooped a glass of champagne from the tray of a passing waiter before heading into the house. The party must have started some time ago as it was in full swing. He scanned the crowd, searching for Lizzie, but she wasn't to be seen amongst the guests.

Nodding greetings to actors he knew, Kendrick weaved his way onto the wide veranda that circled the house. Models with barely-there bikinis and young men who looked as if they spent every minute in the gym posed around the infinity pool, hoping to be spotted by Philip or one of the other directors who would be at the party.

Kendrick was looking forward to seeing what Elizabeth would make of all this. He had the feeling she wouldn't be fazed in the slightest and would have some amusing comments to make.

Despite the fact she'd pulled away earlier at the cabin, he was making progress. No woman would kiss a man like she had if she didn't feel something. She was definitely thawing.

But the memory of her face back at the hospital kind of spoilt the satisfaction he was feeling. For once she'd let down her guard and he'd recognised something in her eyes that had shocked him. He'd seen that look staring back at him in the mirror after Amy had died.

Deep in thought, he wasn't aware of someone coming to stand behind him until two slender arms slid around his waist.

'Aren't you gonna ask me to dance, Kendrick?' He was dismayed at the thudding disappointment he felt when he realised the voice didn't belong to Elizabeth. He unwrapped the arms from around his waist and turned towards the heavily made-up woman standing behind him. He would take Elizabeth's natural beauty any time.

'Hello…' What was her name again? Fiffy? Foofy? Something that sounded like a poodle's name at any rate.

'It's Fiffy. Don't tell me you've forgotten me already?' Fiffy pouted, trailing a manicured nail down the open neck of his shirt.

Something had upset Elizabeth back at the hospital. What was up with her?

'We could have a swim. Or a dance.' Fiffy entwined his arm in hers. 'Or we could go to your place.' Fiffy's plaintive voice brought him back to the present.

How did Fiffy know about his cabin? He made it a rule not to take anyone there. Until Elizabeth, that was.

A month ago, he would have taken up the invitation in Fiffy's eyes like a shot, but that had been before…before his head had become filled with thoughts of Elizabeth Morgan.

'Fiffy,' he said quietly, 'I can't get you a part in a movie. I've explained that before. And I mean it.'

Fiffy's eyes flashed with annoyance and Kendrick sighed. No matter how beautiful and desirable the woman, anything less than honest, mutually satisfying sex wasn't for him. He had always been completely upfront about that. These parties were losing their appeal. Maybe he had been to too many of them.

Kendrick grabbed Jack as he passed. 'Have you seen Lizzie?'

'She's not coming,' Jack said. 'Something about a headache.'

Kendrick turned back to the starlet. 'Fiffy, I really have to go. I'm happy to put a word in with Philip for you.' Without waiting for a reply, he walked away. He needed to find Lizzie and check that she was okay.

* * *

Elizabeth knew she'd made the right decision not to go to the party. It wasn't as if she would be missed. Seeing Sunny's kids today had shaken her to the core. There was no way she would have been up to making small talk.

She was interrupted from her musing by the roar of a motorbike and a part of her was unsurprised to see Kendrick pulling up outside. Instinctively she wrapped her arms around her body. She was only wearing pyjama bottoms and a T-shirt as she'd planned to go to bed soon.

'Kendrick!' She stood up and leaned over her first-floor balcony. 'What are you doing here? Is anything wrong? Does someone need me?'

'No, everything's fine. I came to see if *you* were okay.'

'Okay with me? Why shouldn't it be?'

'Look, Lizzie. Can I come up? I'm beginning to feel like Romeo to your Juliet down here.'

Elizabeth laughed, and some of the sadness lifted from her heart.

Truth was, she was glad to see him. She'd had enough of her own thoughts.

'I'll open the door for you.'

But before she had a chance, Kendrick had jumped onto the side railings of the veranda below and with a leap that belied his size grabbed her railings and swung himself onto her balcony.

'Can't you use the door like everyone else?' She smiled.

Kendrick shook his head. 'Nope. Not while there's an opportunity to impress a lady. You were impressed, weren't you?' he asked in mock dismay.

Elizabeth had to laugh. It felt good. And it felt even better that Kendrick was there.

She caught his eye and her breath froze in her throat.

Every instinct in Kendrick's body was telling him that he should leave this woman well alone, but yet he couldn't pull away from her. His heart was pounding as she looked up at him with luminous eyes.

He placed his hands on either side of her neck, letting his thumbs rest just under her jaw. Very gently he raised her face until her mouth was inches from his. Her eyes were dreamy, half-closed, but he could see in the dilation of her pupils that she wanted him too. And that was all it took.

He bent his head and found her mouth, tasting the sweetness and running his tongue over the softness of her lips. Taking his time, he explored her mouth with his tongue, increasing the pressure until she gasped and began kissing him back with a hunger that surprised but delighted him. Her body was pressed into his, and he dropped his hands to her hips to pull her closer. The last coherent thought he had as they tumbled onto her bed was that she wasn't an ice maiden after all.

Elizabeth lay with her head on Kendrick's chest, listening to the beat of his heart. Judging by the matching slow, steady rhythm of his breathing he had fallen asleep. Why did men always do that after making love? She, on the other hand, could have jumped out of bed, and…whatever. Not that she wanted to leave Kendrick's arms. It felt too good. Even while she knew it was a mistake.

But had it been? Kendrick wasn't Simon. And if he didn't want a relationship, neither did she. She was here for another month and after that who knew? She and Kendrick would go their separate ways. Why shouldn't she find some peace in this man's arms, if only for a little while? It wasn't as if she was planning to fall in love with him.

But haven't you already? a voice inside her whispered. *Even just a little bit?*

The voice was wrong. Dead wrong. She was attracted to Kendrick—sure. She found him unbelievably sexy, but part of what attracted her was the firm knowledge that whatever there was between them wasn't meant to last.

She traced the bullet hole on his shoulder with a fingertip and let her hand trail over the defined muscles of his chest, before trailing her hand down to where she could feel every muscle of his hard abdomen.

He groaned as she moved her hand lower still, exploring the ridges and contours of his body.

Suddenly he flipped her on her back and was staring down at her with glinting blue eyes.

He raised her hands above her head and pinned them there with one of his own.

'Do you trust me?' he asked huskily.

Her mouth was too dry to speak so she simply nodded.

'Then I want you to lie there and not move. Not a muscle. I want to kiss every inch of you slowly and watch your face while I do that.'

As he kissed her throat behind her ears, his lips moving slowly, inexorably downwards, her heart was thumping so hard against her ribs she thought it might just stop.

His mouth was on her breasts, taking each nipple in his mouth by turn, and she arched her back, wanting him. He stopped what he was doing for a second and looked at her, his eyes triumphant. 'You think that feels good? I haven't even started yet.'

Later, dressed once more—if you could call it that—in panties and her T-shirt, she sat between his long jeans-clad legs and leaned against his bare chest, nibbling on the cold lobster he had brought with him from the party. She had grabbed a blanket from the bed and laid it on the wooden balcony. He wrapped his arms about her, keeping her close. The night was warm, with just the merest hint of a breeze, and the sky was studded with stars.

The crickets chirped in the distance and somewhere an owl hooted.

'I never thought I'd end up in bed with you,' she said.

'I knew we would,' he replied.

'Sure of yourself, aren't you?' She knew she should have been angry or offended or something, but she wasn't. She liked his honesty. She couldn't have borne it if he'd lied to her. All she wanted from him was this simple, direct and honest need for each other.

As daylight seeped through the window of her hotel, Elizabeth slipped out of bed and pulled her oversized T-shirt over her head. Kendrick was still sleeping. He slept as he did everything—with utter abandon. He lay on his back with his arms flung over his head and the sheet tangled between his thighs. Thinking about his thighs made the heat rise in Elizabeth's face. Their love-making had been everything it had never been with Simon. Passionate, caring and adventurous. Was she doing the right thing, getting involved with Kendrick? If she hadn't needed to be comforted, would she have slept with him? But it hadn't been just comfort, she had to admit. In his arms she had felt alive for the first time since Charlie had died.

Kendrick stirred in his sleep and frowned. Could it be that his dreams were as haunted as hers? Elizabeth realised with a jolt that last night, wrapped in his arms, had been the first time she hadn't dreamt of Charlie. Although she would never see Kendrick once she had left here, he was helping her to heal inside and she couldn't regret that.

His eyes flickered and immediately he was alert.

He sat up in bed and grinned at her. 'Hey,' he said softly, reaching an arm towards her, 'why don't you come over here?'

Elizabeth wrapped her arms around her body.

'What is this, Kendrick?'

He tossed the tangled sheets aside and came to stand in front of her. His nakedness was doing all sorts of crazy things to her insides.

'It's what we want it to be. Two people enjoying being with each other.'

'Because you have to know I'll never get married again,' she blurted, then felt such an idiot. No one had mentioned marriage. She didn't even know if they had a future beyond last night.

'Who said anything about getting married?' The air seemed to cool between them. 'I was being honest when I said that marriage wasn't on the cards. If I misled you, I'm sorry.'

'I know you did and I know you meant it, but so do I. I don't even think this was a good idea.' She swept out her arm, taking in the crumpled bedclothes.

The corners of his eyes creased. With his tousled hair and the heat in his eyes he had never seemed so sexy or so dangerous. 'I think it's a very good idea. You said last night you didn't want to think about the past or the future, and neither do I. Why don't we see what each day brings? No promises on either side. It seems to me as if you need some lightness in your life and, for the record, so do I.' He pulled her closer and his hands were on her hips underneath her T-shirt. As he ran his hands across her bottom and up across the small of her back she melted into him.

CHAPTER SIX

ELIZABETH clutched Kendrick's waist as if her life depended on it, and maybe it did. Who did he think he was now? Not that it mattered, she thought, suppressing a scream as they tore around another corner, the bike leaning so far it was almost caressing the tarmac.

She yelped as they passed between two cars. Kendrick was so carefree and full of life it was liberating.

The realisation hit her like a ton of bricks. Since Charlie had died, hadn't a part of her longed to be with her daughter? Wasn't that why she'd run, taking this job, knowing if she stayed a moment longer in the home that reminded her of Charlie she would drown in her grief? Now she knew without a shadow of doubt that she wanted to live. Even if the future still seemed bleak.

They were behind a bus now. It was probably heading towards Palm Desert, as they were. Elizabeth was about to yell in Kendrick's ear that he should slow down when all of a sudden there was an almighty bang and the coach weaved from side to side.

Kendrick braked sharply and only managed to miss the out-of-control bus by a whisker.

As he brought the bike to a halt at the roadside, the sound of screeching metal increased until the air was filled with it. Horrified, Elizabeth watched as almost in slow motion the bus tipped onto its side. For a second she thought it was going to right itself, but it was too late. The weight of the bus was already too much on the left and it was sliding on its side along the tarmac. Kendrick and Elizabeth were so close they could hear the screams from inside the bus.

There was a moment of shocked, eerie silence then she and Kendrick were off the bike and running towards the bus.

Kendrick was punching numbers into his phone as he ran.

'I've alerted the emergency services,' he called as he caught up with her. 'I've told them to send fire engines as well as Ambulances.

Elizabeth's heart was pounding so loud she could hardly hear him.

'We're going to have to triage them,' she said. 'Can you help me?'

'Don't worry,' he said grimly. 'I've done this before.'

Already some of the passengers were climbing from the wreckage, looking dazed.

'Please, sit down over there.' Elizabeth pointed to the roadside. 'Keep away from the road itself, and wait until either I or the emergency services gets to you.'

She was about to clamber through one of the open emergency windows when she felt a hand on her arm.

'I'll go first,' Kendrick said.

She shook his arm away. 'Kendrick. I'm the doctor. Those people inside need me.'

But he had already slipped past her and was disappearing inside the bus. Elizabeth followed.

It was difficult to see what was going on inside. The bus being on its side had tossed everyone sitting on the right over to the left and there was no way to tell how many injured lay under the mass of bodies.

Kendrick was systematically picking his way through the

wreckage, stopping at each passenger and giving them a brief once-over, pointing those who could walk to the safety of the emergency exit. As he moved through the coach several more people struggled to their feet and Elizabeth helped them out.

'Lizzie. Over here!' Kendrick called her over.

She squeezed her way past the exiting passengers until she was next to him. He was bent over an elderly lady who was clutching her chest, clearly in shock.

Elizabeth felt for a pulse. It was more rapid than normal, but that was only to be expected, given the circumstances. As far as she could tell, the woman was in no immediate danger.

'My Bill,' the elderly woman gasped. 'Where is my Bill? He was sitting next to me.'

A glance at Kendrick told her he was thinking the same thing. Bill was very likely trapped underneath the twisted metal.

'What's your name, honey?' Kendrick asked.

'Martha. But please.' She clutched Kendrick's shirt. 'You have to find my Bill.'

'Take it easy, ma'am,' Kendrick said gently. 'I'll find him, don't you worry. But first we're going to have to get you out of here. Do you think you can stand for me?'

While Kendrick was seeing to Martha, Elizabeth clambered back towards the front. She had to check the driver, although she doubted he would have stood a chance. And she was right. The driver was staring upwards, his neck at an unnatural angle, his unseeing eyes staring into space. Elizabeth leaned over him and gently closed his eyes before turning back to the rear of the bus. With most if not all the walking wounded having made their way out of the bus, only now would they be able to determine whether anyone was trapped and hurt—or, God help them, dead.

Kendrick squeezed past her, supporting Martha. As he

passed he shook his head. Either Bill was dead or he couldn't find him.

Elizabeth stepped over the wreckage, stopping every foot or so to lift a piece of metal. She could hear Martha's cries for her husband coming from outside and Kendrick's voice, low and reassuring. If Bill was in here, she had to find him.

And then she saw it. A foot sticking out from beneath tangled metal that must have been a seat at one time. Dropping to her knees, she called out to Kendrick, frantically trying to lift the twisted bits of steel. God, could anyone have survived underneath this?

She was almost crying with frustration when she felt Kendrick beside her. She was lifted and set aside.

'Let me,' Kendrick said. 'I'm stronger.'

Within a few minutes Kendrick had exposed Bill's head. Although there was a deep gash in the old man's forehead and he was deathly pale, he was still alive. She had to get better access to him. Suddenly she became aware of smoke and raised her head. Flames were licking at the back of the bus.

'Elizabeth, you need to get out of here. If the fire takes hold, the bus could explode.' Kendrick's voice was calm.

'I'm not going anywhere,' Elizabeth said. 'Not until Bill's okay.'

Kendrick held her stare and she saw something flash in his eyes. Incongruously he grinned. 'Then we'd better get Bill stabilised and hope that the fire service gets here soon.'

As Kendrick continued to pull the remains of the seat away, more and more of Bill came into view. Elizabeth felt along his legs and up across his torso. As far as she could tell, nothing was broken. That was good. But she couldn't tell how badly he'd injured his head or whether he'd hurt his neck. If they attempted to move him without supporting his neck, they could paralyse him. Damn. If she'd been driving her own car, she would have had a neck brace. It was no use thinking like that. She had nothing. Only her hands…and Kendrick.

Kendrick was removing his shirt and twisting it into a snake-like scarf. Immediately Elizabeth guessed what he was doing. As a makeshift neck brace, it wasn't prefect, but it could make the difference.

The flames were higher now and the interior of the bus was filling with smoke. If they didn't get Bill out, he could die from smoke inhalation. They all could. If fire didn't get them first.

'It's okay, Lizzie,' Kendrick said quietly. 'The bus runs on diesel. It's less likely to explode. But we should get out soon.'

She was easing the makeshift neck brace under Bill's neck.

'You go. I'll carry Bill.'

'It'll be safer if we lift him between the two of us.'

Kendrick looked as if he was about to protest, but he nodded as if he knew he'd be wasting time arguing with her. Crouching, he manoeuvred himself into the space behind Bill and placed his hands under his arms. When Kendrick gave her a sign to let her know they were ready, she took hold of Bill's legs and together they lifted the injured man. Inch by inch, aware that the flames were getting closer, they made their way along the bus to the open emergency exit.

Just as they were reaching the exit, the sound of sirens filled the air. Elizabeth's legs almost buckled with relief. Getting their patient out of the bus was a far trickier procedure than lifting him along the narrow corridor of the bus. They could wait here for the rescue team to arrive. There was enough fresh air for them to breathe and in the meantime she could monitor Bill's breathing.

Catching Kendrick's eyes, she knew he was thinking the

same thing. He was in a more precarious position than she was. His escape route was blocked by Bill and her.

'I'm okay,' he said. 'Just do what you have to. They'll get us out in no time.'

Kendrick and Elizabeth watched as the last of the walking wounded were lifted into ambulances and taken to hospital to be checked over. The fire service trucks and police would remain at the accident scene until the bus had been towed away and the crash scene returned to normal. She looked down at her gold blouse, noting it was covered in blood from Bill's head wound.

As the adrenaline seeped away, Elizabeth started to shake.

Kendrick picked up his leather jacket from the ground and placed it over her shoulders.

'Are you okay?' he asked.

'I'm glad you were with me,' Elizabeth said. 'I don't know how I would have managed if you hadn't been here.' And it was true. Kendrick had been calm and methodical, as if he were used to dealing with multiple casualties every day.

'You would have coped.' He looked at her with admiration in his eyes. 'Bill owes his life to you.'

A silence stretched between them as their eyes locked. Why couldn't Simon have been more like this man? She couldn't imagine Kendrick deserting his wife and child when the going got tough. Despite his casual, laid-back manner there was something solid and dependable about Kendrick and despite the alarm bells going off in her head she remembered what it felt to be held in this man's arms. Safe, secure, but also dangerous. And dangerous was the part she had to remember. She shouldn't confuse his ability to cope in an emergency with dependability. She had no reason to think Kendrick was any different to Simon. But at least Kendrick wasn't making any promises.

'Come on, then,' Kendrick said, 'There's nothing more we can do here.'

As if he knew she had had enough excitement for one day, the journey back to the film set was taken at a much gentler speed. Tiredness washed over her and she leaned herself against his back, savouring the solid feel of him.

'I'm going to shower,' Kendrick said when they arrived back at the set, deserted except for the security personnel who waved in with a nod and a smile of recognition. 'I suggest you do the same. Then I'll rustle us up something to eat.'

Elizabeth shook her head. 'I'm not hungry.' But then, as another wave of tiredness and dizziness washed over her, she swayed.

'Hey, hey, hey,' Kendrick said, and before she knew it she was being swept up into his arms.

She wriggled, but it was no use. Kendrick held her too firmly.

He kicked open the door of her trailer with his boot and pushed his way inside. He placed her gently on her sofa and turned towards her bathroom.

'Take off your clothes,' he said, 'while I turn on the shower. Then you're going to get into bed while I organise us some food. You should have something.'

'I'm okay,' Elizabeth mumbled, too tired to protest. 'Perfectly able to get myself showered. I might have a little nap first.'

Reaching behind the bathroom door, he found her robe and tossed it to her.

'If you don't remove those clothes, I'll do it for you.'

The tone of his voice left her in no doubt he meant what he said. She struggled to her feet and picked up the robe.

'Okay, okay. Are you always this much of a bully?' But it felt good. Somebody else was making decisions. Someone was looking after her for a change. She swallowed the lump that rose in her throat. How long had it been?

When Kendrick left, she stepped into the shower and let the warm water wash over her. Her clothes were ruined, but she didn't care. At least she had been able to save a life today. There would be a family who wouldn't have to go through what she'd been through, and despite her exhaustion that felt good.

After her shower, she wrapped her hair in a towel turban style and slipped her robe back on. Kendrick would be back with food soon and she should really get dressed. But she had no energy to do that. All she wanted right now was to sleep. She prayed that for once it would be dreamless.

She pulled the over-large T-shirt she used as a nightie over her head and slipped into bed, pulling the sheets up to her chin. Surely not even Kendrick could mistake her actions for anything more than a desperate, overwhelming urge for rest? She closed her eyes, just for a moment. She would hear him return and then she'd persuade him that she was perfectly all right and just needed to be left alone.

Kendrick stood, tray in hand, looking down at Elizabeth. In sleep she looked younger, more vulnerable. Something shifted in his chest. He had started out wanting to sleep with her, but now? Now he wanted more. He found himself wanting to know more about her. And that hadn't happened for a long, long time.

She was beautiful but she didn't even seem to notice. He placed the tray on the floor and sat on the edge of the bed. Were those dried tears he saw on her cheeks? It surprised him. Until last night he would have said she was incapable of much emotion, she was so much the ice maiden. Yesterday at the hospital he'd seen a wave of sadness cross her face. But she had dealt with the bus crash calmly and efficiently. This was a woman he'd want around if ever he got into trouble in one of his stunts. Come to think of it, this was a woman he wanted around, period.

The thought took him by surprise. He was treading on dangerous ground, letting Elizabeth get under his skin.

He was about to creep away when she whispered, 'No!' For one crazy moment he thought she knew he was there and was begging him not to go, but she cried out the word again and fresh tears leaked from her eyes.

Then she was crying in earnest. Deep, racking sobs that shook her body. Instinctively he pulled her into his arms.

'Shh,' he whispered. 'Wake up, Lizzie. You're having a bad dream.'

Her eyes snapped open and what he saw there made him suck in a breath. He had never seen such naked pain before and it did something to his insides.

'Charlie,' she said urgently. 'I want Charlie.'

'Who is Charlie?' he asked.

The confusion in her eyes cleared and he saw that she had woken up from whatever dark place she'd been. Who was this Charlie?

'Kendrick?' She struggled to sit up, brushing the tears away from her cheeks with a trembling hand. 'What…what time is it?'

'It's seven,' he said. 'I brought you some food. I think you should eat something.'

She smiled wanly. 'A true knight in shining armour. Maybe I could just have a coffee.'

He stood back to let her get out of bed. She was wearing a too-big T-shirt that slipped off her shoulder, revealing an exquisite glimpse of the swell of her breasts. The T-shirt skimmed the tops of her thighs. He swallowed a groan. God, he wanted her. Had she not just a few moments ago been held in the grip of a nightmare he wouldn't have been able to stop himself from kissing her. But then she reached out for him and he was lost.

'Who is Charlie?' Kendrick asked much later. At his words she felt herself stiffen.

'Why do you ask?' She was sure she hadn't mentioned Charlie to him.

'You were dreaming when I brought you the food. You were crying and you said his name. Was he your ex-husband?'

Her blood chilled. She didn't want her past to have anything to do with this…whatever it was. If she told him about Charlie, it would change things. She wanted this to stay simple.

'No. Someone else.' *Forgive me, Charlie. I never thought I'd deny you.*

She turned around in his arms until she was facing him. 'I don't want to talk about Charlie,' she said. 'For whatever time we are together I want to pretend there is no past and not try to pretend there is a future. I want to live for the here and now. Can you accept that?'

His smile widened. 'Hey, that's usually my line.'

She leaned towards him, caught his bottom lip between her teeth and bit it gently. As his arms tightened about her she felt a flicker of triumph. It was her turn to make him crazy.

When Elizabeth woke again, the sun was shining through the curtains of her trailer and she was alone. Some time during the early hours of the morning she'd been aware of Kendrick kissing her and saying softly that he was going back to his trailer before the others arrived back.

She lifted her arms behind her head and stretched languorously. Then she glanced at the clock. Nine o'clock! She hadn't slept that late for years!

Leaping out of bed, she hurried to the shower. Although there wouldn't be any filming today, it was possible one or more of the cast might have returned early and come looking for her. Finding their doctor in bed was not the image she wanted to engender.

As she lathered herself she thought back to the last couple of nights. The truth was it was difficult to think of anything but Kendrick. She sighed. Had she made a mistake, sleeping with him? It hadn't been planned but the need for comfort, the need to be held, the need to forget about her pain had been too strong. But that didn't explain the other times they had made love. She blushed at the memory. That had been pure lust.

By the time she emerged from her trailer she was feeling distinctly panicky. How would Kendrick behave towards her? Would he act as if nothing had happened? Would he ignore her—heaven forbid—or would he try to pick up where they'd left off? And what did she want? Damn. She felt like a girl with her first crush.

Kendrick looked up from his coffee as she entered the mess tent. He was chatting to Josh.

Her heart beating wildly, Elizabeth knew she had no option but to join them. She just wished she didn't feel like a school-girl on her first date.

'Morning, Lizzie,' Kendrick greeted her, his eyes dancing. 'Did you sleep well?'

'Very well,' Elizabeth responded primly, hoping her face wasn't as red as it felt. 'Do you mind if I join you?' Now she knew she sounded as if she were at some tea party. The gleam in Kendrick's eye told her he was enjoying her discomfort.

'Of course.' Kendrick made space for her to sit next to him. 'We're just discussing one of our gags.'

'Gag?' Elizabeth was confused.

'It's what we stuntmen call the stuff we do.'

Suspecting she wouldn't like the answer, Elizabeth thought it best if she didn't ask why.

'So what is it?' she asked, taking a fork full of her scrambled egg.

'It involves a car crash and a hot burn,' Kendrick said, with a glance at Josh.

'A hot burn?' She was liking this conversation less and less.

'It's where I have to look as if I'm on fire,' Kendrick said. 'But don't worry,' he added hastily. 'We know what we're doing. We've done it before. We make sure there are folk around with fire extinguishers and I'll have stuff on that keeps the flames from burning.'

'As long as they get to you in two minutes,' Josh said darkly.

'They will,' Kendrick said.

It did nothing to allay Elizabeth's fears. It sounded as if there was a great deal that could go wrong. It was one thing watching Kendrick doing his stunts when she wasn't…what? Involved? Sleeping with him? Crazy about him? The thought stopped her breath. She wasn't crazy about him. She liked him. He was good for her at a time in her life when she wanted to pretend that she was someone else. That was all.

But the way he was looking at her and the way her heart responded—kicking against her ribs—made her wonder if that was true.

Confused, she realised she'd lost her appetite and pushed her plate away, reaching for her coffee instead.

'Are the others back yet?' she asked. She didn't want to think those thoughts.

'Some of them. The rest won't return until after lunch. In the meantime, Josh and I are going to go over the gags we'll be doing tomorrow.' He leaned back in his chair, looking like a man who was satisfied with life and no wonder.

'I'll make sure I'm around.' Elizabeth picked up her tray. 'What time?'

'Straight after we're finished here. We work it out on paper first then we build the stunt up bit by bit. You can stay and listen to how we do it, if you like.'

But Elizabeth was already on her feet. She wanted to get away from Kendrick and his searching looks so she could compose herself.

'I won't if you don't mind. I'm going to go to the medical trailer and see if anyone's looking for me. I also need to check my supplies.' She knew she was over-explaining but she didn't want him to know how much being near him was flustering her. She was beginning to think that not feeling was better than this acute anxiety coiling in the pit of her stomach.

Across on the other side of the set she was surprised to find Jack leaning against the door of the trailer. He was alone, which in itself was unusual. Every other time Elizabeth had seen him he had been followed by an entourage of assistants, make-up artists, stylists and who knew what else. They all shared one thing in common. Simpering adulation of the great man. Personally Elizabeth didn't get it. He might be rich, successful and good-looking—although not in the masculine way Kendrick was—and a film star, but he was arrogant and disinterested in anyone else to the point of rudeness sometimes. She wondered what had brought him to seek her out.

'Jack, what can I do for you?' Elizabeth asked, unlocking the door of her trailer.

For the first time he looked unsure of himself. He kicked a pebble away with the toe of one of his expensive shoes.

'Why don't you come in out of the heat?' she continued as Jack still didn't say anything.

'We missed you the other night,' Jack said eventually,

flashing her the famous grin she had seen on the large screen many times before.

'I'm sorry. It sounded like a great night,' Elizabeth replied.

'I heard there was some sort of accident on the road up here last night and that you and Kendrick helped out. Is that right?'

Elizabeth nodded to a chair. 'Please, make yourself comfortable.' She was pretty sure he hadn't come to talk about the accident. 'Yes. It was a shock. Thankfully everyone we rescued is going to be all right. It was lucky Kendrick was there to help.'

'Ah, Kendrick. Our very own real-life hero.' Elizabeth didn't like the way he said it. He couldn't envy Kendrick, could he? She hid a smile. It was quite possible Jack didn't like the competition. He had made his money pretending to be a hero, whereas Kendrick really was one.

'Is it Kendrick you came to talk to me about?' she asked coolly. 'Or was there something else on your mind?'

Suddenly Jack paled. Elizabeth only just had enough time to grab a sick bowl before he doubled up and vomited violently.

She held his shoulders as he heaved. This was why he was alone. He'd hardly want anyone to see him like this.

Eventually, after Jack had stopped being sick and had wiped himself down with the cool cloth Elizabeth passed him, he sank back into the chair looking distraught.

'How long have you been feeling like this? Any other symptoms?' Elizabeth asked.

Jack nodded. 'I've been feeling this way for the last couple of hours. I must have been sick at least four times. Am I having a heart attack or something? I sure feel like hell.'

'I doubt you're having a heart attack. Far more likely it's something you ate. Perhaps in the last few days?' If so, it was unlikely Jack would be the only victim. 'Can you remember what you ate?'

'Lobster, oysters, salad, the beef, other things. A bit of salad.'

She had nibbled the lobster Kendrick had brought from the party. Come to think of it, her stomach was feeling decidedly queasy. Great. A set full of ill people and if she was right, only a sick doctor to look after them.

'I'm going to help you back to your trailer and make sure you're comfortable. If you don't stop being sick in a couple of hours I'll give you an anti-emetic to help, although if it is food poisoning it's best to let your system get rid of any toxins. I want you to take sips of water. If you can't keep that down, I'll give you some electrolyte fluid. Do you know if anyone else is having symptoms?'

She helped Jack to his feet. All his earlier bravado had disappeared. Now he was just another sick patient feeling understandably sorry for himself.

'I don't know. I haven't seen anyone else since I arrived back this morning. I sent my assistant away. I didn't want her around to see me being sick.'

As soon as she'd settled Jack she would go and check up on everyone else. It was possible others had been afflicted and were too ill to leave their trailers.

And she was right. There were at least four others in the same boat as Jack and no doubt others had yet to become ill. She phoned public health to let them know that there was an outbreak of food poisoning but as it had been most certainly from the food at a private party there was nothing they needed to do except be aware if any other family doctors phoned in to let them know about patients. Everyone who was ill had eaten the lobster and Elizabeth knew it was likely she would get ill herself. In the meantime, she needed to make sure that Philip was aware of what was going on.

As she crossed the camp to find the director, she passed Kendrick and Josh, who were practising some complicated-looking somersault on a trampoline, presumably to perfect it before shooting a stunt.

She walked over to them and waited until they had finished. Kendrick noticed her and came across straight away. 'We don't need you on standby just yet,' he said. 'I'll let you know when we start practising it in earnest.'

'Make sure you do. But that's not why I'm here. Did either of you have lobster at the party?'

Kendrick shook his head. 'Can't stand them. Taste of the sea and salt, that's all.'

'What about you, Josh?'

'Don't care much for them either. Give me a good steak any day.'

'Why are you wanting to know?' Kendrick asked. 'Don't tell me they were off?' He broke into a wide grin. 'I can't imagine Jack being best pleased about that. He likes to think he throws the best parties, not ones that make his guests sick.'

'It was probably just a bad one. But if you two are okay, I need to get on.' A spasm of pain sliced through her abdomen and she pressed her stomach with a hand. Perhaps she should give herself an anti-emetic? That might keep the symptoms at bay long enough for her to make sure everyone else was okay.

'Are you all right? Here, come and sit down.' Kendrick placed an arm around her shoulders and made to lead her away. Elizabeth shook her head and tried to push him away.

'You had the lobster too.' He was no longer smiling.

'I'll be okay.'

But before she could protest Kendrick swept her up in his arms and was striding across to her trailer.

'Will you put me down?' Elizabeth snarled, mortified. 'I

have to see to my patients.' She could barely speak. Nausea was rising and her stomach was churning. Please, God, don't let me be sick. Not now, all over Kendrick and in front of everyone.

Kendrick kicked open the door of her trailer and placed her on her sofa.

'Okay. You stay here. Tell me what you want me to do.'

'Go and see who is ill and make sure that someone is looking after them.' As the nausea rose in her throat she pushed him towards the door. 'Go!'

Later that evening, when Elizabeth was beginning to feel a little more human and contemplating a shower, there was a knock on her door.

Without a shower, she wasn't in a fit state to see anyone. Her hair was matted, her make-up smudged and she had discarded her clothes on the floor and curled up in bed wearing only her bra and panties.

Before she had a chance to tell whoever it was to go away, the door opened and Kendrick strode in uninvited. She should've guessed. Even if she'd barred her doors and windows the man would probably still have found a way in. She wouldn't even put it past him to remove a door from its hinges if it got in his way.

'Go away, Kendrick,' she groaned, hiding her head under the blanket. 'I'm not human enough to have visitors. So unless you're here to tell me that someone needs my urgent medical attention, just go away—please.'

'I brought you some fruit juice,' he said. 'And I thought I should tell you there are about ten of you who are suffering from eating lobsters. I've coerced those of the cast who are okay into keeping an eye on the rest. Holding sick bowls isn't really my—er—thing. At least you don't have to worry about the others.'

There was silence for a moment and she wondered whether he had left. She peered over the top of the sheet and her heart stopped. He had picked up the photograph of Charlie she had left on the bedside table and was scrutinising it.

'Who is this?' he asked softly. Elizabeth had to resist the impulse to snatch the photo from his hand. Usually she left it in her drawer for exactly this reason. She didn't want un-expected visitors to her trailer asking questions she wasn't ready to answer. But she had taken it into bed with her when she'd been feeling so dreadful and at some point during the day had placed it back on the table next to her.

'It's my daughter. Charlie.'

'So this is Charlie. What happened to her, Lizzie?'

She held out her hand for the photograph and when Kendrick passed it back she traced Charlie's sweet face with the tip of her finger. She could hardly force the words past her closed throat.

'She died,' she said simply.

'Lizzie, I'm so sorry.' Kendrick sat down on the bed and pulled her towards him so that she was nestled against his chest. 'You don't have to tell me if you don't want to.'

But she did.

'She was born with Gauther's disease. It's a life-limiting illness. I knew almost from the start that she wasn't going to be with me very long.'

Kendrick said nothing but she felt his arms tighten around her.

'I gave up work to look after her. She needed full-time care and I wanted to do it myself. I wanted to spend every second of her life with her.' Her voice faltered and she sniffed loudly. 'She died three months ago. She was only eighteen months old. Kendrick, no mother should outlive her child. That's why I'll never have any more. I couldn't bear to go through that again.'

'What about her father? You said you were married?'

Elizabeth sighed. 'Simon? He couldn't take it that he had a child with disabilities. It was as if it was a slur on his manhood. Can you believe he wanted me to give her up for adoption? He said that way we could try for another. As if Charlie was a toy that could be thrown away just because she didn't live up to his expectations.' Anger pooled in her chest at the memory. 'I thought that Simon would come to accept Charlie, given some time, but he didn't. When I wouldn't hand Charlie over to foster-carers, he left.'

'He left you and Charlie alone?' Kendrick's voice was threaded with steel.

'We coped. You know, the next time I saw Simon was at Charlie's funeral.'

She shook her head. 'I could have forgiven him for leaving if only he'd kept in touch with Charlie. But once he walked out of the door, it was as if she—we—no longer existed for him.'

She managed a shaky breath. 'So you can see I'm serious about never marrying again. I'd rather be on my own than go through that again. It's simpler.'

'Not all men are like your ex-husband,' Kendrick said, but there was something in his voice that made Elizabeth's blood chill. He sounded distant, unlike the man she had shared her bed with.

He stood. 'I'd better get going.'

He looked down at her. There was a wariness in his expression that hadn't been there before. 'I'll come and check on you later.'

As Elizabeth had expected, the food poisoning took around twenty-four hours before everyone was over the worst, herself included. Kendrick kept popping in through the day to see how she was and to bring her news of the other afflicted members of cast and crew, but something had definitely shifted between them. He was friendly but the teasing spark in his eyes was gone.

And it made her feel like she'd been kicked in the ribs.

So much for telling herself that she didn't feel anything apart from lust for Kendrick. What an idiot she'd been. All she could hope for now was to salvage some pride. She wouldn't let him see that he'd hurt her, not even if it took all her acting skills. At least he wouldn't have that satisfaction.

He told her that Philip, who, like Kendrick, had been unaffected, was carrying on filming with those who were still on their feet.

'Not one to waste any time. Not that I can blame him. Every day we're not filming costs money.' He peered at her. 'You look as if you're on the mend.'

Elizabeth felt as if a steamroller had run over her and then reversed and done the same thing again. Kendrick, on the other hand, looked disgustingly healthy. Gorgeously, sexily, healthy.

She struggled to her feet. 'I'm going to see how everyone is,' she said. 'No, really, Kendrick, I'm fine,' she added as he looked about to protest. 'You've been really sweet, but I need to get on and do my job.'

Kendrick looked doubtful for a moment then he must have seen the determination in her face as he stood aside. Good, she had managed just the right tone.

'Okay, Lizzie. Have it your own way. I really need to get on and do some practice with Josh. Philip wants to film a stunt tonight, I'm afraid. Whether you're fit to be there or not.'

'I'll be there,' Elizabeth muttered. 'Just let anyone try and stop me.'

Later that afternoon, after she'd made sure all the afflicted patients were recovering, Elizabeth wandered over to where they were setting up for the stunt. She still felt weak but she knew by the time tomorrow came she'd be almost back to normal. Jack had insisted on being flown back to LA as soon as he had stopped vomiting and was expected back in a day or two.

'Without my lead man, I need to get as many of these stunts in the bag as we can,' Philip was saying. 'At least then I won't lose too much time.' He glared at Elizabeth as if it was all her fault. Kendrick winked at her behind Philip's back.

'What about if we do the car-chase scene out in the desert?' Kendrick suggested. 'Josh and I have that one pretty much worked out.' He sketched a wave behind him. 'I know what I have to do with the burning building. That can wait until Jack is back.'

Philip looked somewhat appeased.

'How about you, Doc?' he asked Elizabeth. 'Are you up to being around?'

Kendrick frowned. 'I'd forgotten the doctor needed to be there. I'm not sure it's a good idea for her to be standing around in the sun when she's been ill.'

'I'll be fine.' Although Kendrick was intervening for the best of reasons, she wasn't about to let him tell her how to do her job. How would he feel if she tried to tell him how to do his? She suppressed a smile at the thought of her directing his stunts. If she had her way he'd jump from no more than two feet off the ground and somehow she doubted that was going to happen. However, it felt good that someone cared enough to think about her welfare. It had been so long since anyone had. The thought jolted her. She was used to coping on her own. Did she really want someone to involve themselves in her life?

'Good,' Philip said before Kendrick could protest further. 'Let's get the crew that are okay on their feet and out of here. I want to film the scene while there's good light.'

'I'll go and get my medical bag,' Elizabeth said, turning towards her trailer.

Kendrick fell into step alongside her.

'Are you sure you're up to it?' he asked. 'Because I could refuse to do it today and he'll have no option but to postpone it.'

Elizabeth stopped in her tracks and faced him. 'Kendrick, I appreciate your help and your…' she sought for the right word '…concern. But I'm as professional as you. If I'm needed, I'll be there. Don't worry, I'll take a hat and plenty of water, as well as extra for everyone.'

Kendrick looked far from being reassured. 'It'll be a long day.'

'And I'll be fine. Go and do whatever you need to while I get organised.' She looked at him for a long moment. 'This stunt is going to be safe, isn't it?' It was different from watching him before. Before what? She'd slept with him? Started to care about him? She shook her head, dismissing the thought. She didn't care about him in *that* way. *Don't you?* a little voice whispered. *You don't tend to sleep with men you don't care about. Who are you trying to kid?* She was determined she was going to ignore the voice. She could not afford to care about anyone. Not ever.

Kendrick was grinning at her. 'I'll make a deal with you. You let me look after my side and I'll let you look after yours.' He placed a hand on her shoulder. 'Don't worry, Lizzie, we make the stunts as safe as possible. It's my job to look out for Josh and make sure he stays in one piece. He used to drive rally cars for a living. He's the best there is, you have my word for it. We only need you there as insurance.'

It took another hour before the trucks were loaded and ready to go. Philip had explained that it would be a chase across the desert, culminating in a crash of the car Josh was driving, as Jack's double, into a lorry that would be parked on the side of the road. None of that reassured Elizabeth. What if something went badly wrong? They had the helicopter standing by with a pilot to airlift Josh to hospital should the need arise. She hoped it wouldn't be. She'd inspected the helicopter thoroughly when she'd first arrived. It had a defibrillator as well as monitoring equipment and oxygen. She had to admit it was as well equipped as anything she'd encountered when she'd worked as a member of the BASICs team. But that had been different. There she had been part of a team. Here she was on her own. Here she was expected to look after people who, for all her determination to keep her distance from them, she was beginning to think of as her friends. And that was without whatever it was she felt for Kendrick.

Nevertheless, she knew she could handle most eventualities. And hadn't Kendrick promised her that he was safety conscious? Apart from the odd cut and bruise, so far he had shown himself pretty adept at minimising any damage to himself.

One of the crew, a woman called Julie who was one of the sound recordists, came to stand next to her. Elizabeth offered her a drink of water and Julie took it gratefully.

'Some heat, huh? The weathermen keep promising it's going to get cooler.'

Elizabeth wiped her brow. 'Can't come soon enough for me.'

They watched together as Kendrick strapped Josh in the driver's seat of the car.

'Have you worked with Kendrick and Josh before?' Elizabeth asked.

'Kendrick, about five times. He's one of the best at what he does so the directors like to use him. Josh, I think I might have worked with once before. The stuntmen tend to keep themselves to themselves on a set as a rule. Kendrick is a bit unusual in that he mixes more.' She sighed. 'He's so gorgeous.

I keep hoping he'll ask me out, but so far no luck. Perhaps he's got an eye on Tara. He usually goes for the female lead.'

A shock ran through Elizabeth's body that felt uncomfortably like jealousy. Why was she surprised? Kendrick had made no secret of the fact he liked female company.

'He and Tara had a fling a couple of years ago. It lasted the whole of the time we were filming, but then it seemed to peter out. I guess Kendrick isn't in it for the long term. Do you know stuntmen are just as likely to get divorced as stars?' Julie took a final swig of her water. 'Oh, well, I suppose I'd better get back to work.'

The nausea had returned. Was Julie trying to send her a not-so-subtle warning? Had people noticed that there was something between Kendrick and herself?

It was one thing thinking she knew about Kendrick, quite another hearing that she was no more than another notch in his bedpost. Anxiety and anger coiled in her stomach. She'd been an idiot to let him get under her guard. On the other hand, it wasn't as if he'd forced her. In fact, hadn't it been his lack of commitment that had attracted her in the first place? Why, then, did she feel so bereft?

CHAPTER SEVEN

BY THE next day, the camp was crowded with cast and crew once more. Jack still hadn't returned but everyone was in good spirits after their short break and there was a buzz of excitement.

'Okay, folks, gather round.' Philip's megaphone was back in action and even the usually surly director appeared in good form. Once everyone was assembled he lowered his megaphone.

'I think we have only a couple of weeks left before it's a wrap.'

A cheer went up at his words, but Elizabeth felt a sinking sensation in her chest. Soon Kendrick would be out of her life for good. She still hadn't decided what to do when filming finished, although she had sent a letter to her former employers to ask whether there was a vacancy for her.

Once filming was under way, Elizabeth strolled across to her medical trailer.

This morning there were more than the usual one or two patients waiting. She dealt with a sprained ankle, a mild chest infection and a bad rash. When the last patient had left, she heard a tap on the door. It was Tara. They hadn't spoken much but when they had, Elizabeth had found the actress self-deprecating and witty.

'Hi, Elizabeth, I had a few moments free so I thought I'd come and find you,' Tara said.

'Is there anything wrong?' Elizabeth asked.

'Not really,' Tara said evasively. 'I just wondered if you had a pregnancy test.'

'Of course,' Elizabeth said. 'How sure are you?'

'Pretty sure. I've been pregnant twice before so I know the symptoms. I'm two weeks late, and I'm never late.'

Elizabeth reached into a drawer and handed Tara a couple of tests.

'I didn't know you had children.'

'I have a son. He stays with his dad when I'm filming. I miscarried my last pregnancy.'

Tara's eyes filled and Elizabeth reached for her hand. 'I'm so sorry.'

'It happens, or so they tell me. I just hope nothing happens to this one. If the test is positive.'

'There is no reason at all if you've had one healthy baby why you shouldn't have another. And I'll be here to keep an eye on you. Why don't you nip into my bathroom and do the test and then I can check your blood pressure? Unless, of course, you'd rather be on your own when you do it. I suspect your husband might want to be the first to hear.'

'I don't want to tell him. I don't want him to know. If I am pregnant I want to get beyond the first twelve weeks before I get his hopes up.'

'That's a big thing to ask of yourself, not to have anyone to share your anxiety with. Look, go do the test and if it's positive we can chat some more.'

While Tara was in the bathroom, Elizabeth closed her eyes and remembered. The dizzy excitement when she'd thought she was pregnant. Doing the test and seeing the blue line. Stopping herself from phoning Simon at work, but instead getting off work early, wanting the moment to be perfect when she told him. They had been trying for a couple of years and were just about to embark on a course of IVF when she'd fallen pregnant naturally. Since then she'd thought of Charlie as her miracle baby.

On the way home from work, she'd been unable to stop herself going into a toyshop and buying a snowy-white, baby-soft Jemima Puddleduck with her jaunty blue hat and scarf. The books of Beatrix Potter had been her favourite when she'd been a child.

At home, she had done everything she'd always read about. Cooked a meal. Set the table with candles. Placed Mrs Puddleduck on the bedside table, not wanting to give the game away too soon.

She had hardly contained herself until Simon had come home. One look at her face had been enough. He had danced her around the room and later, after they had eaten, they had sat in front of the fire wrapped in each other's arms, dreaming about the future. Discussing how this time next year there would be three of them. And maybe in another couple of years another child. Her life had seemed so perfect back then.

Tara emerged from the bathroom, a nervous smile on her face.

'Positive. It says positive. But I think I should do another one, just to be sure.'

The second one was also positive, as Elizabeth knew it would be. She spoke to Tara, established she had been taking folic acid and that during her first successful pregnancy she hadn't any problems.

'From your dates I think you must be about six weeks,' Elizabeth said. 'There's no point in having a scan until you're a bit further on, but I can arrange that for you if you like. Or you can see your own ob/gyn when you're next in town. Come to think of it, that might be best. He or she knows your obstetric history.'

'But you can look after me while I'm here?' Tara said. 'That would be okay, won't it? My ob/gyn is a friend of my husband.'

'He won't be able to tell your husband anything without your express permission,' Elizabeth said.

'I know, but I'd rather not take the chance that he wouldn't let it slip.'

Elizabeth took one of Tara's hands in hers. 'I think you should reconsider telling your husband, you know. That's what they're there for.'

As she said the words she knew that in her case, at least, it had been a lie. Simon had been totally unable to support her when she'd needed him most. She would never make the mistake on counting on anyone else ever again. Not that she planned ever to need anyone's support. Her life, with just her in it, was her business and how she lived it was up to her and her alone.

'I'll think about it,' Tara said. 'I promise.'

She laughed as the sound of Philip on his megaphone blasted though the walls of the trailer. 'I think we're being summoned.'

Back on set, Kendrick and the rest of his team were in a huddle, setting up the next stunt.

'He's cute, don't you think?' Tara said, watching Elizabeth from the corner of her heavily made-up eyes. 'He and I were together a few years ago, before I met my husband. It didn't last long but while it did, it was fun.'

Elizabeth felt something uncomfortably like jealousy coil in her chest.

'I need to get to Make-up,' Tara excused herself. 'I'll see you later.'

As Tara walked away, Elizabeth watched Kendrick do the stunt they had been setting up. Now she knew what the practising with the trampoline had been about. Kendrick used it to gain enough height to do a somersault just as Josh and some of the other members of the crew let off a mock explosion. From where she was standing it all looked very real. As if Kendrick really had been blown up and had been sent flying by the force of the explosion.

After the third take, Kendrick caught her looking at him and for one long moment their eyes locked.

She thought she saw something in his eyes but then the shutters came down and he turned away. A chill ran up her spine. Had Tara been right to warn her? Now Kendrick had slept with her, was he regretting it? Preparing to move on to his next conquest? A wave of anger washed over her. That was up to him. Neither of them had made any promises, but she was damned if she was going to be fobbed off like some unwelcome guest at a party. She made up her mind. She would speak to him, make it clear he had nothing to fear on that score. She was grown up and was perfectly able to deal with what had happened like an adult, and she would make damn sure he gave her the same courtesy.

Kendrick was sitting outside his trailer, carving a piece of wood and whistling under his breath. He jumped to his feet when he saw her coming towards him.

'Lizzie. How're you doing?'

'I'm fine.' She sucked in a breath. 'Kendrick, can we talk?'

'Sure,' he said, drawing up a chair for her to sit. The wary look was back in his eyes.

Elizabeth looked around. The set was teaming with people visiting one another, walking around or playing a board game under the outside lights of their trailers. Others were sharing a beer at the makeshift bar.

'Not here,' she said. 'Let's take a walk.'

Kendrick got to his feet without saying anything and they walked into the desert in silence until they had left the camp behind.

Taking a deep breath, Elizabeth turned to face him. 'You've been avoiding me. Do you want to tell me why?'

Kendrick looked at her with cool blue eyes. There was no trace of his usual grin.

'Lizzie…' he started to say, then stopped. 'No, you're right. I have been avoiding you,' he said at last. 'I refuse to play games with you.'

Elizabeth propped her hands on her hips.

'Have you decided that sleeping with me was a mistake? Because I have to tell you, Kendrick, I'm a big girl.'

For a moment the smile was back. 'No, sleeping with you wasn't a mistake,' he said. 'It's just… Look, Lizzie, I wanted to make love to you, I thought we could, you know, have something going for a while. We're both adults. We knew what we were doing.'

'So?'

'But that was before I knew about Charlie.'

'And just what does Charlie have to do with it?'

'You're vulnerable. Lizzie, your child died only a few months ago. I would never have slept with you had I known.'

Anger flooded Elizabeth's body. 'When do you get to decide what is right for me and what isn't? Where do you get off deciding whether I'm too vulnerable to sleep with you? Who gives you the right to decide? Kendrick, if you want to end it, at least have the decency to be truthful.'

'I wanted to make love to you, Lizzie. Not feel responsible.'

For a moment she wanted to take a swing at him. 'Feel responsible for me?' She almost spat the words. 'What the hell makes you think I want anyone to feel responsible for me? I told you about Charlie because you asked. Would you have preferred me to keep her a secret? Would that have made you feel better?'

'Lizzie…' He reached for her but she stepped back. She was so angry she could feel the blood pumping in her veins.

'You caught me at a vulnerable moment, I'll give you that. But I slept with you because I wanted to. I slept with you because it helped me blot out the pain, even if it was only for a short while. Do you have any idea how much I ache inside?'

'Lizzie…' Even in the moonlight she could see that he had paled. He stepped towards her again, but she didn't want him near her.

'You think that wanting comfort means I want you in my life permanently? You couldn't be more wrong. I will never marry again. I will never love again. I will never have another child. So don't you dare tell me what I want.' She was breathing hard. The tightness in her chest was getting stronger.

'I can look after myself. I want to look after myself. I will never rely on another man again. Least of all you.' She took a deep, steadying breath. 'We had sex, Kendrick. That was all. Don't make it into something it wasn't.'

She turned on her heel, knowing that if she didn't get back to the safety of her trailer, she would break down in front of him, and that was the last thing she wanted. It would just confirm to Kendrick everything he thought. That she was vulnerable. The word made her temper rise all over again and she whirled back to face him.

'And stop calling me Lizzie.'

Kendrick watched her furious figure stomp away. That hadn't gone well. Despite being taken aback by her anger, he felt a smile tug at his lips. Why had he ever thought she was an ice maiden? She was a tiger when she got going.

He stared out into the desert. What he'd told Elizabeth hadn't been exactly the truth, but he could hardly have told her the real reason he was keeping his distance from her. When she'd told him about her daughter Charlie, he'd wanted nothing more than to pull her into his arms and protect her from ever being hurt again. He prided himself in not being afraid of anything—but that kind of emotion scared him witless. He didn't want anyone to rely on him. He didn't want anyone to expect anything of him. He had no illusions. He wasn't the kind of man a woman should marry. He didn't want children, he'd be a lousy father and he wasn't going to subject a child to that. Look at how things had turned out between him and his father. All his father had ever wanted was a carbon copy of himself. Someone to follow in his footsteps. Someone to make him proud. And Kendrick had failed on all counts. He was done with failing people. And the best way to do that was by not making promises he couldn't keep.

He rubbed his chin.

But Elizabeth was different. She no more wanted a relationship, a future, than he did. Then he felt a moment's chagrin. She had slept with him for comfort? That didn't sit well either. He wanted her to have slept with him for the same reasons he had wanted her. Because of overwhelming lust.

He kicked at a stone with the tip of his boot. He believed every word that she'd said. She didn't want a long-term relationship. After all, she'd said she could look after herself. That was abundantly clear. Why, then, did he feel this strange sense of disappointment?

CHAPTER EIGHT

HEARING raised voices, Elizabeth looked across to the other side of the camp. A woman with long black hair was standing in front of Kendrick with her hands on her hips, shouting something Elizabeth couldn't quite make out while gesticulating to a Jeep parked behind her. Even from this distance Elizabeth could tell that whatever she was saying wasn't making Kendrick very happy. Intrigued, Elizabeth wandered over to them.

'He's your flesh and blood too,' the dark-haired woman was shouting. 'Don't you think it's time you helped out?'

'I'm working.' Kendrick folded his arms.

The woman reached into the back of the car, reappearing a few moments later with a child in her arms. Judging by its size, it couldn't have been more than eighteen months old.

'It's just for today. You can take him to the ranch tomorrow and I'll collect him from there. C'mon, Kendrick, you owe me.'

Elizabeth's mouth was dry. It looked as if the woman doing the shouting was an ex-lover of Kendrick's. Dropping off the child with his father. And from what she was saying it seemed Kendrick hadn't taken much responsibility. The realisation made her feel ill. If ever she needed proof that Kendrick was just like Simon, here it was.

The woman pushed the child towards Kendrick, who was

forced to accept the toddler. Kendrick held it at arm's length, a look of puzzlement on his face. Clearly he had no idea what to do with the little person he had been handed.

Appalled, Elizabeth watched as the woman jumped into her Jeep and with a flurry of dust drove away. Turning on her heel, Elizabeth headed back to her trailer.

Inside she sat on her bed, trying to get her thumping heart under control. Kendrick had a child, one that he was clearly trying to avoid taking responsibility for. He was a snake. Not much better than Simon, and it was good she had discovered this now. What had she been thinking when she'd thought he was different? Her judgement when it came to men was clearly flawed.

She stood up and began to pace. Okay, so she had misjudged Kendrick. Where did that leave her? She had coped on her own before and she could do so again.

She picked up the photograph of Charlie and held it to her. Her heart ached as she remembered her little girl looking up at her with trusting eyes, relying on Mummy to take the pain away, to make everything better. But she hadn't been able to. She'd had no option but to watch Charlie suffer. And that despicable man outside couldn't even be bothered to look after his child for one day. More importantly, could she let another child of hers go through that again?

Hating the way she felt disappointed in Kendrick, realising now how much she'd wanted him to be different and wondering if she'd ever be able to look at another child without feeling torn in two, Elizabeth sat down on the bed and sobbed.

Once she had cried herself out, she washed her face and repaired her make-up. She still had a job to do. Filming was due to start and after that she would be in her trailer for any of the cast who needed medical advice. Whatever she decided to do, whatever agonies of indecision she was going through would have to be put aside until she was alone again.

Walking back onto the set, she saw that whoever the woman with the child was had got her way. Kendrick was sitting outside his trailer, looking on with bemusement as Josh walked up and down, trying to comfort the child, who was screaming as if its heart would break.

Whatever Josh was trying to do clearly wasn't working. The cries ripped through Elizabeth and she tried to close her ears. This wasn't her problem. Hadn't she come here so that she wouldn't have to face children? Steeling her heart, she went to pass by but Josh called out to her.

'Doc, could you help us here? I think Kip is in pain. Something serious has to be up with the kid.'

Elizabeth stopped in her tracks and sighed. She had no choice. It was possible that the child was in pain, although she doubted it. The cries sounded much more like those of a toddler who was overtired or hungry, or both. Nevertheless, whatever her own feelings, she couldn't stand by and ignore a distressed infant.

'Let me have a look,' she said.

Kendrick was waving his car keys in front of the child's face, but if he thought that was going to do anything to calm it down he was badly mistaken. Instead, the cries rose in pitch and the little face screwed up with fury.

Elizabeth removed the screaming infant from Josh's arms. Almost immediately, as if the child knew he was in the hands of someone who knew what they were doing, the cries tailed off. Brown eyes fixed on hers.

'Name?' Elizabeth said brusquely. The familiar feel of a small warm body in her arms, the particular baby smell, the familiar look of trust and entreaty, was breaking her up inside.

'Kip,' Kendrick said. 'What's up with him? I didn't know something that small could make a sound so loud.' He pulled a hand through his hair. In the time that Elizabeth had been gone he seemed to have aged. He wasn't the cool, collected Kendrick of earlier. In his place was a man who looked at the end of his tether.

'I think Kip might be hungry, or sleepy, or—' she wrinkled her nose as the smell of ammonia drifted up her nostrils '—wet. Most likely all three. Do you have nappies? Food?'

Kendrick looked around as if expecting to find those things behind him. He turned impassioned eyes on Elizabeth. 'Where am I supposed to find those things?'

'What about the bag Kendall left for you?' Josh interrupted. He was looking more relaxed now that Elizabeth had appeared.

'Oh, yes. Of course.' Kendrick lifted a small leather bag from the ground next to him. 'I think it's all in here.'

Elizabeth balanced a hiccupping Kip on her hip and dug around in the bag. There were disposable nappies, bottles and a change of clothes. She hauled out one of the bottles and handed it to Josh. 'Could you get some boiled water and add it to the powder? Then bring it back. C'mon, Kendrick, let's go inside so you can change your son.' At his look of incredulity she snapped, 'You'll have to learn some time.' She was so angry with him she could barely talk.

'Son?' Kendrick said. Then he laughed. 'You think that bundle of fury belongs to me? You have to be kidding.'

'He's not yours?' Elizabeth tried to ignore the feeling of relief that swept through her.

'He's my nephew,' Kendrick said. 'His mother, my sister, just dumped him on me. Said she has an audition she just can't miss. I'm to take him to my parents' ranch. Apparently my harebrained sister didn't have time.'

'Then,' Elizabeth said firmly, 'he does belong to you. As his uncle it's your responsibility to look after him.' She walked into his trailer, leaving him to follow.

It was the first time she'd been inside his trailer and she

looked around with interest. Almost the mirror image of hers, it was tidy. A guitar was set against a wall, the bed neatly made and the counter clear of dishes. It reminded her of army barracks. Clearly his time in the forces had left its mark on Kendrick.

She placed a tearstained Kip on the sofa and undid his nappy. She handed the sodden bundle to Kendrick, who couldn't have treated it with more dismay had she passed him a hand grenade.

She used the wipes she had found in the bag Kendall had left and soon had Kip a clean nappy. As she worked, the child's large brown eyes clung to hers and she found herself talking to him in a low, soothing voice.

'It's okay, baby. We'll soon have you feeling all comfy again. Then we'll give you your bottle and you can have a sleep. Mummy will be back tomorrow and in the meantime Uncle Kendrick…' she slid a look at Uncle Kendrick, who was watching her with a confused look on his face '…will look after you.'

'Can't you?' Kendrick said helplessly. 'I mean, I don't know how to look after a baby. Besides, I have to work. How can I work while looking after a baby? It's just not possible.'

'When did you last see your nephew, Kendrick?' Elizabeth asked. 'Doesn't he know you at all?'

'I saw him after he was born. He's changed since then. I would hardly know this is the same kid.'

'Then you'll have to learn how to look after him. At least until you take him to your parents'. I have to work too, so I can't look after him for you.'

Not just wouldn't—couldn't. Every moment she spent with this baby was tearing her in two.

Josh arrived back holding a full bottle of formula triumphantly. 'Sorted,' he said. 'What do we do now?'

Elizabeth chose to ignore that 'we'—at least for the time

being. For now, she needed to ensure Kip was fed and put down for a nap. After that it was up to Kendrick.

She tested the milk on the inside of her wrist. Too hot. It needed a few minutes to cool down.

She pointed to Kendrick and then to the single armchair in the room. 'Sit there.'

Kendrick looked mutinous, but did as he was told.

Elizabeth placed Kip in his arms, and her heart cracked a little as the tiny boy was dwarfed in Kendrick's muscular arms. He was holding the child away from his body as if unsure what to do with him. Elizabeth suppressed a smile.

'He's not a sack of potatoes or live ammunition, you know. Hold him close to you.' She leaned over Kendrick and adjusted the child in his arms until he was lying snugly against Kendrick's chest. Kip smiled at his uncle, revealing two front teeth.

'Hey, did you see that?' Kendrick said, a note of wonder in his voice. 'The kid actually smiled at me. I think he likes me. Hey, kid, maybe later I can take you for a ride. Would you like that? Go on a horse with your Uncle Kendrick?'

'He's too small to go on a horse, Kendrick,' Elizabeth said. 'Here's his bottle. Tip it up so he doesn't suck on air.'

Kendrick did as he was told and soon Kip was sucking hungrily. Elizabeth watched them for a moment. The sight of macho Kendrick holding the little boy was incongruous, yet melted her inside. This was how he would be with his own child. Eventually. Once he had some training. And if that child wasn't disabled. She couldn't imagine someone as sure of his own masculinity, so physical, coping with a child who wasn't. She could barely see him with a child who was fit and healthy.

Kendrick glowered at Josh, who was standing watching with a broad smile on his face. 'If you so much as breathe a whisper of this to the others, I'll have your guts.'

'Hey, you're a natural. What is there to be embarrassed about?'

Kendrick tried to squint at his watch without disturbing the feeding child. 'We need to be on set in ten minutes.' He looked hopefully at Elizabeth. 'Do you think he'll be finished by then?'

'What? So you can leave him sleeping in the trailer? On his own?'

'Hell, I never thought of that. I don't suppose you…?'

'No, Kendrick. I have my own job to do. I can't look after a child.' Can't. Won't. Didn't want to. 'He's your responsibility. All yours.'

'I wonder if Imogen will look after him.'

'Imogen is in the next take,' Josh said. 'You're not.'

'In that case, I'll have to bring him on to the set with us. There must be something we can put him in.'

Elizabeth was exasperated. Did Kendrick really have no idea? But as long as the child came to no harm, it was none of her business. As she turned to leave them to it, she couldn't resist another quick peek. Now that he was fed and changed, Kip's eyes had softened and half closed as he surrendered to sleep.

Elizabeth swallowed the lump in her throat. Although she knew she could never risk having another child, it didn't mean she didn't long for another baby deep down inside. She blinked away the hot tears that burned behind her eyes. Hadn't she resolved to make the best of her life, to make the most of the cards she'd been dealt? There was no point in wishing for what she could never have.

Later that afternoon Elizabeth found herself in a Jeep with Kendrick and Kip. Not for the first time, she wondered why she'd let Kendrick persuade her to come with them to the ranch. The reason she had given herself—that she couldn't leave a defenceless child to the ministrations of his uncle—wasn't entirely true. She was curious to see where Kendrick had been brought up. But that wasn't totally true either. She was here because she wanted to be with Kendrick. Filming was due to finish soon and then Kendrick would walk out of her life for good. The thought was almost unbearable. How could she have let herself fall for this man? Hadn't she sworn to herself that she would never depend on anyone again, never lay herself open to being hurt? Yet here she was with a man who could only break her heart. And do it without noticing.

'Here we are,' Kendrick said as they turned into a dust road. His face was set, his usual grin absent. He didn't look happy about being home.

Elizabeth couldn't see anything that looked like a ranch. All she could see were miles of fields with horses feeding contentedly.

'Hey, Kip. Do you see the horses?' Kendrick asked. But Kip was too busy looking the other way. At a clump of grass or a tree that must have caught his attention.

'Are they yours?' Elizabeth asked.

'My father's,' Kendrick said tightly. 'He owns around thirty. Some he uses for stud, the others on the ranch.'

'So he's a cowboy,' Elizabeth said, trying to make Kendrick smile. She was nervous enough, without dealing with the tension that was rolling from Kendrick in waves.

'Mmm. He doesn't do much of that. Luckily he leaves it to the guys who know what they're doing.'

After driving for another ten minutes along the bumpy track they pulled up outside a low-slung, sprawling ranch house. In front of the house and to their right was a paddock where a man who looked every inch a cowboy was standing in the centre as a horse galloped in a circle around him on a long rope. Every now and again the horse would lift its rear legs and kick the air as if frustrated.

Kendrick leaped out of the car and called over. 'Hey, Tim, how's it going?' He reached into the back seat and with some difficulty removed Kip from his baby seat. Holding him awkwardly in his arms, he went over and opened the car door for Elizabeth. It was on the tip of her tongue to tell him she was perfectly able to manage opening a car door herself but she bit back the words.

'Let's go and see what Tim's up to,' Kendrick said.

Elizabeth had no idea whether he was addressing her or the toddler but followed him across to the paddock fence. Kendrick perched Kip on the fence so he could see what was happening.

The horse reared when he saw them and Tim struggled to hold onto the rope.

'Looks like you need a hand there,' Kendrick said. A smile was playing in the corner of his mouth.

'He's a tough one,' Tim grunted. 'I've been trying to get a saddle on him this last week, but he's having none of it.'

'Could you hold Kip for a bit?' Kendrick asked. Before Elizabeth had time to protest, Kendrick was holding Kip towards her and she had no choice but to take the toddler from him. Kip reached out a chubby fist and grabbed the front of Elizabeth's blouse, twisting around so he could follow Kendrick with his eyes.

The feeling of the child in her arms made her throat tighten.

Kendrick vaulted over the fence and strode towards Tim. 'He doesn't trust you yet,' he said. 'Want me to give it a go?'

'You're the boss man,' Tim said. 'If anyone can get him to settle, it'll be you.'

The horse had come to a halt and was breathing heavily, its flanks tipped with frothy sweat. As Kendrick walked towards him the horse sidestepped and rolled his eyes.

'Hey, big fellow,' Kendrick said softly. 'No one's going to hurt you. No one's going to make you do anything you don't want to.'

The horse lowered its head and snorted, still eyeing Kendrick warily. Elizabeth held her breath. If the horse reared and caught Kendrick with one of its hooves, it could be nasty. Very nasty. She wanted to call him back, but she forced herself to swallow the words. Any sudden noise might make the horse react and do the very thing she dreaded. Kip was pointing and saying a stream of words in his own baby language. Elizabeth found herself squeezing him tighter. The warm body tucked against her felt painfully good.

Kendrick was still approaching the horse, talking quietly. As he spoke the horse calmed, its snorting and rolling eyes becoming still. Its ears pricked up and it looked at Kendrick. Tim had backed away before vaulting over the fence, and came to stand next to Elizabeth.

'Hey, Kip,' he said. 'How d'you do, ma'am?' He tipped a finger to his hat, making Elizabeth smile. It seemed as if she'd moved from one movie set to another.

Men were beginning to gather around. Without saying anything, except nodding in Elizabeth's direction, they positioned themselves along the fence to watch Kendrick.

'Bet you fifty dollars he doesn't get the saddle on Satan,' one of the watching ranch hands said to Tim.

Satan? The horse was called Satan. Elizabeth was torn between covering her eyes or Kip's so that they wouldn't have to watch.

'Bet you a hundred he saddles him and rides him,' Tim said calmly.

'Ain't no one can ride that crazy animal. Not even Kendrick,' the man replied. 'But if you want to throw your money away, don't let me stop you.'

There was a flurry of activity while money changed hands.

It seemed that all the watching men wanted to bet on whether Kendrick would be killed. If Elizabeth could have stopped this, she would have. On the other hand, she had seen enough of Kendrick in action to know that if anyone could do what the men were betting on, it would be him.

By this time Kendrick was stroking Satan's neck, still talking in a low voice. The horse nickered and tossed its head, but otherwise remained calm.

Kendrick held the rope near the horse's head and walked him around for a little while.

'Can you bring me a saddle?' he called over to Tim.

Tim cast a told-you-so look at the others and, picking up a saddle from the fence, carried it across to Kendrick. Satan skipped sideways again as he approached but Kendrick soothed him until he was standing still again. Kendrick waited until Tim was once more on the other side of the fence before he placed the saddle on the horse's back.

Elizabeth held her breath. Kip moved his hand and grabbed hold of her bottom lip and clung on for dear life. Elizabeth was too mesmerised at what was happening a few yards away to try and move his hand.

Feeling the weight of the saddle, Satan rose on his hind legs, scrabbling at the air with his front hooves and only narrowly missing Kendrick's head.

Undeterred, Kendrick waited until he calmed a little. There was another flurry of movement beside her as more money changed hands.

Then, with one easy movement, Kendrick leaped onto Satan's back. This time the horse reacted. Bucking and rearing as he broke into a canter. But Kendrick held on. Round and round they went until the horse stopped bucking and settled into a smoother gait. Then Kendrick turned Satan towards the fence and with an almost undetectable movement of his feet sent the horse soaring up and over the fence and into the plains stretching into the distance. As horse and rider disappeared there was a collective sigh from everyone watching.

'Okay, everyone, pay up and get back to work,' Tim said, holding out his hand.

'Will they be okay?' Elizabeth asked. 'I mean, what if Kendrick comes off? What if he hurts himself?' She tried to act as if her concern was nothing more than the natural concern of one human for another but judging by the speculative look in Tim's eyes he wasn't convinced.

'Don't worry about Kendrick. He'll be fine. If Satan tosses him, he knows how to fall. He'll be okay. Satan will come back and I'll send one of the lads to look for Kendrick. But as I said, I don't think that'll happen.' While he was talking he was counting the money in his hand with a satisfied smile. 'Those boys don't know Kendrick the way I do, otherwise they would never have bet against him.' He seemed to remember his manners. 'Come inside out of the heat, ma'am. I'll get you and Kip here a drink.'

'Have you known Kendrick long?' Elizabeth asked as they walked towards the house.

Tim's face lit up in a smile. 'Ever since he was about Kip's age. He learned to ride almost as soon as he could walk. Always had a way with horses too. Seems he can talk to them in a way they understand. He should work the ranch instead of doing that crazy job. His father could do with someone to take over.'

The more she learned about Kendrick, the more she realised how little she knew about him.

'When are his parents due home? We'll be heading back as soon as we've passed Kip on.'

'They're due back later this afternoon. How is the boy anyway? He's up here with his mama most weekends. She rides too. Nothing like Kendrick, but not bad for a girl.'

Tim ushered Elizabeth into a chair on the veranda and left

her while he went to fetch them a drink. She bounced Kip on her lap, before giving in and putting him on the floor.

'No wonder your uncle is planning to put you on a horse, young man. Looks like you're pretty fond of bouncing around.'

A cloud of dust in the distance caught her attention. As it got closer she could see it was Kendrick and Satan. He slowed the horse to a walk a few yards away and when Tim came back out with the drinks, he left them with Elizabeth and walked towards horse and rider. Kendrick swung his leg over the front of the saddle and jumped down. 'You should walk him around for a bit to cool him down. I think he'll be okay to ride now,' he told Tim.

'Very impressive,' Elizabeth said as Kendrick walked towards her.

Kendrick grinned. 'You think so? I like to impress.' He bent over and swung Kip into his arms. The little boy giggled with delight.

'Hey, Kip. What about something to eat? Then I'll take you on the horse. How does that sound?'

'You're not seriously thinking of taking him on Satan?' Elizabeth said, horrified.

'Of course not. We've plenty of well-behaved horses he can ride. Besides, he'll be with me.' He placed Kip back down on the floor, where the child found some ants to study. 'You could come too. I promise you, you'll be perfectly safe.'

Elizabeth stretched. 'Maybe later. Right now I'm just enjoying being here in the sun.'

Kendrick pulled a chair alongside hers. 'Then that's what we'll do.'

They sat in silence for a while, watching Kip as he crawled after the ants. Every now and again Elizabeth or Kendrick had to reach down to stop him putting one in his mouth.

'Tell me about your parents,' Elizabeth asked. 'Do you see them often?'

Kendrick's expression darkened. 'Not really. I'm always travelling and, well, my father and I don't exactly get along.'

'How come? I would have thought you had a lot in common. Horses. This ranch.'

Kendrick stretched his long legs in front of him and placed his arms behind his head. Elizabeth sucked in her breath. Every part of her seemed to respond to his closeness. It was as if there was a string pulling her towards him. As if there was some kind of force field surrounding him that drew her. She had never felt like this before. Never felt every nerve cell in her body react this way to someone's presence, and it disturbed her. She'd thought she'd loved Simon, and maybe she had, but she'd never felt that constant pull towards him that she was feeling towards this man. Was this what it was like to be in love? The need to be close to someone. The feeling that the world was a darker place whenever they weren't around. The feeling of coming home, of being at peace whenever they were. It was more, so much more than just wanting to be in his arms or his bed.

'We were close once,' Kendrick said. 'He was in the army and when I got into West Point he couldn't have been prouder.'

Elizabeth waited. It was quiet, only the faint sounds of the men shouting as they worked the ranch disturbing the silence.

'Then when I got my helicopter pilot's licence and was given a commission, it was as if he'd fulfilled his life's ambition. I don't know if I said, but he was a colonel before he retired. I knew I had to be better than everyone else so no one could say it was nepotism.'

Kendrick's smile was rueful. 'I wanted him to be proud of

me, so I worked my butt off. If I was asked to run ten miles with full kit, I would run twenty. If I was asked to do twenty press-ups, I would do thirty. If the best got their helicopter's licence in four months, I wanted to do it in three. And I did.' He stood up to remove a crawling Kip from the edge of the step. 'I made Major before anyone else in my intake.' There was no arrogance in the words, just a sense of certainty. 'But then, when I was in Iraq, something happened. They busted my butt because of it. My father intervened and they agreed to put me on desk duty. But I didn't want to stay in the army to do that. If I couldn't fly, I wanted out.'

'What incident?'

Kendrick frowned. 'It's not something I like to talk about.'

'Tell me, Kendrick.' She wanted to know. She wanted to understand everything about this man. 'I can't imagine what you did to be busted.' A thought struck her. 'Unless you stole a helicopter to do a stunt?'

Kendrick gave her a slow smile and shook his head. 'I like it that you're on my side,' he said. 'And of course I didn't steal a helicopter. 'But I was in the wrong. I disobeyed orders and put my gunner's life at risk as well as the helicopter. Those babies cost millions and the army doesn't like its pilots to mess them up. And mine got pretty messed up. I was lucky to get away without a court-martial.'

That didn't sound right to Elizabeth. Kendrick was reckless, but she had seen the way he watched out for the others in his team.

Kip tottered to the edge of the step again and this time it was Elizabeth who got up to retrieve him. Her heart ached as she remembered that she'd never had to do this for Charlie. She had never crawled.

'Dad was furious,' Kendrick continued. 'He's an army man through and through. Obeying orders, being part of the team is what counts. It almost killed him that I could have been court-martialled for my actions.' A cloud passed across Kendrick's face. 'But I would do the same thing all over again if I had to.' Something in the air between them chilled.

'Dad pulled out all the stops to stop me facing a military court. Called in favours, used every bit of influence he had, and believe me that was some, to stop it. And he succeeded. So when I decided I was going to leave the army anyway, we fought.' Kendrick's lips flattened. 'Not physically, of course. Until then I had always done more or less what my father wanted. But his fury when I told him I was leaving the army was nothing compared to what he had to say when he learned I had decided to work on movies as a stuntman. He found it shameful. If I had used my pilot's licence to get a civilian flying job, he might have come around eventually, or if I'd taken over here from Tim as ranch manager, he might have lived with that. But a stuntman? In an industry he has nothing but contempt for? No way.'

'Why did you choose to become a stuntman? Why not the other options?'

'This way of life suites me. I'm considering doing some directing.' He smiled ruefully. 'One day I'll be too old to do stunts, or too injured.'

'What about the risks? Don't you care that you could get killed? Or paralysed?'

'Of course I care. But it's no more dangerous than being in the army. And as for the risks, I do the same as I did then. I try to make sure that the danger is minimised.'

He shifted in his seat. 'Enough about me. I want to know more about you. I suspect your folks were proud of you.'

'Yes, they were. My father was in the oil industry. He worked in Texas for years. He took early retirement and they moved back to England for a while. When my mother died he went to live near his sister in Canada. I was married by that time so I stayed here.'

'Where did you meet your ex-husband?'

'Simon? He worked at the oil company my father worked for.'

'Did you love him?'

'I thought I did. But I guess I didn't really know him.'

'What happened? Can you tell me?'

Elizabeth swallowed hard. 'Charlie happened.'

She bent down, picked Kip up and held him tight. The familiar, sweet, precious baby smell was instantly painful. But it felt so good to hold the small bundle in her arms. Elizabeth rubbed his cheek gently with her finger.

Kip snuggled into her and yawned. He was clearly ready for his afternoon nap. She sat on the seat swing on the veranda and Kendrick sat down next to her.

Kendrick eyed the sleeping baby apprehensively. 'Ah, peace for a while. Although he is kind of cute, I have to admit I'll be glad to pass him back to his mother. Kids aren't my style. But he obviously feels comfortable with you. It must be because you're used to children.'

Elizabeth flinched and Kendrick hit himself on the forehead.

'I'm sorry, Lizzie. That was a tactless thing to say. Sometimes I'm an idiot.'

'It's okay. I need to talk about Charlie. I thought it would be better if no one knew about her so I wouldn't have to tell them what happened, but I can't pretend my daughter never existed.'

'How did she die?'

'She had a rare wasting illness called Gaucher's disease. When she was born, when I first held her in my arms I was so happy. I thought my life was prefect. Perfect husband, perfect child, perfect job. I knew I was blessed.' She smiled as she remembered the first time she'd held her daughter. The tiny rosebud mouth, the silky-soft skin, her tiny hands, the feel of her skin on her skin. 'But even as I held Charlie to me, I knew in my soul that something wasn't right. But I shook the feeling off. I told myself it was just new-mother anxiety.'

'Go on,' Kendrick prompted.

'As she got older that feeling grew stronger. I tried to tell Simon, but he didn't want to know. He was so caught up in his career I guess he thought I had too much time on my hands and that I was looking for something that wasn't there.'

'But when she should have been lifting her head, beginning to sit up, none of that was happening. I took her to the doctor, but like Simon he told me I was being an over-anxious mother, that Charlie would do all of it in her own time. I knew they were wrong. Mothers know. We know,' she repeated.

Kendrick put his arm around her shoulder and pulled her close to him. 'I'm sorry,' he said simply.

'Eventually I got tired of everyone telling me that everything was okay when I knew it wasn't. So I took her to a private clinic. The doctor referred us straight away to a specialist children's hospital. They did tests, hundreds of them, it seemed. I can't tell you how often I wondered whether I was doing the right thing every time Charlie cried when they took blood. I felt like a monster putting her through all of that and I didn't even know whether anyone could help her.'

'Where was your husband during this time?'

'He had to work. To be fair, there wasn't much he could have done.'

'Except be with you,' Kendrick growled. 'He was Charlie's father. Your husband. It was his duty.'

'Ah, duty,' Elizabeth said softly. 'I didn't want duty. I never want duty.'

'Then what happened?'

Elizabeth's chest was tight. Although she'd told Kendrick that she needed to talk about her child, this was the first time she had talked to anyone about those awful months and it was like opening a wound and squirting acid into it.

'Eventually we got a diagnosis. Gaucher's is a genetic, irreversible wasting disease that can either affect the nervous system or muscles, or, as in Charlie's case, both.' Her throat was so tight she could hardly speak. The day she had learned for certain that Charlie's illness was both irreversible and terminal had been the worst day of her life. Simon hadn't even taken the day off work the day the doctors had given their diagnosis.

'Once I knew that there was nothing more anyone could do, I took Charlie home. Simon was livid. He thought I should have left her in hospital and then have her put in foster care. He said she was better off there. How can any child be better off without her mother? But I would have stayed with her at the hospital, I would have let them go on sticking needles in her if I'd thought there was any chance, any chance at all they could help her. As it was, all they were doing was causing my poor baby pain.'

She buried her face in Kendrick's shirt as the tears began to fall as she remembered those days—the terrible fights with Simon, the ache of not being able to help her baby.

Kendrick's hand was in her hair, and he was murmuring to her as if soothing a child.

'One day, Simon left. I woke up to find him standing at the door, with his suitcases all packed. He said he couldn't bear to watch Charlie die. That wasn't the truth. He couldn't bear it that his child was disabled. It wasn't part of the perfect image he had of himself and his life. I let him go. I didn't want him if he didn't want his own child. I stopped loving him that day. I wonder now if I ever truly loved him.'

Kendrick held a hanky underneath her nose and she took it gratefully.

'The next time I saw Simon,' she said, 'was at Charlie's funeral.'

Kendrick kicked Satan into a gallop. Elizabeth had taken Kip into one of the bedrooms and had asked Kendrick to leave her alone for a little while.

He wanted to think—no, strike that. He wanted not to think and so he was doing the only thing he knew that would stop the thoughts tumbling around his head, driving him crazy. Just as Lizzie was driving him crazy. He would have preferred to go big-wave surfing or BASE jumping, that would really have sorted his head, but he was stuck here in the desert with no waves or nearby cliffs.

So riding Satan as fast as the horse would go would have to do.

What Elizabeth had told him had shaken him. The thought of Elizabeth, his Lizzie, going through all that on her own filled him with rage. How could any man do that to his wife and child? He would never let Elizabeth face a trip to the dentist without being there for her.

How could any man leave a woman like Elizabeth? She was warm, caring and loyal even though she had been to hell and back. She had faced the worst life could throw at her with dignity and courage. He, on the other hand, had tried to run away from his guilt and loss. She was a better person than he was. A woman any man would be proud to have by his side.

The realisation hit him like a blow to the chest. He was falling in love. He didn't know when or how he had started to feel like this, but he knew he wanted to be with Elizabeth more than any other woman. He could race Satan to the back of beyond but that wasn't going to change the way he felt.

When Kendrick got back to the ranch, he still didn't know

what he was going to do or say to Elizabeth, if anything. Maybe whatever this was would go away if he gave it enough time.

To his dismay, by the time he'd rubbed Satan down and walked over to the house, he saw that his parents had arrived. Hell. He wasn't expecting them back for another couple of hours at least. His mother was sitting next to Elizabeth with Kip in her arms. The two women looked as if they'd already made friends.

'Kendrick!' His mother passed Kip to Elizabeth and came across to greet him with a smile. 'It's so lovely to see you. Why does it have to take Kip to get you to come and see us?'

'Mom.' He kissed the papery cheeks and gave her a hug. 'I see you've met Dr Elizabeth Morgan?'

'Yes, Elizabeth and I have been getting to know each other.'

Uh-oh. He recognised that look on his mother's face. She was always asking him why he hadn't settled down yet.

His father came out onto the veranda and Kendrick's heart sank. Every time he and his father met, things ended in an argument. Perhaps with Elizabeth being here they could remain civil for the next couple of hours. Or perhaps he should just leave straight away. He had done what Kendall had asked and delivered Kip. He had done his duty.

'Are you staying the night, Kendrick?' The hope in his mother's eyes made him flinch.

'We need to get back to the set, Mom. Maybe another time?'

She tried to hide her disappointment, but not quickly enough. This was exactly why he didn't need or want relationships. It only brought trouble. He had to remember that.

Elizabeth stood. 'But as long as we get back before tomorrow morning, it'll be okay. Won't it, Kendrick?' Now she was ganging up on him too.

He relented. 'Sure. We'll stay for dinner, if that's okay?'

The look of delight in his mother's eyes was reward enough.

'Kendrick!' His father strode towards him with his hand outstretched. 'Good to see you, son.' They shook hands, more like acquaintances than father and son.

'Hello, Dad. Did you have a good trip?'

From the corner of his eye he could see that Elizabeth was watching the exchange with a look of bafflement on her face.

'I did. And I have some news for you. Good news.'

'I think it should wait until after dinner, Hughie,' his mother interrupted hastily.

Kendrick knew then that whatever news his father had for him, it wasn't something he wanted to hear.

'Now, why don't you watch Kip, while I show Elizabeth where she can freshen up?' his mother continued.

Kendrick managed to hold a conversation with his father long enough for Elizabeth and his mother to return. It helped that they had Kip to divert them. Kendrick had never known that toddlers required so much watching and after a few minutes of constant chasing after the lively toddler his father had suggested they saddle one of the horses and Kendrick take Kip up in front of him. It had worked like a charm. The rocking movement of the horse had sent the boy to sleep almost immediately.

'It used to work with you,' his father said. 'Mind you, you were riding on your own when you were three years old. You always refused to be led.'

It was a revelation to Kendrick. Nowhere in his memory was there an image of his father teaching him to ride.

'You had barely started at school when you were clearing jumps twice the size of yourself.'

Kendrick thought he must be mistaken. Surely that wasn't pride he heard in his father's voice?

'Come on, you two,' his mother called from the doorway. 'Supper's ready.'

It was strange sitting down to a meal with his parents in his childhood home. He couldn't remember the last time he'd done that. And even stranger seeing Elizabeth opposite him. His mother was too polite to ask Elizabeth too many searching questions, even though he could tell the curiosity was almost killing her.

'Oh, honey, I meant to tell you and I completely forgot!' Kendrick's mother, Susan, said, a look of dismay on her face.

'What is it? Is something wrong?' Kendrick replied, sounding alarmed.

But his mother was smiling widely. 'No, not wrong at all. Your Aunt Camilla phoned me while I was away to tell me that Fabio is getting married. He's finally found the girl for him. Like you should.' Susan flicked a look in Elizabeth's direction. She couldn't have made it more obvious if she tried.

'Fabio! Getting married. Well, I'll be damned. Sorry, Mother.' Kendrick turned to Elizabeth. 'My cousin Fabio is the last man I'd expect to tie the knot.'

'That's what happens, darling, when you fall in love,' his mother said with another pointed look at Elizabeth. 'They're getting married in Brazil. In three weeks' time. I know he would like you to be there.'

'I'm surprised he didn't let me know himself. Perhaps he was frightened I'd talk him out of it.'

His mother's frown told him he'd said the wrong thing. Couldn't she just accept he wasn't going to get married? 'But wild horses wouldn't keep me from Fabio's wedding. Filming should be finished by then.'

'What about you, Elizabeth? Will you go?' Susan asked.

Elizabeth gave a small shake of her head. The sad look on her face made his chest tighten. He should have kept away from her.

Finally, the meal over, Susan served the coffee.

'We should leave soon, Mom,' Kendrick said. 'If we're to make it back before midnight.'

His father cleared his throat and Kendrick knew he was ready to have his say.

'I was talking to your commanding officer a couple of days ago,' he said.

'Ex-commanding officer,' Kendrick corrected mildly.

'Yes. Well. That's the point. He wants you back. Says he's prepared to forget all about that other business.'

'I'm not going back to a desk job, Dad,' Kendrick said tiredly. He had lost count of how many times they'd had this conversation.

'It's a good life, son. They'll give you back your rank in a year. Maybe sooner. And, besides, it's not a desk job.'

Kendrick's ears pricked up. The main reason he'd left the army had been because they wouldn't let him fly after he'd damaged their helicopter. Okay, so maybe it wasn't just because of the damage, more to do with disobeying orders, but that hadn't been the only reason he'd left.

'I'm not going back to fight in Iraq, Dad. I know you don't want to hear that.'

A look of dismay—or was it repugnance?—crossed his father's face. As a colonel and a career soldier, Kendrick's disgrace had reflected badly on him. But he was done trying to be the person his father wanted.

'They want you to come back and teach new pilots how to fly Apaches. They say no one knows how to do it better than you.'

That was different. He'd be flying again. And teaching the

kids straight out of flying school how to keep themselves in one piece.

'What is an Apache?' Elizabeth asked. She'd been sitting listening quietly.

Hugh explained and Elizabeth looked even paler than she had done earlier.

'I don't know, Dad. It's a possibility. How long do I have to think it over?'

'As long as you like,' Hugh said. His smile was the first genuine one Kendrick had seen in three years. 'But he's keen to know your answer.'

'I'll think about it,' Kendrick said. He drained the last of his coffee and stood up. 'I want to ride Satan one more time before we leave, if that's okay with you, Elizabeth?'

'Sure. I'll help your mother clear away while you're gone.'

'You don't have to help,' Susan said as Kendrick and his father left the room. 'Why don't you take your coffee back outside onto the veranda? I'm used to having the kitchen to myself.'

'I'll have it at the kitchen table if that's okay?'

When Susan nodded, Elizabeth sat down and took a sip of her coffee. She liked it here. Despite the tension between Kendrick and his father, it felt comforting to be in someone else's kitchen.

'Do you think Kendrick will go back to the army?' she asked Susan.

Susan wiped her hands on a tea towel and studied Elizabeth for a moment. 'I don't know how much you know about the reason he left,' she said slowly.

'I know he got into trouble for disobeying orders,' Elizabeth replied. 'He told me.'

'Did he tell you that the reason he got into trouble was because he went to rescue a group of soldiers who were pinned down by enemy fire and that one of the soldiers who was caught in the ambush was his girlfriend Amy?'

Elizabeth was stunned. 'No, he didn't.'

Susan folded her lips as if Elizabeth's response was what she'd expected. 'Just as I thought. He doesn't talk about it to anyone.' Susan turned away and looked out of the window. 'We all loved Amy, especially Kendrick's father. We hoped that they would get married, that at long last Kendrick would settle down.'

'Loved her?' Elizabeth's throat was dry.

'She died before Kendrick could reach her. He left his helicopter to try and get to her. She was the reason he disobeyed orders. But it was no use. He was too late. He managed to pull two other soldiers to safety, but he blames himself for not getting to Amy sooner. I sometimes think his father blames him too.'

Elizabeth's head was swirling. It explained so much about Kendrick. The haunted look she saw in his eyes when he thought no one was looking. His attitude as if every moment had to be squeezed out of life. His reluctance to get involved. Like a jigsaw, all the pieces fell into place.

'But now he's met you.' Susan turned back to Elizabeth. 'Maybe he'll have a reason to think about the future. Maybe he can find happiness again.'

It was on the tip of Elizabeth's tongue to tell Susan that she wasn't the person to bring Kendrick happiness. She had too many of her own demons to deal with, but she swallowed the words. Perhaps she and Kendrick could find some solace together, if only for a little while.

Elizabeth waited until they were a good bit along the road before she raised the question that had been bothering her.

'Your mother told me about your girlfriend,' she said.

The darkness hid Kendrick's expression from her.

'Did she now,' he said softly.

'Why didn't you tell me?'

'There was nothing to tell. I loved her. She's dead.' He couldn't hide the pain in his voice.

'So that's why you risked everything? To try and save her?'

'How the hell did anyone expect that I would leave her there? Even if I knew she was dead, I couldn't leave her.' His voice was ragged and it tore through Elizabeth. She knew his pain.

'Pull over, Kendrick,' she said.

'Why?'

'Just do as I ask.'

He pulled the car onto the side of the road and they sat in silence for a few moments.

'Is the reason you've been avoiding me anything to do with her death?' Elizabeth asked.

'Lizzie,' Kendrick said. 'Every time I look in your eyes. Every time you talk about your child, I'm reminded. And I don't want to be reminded. I want to forget.'

'Is that why you live the life you do? I know that feeling, Kendrick. I know what it's like to not want to feel. To keep your mind full so you won't think. It only works for a little while.' She reached over and took his hand in hers. 'I think what we have is good for us both. It helps us both. We'll never forget them, Kendrick, but what's wrong with finding peace where we can?'

He took a long, shuddering breath. 'I don't want to hurt you, Lizzie. You've been hurt enough.'

Reaching up, she threaded her hands behind his head. 'Nothing can hurt me any more,' she said. She pulled his face down to hers and tasted a salty wetness that made her heart ache. 'I want you, Kendrick. Even for a short while. I know once we leave here we'll go our separate ways, but for now just love me.'

CHAPTER NINE

As FILMING drew to a close, the days on the film set were quieter. Every evening, when filming had finished for the day, Kendrick saddled up Buster and they went riding. Elizabeth was delighted to find that she and her mount had developed a rapport and soon she was happy to canter for long distances.

Sometimes they stayed out after night had fallen and Kendrick would make camp. They would sit with their arms wrapped around each other, listening to the sounds of the desert. They talked a little but never of their lives. Mostly they made love. Every evening Kendrick came to her and spent the night, rising before dawn so as not to draw attention, although Elizabeth doubted they were fooling anyone. It was the happiest she had been since Charlie had died and she tried to forget that one day soon it would be all over. Kendrick would walk out of her life and she out of his and they would never see each other again.

She pushed the thought to the back of her mind. She would face the future when she had to and not a moment before. All she knew was that she wouldn't be going back to her home in the UK. It had been sold and a new family was due to move in before she got back. Elizabeth hoped they would be happy.

Jack still hadn't returned. Philip was on edge and his anxiety permeated the camp. Kendrick told her that Philip had filmed all the stunts he could, but now had to wait for Jack's return before filming could start again.

'He's worried,' Kendrick said. 'If the film goes over budget, it's his responsibility.'

'There's nothing he can do about Jack being ill.' Elizabeth did wonder though. Jack's food poisoning should have disappeared by now.

'Gossip has it that he's taken himself off to Las Vegas for a couple of days,' Kendrick said. 'Whatever, Philip can't continue until he's back. Luckily he was ahead of schedule so has a couple of days in hand before he falls behind. In the meantime, he's given everyone the weekend off. He's determined filming will start again on Monday. I suspect I'll be sent to strongarm Jack back to the set if he doesn't appear on Sunday evening.'

Kendrick studied her with a crooked smile. 'What do you say we take ourselves off for a couple of days? I'll go crazy if I have to hang around here with nothing to do.'

Elizabeth hesitated. 'What do you have in mind?'

'A day in LA, then we could drive up the coast. Remember that place I told you about? Built into the cliff? I've booked us a night.'

Still Elizabeth hesitated. She was unsure why. Perhaps it was because she could no longer kid herself that she wasn't falling for Kendrick. She felt an unexpected ache in her heart.

'Why not?'

The next couple of days were the happiest Elizabeth could remember since Charlie had died. They did all the touristy stuff in Los Angeles. Trying to fit their handprints in those of the famous film stars, walking down Sunset Boulevard.

They spent the first night in Kendrick's cabin, sitting on the beach in the moonlight, watching the surf rolling in. Kendrick sitting behind her with his legs on either side, her leaning against his chest. He taking her by the hand to his cabin where they made love, the sheets tangling in their limbs, laughing at nothing, nibbling on salt crackers and cheese.

Then setting off up the coast on Kendrick's motorbike, she holding him tightly as he whizzed along the road. Stopping for a picnic lunch of fruit, cheese and bread that Elizabeth had picked up from a delicatessen. Back on the bike with the wind in their hair.

Elizabeth was smiling when, just as evening was falling, they reached the place Kendrick had booked for the night.

The hotel was built into a mountain, the rooms set so far into the cliff they were almost invisible to the naked eye. Each one was like an isolated pod, with an open fire for cooler winter evenings and a large double bed covered in soft throws. A small plunge pool in front of their room looked out over the cliff and out to sea. Each cabin had been positioned for maximum privacy. As Elizabeth looked down on the crashing surf below an eagle flew past, almost at eye level.

She sighed. It was perfect.

'Would you like to have dinner or do you fancy a swim first?' Kendrick said. His eyes darkened as he looked at her and Elizabeth felt the familiar feeling of lust coil in her belly. She could never get enough of him. But it wasn't just lust.

When he grinned, his eyes crinkled at the corners and his eyes seemed to glint like diamonds. Whenever she was with him, it was as if the outside world disappeared and nothing mattered except that they were lost in each other.

Thinking about Charlie still made her heart splinter, but it was no longer unbearable. Instead of the all-consuming pain, she was occasionally able to think about her child without wanting to curl into a little ball and shut out the world. Was her heart at last healing a little? She would never forget her child, there was no question of that, but she was beginning to envisage a time when she could remember her daughter with gratitude for the time they'd had together. The pain, the desperate sense of loss would never go, but she welcomed the temporary lifting of the searing grief she had been carrying around with her these last few months.

Kendrick had pulled her towards him and was slowly unbuttoning her blouse, looking into her eyes all the time.

She had this man to thank for easing some of her pain.

He slipped her shirt off her shoulders and moved his attention to the top button of her jeans. Elizabeth moaned softly as he undid the button and eased her jeans over her hips.

'I think dinner and swimming might have to wait,' Kendrick said, his mouth on her belly.

As heat spiralled through her she knew that somewhere along the way, despite her resolve not to, she had fallen for this man. She was in love. For the first time in her life. What she'd felt for Simon had been nothing compared to how she felt about Kendrick. She loved him heart and soul. For ever.

The realisation chilled her to the core. This wasn't how it was supposed to be. Hadn't she told herself that the only reason she was with him was because he didn't see a future for them any more than she did?

And then as he picked her up and into his arms, all thoughts were swept away.

CHAPTER TEN

ELIZABETH looked at the faint blue line and felt ill.

Pregnant.

Definitely pregnant.

At first she'd tried to pretend that the tender breasts and nausea were signs her period was due, but as the days passed, the gnawing suspicion wouldn't go away. Then when Tara had come for her antenatal check-up, the penny had dropped. The symptoms Tara was experiencing were exactly those Elizabeth was going through.

She had been in denial. It hadn't occurred to her she might get pregnant. Charlie's conception had been almost a miracle. She was certain there was no way another one could happen. And just in case, she had put herself on the Pill. No way did she ever want to get pregnant again. She simply couldn't cope with the possibility of having another child who could die. Neither had she expected to be in a position to find herself pregnant. After Simon she had told herself she was done with men. Yet she had slept with Kendrick and now the worst had happened.

She was pregnant. The food poisoning. Why hadn't it occurred to her that being sick might have made her contraception unreliable? Because she hadn't been thinking. At least, not with her head.

What was she going to do about it?

She got to her feet and began to pace. Although the chances of Kendrick having the defective gene were remote, it wasn't impossible. What if the same thing happened to this baby as had happened to Charlie? How could she bear to go through all that again? What, then, was the alternative? To terminate the pregnancy?

Elizabeth slid down the wall until she was on the floor. What choice was that? A termination or loving and losing another child? But this baby was another miracle. Twice in a lifetime was almost unbelievable, but three times? No, she would never fall pregnant again, even if she wanted to. Terminate this pregnancy and she would never have another child. No question.

'What should I do, Charlie?' she whispered. 'Would it have been better for you not to have lived at all than to have lived your life?'

The image of her child, smiling at her as she inspected her toes came flooding back, to be replaced almost immediately with one of her in pain. Not understanding why Mummy couldn't take the pain away. Not understanding why doctors had to poke and prod her. It was one of the reasons Elizabeth had taken her home. There had been no point in letting the doctors run constant tests on her child if it was not going to change the outcome. When she had finally made herself accept that, it had been almost liberating. Away from the hospital, at least she and Charlie had had some sort of life together. And among the sadness and grief there had been happy moments. Moments when she had held her child against her, knowing that her touch had let Charlie know she was loved.

But do it all over again?

When Simon had walked out, she'd been almost too caught up with Charlie to bring herself to care. But it had been hard and there had been many, many long and lonely nights when she had longed to have someone hold her, comfort her. She and Simon had only moved to the sprawling London suburb a short while before Charlie's birth and over the time she'd lost touch with the friends she'd once had. Without her mother and with her father in Canada there was no family member to help.

Should she tell Kendrick? At least talk it over with him. Didn't he have the right to be involved in any decision she might make?

But what was the point? If she told him she was pregnant, he'd probably offer to support her, he was that kind of man, but he was also the kind of man who wouldn't stick around. He'd made it clear that he didn't see a wife and child in his future. Besides, if she decided not to continue with the pregnancy what was the point in telling him?

Her head was spinning.

How far on would she be? She calculated dates in her head. About five weeks. So there was time to think about what she wanted to do.

She pulled her knees to her chest and rested her head on her knees. She'd never felt so alone.

She allowed herself a few more minutes of self-pity then got to her feet and washed her face.

Hollow eyes stared back at her. Picking up her make-up bag, she applied lipstick, some blusher and mascara. Whatever was going on inside, she didn't need the world to know.

Kendrick watched as Elizabeth walked onto the set. Something was wrong. He would bet his life on it. Although she was perfectly made up, her hair falling in a curtain of liquid gold around her shoulders and she took his breath away, there was a tiny pucker between her brows, a shadow in her eyes that concerned him.

As she came closer, he could see that her eyes were a little puffy. Had she been crying? His Elizabeth?

He felt an unexpected stab of fury. Had someone said something to her? If so, he'd personally grab them by the shirt collar and shake them until their teeth shook. But that didn't ring true. Elizabeth wasn't the kind of woman to let anyone rattle her. She was too collected for that. Which made the fact that she'd been crying even more worrying.

Had she had bad news from home? A friend in trouble, perhaps?

He jumped to his feet. Whatever it was, he'd get it out of her and then he'd be able to help. Surely there wasn't anything wrong that couldn't be fixed.

'Lizzie, honey, what is it?' He took one of her cold hands in his and rubbed it gently, wanting to get some warmth back into her. Was she ill?

She smiled but it didn't reach her eyes. It was as if she had gone to some place he couldn't reach. 'I'm fine. A bit of a headache, that's all. I've taken some painkillers, so I should be fine in a minute.'

She was lying. He was sure of it. But he'd come to know enough about this woman not to challenge her head-on. He'd get it out of her one way or another, but he'd have to leave his normally cack-handed methods and get there slowly. But get to the truth he would.

'Are you okay to work? Do you want me to tell Philip that you can't make it this evening? I'm sure he can get another doctor to fill in. This is LA after all. There's bound to be a couple of thousand who'd leap at the chance to work on a film set.'

She frowned at him and tightened her mouth in the way he knew meant she was annoyed.

'Kendrick, when will you realise that I'm perfectly capable of deciding whether I'm fit to work? I am not a child. I am not your responsibility.' She said the last words with such venom he recoiled. What had brought that on? Elizabeth might be feisty, but she was never outright rude.

'I'm sorry,' she said, and touched him on the shoulder. He had to force himself not to pull her into his arms and plead with her to tell him what was wrong. In her current frame of mind that would be exactly the wrong thing to do.

'Remind me what we're doing tonight.'

That too was unlike her. Normally Elizabeth insisted on getting the details of planned stunts in advance so she could be prepared for any eventuality. Although this part of the filming was taking place in a sectioned-off part of an LA freeway and there would be medical services close at hand should anything go wrong, she would still be the first person on the scene.

'We're doing a car chase. Josh will be crashing his car again. I'll be driving the motorbike that is trying to force him off the road.'

'Great,' said Elizabeth. 'Just what I need. You trying to get yourself killed.'

She looked so woebegone that this time he couldn't stop himself. Uncaring that anyone could see them, he took her face between his hand, forcing her to look into his eyes. What he saw dismayed him even more. Her blue eyes were luminous with unshed tears. In that moment he knew. He was in love. Not just falling, he was deeply, irrevocably in love.

He was in a load of trouble.

'What is it, Lizzie? Please tell me.'

The silence stretched between them and as her lips moved he thought she was going to tell him. But then she shook her head and pulled away.

'You'd better get ready,' she said. 'Don't you have to get suited up?'

He dropped his hands to his sides, knowing he'd get nothing more from her. Later, when the filming was over, he'd find her and make her tell him. As for being in love? Damn. He could only hope he'd get over it when she left. He had nothing to offer her apart from a nomadic existence moving from set to set. Even if they married. Where had that thought come from? He didn't want to get married. He'd be useless at all that nine-to-five, slippers-and-newspaper routine. It would drive him crazy. And as for children, Elizabeth said she didn't want any and he believed her. But what if she changed her mind? What then? He'd be even more trapped.

But he let his mind wander. Would it be so terrible to have kids? If it was a boy, he could teach him how to ride a horse, fly aeroplanes, ride a skateboard. He could even take him surfing. Not out to the big waves, naturally. At least, not until he was fourteen. And if it was a girl? He could teach her the same things.

He let the fantasy roll around his head for a moment. He could go back to the ranch. Take over from his father who wasn't getting any younger. It could be a good life. A satisfying life. Elizabeth wouldn't need to work, but if she insisted, well, there were always shortages of good doctors in the rural parts. Suddenly the idea of being a husband and father didn't seem quite as outrageous as it once had.

He slid a glance at Elizabeth. She was chewing her lip in that cute way of hers that meant she was mulling something over. He could see her on the ranch, sitting on the rocking chair on the veranda, he sitting next to her as they talked about their day.

Kendrick forced his thoughts away from Elizabeth and his fantasies. Right now he had a big scene to do and it needed every bit of his concentration, but once filming was over for the night, he would talk to her. Find out what was bothering her and maybe even tell her he loved her.

The evening was warm as they stood around, waiting for the scene to be set up. Elizabeth tried to focus on what was happening around her instead of what was happening inside her. Every hour the cells of the baby would be dividing and multiplying as the baby developed inside her. She couldn't think of it as a baby. She mustn't think of it as a baby. Much, much better, if she had to think of it at all, was to remember it was only a cluster of cells. It wouldn't even have a beating heart yet.

'Okay,' Kendrick was saying as his team of stuntmen and women huddled around him. 'I think we're all pretty clear on how this has to work. Josh, remember to duck below the dash just before you ram into the truck. I'll be on the motorbike, next to you. We have to get the timing spot on. I don't want you knocking into me and sending me flying across the road.'

'Hey, boss, when have I ever bumped into you?' Josh said good-naturedly. 'You make sure your timing is spot on, and I'll look after mine.'

'The rest of you who aren't in this scene stand by to help Josh out of the car when it crashes. I don't want to take any chances it'll explode with him in it.'

Great. Just great. They were talking crashes and explosions and who knew what else they had planned. It would be a miracle if they all came out of this without a scratch. At least there was an ambulance with a couple of paramedics on standby as well as her. Elizabeth prayed none of the precautions she'd taken would be needed.

Over the last hour she had watched as Kendrick and Josh had set up some kind of track along the road barrier. Imogen had explained that they needed to do that in order to keep the car Josh would be driving sideways once it had been hit. It would then race along the barrier for a few hundred metres before landing back on four wheels. The rest of the crew had lined up old cars along the side of the road to act as a crash barrier on the other side.

What kind of people were these? Elizabeth wondered, not

for the first time. Despite what Kendrick had told her, she couldn't accept that they didn't know that one false move could end in tragedy.

Imogen must have been thinking the same thing. Either that or she'd read Elizabeth's mind.

'We're not reckless, you know. All the stuntmen I've ever known, apart from a couple, died either from natural causes or in accidents where they weren't working.'

Was that meant to reassure her?

'You'll see. They do everything they can to make the stunt safe. And as far as I know, Kendrick hasn't lost anyone on his watch.'

They watched in silence for a little longer. 'Of course, Kendrick does like taking risks. That's why he left the army.'

Did everyone know more about Kendrick than she did?

Imogen smiled. 'I'm sure if Kendrick had wanted to stay, his father would have found a way to keep him.'

Elizabeth stayed silent, hoping Imogen would carry on musing if she wasn't interrupted.

'But I guess even the colonel couldn't get Kendrick out of trouble when it came to endangering his crew and practically writing off a multi-million-dollar helicopter. Personally I can't see what else Kendrick could have done, but I guess I'm not in the army so what do I know? All I do know is that if I were in trouble, it's Kendrick I would want to get me out of it.'

Endangering his crew? Writing off a helicopter? This was more than Susan had told her.

The more she learned about Kendrick, the more confused she became. Did she know him at all? She placed a hand over her stomach, feeling the familiar, but unwelcome, protective urge.

Josh brought Elizabeth a cup of coffee and she smiled her thanks.

'Are you sure he knows what he's doing?' she asked anxiously.

'Who? Kendrick? I trust him with my life,' Josh said simply. 'I've worked on other sets and, believe me, ones where Kendrick is the co-ordinator are the safest by far.'

'And you believe this. Even knowing why he had to leave the army?'

Josh slid her a look. 'Hey, Doc, I don't know who's been talking to you, but Kendrick only did what he had to. If I had the guts I would have done the same in his place. His girl was hit, he needed to get her out of there and he was the only one who could do it.'

'His mother told me about his girlfriend.'

Josh took a swig of coffee and studied his drink pensively. 'I doubt she knows the whole story. The horror of what he must have gone through. I'm only telling you what I've learned over the years. Kendrick doesn't talk much.' He flashed Elizabeth a smile. 'I guess you know that by now. Anyways, he was flying one of those helicopters. You might have seen them in the movies? The ones that offer support to the men on the ground?'

Elizabeth nodded.

'The way I heard it, some soldiers were involved in an unexpected ambush,' Josh continued. 'They radioed for help and Kendrick was one of them who was sent. He knew his girl was part of the platoon, but he didn't know she was dead already. It eats him up that he couldn't save her. There were a couple of soldiers who were still alive and he got them out of there while under heavy fire himself. Folk still talk about it. Trouble was, the big brass didn't see it that way. As the pilot, Kendrick wasn't supposed to leave his chopper in the hands of his gunner. The brass said any of the enemy might have got it. As it was, it took a few bullets as they were taking off. Made a mess of their expensive machine. They didn't seem to care too much about the two soldiers who almost certainly wouldn't have made it out of there alive if it hadn't been for Kendrick. I guess they didn't know whether to give him a medal or court-martial him. As it happened, his father tried to intervene. Argued that Kendrick should stay in the army but in a desk job away from the action. But Kendrick was having none of it. Said if he couldn't fly, he wasn't staying. So here he is. This way he gets to fly sometimes. I heard he and his father haven't spoken much since.'

Elizabeth was stunned. No wonder there was tension between Kendrick and his father. But his father was wrong. He should be proud of his son. Just as any child would be proud to have a father like Kendrick.

In that moment she knew. She would never terminate the pregnancy. This child would be loved, however he or she turned out.

A burst of happiness lit her up inside. She had made her decision and it was the right one.

But should she tell Kendrick? Everything she knew about him told her that he would never leave her to have the child on her own. She didn't want him to stay around out of a sense of duty. Eventually the burden of responsibility would change him, he'd feel trapped and want to leave but wouldn't. She couldn't bear to do that to him or her child.

She loved Kendrick. She would always love him. But she'd coped on her own before and she would again.

She looked over to the man who had her heart and always would, and her insides churned at the thought of leaving him. She took a deep breath and squared her shoulders. She'd make the most of any time they had left together. At least now she knew she had the strength to face the future, whatever it brought.

CHAPTER ELEVEN

THE last day of filming came round all too soon. Philip had brought in caterers for the wrap party and there was a real carnival atmosphere. Kendrick watched Elizabeth as she spoke to some of the crew, her head tilted back, laughing. She looked more beautiful than he'd ever seen her. The sadness he'd seen a few days earlier had disappeared. He'd tried to ask her about it but she'd brushed his questions away with a smile. There was a glow about her, as if she was beginning to live again. And he wanted to be part of that life. It was no use. He knew it now. He was in love with Elizabeth Morgan. Completely in love. He hadn't recognised it before because he hadn't wanted to.

It was too late to fight it. He couldn't let her leave. He couldn't imagine life without her. He wanted her to be with him for the rest of their lives. He wanted to grow old with her. For her to have his babies—the whole shooting match.

With the acknowledgement something inside him quietened down and for the first time in his adult life he felt at peace with himself. He would have to bite the bullet and ask her to marry him.

But not here. In Brazil. After Fabio and his wife-to-be tied the knot. On the beach somewhere. That was how the romantic movies did it, so it must be right. He didn't have a clue. It wasn't as if he'd ever proposed before. He would buy a ring, wait until he had her alone and go down on one knee. She would have to accept him then. A knot of anxiety tugged away at his gut. What if she said no? She'd been pretty adamant she didn't want to get married again. He dismissed the thought.

He was sure she loved him.

'Will you come with me to my cousin's wedding?' he asked as soon as he found the opportunity to get her on her own.

She looked at him with those steady blue eyes.

'In Brazil?'

'Why not? You're not rushing back to the UK, are you?'

She shook her head and he saw a shadow cross her face. No doubt she was remembering the last time she'd been there. If—no, when—she married him, he would spend the rest of his life making good memories for her.

She hesitated and the earlier knot of anxiety returned. What if he'd got it all wrong? No. It was impossible. He knew women.

'I suppose,' she said reluctantly. That wasn't exactly the response he was looking for, but it would have to do. Perhaps she was wondering what the point of dragging out their relationship was? For a second he was tempted to ask her right there and then, but he controlled the impulse. He wanted it to be perfect.

As Elizabeth stepped off the plane a fragrant breeze tickled her nostrils. They had flown to Brazil, then a smaller plane hired especially for the wedding guests had taken them out to the nearby island of Florianópolis.

The runway was only a short distance from the beach and Elizabeth saw palm trees and sand the colour of coconut milk. Whatever she'd expected, it hadn't been this.

A tall, lean man with olive skin and dark hair stepped forward and slapped Kendrick on the back.

'Hey, Kendrick. I'm glad you could make it.'

'I wouldn't have missed my little cousin getting married for anything.' Kendrick grinned back.

Not that the man in front of her was little. Although Kendrick topped him by a good two inches, Fabio had to be six feet at least. He was good-looking, almost beautiful, but Elizabeth preferred Kendrick's ruggedness.

Green eyes turned to Elizabeth and an eyebrow was lifted in question.

'This is Dr Elizabeth Morgan,' Kendrick introduced her. 'Just don't call her Lizzie. She might take a chunk out of you.'

'I'm delighted you could come. I hope you'll enjoy your stay,' Fabio said with a quick glance at Kendrick.

'I'm sure I will.'

'So where's the bride?' Kendrick asked. 'Have I met her?' He narrowed his eyes at his cousin. 'Wait a minute. Don't tell me. I'm betting it's that cutie you were with at the film première.'

Fabio broke into a wide grin. 'And you'd be right. She's up at my mother's right now, going over final arrangements.'

As they talked they headed out of the airport, pausing only to pick up their bags. They had cleared Immigration when they'd first arrived in Brazil.

'And how is Camilla?' Kendrick asked. 'Sounds to me as if you two have come to some sort of understanding.'

'You could say that. Katie has Mother eating out of her hand. The only problem is that she's insisting that she'll never be called Grandmother.'

Kendrick came to a halt. 'Are you…? Is Katie…?'

Fabio grinned. There was no mistaking the happiness in his eyes. Elizabeth's heart twisted. What would it be like to be loved like that? To know that you were the centre of someone's universe? Once, she too had thought the future was all mapped out and that only happiness lay ahead. How soon it had turned to dust. She shook the thought away. Hopefully life would be kinder to Fabio and his Katie.

'Yes, she's just over eight weeks pregnant. Don't say anything, though. She's a little superstitious about it.'

Elizabeth's heart twisted again. She too remembered the excitement of being pregnant the first time but it hadn't crossed her mind to be anxious and she'd been totally unprepared for having a child with a terminal illness. Not that she would have not had Charlie in her life.

She was scared to death about this pregnancy, but this time she'd be prepared. She'd arranged for an appointment at the hospital in a couple of weeks' time. This time, if there was anything wrong with her child, at least she'd be prepared.

'I thought you could stay with us at the house,' Fabio was saying. 'I hope that's okay. Mama has invited half of the Brazilian population as well as most of the film world to the reception so accommodation is booked solid on the island. Fortunately, she's accepted that it's only close friends at the actual wedding service.'

As they pulled up in front of the house a woman ran down the steps to meet them. After a resounding kiss from Fabio, she turned to them.

'Hi, I'm Katie. It's so good to meet you again, Kendrick.'

'Me too, ma'am. This is Elizabeth.'

Katie took one of Elizabeth's arms in hers. 'Come, you must be exhausted. I'll show you to your room.' She turned around briefly. 'Be a darling, Fabio, and take the bags up to the room for our guests.'

Katie was beautiful and the added light in her eyes made her seem to glow. She was petite, only coming to Elizabeth's shoulder.

'Congratulations,' Elizabeth said as they walked up the sweeping staircase. 'You look very happy.'

'I've never been happier,' Katie said simply. She showed Elizabeth into a bedroom that was at least twice the size of her sitting room back in England. She walked over to the window and flung the shutters wide.

'We keep them closed during the day to keep the heat out. But it seems a shame to block out the view,' Katie said.

And it was some view, Elizabeth had to admit as she stepped out onto a small balcony. The beach was only a few metres away and the sea rolled gently onto the sugar-white sand.

'I wasn't sure, but do you and Kendrick want to share?' Katie asked, her grey eyes looking anxious. 'There's another room along the passage Kendrick could have.'

Elizabeth smiled. 'No, this will do perfectly.' Her heart thumped. Another couple of days and then it would be over.

'I'll leave you to freshen up. After lunch I'm afraid I'm going to have to leave you in Kendrick's hands. There's still so much to do before tomorrow. More guests—people from the practice where Fabio and I work are arriving this evening. Fabio's mother has arranged a barbecue for everyone tonight, so I'll see you there.' And then in a flurry Katie was gone.

She had just left when there was a tap on the door and Kendrick entered.

'Okay?' he asked.

'I'm fine. It's so beautiful here.'

'Fabio is a lucky man,' Kendrick said. 'Things haven't always been easy for him.'

'Why?'

Kendrick took her by the arm and they went out onto the balcony. Elizabeth rested her back against his chest, savouring the feeling of his arms around her, wanting to make the most of every last minute they had together.

'He hasn't always got along with his mother. Remember I told you about his parents on the plane out here?'

When Kendrick had told her that Fabio's parents were Camilla Salvatore and Tom Lineham, Elizabeth had immediately known who they were. Tom Lineham, although dead for many years, was still a legend.

'Fabio's childhood was pretty isolated. I never thought he'd fall in love and settle down. His relationship with his father—my mother's brother—was fraught even before my uncle died. A bit like mine with my father.'

He rested his chin on the top of her head. 'Speaking of which, I'm seriously considering going back to the army.'

Elizabeth's blood ran cold. It was one thing her making plans for a future without him, quite another to hear him doing the same. She only prayed he wouldn't be going back to the front line.

'If you do, will you go back to active service?' she asked.

'I'm not sure. At this stage, it's only tentative. I haven't said yes—yet. I'd like to train other pilots. But once I'm back in the army they can send me where they like. And anyway,' he said thoughtfully, 'I don't know if I could train pilots without flying with them on missions.'

This was worse than anything she'd expected. Over the time she'd watched Kendrick work, she'd come to realise that he managed the risks and while the stunts were still dangerous, at least they were carried out in controlled conditions with her close by to help if she were needed. Out there, there was no way to control the risk. She swallowed the lump in her throat. She wouldn't say anything. What was the point? Kendrick had made it clear that he didn't want the responsibility of worrying about someone else and she knew instinctively that he wasn't the kind of man to change his mind once it was made up. Maybe it was for the best they were never going to see each other again. She couldn't bear the thought of someone else she loved dying.

'Fabio wants me to go and play polo with him this afternoon. Would you like to come and watch?'

Elizabeth shook her head. She needed time alone so she could absorb what Kendrick had just told her. Fixing a smile on her face, she turned in his arms and pulled his head down towards hers. 'What time is lunch?' she asked.

Kendrick glanced at his watch behind her back. 'Not for another hour.'

'In that case,' she whispered, raising her mouth to his, 'I think we have just enough time.'

After lunch Kendrick headed out with Fabio. The memory of Elizabeth in his arms made him smile. Then he frowned. There had been something desperate in their love-making this time, something urgent, as if she had been trying to memorise every line and plane of his body. She didn't know yet, of course, that this wasn't goodbye. For a moment, when he'd told her about possibly going back to the army, he'd been tempted to propose, to tell her that he wouldn't go unless she could go too, but he'd held back, not wanting to spoil his planned proposal.

There was no time to think too much about it as shortly after they reached the polo field they were mounted and, on the opposing team from his cousin, soon immersed in their game.

Later, after they had showered and the other players had gone, Kendrick decided to share his plans with Fabio.

'You're not the only one who's going to get married,' Kendrick said. The look on his cousin's face was priceless.

Fabio slapped him on the back. 'Why didn't you say before? I would have congratulated Elizabeth.'

'She doesn't know. Not yet. I'm going to spring it on her

tomorrow. After your wedding. I didn't want to steal your thunder. I've done that too many times in the past.'

Fabio grinned back. 'I think the score is pretty even, mate. Although you're bound to catch up soon. I don't go surfing and BASE jumping so much any more. I've somehow lost the urge. Falling in love and becoming a father tends to do that. I kind of realise that I can't take the risks we used to. I have responsibilities now.'

He grinned again and although Kendrick had never thought he'd hear the word 'responsibility' uttered by Fabio with a smile, he knew how his cousin felt. Was it fair to be thinking of proposing to Elizabeth if he might go back to the front line? He had the uneasy feeling it wasn't. He only hoped she would understand.

CHAPTER TWELVE

IT WAS a perfect day for a wedding, Elizabeth thought as she stepped out onto the balcony. Kendrick was still sleeping, his arms and legs splayed out in careless abandon.

It had been late when he'd come back last night and he had crept into bed quietly so as not to wake her. He wasn't to know that she had been staring wide-eyed at the ceiling until she'd heard his footsteps outside the door. For once she'd pretended to be asleep. She hadn't been able to bear him to read the truth in her eyes.

A cool breeze rustled the palm trees. One more day and they would be saying goodbye. She was flying back to London to see her obstetrician.

She shivered and hearing footsteps behind her turned to see Kendrick, completely comfortable in his nakedness, coming towards her. Wrapping his arms around her, he hugged her close. 'You're cold,' he said. 'Come back to bed so I can warm you.'

But even as she gave herself up to him, she wondered if she'd ever feel warm again.

The wedding was a simple affair but no less moving for that. The bride wore a simple dress in a gauzy, almost diaphanous material with her hair in a chignon. The groom was in a white shirt and white linen trousers.

The service was held under a palm tree on the beach in front of Camilla's home. True to form, the groom's mother sniffed her way through the service. As the bride's father was no longer alive, Kendrick gave her away to Fabio. The permanent grin on his face was even wider, if that was possible.

As Katie and Fabio made their vows to each other, Elizabeth had to blink tears away. The couple were so much in love and had the rest of their lives together.

Elizabeth's mind strayed to the life growing inside her. In a different world the couple standing before her could have been Kendrick and herself, the baby growing inside her a source of happiness and joy, instead of fear and anxiety. At that moment she knew. She had to tell Kendrick. Whatever she decided to do, he had the right to know.

After the photographs and the toasts everyone made their way back to the house where the wedding feast was to be held. After that there would be dancing and the couple would be leaving for the airport. Apparently they were to honeymoon in Istanbul, a city that had special meaning for them.

As Elizabeth was about to follow the other guests back to the house, Kendrick appeared by her side.

'Elizabeth, will you walk with me?' The unusually formal language and the out-of-character nervousness on his face made her wonder.

'Sure,' she said, and as he took her hand in his she let herself be led along the beach. They walked in silence. Several times Kendrick opened his mouth as if to say something, then closed it again. Suddenly Elizabeth had had enough. She had to tell him now. Before she lost her courage.

'I'm pregnant, Kendrick,' she blurted.

'Pregnant?' He seemed stunned.

Oh, my God. This was harder than she'd expected. Deep down, she wanted him to be happy, to be delirious. To love them both.

She turned to face him, her eyes searching his. If only she could see a glimmer of joy in his face, if only…

Then his mouth split into a wide grin. 'Pregnant? When, how, what…?' His hand reached over and gently rubbed her stomach. 'We're having a baby?'

Elizabeth nodded.

The look of wonder in his eyes almost ripped her in two. 'That's great, Lizzie.' He picked her up in his arms and whirled her round.

Then, to her amazement, he dropped to one knee and looked up at her.

'I feel like such an idiot down here.'

He looked so woebegone that Elizabeth swallowed the bubble of laughter that rose to her throat.

'Elizabeth Morgan,' Kendrick said, taking her hand, 'would you do me the very great honour of becoming my wife?' He rose to his feet and smacked the sand off his trousers. 'Sorry. Can't do the kneeling thing. Doesn't do it for me. There's only one way to do this that feels right.'

He dropped his hands to her waist and she swayed towards him. He looked her directly in the eye and she saw hope and fear and love there.

'I love you. I never thought I'd say that, but I do. I want you to be my wife.'

She knew what she wanted to say, but she couldn't. Had he only proposed because she was pregnant? What if he walked away, like Simon, leaving her on her own? She couldn't go through all that again. She simply wasn't strong enough.

He was waiting for her answer.

'No, Kendrick, I'm sorry, I can't.'

He frowned. Clearly her reply wasn't what he was expecting. 'What do you mean, you can't? You love me, don't you?'

Elizabeth ran a hand across his face. 'I don't think you

realise what the implications of this pregnancy are. This baby—our baby—might be born with the same condition that my darling Charlie had. Can you cope with that?' She dropped her hand, tears welling in her throat.

Kendrick's fingers bit into her shoulders. His eyes burned into hers. 'I'm not Simon. I'll never be like Simon—you have to believe me, Lizzie. You mean more to me than my own life—and if our child is less than perfect, we'll see it through. Together. I promise you that.'

She wanted so much to believe him. Wasn't love about trust? Elizabeth wrapped her arms around his neck and he hugged her with such ferocity she thought he'd never let her go. Then he was kissing her, sweet, desperate kisses. So this was what real love felt like.

Nevertheless, although it broke her in two, she knew what she had to do. She pulled away.

'Love you, Kendrick?' She made herself frown. 'I thought I made it clear from the start that this wasn't going to end in happy-ever-after?'

He laughed harshly. 'That was then. We both said things but that was before we knew we were going to fall in love.'

There was a glint in his eye, the beginning of a hardness she couldn't bear to see. But she knew she had to twist the knife one more time.

'I'm not in love. And I suspect you aren't, either. Not really. You're thinking of going back to the army after all. You decided to do that without talking to me. Don't you think, Kendrick, that was a decision you should have discussed with the woman you purport to love?'

His eyes narrowed. The smile was gone. 'So that's what this is about,' he said softly. 'Me going back to the army. Maybe I should have talked to you first,' he said, 'but I'm used to making my own decisions. It's a habit. I'll get used to consulting with you in time.'

Elizabeth stepped back. 'I'm sorry, Kendrick. I don't know what gave you the idea I could marry you. And if you think I'm going to wait at home, worrying that you might get killed, you have another think coming.'

'So that's what this is about, Lizzie.' The darkness in his eyes cleared. 'I'm an idiot. Of course, given what happened with Charlie, you're bound to be more worried about me. But don't you know by now? I can look after myself.'

She reached across and opened the button of his cotton shirt. She found the bullethole and circled it with her finger. 'Like you looked after yourself then? You could have been killed that day. You have a death wish, Kendrick, and no one is going to get that out of you. Least of all me.'

Her throat was getting tighter and she could hardly bear to look him in the eyes. If he saw them, he would know she was lying.

'I need to know if this baby has the slightest chance of having the same syndrome Charlie had,' she said. 'So, if you do love me, there is one thing you can do for me. I have an appointment with a geneticist at a specialist children's hospital. Meet me there. He'll need a blood sample from you as the father. If, after having time to think about being a husband and a father to a possibly disabled child, and you decide that's still what you want, we can talk again.'

'I won't change my mind, Lizzie,' he said. 'You should know me by now. I'd follow you back to England right now if I could, but I can't. Philip needs me back in LA for a couple of days to review the film of the stunts, but after that, nothing will keep me away from you or our baby.'

Elizabeth wanted to believe him. If he'd proposed to her before she'd told him about the baby, perhaps she would have. Giving him a way out was the right thing to do. If, after time apart, he still wanted her and their baby, maybe she'd let herself trust in him.

She turned away. 'I'm going back to the house, Kendrick. And from there I'm catching the first plane back to London. You take your time and think long and hard before deciding to come to London.'

He pulled her back into his arms.

'I'll be there, Lizzie. I promise.'

CHAPTER THIRTEEN

KENDRICK smiled. In a couple of days he'd be with Elizabeth and he was never going to leave her or their baby again. At least, not if he could help it. Sure, there would be times when he'd have to go away—he had to work—but he'd made sure the weeks after the baby was born he'd be free to spend every minute with his new wife and child.

If Elizabeth thought he would ever abandon his child, regardless of how it turned out, she didn't know him. Not that he could blame her. Up until he'd fallen in love with Lizzie, a wife and child hadn't figured in his plans. Now there wasn't anything he wanted more.

They would get married as soon as possible. He didn't care where, that was up to Elizabeth. They could get married on the moon if she wanted. He would spend the rest of his life making sure she had whatever she wanted. These last couple of weeks had been the longest of his life.

He checked his parachute and his buckles one more time. It was unfortunate that Philip had wanted to reshoot the stunt, but the director had been right. The scene wasn't perfect and Kendrick wasn't happy with anything less.

Philip had asked him again whether he would be second director in the next movie. It would mean not taking up the training position with the army and less actual stunt work, but it was an interesting proposition. He would wait until he'd spoken to Elizabeth before making his decision.

He smiled again. Who would have thought that he would be glad that he had someone to talk over decisions with? He'd always made up his mind without having to consult anyone else. But this felt good—and right.

'Ready when you are, Kendrick,' Philip shouted. The megaphone screeched in the silent desert air.

Kendrick climbed into the car. It was the same routine as before. He'd wait until the second the car went over the cliff, with him clearly visible at the wheel, then he'd scramble out the removed rear window and jump away. It required split-second timing, but he'd done it before without mishap. It was a dangerous stunt, one only a few of the most experienced stuntmen would even attempt, but he had all the skills it required. It might be his last stunt, so he'd make sure this one was perfect. Then he could get home, throw his few belongings into a bag, including the teddy bear he'd bought for the baby, and head for the airport.

'Okay, let's roll,' Philip shouted.

Kendrick grinned. Life was good.

When Kendrick opened his eyes he was in hospital. At least, that was where he thought he was. His mother was sitting by his bed, looking pale and frightened.

All he could remember was redoing the stunt with the car going over the cliff and then struggling to open his parachute, which had somehow become tangled…then nothing.

He tried to reach out to his mother, to touch her and take away the bleak look in her eyes, but he couldn't. He couldn't move anything. It was as if he was trapped inside some kind of torture device.

A nurse leaned over him and cool, practised hands touched his forehead. 'You're awake, then,' she said. 'I'll go and get the doctor.' She scurried out before he had a chance to say anything.

His mother leaned over and kissed his cheek. Standing behind her was his father. If he didn't know better, he would have sworn he saw tears in his father's eyes.

'Why am I here?' Kendrick asked.

'Try to keep still,' his mother whispered.

He almost laughed. He couldn't move if he tried.

More images came back to him. The desperate attempt to open his parachute, knowing he had only moments left. The sickening sensation of slamming against the side of the mountain. Then nothing.

'Why can't I move?' Even as he said the words, a terrible realisation was dawning.

'You hurt your spine in the fall,' his mother whispered. 'They don't know how badly. Not yet.'

A chill was seeping into his bones. This is what he'd always dreaded. What all stuntmen and women dreaded. The thing they never talked about. The thing that was worse than death.

Where was Lizzie? There was something about Lizzie he had to remember but he couldn't.

He closed his eyes.

When he came to again, his parents were still there. His mother was pretending that she hadn't been crying and his father was talking to the doctor in a low, urgent voice. There were dark circles under his mother's eyes. She should go and get some rest. Hadn't he told her to go?

'Could I ask you all to leave us for a moment?' A masculine voice came from his left. Kendrick turned his head—at least that was one part of his body he could move. The voice came from a man about his age dressed in blue hospital scrubs.

Reluctantly his visitors stood. 'We'll be just outside the

door,' his father said gruffly, and placing his arm around Susan's shoulders led her out of the room.

'I'm Dr Urquhart,' the figure introduced himself. 'How much do you remember of what happened?'

CHAPTER FOURTEEN

ELIZABETH waited outside the doctor's consulting-room.

Whenever the doors of the clinic swished open she'd look up, expecting to see Kendrick striding towards her, and every time it wasn't him her heart sank.

She glanced at her watch for the hundredth time. Ten past four. The appointment had been for four o'clock.

The feeling of dread was growing stronger. Why wasn't he here? Had he decided after all that, however slim the chances were of having a disabled child, he couldn't cope? He had phoned once since they'd left Brazil and after that—nothing. When he'd phoned he'd been certain he was coming.

Elizabeth twisted the handkerchief between her fingers. She'd been right to trust her instincts. Two weeks apart had been enough for Kendrick to realise that even if he did love her—and she could have sworn that he did—he couldn't commit to the responsibilities of being a husband and father.

She shifted in her seat. She'd been so sure he loved her. But had she really believed it? Wasn't that exactly the reason she'd imposed this time-out? Because she wanted him to be a hundred per cent certain? Because she couldn't bear to go through again what Simon had put her through?

She'd been crazy to allow herself to hope. She should have known that it had all been too good to be true. As soon as he'd had time to think about the pregnancy, he'd got cold feet, just as she'd feared he would.

She brought her hands to her stomach. It didn't matter. Kendrick or no Kendrick, this baby would be loved with all her soul. But it hurt. She'd let herself believe in Kendrick. Let herself think that he was different. That he wasn't the running-away type, and she had been wrong.

A tall shape paused behind the frosted glass of the double doors and Elizabeth's heart leaped to her throat. Kendrick! He was here. He was late, that was all. She should never have doubted him.

As happiness soared through her, she stumbled to her feet, ready to fling herself into his arms.

But as the doors swung open and it wasn't Kendrick her heart crashed again. All of a sudden with a certainty that stole her breath she knew he wasn't coming.

Everything blurred and she felt behind her for the seat. He wasn't coming. He didn't love her enough. She had to accept that. She cupped her stomach with her hands, feeling a primeval surge of protectiveness.

'It's just you and me, darling,' she whispered. 'But we'll be okay.' Whatever and however this baby turned out, she would love it with every fibre of her being.

Six months later, Elizabeth stood back and surveyed her handiwork. Not bad. She'd decided on pale yellow paint for the walls. That way, whether it was a boy or a girl, all she'd have to do would be to add accents in the appropriate colour. It was hard to believe she'd been back in the UK for two months, having spent four months of her pregnancy with her father in Canada.

She had found this place after a couple of weeks of searching and although it wasn't perfect, it would do her and the baby for the time being.

As the baby moved inside her, she placed her hands on her abdomen. 'Hey, something tells me you're going to be like your daddy. Never happy unless you're on the move.'

The thought of Kendrick brought a lump to her throat. She still loved him—even though he'd hurt her more than he'd ever know. But she couldn't wallow in her misery or self-pity—she'd a baby to think about. Her doctor had told her that Kendrick had tested negative as a carrier of Gaucher's disease. But that was all he could say. At least Kendrick had kept that promise. Not that the result made any difference. Even if Kendrick had tested positive, she wouldn't have changed her mind about having the baby.

She picked up the photograph of Charlie and smiled. Although the memory of her daughter still made her heart ache, at least she could think of her without the heart-breaking sadness of before.

'Hey, Charlie,' she whispered, 'do you think your brother or sister is going to like their room?'

The air ambulance service had hired her and she was to take up her post six months after the baby was born. By that time she would need to have sorted some sort of help. There was no room in the flat for a live-in nanny, but if she was careful, she could afford to pay someone to come in Monday to Friday. She could manage. All this child really needed was love…and she had plenty of that to give.

As usual her mind turned to Kendrick. What was he doing? Had he gone back to the army? Was he even now on the front line or training pilots somewhere closer to home? She pushed the thought away. Kendrick was out of her life.

Taking the paintbrush with her, she walked into her kitchen. Suddenly she felt a twinge in her abdomen. It was ten days earlier than her expected due date so it was likely it was Braxton-Hicks' contractions. But the baby could be on its way. At least she had finished painting the nursery. Her bag had been packed for a couple of weeks now. All she had left to do was assemble the cot.

Back in the nursery she surveyed the pieces with dismay. Then she gritted her teeth, picked up the instructions and set about her task.

The cot was almost half-completed when she heard a ring at the door. It was probably the postman with the stuff she'd ordered from the baby shop.

The doorbell rang again, more insistently, followed by loud banging.

'I'm coming,' she called, pushing a lock of hair behind her ears.

When she opened the door her heart crashed against her ribs.

'Lizzie. Can I come in?' Kendrick said.

Unable to speak, she stood back and without waiting for an invitation he stepped into her small hall. He was thinner than she remembered, but it wasn't that that caught her attention. He was limping and leaning heavily on a cane. She had to grip her hands together to stop herself reaching out to him.

'What are you doing here?' she asked. But Kendrick, never one to let a lack of an invitation stop him, walked into her lounge. He sat himself down on her sofa and stretched his legs in front of him. He winced.

Elizabeth hid her anxiety. How had he hurt himself?

'You're looking well, Lizzie,' he said. She couldn't read the look in his eyes.

'I'm fine. The baby's fine.' Another twinge, more like a real contraction this time, squeezed her abdomen. 'How did you find me?'

Kendrick grinned and her heart somersaulted. She'd hoped that by now she'd have got over him a little. The way her pulse was beating told her otherwise.

'With great difficulty,' he said. 'But eventually I tracked you down though the employment records of the film company.'

'That information is supposed to be confidential.'

'Ah, Lizzie. Don't you know there are ways and means if you want something badly enough?'

'You had no right, Kendrick. And you still haven't told me why you're here. If your conscience has got the better of you, please don't worry. As you can see, I'm doing fine.'

He glanced over at the cot, which was standing in the same lopsided position as she'd left it. She never had been much good with reading instructions.

'I can see that.' He stood and limped across to the cot. 'You haven't done so well with this.'

Tears of fury pricked her eyes. Who did he think he was, coming in here and making her feel all sorts of stuff she didn't want to feel?

'I want you to leave,' she said through gritted teeth. Just then another contraction ripped through her body and she turned away so he wouldn't see her grimace. But he was too busy taking the cot apart and reassembling it to notice.

'What happened to your leg?' she asked, curiosity getting the better of her. 'Did you crash your helicopter?'

'Not exactly,' he said. 'Give me a minute, will you?'

Give him a minute? He had five before she should call the hospital.

'Kendrick, I want you to leave,' she said again. Then another pain sliced through her and this time she couldn't help the involuntary cry that slipped out.

'Lizzie. Is it the baby?' Instantly he was by her side and easing her into a chair.

'Say what you have to then leave me alone,' she snarled through gritted teeth. As another contraction seized her, her nails dug into his arms. God, the contractions were coming too soon. No more than three minutes apart. If she didn't want the baby born here, she had to get to the hospital.

'Explanations can wait,' he said grimly. 'First I think we need to get this baby delivered.'

He insisted on taking his car, which he had parked outside. Carefully he helped her into the front seat.

'My bag,' she gasped. 'I left it upstairs.'

He took one look at her. 'I'll get it later,' he said. 'Which hospital?'

Clearly he thought he was driving a stunt car, Elizabeth thought between the pains cramping her body. Kendrick was driving as if he was being chased by a man with a machine-gun, overtaking when he had the slightest gap and going up on the pavement to pass stationary cars. It would be a miracle if they weren't stopped by the police.

'Slow down or you'll kill us all,' Elizabeth ground out between clenched teeth.

But it seemed as if Kendrick was determined to beat the record for crossing London. Before Elizabeth knew it, they were pulling up outside the maternity unit of the hospital she had booked into and Kendrick was demanding that someone bring a wheelchair and a doctor right this second.

'My girl is having a baby. Our baby,' he told the porter who arrived with a wheelchair. The look of pride and fear on his face would have made Elizabeth laugh if she'd been less angry with him and in less pain.

'I'm not his girl,' Elizabeth told the porter as he steered the chair into the hospital. 'He's just some madman. Tell him to go.'

'It's all right, love,' the porter said. 'A lot of mothers blame the bloke at this point. You'll see—once you have the baby, you'll feel differently.'

'I will not feel differently in a hundred years,' she said.

'He didn't bother to turn up to the doctor's appointment six months ago. This is the first time I've seen him since.'

The porter glanced across at Kendrick and frowned disapprovingly.

'I was in hospital, mate. I couldn't get out of bed, let alone make it to the appointment.'

In hospital? This was the first Elizabeth had heard of it. No doubt Kendrick was trying to find excuses to make himself look better in the porter's eyes, but this was going too far.

'Even if that's true...' she glared at Kendrick as another contraction hit her '...there are telephones. Mobiles even. I think they have them in the US too?'

Nurses were coming towards them. Hands were reaching out. They were asking her questions. How long had her contractions been coming? How far apart? Her partner could have a seat outside while they examined her to see how far along she was.

'My husband?' Elizabeth spat. 'He's the last man on earth that I will ever call my husband.'

Then she was on a bed and they were giving her gas and air. A couple of lungfuls and she started feeling as if she was floating above herself. When she looked around, Kendrick was standing over her, smiling. Who had let him in? Hadn't she said she didn't want him here? This was her baby. Kendrick could have visitation rights. Maybe. Once he proved he could be a reliable father.

'You're doing fine, Lizzie,' Kendrick was saying. 'It looks like our baby is going to be born quite soon.' Kendrick was wearing a green gown and mask. All she could see were his blue eyes.

The nurse injected something into her thigh and the euphoric feeling got better.

'Hey, did I ever tell you that I love your eyes?' Elizabeth said out loud. Where had that come from? She didn't like anything about the lying, miserable no-good man in front of her who had chickened out when he'd known she was having his baby. His baby, who for all he'd known at that time, could be born with a terrible illness.

'You know this baby is okay, don't you? You found out, and you decided it would be quite cute to have a child after all for the occasional trips to the park. Wait a minute…' She wagged a finger at him. 'You probably want help on the ranch, is that it? Maybe you want to teach him or her to fly a helicopter.'

Crazy words were coming out of her mouth but she couldn't stop them.

'Is that it? Men like you always decide sooner or later that they want a kid. Some kind of macho need to spread your genes, and even better if you don't have to take responsibility.' She was proud of the way she managed to put emphasis on the last word. If he had a modicum of intelligence he'd remember that she'd told him quite clearly, once, that she didn't need or want him to be responsible for her.

'I'm here because I love you. I want to marry you. Have babies with you.'

Now she was hallucinating.

'Hah! You can't fool me,' she said. 'I may be drugged up to the eyeballs and I may be in love with you…' Double oops. She had slipped up badly that time. 'I mean, I may have thought I was in love with you, but I was wrong.' Now she'd forgotten what she was going to say. Something about him being in love with her. Something about how that couldn't be right.

''Cause if you loved me, you would have come to the hospital, or if something stopped you, you could have phoned me,' she continued. At least he could have. Up until a month ago when she'd lost her mobile and had had to get a new number. But that had been five months after he'd promised to meet her. No one took five months to work out whether they loved someone enough to risk having a child who might not be perfect with them.

'I couldn't come before, Lizzie,' he said, so quietly she had to strain to hear the words. 'I came as soon as I could, I promise.'

'I think we're going to have a baby,' the nurse said from somewhere down between Elizabeth's legs.

Kendrick stepped towards the end of the bed and Elizabeth grabbed him by the hand. 'Oh, no, you don't, mister. You're not going anywhere south of my head. So unless you want to be kicked out for sure, don't you dare move a muscle.'

Thirty minutes later, Elizabeth was holding her son in her arms. He was perfect. His mouth like a rosebud, tiny fingers and toes all accounted for, and blue eyes, although of course that could change.

Kendrick was gazing at his child with a look of wonderment on his face.

'Is he…?' He cleared his throat. 'Is he all right?'

For a moment Elizabeth wondered what he meant. 'Do you mean you don't know?' she said. 'But you gave a blood sample to be tested. Didn't you get the results?'

Kendrick shook his head. 'I didn't want to know. I never doubted I'd love our child, perfect or not. But until I knew I could be a father, I knew I had to stay out of his life. Both your lives.'

'What do you mean?' Elizabeth kissed the wispy hair on her son's head as he suckled. The nurses had left them on their own, promising to come back in a little while to check up on mother and son.

'The reason I didn't meet you as I promised is because I was in hospital.'

Elizabeth looked up from her child, seeking the eyes of the man she knew she would never stop loving.

'What happened?' she asked.

'Remember I told you in Brazil that I needed to go back to California?'

Elizabeth nodded.

'Philip decided he needed to do the car-off-the-cliff stunt again. Something went wrong. I was pretty badly hurt.'

Elizabeth felt her heart squeeze. He'd been hurt and she hadn't even known.

'I had a compressed fracture of the spine and they thought I might not walk again,' Kendrick said. 'I knew then that I couldn't come to you. I couldn't put you through all that again. Caring for me like you had to care for Charlie. I love you too much to do that to you.'

'You should have told me!' The cry was wrenched out of her. Kendrick had been hurt, had needed her and she hadn't been there. 'I would never have left you on your own. I would have looked after you. You should have trusted me.' And she should have trusted him.

The look he gave her was one of ineffable sadness. 'I know you would never have left me, Lizzie. That's why I couldn't tell you.'

He sat on the bed next to her and pulled her into his arms.

'I wanted to be with you. I wanted to be a father to our baby. It was what gave me the strength to fight. I wouldn't give up. Every small movement I regained brought me closer to you and our child.' He looked down at their baby and smiled.

'It took me all this time to learn to walk again,' he said. 'But I did it. When you walk down that aisle to become my wife, I wanted to be standing there waiting for you. On my feet. Without support.'

'But isn't that what people who love each other do, Kendrick?' she said. 'Support each other? In sickness and in health? The works?'

'It's what you do and what I would do for you. But can you try and understand why I couldn't come to you before now? It's because I love you that much I would rather walk away than see that love diminished over time as you cared for me. I'm not the kind of man who could accept that. I wanted you to have me whole or not at all.'

Her heart was beating fast within her chest. He loved her. She knew that now. He loved her as much as she loved him. There would be no more leaving, no more doubts, only certainty and love.

She looked up at him. 'What does a woman need to do to get kissed around here?' she said.

EPILOGUE

ELIZABETH bent and placed a posy of flowers on her daughter's grave. Kendrick was standing a step behind her, holding their baby in his arms. Tomorrow they'd be going back to the States. Kendrick's leg would never heal well enough for him to go back to the army. Flying helicopters demanded peak physical condition and it was likely he'd always walk with a limp. He wouldn't be going back to stunt work either. Instead, he'd be working behind the scenes as a second director, with full control over organising and ensuring the execution of the stunts. He'd told Elizabeth that it had always been part of his plans.

She had told the ambulance service that she wouldn't be coming to work for them after all. When baby Josh was old enough, she would probably retrain as an emergency specialist. It was what she enjoyed doing most.

She stepped back and took their baby from Kendrick, holding her child close, knowing that this one would never replace the one she had lost. Kendrick pulled her against him and she leaned against him, savouring his strength and his love.

'Sleep tight, my darling Charlie,' she whispered. 'Mummy will never forget you.'

She stood in the circle of Kendrick's arms, holding their

child, and as the wind pushed the clouds away and the sun beat down on her shoulders she knew that life was going to be good.

0711/03a

Medical Romance™

CAREER GIRL IN THE COUNTRY
by Fiona Lowe

Dynamic city surgeon Poppy can't believe she's been sent to work in the rural Outback! Her gorgeous colleague, emergency doctor Matt, thrives on the small-town solitude, but Poppy knows he's hiding from something…and she's determined to make him face his secrets!

THE DOCTOR'S REASON TO STAY
by Dianne Drake

After finding his little ward Molly the loving parents he never had, brooding surgeon Dr Rafe Corbett intends to leave town for good. Edie Parker intends to make Rafe realise *he* is the father Molly needs. But can she convince him to stay—because Edie is losing her heart to them both…

WEDDING ON THE BABY WARD
by Lucy Clark

Determined to deliver her best friend's precious twins safely, Dr Janessa Austen calls on neonatal specialist Miles Trevellion's expertise. These tiny baby girls must be Miles' *only* priority—the beautiful Janessa can be nothing more than his colleague. For now…

SPECIAL CARE BABY MIRACLE
by Lucy Clark

New mum Sheena's newborn girls are fighting for their lives and paediatric surgeon Will Beckman is the man to save them—the same Will who was once the love of Sheena's life! Sheena's hoping for two little miracles—but perhaps an unexpected third dream might also come true?

On sale from 5th August 2011
Don't miss out!

THE TORTURED REBEL
by Alison Roberts

Beautiful helicopter pilot Becca Harding has spent long years trying to forget SAS medic and emergency specialist Jet Munroe, but she's never been able to forgive him. Now, thrown together again, it's time to stop running from their past, and the scorching attraction still lingering between them.

DATING DR DELICIOUS
by Laura Iding

It's Hannah Stewart's first day as a surgical intern at Chicago's busiest hospital and she couldn't be more excited—then she meets Dr Jake Holt, her new boss…the man she had a completely out-of-character, one-night stand with! Jake has a strict "no relationships at work" rule, but his new intern is proving to be a distraction impossible to ignore…!

On sale from 5th August 2011
Don't miss out!

2 FREE BOOKS
AND A SURPRISE GIFT

We would like to take this opportunity to thank you for reading this
Mills & Boon® book by offering you the chance to take TWO more
specially selected books from the Medical™ series absolutely FREE!
We're also making this offer to introduce you to the benefits of the
Mills & Boon® Book Club™—

- **FREE home delivery**
- **FREE gifts and competitions**
- **FREE monthly Newsletter**
- **Exclusive Mills & Boon Book Club offers**
- **Books available before they're in the shops**

Accepting these FREE books and gift places you under no obligation to buy, you may cancel at any time, even after receiving your free
books. Simply complete your details below and return the entire page
to the address below. You don't even need a stamp!

YES Please send me 2 free Medical books and a surprise gift. I
understand that unless you hear from me, I will receive 5 superb new
stories every month including two 2-in-1 books priced at £5.30
each and a single book priced at £3.30, postage and packing free. I
am under no obligation to purchase any books and may cancel my
subscription at any time. The free books and gift will be mine to keep
in any case.

Ms/Mrs/Miss/Mr _____ Initials _____

Surname _____

Address _____

_____

_____ Postcode _____

E-mail _____

Send this whole page to: Mills & Boon Book Club, Free Book Offer,
FREEPOST NAT 10298, Richmond, TW9 1BR